THE MONSTER'S
LAMENT

Robert Edric

Doubleday

LONDON · TORONTO · SYDNEY · AUCKLAND · JOHANNESBURG

TRANSWORLD PUBLISHERS
61–63 Uxbridge Road, London W5 5SA
A Random House Group Company
www.transworldbooks.co.uk

First published in Great Britain
in 2013 by Doubleday
an imprint of Transworld Publishers

A CIP catalogue record for this book
is available from the British Library.

ISBNs 9780857520043 (hb)
9780857520050 (tpb)

Addresses for Random House Group Ltd companies outside the UK
can be found at: www.randomhouse.co.uk
The Random House Group Ltd Reg. No. 954009

The Random House Group Limited supports the Forest Stewardship
Council (FSC®), the leading international forest-certification organization.
Our books carrying the FSC label are printed on FSC®-certified paper. FSC
is the only forest-certification scheme endorsed by the leading environmental
organizations, including Greenpeace. Our paper procurement policy can be
found at www.randomhouse.co.uk/environment

Typeset in 12/15pt Granjon by
Kestrel Data, Exeter, Devon.
Printed and bound in Great Britain by
Clays Ltd, Bungay, Suffolk.

2 4 6 8 10 9 7 5 3 1

MIX
Paper from
responsible sources
FSC® C016897

THE MONSTER'S LAMENT

www.transworldbooks.co.uk

For Gwennyth Venn

One is always wrong to open a conversation with the devil, for, however one goes about it, the devil will always insist on having the last word.

André Gide
Journals, 1917

London, April 1945

1

FRANKIE DOLL LOOKED UP AT THE FLYING BOMB AS IT MADE its noisy, faltering way across the cloudless sky. It was seven in the morning, and the sun was already high above the rooftops of Archer Street, filling the far side of the narrow road with its yellow light, and casting Frankie Doll and the doorway in which he stood into deep shade.

Others gathered further along the street and gazed up-wards in an effort to spot the small rocket. A girl came out of the doorway beside Frankie Doll and collided with him. She, too, looked quickly up, but then turned her attention to the shoes she carried, and after that to her bare feet on the cold paving. She leaned on Frankie Doll while she pulled on her shoes.

Frankie Doll knew her from the Regency – Ruby some-thing. Something Irish. Nolan, Dolan. Definitely an Irish accent. Red hair. Like him, she would have just worked through the night and was now leaving and on her way home. He looked down from the sky for a moment and wondered what – if anything – to say to her.

The girl fastened her straps and let go of Frankie Doll's shoulder. She asked him for a cigarette and he gave her one and lit it for her.

'Hardly right, is it?' she said, nodding upwards. 'Hardly fair. Not this far on. Not after all this time.'

At first, Frankie Doll didn't understand her.

Above them, the small, shiny rocket continued along its noisy course.

'Everybody's saying it's all over bar the shouting and the reckoning,' the girl said.

Frankie Doll remembered her name. Nolan. Ruby Nolan. He looked at her again. She probably wasn't even twenty yet. The Irish all sounded the same to Frankie Doll. He wondered what she called herself in the club. Or perhaps Ruby *was* her club name. More than likely. It was a world full of Rubys and Pearls, Scarlets and Sabrinas.

'What reckoning?' he said.

'You know. Slicing things up. What is it? "The Spoils of War".' She was pleased with the phrase and repeated it. She rubbed at a mark on her leg.

Frankie Doll finally understood her.

Above them, the flying bomb gave its first unmistakeable stutter, followed by a few seconds of silence, followed then by the resumption of its engine. Frankie Doll knew something about engines. Engines and fuel. The rocket noise always sounded wrong, badly tuned, a loose piston-housing, poor fuel mixture, low grade. A burned-out fly-boy had once pointed out to Frankie Doll that it hardly mattered how good or poor the fuel was or what shape the engines were in as long as they got the rockets to roughly where they needed to be; because wherever they fell, they did their dirty work. And perhaps it was even deliberate, them sounding like that, the same fly-boy had suggested, putting the fear of God into everybody who heard the things coming and who knew what all that spluttering noise and those ominous broken silences now meant.

There was a further missed note, followed this time by a longer silence, one, two, three seconds. Frankie Doll wondered how many others would be making the same heart-stopping calculation.

'Here we go,' Ruby Nolan said, now standing even closer to him.

Along the street, someone called out and pointed.

Frankie Doll looked up again and saw the rocket passing directly overhead, disappearing as it crossed close to where the sun hung low in the sky, and then reappearing as it continued somewhere north over Oxford Street.

'Not much longer now,' Ruby Nolan said. She rubbed her hands and stamped her feet on the ground.

'You can see it,' Frankie Doll told her.

She glanced up, but then shrugged and looked back down again. She seemed more interested in her feet. 'These shoes,' she said, 'I borrowed them. Do they suit me, do you think? Never worn heels this high before.'

Frankie Doll looked at the girl's feet, but said nothing. He was thinking now about what she'd said – about the unfairness of people being killed this close to the war's end. And then he looked back to where the invisible rocket continued on its way across the London sky.

'You'd never be able to tell where it was exactly when you couldn't see it,' the girl said. 'You hear it, then you don't hear it, and then you wait. And if you hear it explode, then that's you off the hook for another day and it makes no bloody difference either way.'

'So do you never think about who might be on the receiving

end when it isn't you?' Frankie Doll said to her. He strained to hear the first tell-tale note of the distant motor cutting out completely.

He'd seen pictures of the things in the newspapers. One had been carried along the Embankment on the back of a tank transporter. Somebody had painted a dragon's face on the sharp end, making it look like a slain creature. Faulty fuse, someone had told him. A dud. Half a dozen soldiers had sat along its silver length, waving to the watching crowds as though they were on a fairground ride. Apart from a buckled fin, there hadn't been a mark or a scratch on the rocket. Someone else in the crowd had said that the whole thing was a con, a bodge-up, propaganda. How, otherwise, would the rocket be undamaged – faulty fuse or not – having fallen out of the sky? A nearby woman contested this by saying that it might have glided to the ground and then landed on a haystack somewhere in a field outside London. Some agreed with her; others laughed at her. Or perhaps it had come down in one of the parks, someone else suggested. This appealed more to the woman and she revised her flimsy explanation of the undamaged bomb.

'Why should I?' Ruby Nolan said, distracting Frankie Doll from his thoughts.

'Why should you what?'

'Think about who might be getting it in the neck. I hardly know anybody else here. Look after number one, that's my motto. Ask me, it's the best way to be. Ask me—'

But Frankie Doll was no longer listening to her.

'It's stopped,' he said.

That same sun-filled, pale-blue sky was filled now with silence. The distant hum of early traffic, a few notes of bird-song, but, essentially, silence.

'One, two, three,' Ruby Nolan started counting.

It struck Frankie Doll only then that it was strange for the rocket to have been launched this late in the proceedings, so close to the final curtain call, so to speak – this rasping baby of a bomb after all those months of the bigger rockets with their silent arrivals and much larger and deadlier explosions.

How does that work, then? Tommy Fowler had asked him. How come you get the bang and *then* you get the noise of the bastard coming? Not right at all. It's a trick. Must be. They send two over, that's it – one with a silent motor, and then one a few seconds later with the usual engine and no bang. Stands to reason. Against the laws of nature, otherwise. Only one thing to be said in their favour, Tommy Fowler said – you never heard your number being called. No standing around and waiting all those long seconds, praying and wondering and working out where you stood and what your chances were. The world was full of other poor, unlucky sods, so what were the odds if you survived and they all stayed poor and unlucky and got what was finally coming to them?

It seemed much longer to Frankie Doll, but Ruby Nolan said, 'Six.'

Along the street, the other men and women had lowered their arms and were all now waiting in silence for the explosion. Some of them, Frankie Doll saw, were braced for the blast, and some of them – and this was a dead cert – were silently praying for their own survival.

In the beginning, Frankie Doll had occasionally tried to plot the course of the bombs, guessing which districts and streets they were flying over. He calculated – or at least he convinced himself that it was a valid calculation – how much fuel was left in the rocket's tank by the noise it made. And then how much further it had to fly – either towards him or away from him – by that same note. And then – and this, he understood, was a considerably more reliable calculation – he worked out how much flight was left in the rocket once it began its faltering descent. Some arrived roaring vigorously and then fell suddenly silent – vertical descent, Frankie Doll reckoned – and others flew stopping and starting for minutes at a time before continuing on their way or beginning their slower, more gentle fall from the sky.

'Seven,' Ruby Nolan said, again interrupting Frankie Doll's thoughts, and the instant she said it, they both heard the distant explosion.

'North,' Frankie Doll said. 'Hendon, Finchley way.'

'Wherever it is,' Ruby said, 'five bob says it won't be Buckingham Palace. And another five bob says that none of that mob will have been within fifty miles of it.'

Frankie Doll heard the cold note of spite in her voice and wondered if this had something to do with her being Irish.

'I suppose not,' he said. He searched along the roofline for any sign of smoke, but already knew by the muted sound of the explosion that the bomb had fallen some miles away. There were no after-noises – no falling masonry, no screams or cries, no crackle of rising flames – only the returning silence of that spring morning.

'Got another?' Ruby said. She dropped the last inch of her cigarette to the ground and rubbed at it with her shoe.

Frankie Doll took out his packet.

'You got family in that direction?' she asked him.

'Got no family whatsoever in any direction,' Frankie Doll said, which was true.

'Only got yourself to worry about, then,' she said, taking two cigarettes from the pack and slipping one into her pocket. 'What will you do?'

'Do?'

'After all this malarkey. When it's all over and done with.' She nodded at the doorway behind them. 'I mean, this place is hardly going to be the same, is it? Not once the Yanks get their marching orders and our own lot get shipped back home.'

'I suppose not,' Frankie Doll said.

Tommy Fowler was already talking about the days ahead. But according to Tommy Fowler, things could only get better, not worse. A thousand laws and regulations would soon be relaxed. No war, no more worries about all those petty restrictions and regulations which were a blight on his current existence. People like you and me, Frankie boy, people like you and me – that's who the future was invented for. We're on our toes, you and me, we know what to expect, we've seen this coming a long way off.

And all Frankie Doll had been able to do was nod vigorously and agree with everything Tommy Fowler had said. Because that was how things worked with Tommy Fowler. Because Tommy Fowler was life and death to Frankie Doll. And even if Frankie Doll had known for certain that Tommy Fowler was wrong, that things were now changing in ways Tommy Fowler would never understand in a thousand years, then Frankie Doll would still have kept his mouth shut and said nothing. Because that was how things worked with Tommy Fowler.

Along the street, someone shouted, and then several others started cheering. Three men and a woman linked arms and danced in a clumsy circle in the road, encouraged and applauded by those who watched them.

'Pathetic,' Ruby Nolan said. 'It missed them, that's all. You ever see those pictures of Dresden?'

Frankie Doll nodded.

'Why try to keep them a secret? So what? Street I lived in near Belfast docks, house took a bomb that killed seven children – seven, and two of them unweaned babies. Mother and father survived, but all seven kids were blasted to smithereens.'

'It sounds—' Frankie Doll started to say.

'It sounds exactly like it was. A bomb out of nowhere doing what bombs out of nowhere do.' She made an explosion with her hands.

This time Frankie Doll wanted to ask her if her lack of sympathy had something to do with her upbringing. He knew that most Irishmen hated most Englishmen, and vice versa. Paddies, Micks and bogtrotters, Tommy Fowler called them – even his so-called Irish friends, and there had been a good number of those over the past six years. But instead, he said, 'It sounds like something you'd never recover from. Losing all those kids, and especially like that.'

'You'd think so,' Ruby Nolan said.

Frankie Doll took several paces into the street, stepping from the cool of the shadow into the surprising warmth of the sun. He closed his eyes and held his face to the sky. He'd been at the club for twelve hours. Tommy Fowler had made an appearance around midnight, patted him on the back, counted the takings and then left less than an hour later.

Along the street, the small, impromptu celebration ended.

People were alive, that was all; they'd been alive a minute earlier and they were still alive now.

'Are you walking?' Ruby called to him. She followed him into the sunlight and shielded her eyes.

Once out of the shadow, she looked much younger to Frankie Doll, a child almost.

All tastes and predilections, preferences and perversions catered for. Another one of Tommy Fowler's.

One of the men from along the road came to where Frankie Doll and Ruby Nolan stood.

'We live to fight another day,' he said to Ruby, clearly expecting her to share his relief.

'The thing was always going where it was always going,' she said, disappointing him.

'I did my bit for King and country,' he said to her. 'Invalided out after Dunkirk.'

'Then you didn't do anything for long,' she said. 'And I bet you spent most of that time running one way and looking the other.'

The man was unprepared for this. 'You're Irish,' he said. 'So?'

The man turned to Frankie Doll. 'You with her, are you?' he said, his meaning clear.

'What if he is?' Ruby Nolan said to him.

Having received no acknowledgement from Frankie Doll, the man was now less certain of himself and he backed away from the pair of them.

'That's right,' Ruby Nolan shouted at him. 'Run away. Again.' She spat at the ground close to the man's feet.

'You and her . . .' the man said to Frankie Doll.

'Me and her, what?'

'She's a tart, that's what.'

Ruby Nolan laughed at him. 'And you're wishing that you'd come across me all alone and that your brave new friends weren't watching you now.'

Frankie Doll saw by the man's reaction that she was right. 'Just go back to them,' he said.

'Or else what?' the man said.

'Or else this,' Frankie Doll said, and he swiftly and deftly took a knife from his pocket, opened out its slender six-inch blade and pointed it directly at the man's face.

'Jesus Christ,' the man said.

Ruby Nolan laughed again. 'No good shouting for him. He won't help you. Not twice in one morning.'

'Just get back to your happy-to-be-alive friends,' Frankie Doll told him. 'Buy a paper later, see where the rocket landed and who it killed instead of you, and perhaps then you'll feel even luckier and you can celebrate all over again.'

The man finally turned and walked away from the two of them.

'I could have handled him,' Ruby Nolan said.

Frankie Doll closed the knife and put it back in his pocket. 'You walking?' she said.

'Might as well,' Frankie Doll said.

2

JOSHUA SILVER STEPPED BACK FROM THE WINDOW AND TURNED to the man behind him. 'Sounded like a bomb,' he said. 'Or perhaps just some building or other finally giving up the ghost and collapsing.' He watched as the torn and yellowing net curtain fell back into place. On either side of the window, the heavy drapes hung equally dilapidated, faded by the light and stained with smoke and a multitude of hands. 'But why now?' he said, resuming their interrupted conversation.

The man behind him laughed at his concerns.

'Surely you must still know someone who knows you, who you are, *what* you are, someone still concerned enough to care, someone with the' – Joshua Silver rubbed his forefinger and thumb together to emphasize the point – '*wherewithal* to make these last few years more . . . more . . .'

'Comfortable?' his companion said. 'Anonymous? Dreary? Endless? Pointless?'

'I was going to say bearable,' Silver said, provoking more low laughter.

'How very *genteel.*'

'You deserve better than this hovel.'

'According to most of the world, and certainly most of this country and its kow-towing, lickspittle, lap-dog press, I deserve all I get, and much, much more. In fact, I don't doubt for one minute that there won't be a day of national rejoicing when I die on this Earth and depart to another, hopefully more rewarding, obliging, appreciative and grateful realm.'

Joshua Silver had heard it all before, but he still flinched at the words. 'But you're—'

'I'm Aleister Crowley,' Aleister Crowley shouted, as though this explained everything, which, as Joshua Silver knew only too well, it usually did. 'And if my baptized name is not enough, then you only have to flick through the dreary pages of that same self-regarding, pocket-lining press to find a dozen further and considerably more appreciated epithets.'

'"The Great Beast",' Joshua Silver said absently. It always sounded too overblown and melodramatic a title.

'See – even *you* have absorbed the trash.' Crowley paused and coughed, taking a minute to clear his throat and then to regain his breath and composure, massaging his chest and then his neck to aid this. 'I ask you – you, Joshua Silver – do I, in any shape or form, look like the Antichrist to you?'

'You look like what you are,' Silver said. 'An old and ailing man.'

'Seventy,' Crowley said. 'Three score and ten. My allegedly allotted span. Tell me, you being a doctor – your discredited expulsion from that august, though equally self-satisfied profession notwithstanding – is that what people still expect? Seventy years? Because if it is, then they're soon enough going to be expecting a lot more. They've survived, they *deserve* more, they deserve *better*. Soon they're going to want at least another decade on top of that, then they'll want to live to a hundred, and then—'

'And after that they'll want what you—' Silver stopped

abruptly and looked back to where Crowley sat in the over-stuffed armchair in the corner of the room, a dim lamp beside him, a cold fire at his feet, its ashes and a few pieces of unburned wood spilled on to the threadbare rug in front of it.

'What I want . . .' Crowley said. But there was neither anger nor reproach in his voice, and Silver heard this.

'All I meant . . .' Silver said.

'You're my old and trusted colleague,' Crowley said. 'I know *exactly* what you meant, as clearly as I understood your intent – would "warning" be more appropriate, do you think? – in making the remark.'

'"Old and trusted"?' Silver said. 'You make me sound like a dog.'

Crowley smiled at the words. 'No, not a dog,' he said.

Silver moved closer to the old man, to the table upon which he had placed his doctor's bag, pushing aside the unwashed crockery and glasses which filled the surface. He opened the bag and took out a stethoscope.

In response to this, Crowley unwound his scarf, opened the heavy, embroidered dressing gown he wore and then un-fastened a button of his pyjama jacket. A greying vest showed through the gap, and he pulled this up to reveal the soft, pale flesh beneath.

Silver went to him, rubbing the pad of his stethoscope against the palm of his hand.

'You seem nervous,' Crowley said.

'Perhaps because I already know what I'm going to hear,' Silver told him.

'A heart?' Crowley smiled at the old joke.

'A failing heart.'

23

'Then why listen?'

Silver pushed the disc against Crowley's chest and told him to stop talking. He moved the stethoscope a few inches left and right, closing his eyes as he silently counted the slow and erratic beats. He finally withdrew and then refastened Crowley's buttons himself.

'Well?' Crowley said. 'Is it still beating? Am I to go marching on into the godforsaken future the same fit and virile man I once was for all eternity?' He drew his dressing gown together and let the scarf fall back over his chest. On his head he wore a small tasselled Turkish cap, and he readjusted this as Silver withdrew from him.

'Ataturk himself gave me this,' Crowley said.

'I believe you already told me that a hundred times.'

'And these slippers.' Crowley raised his feet from the fender on which they rested, groaning slightly at the effort.

'See,' Silver said. 'You can't even lift your feet without it causing you some pain.'

Crowley considered this and then lowered his feet, drawing them closer to him. 'Is there any coal left?'

Silver laughed. 'You haven't had any coal all winter. Salvaged wood, that's all, rafters, joists, laths.'

'Silver linings, eh?' Crowley said. It was another old joke between the pair of them.

'If you say so,' Silver said.

'I do,' Crowley said. 'What, you expect me to show a little more gratitude, appreciation?'

'They pulled enough corpses out with the floorboards.'

'And if you believe the press, then I'd probably rather burn those than the wood.'

Silver shook his head at the words. 'All that's in the past.

People have had other things to worry about for a long time now.'

'Haw Haw said it was incumbent upon me to hold a Black Mass in Westminster Abbey. I do believe Horatio Bottomley devoted a whole edition of his filthy rag to exhorting me to do the same, to see where it got me.'

'That was before—'

'Before he knew the war was won, before he sniffed *that* particular wind and the stink blowing on it.'

'He's another one,' Silver said. 'Haw Haw.'

'Whatever he is, he's certainly going to feel a little tight around the collar before too long. Unless he believes he still has time to make some kind of deal.'

'The authorities won't countenance—'

'I was thinking of an altogether higher power,' Crowley said.

'Well, whichever way the wind blows, he's going to be swinging in it.'

'What a turn of phrase you have,' Crowley said, smiling. He motioned to a tray on the crowded table, and Silver poured them both a cup of tepid tea, after taking out his handkerchief and wiping the rims of both cups.

'No milk or sugar, I'm afraid,' Crowley said. 'Not even a squeeze of lemon or a drop of opium or ether to add a shine to our day.'

'It's scarcely even tea,' Silver said, sipping the bitter liquid and pulling a face.

'You must adapt, doctor. Adapt and survive. Adapt, change, bend in the wind, shift with circumstance.'

'Fine words from the once wealthy to the newly impoverished.'

'I lived according to my means,' Crowley said. 'That's all. Exactly as I am doing now.'

'But now you're old and your health is failing.'

Crowley sipped his own tea as though it were delicious. He licked his lips and let out a long breath. 'Which is precisely why I called you here today.'

'You didn't call me,' Silver said. 'How? I was coming anyway; I come every Monday, Wednesday and Friday.'

'And today is?'

'Wednesday.'

'Of course. How fastidious you remain.'

'To know what day of the week it is?'

'To insist on everyone else acknowledging the fact.' Crowley took another sip.

Silver knew better than to contest the ridiculous point. He had known Crowley for seven years now, ever since their failed Wandsworth Road enterprise. And whereas almost all of his other friends and colleagues had deserted Silver after his disgrace and downfall, Crowley had remained. Silver knew it was an unequal alliance – he would sometimes say 'friendship' – but it was one he accepted and had come to appreciate and depend upon.

'So tell me,' he said.

'Tell you what?'

'Why I was summoned into your holy presence amid these regal surroundings.'

'Because I have a scheme,' Crowley said.

Another scheme, Silver thought. 'To make money – or should I say, to dupe someone out of *their* money – to lure another so-called benefactor? Someone prepared to make your remaining time on Earth – in *this* realm – considerably

26

more comfortable than it appears to be at present?'

'None of those things,' Crowley said, smiling again. 'Though the latter might prove to be a not inconsiderable consequence of ... of ...' He trailed off into a cloud of reverie – something else with which Joshua Silver was also long familiar.

'A consequence of your "scheme"?'

'Of my scheme, yes.' Crowley cupped a hand to his mouth, breathed heavily into it and then sniffed at this.

'Periodontal disease,' Silver told him. 'Poor dental hygiene. You should clean your teeth; drink a glass of water every so often.'

'Water?' Crowley pulled a face and sipped his tea again. His teeth were yellow, some brown, and a few were missing, making those that remained ever more prominent in the tightening flesh of his face.

'It wouldn't kill you,' Silver said. He sniffed the other sour odours of the room – old food, damp, mould, burned gas, unwashed clothes, dirt, stale air – and wiped his mouth with his handkerchief.

'Are you about to recite your litany?' Crowley said.

Silver understood him and said nothing.

'Crabs, phlebitis, gallstones, recurrent migraines, ditto malaria, intermittent neuralgia, uncontrollable flatulence, enteric fever, congestion of the throat, asthma, to say nothing of the whole galaxy of aches and pains, failures and seizures that the ageing flesh is heir to. Did I miss anything out?'

'A diseased liver?' Silver said. 'Incipient and all too obvious dipsomania?'

'Ah, yes, that.'

'And your flatulence is not uncontrollable, merely something you indulge.'

'Ah. And I never even mentioned my paranoia, my arrogance and my egotism, all similarly indulged at considerable expense to others.'

'None of which, strictly speaking, are medical conditions – at least not conditions that fall within my own sphere of expertise and practice. Nothing upon which I might confidently . . .' Silver stopped speaking and turned away from Crowley, looking back to the window and the dim light it framed. He closed his eyes and rubbed his forehead.

After this, neither man spoke for a moment, and the room filled with the heavy ticking of the mantel clock.

'Nor did I mention my testicular varicocele,' Crowley said eventually, causing Silver to smile. 'China,' he went on. 'The malaria. Or it might have been India. Or Egypt. Probably Egypt.'

'You were a young, healthy man then,' Silver said.

'And I'm not now?'

'The flesh . . .'

'It's why I lost most of my friends and acquaintances – my paranoia and arrogance.'

'Not to forget your egotism.' Silver wondered if Crowley had left the word unspoken so that he might say it, another of their slender yet unbreakable bonds.

'Of course. My egotism.'

Six years earlier, Joshua Silver had been exposed, accused, tried and found guilty of gross professional misconduct. After which he had been struck from the medical register. He had known Crowley only a few months when Crowley had introduced him to a man called Dyer, like Crowley an ethyl addict. Silver was in debt and Dyer had loaned him money at extortionate, unpayable rates of interest. At the end of those few months, Silver had been persuaded by Dyer into perpetrating a medical fraud whereby all of Silver's debts and associated concerns would evaporate.

It was a simple plan, and for six months it worked. Any patient presenting to Silver with abdominal pains he diagnosed as suffering from acute appendicitis. He then arranged for an operation to be undertaken, before which the patient would attend Silver's Wandsworth Road surgery and be given a preliminary anaesthetic there while the ambulance was called for. Silver would make an incision and then immediately stitch this back up in his own examination room once the patient was unconscious. The patient would then 'recover' from this anaesthetic in the same room, having been supposedly returned there by the same non-existent ambulance. If any of the sufferers expressed surprise at what had happened, then Silver told them that everything had been planned and carried out to keep their anxiety and pain to a minimum. The 'preliminary', relaxing anaesthetic, he would explain, was in fact the actual operating anaesthetic, and the ambulance was already outside waiting while this took effect. When the stitching was complete, a painkilling injection was given directly into the abdominal wall; sometimes a few punches achieved the expected bruising. A further week-long course of much weaker painkillers was prescribed, by which time the original pain, whatever its cause, had usually ended. Besides, Silver always reassuringly pointed out, some continuing pain and discomfort was only to be expected after such an operation. When patients said they expected to have to remain in hospital to recuperate, Silver would equally convincingly explain to them that modern medical opinion no longer considered this necessary or desirable. Besides, that was where the true cost of the operation lay. Any insistent or suspicious victims were then prodded and poked around their recent stitching to distract them.

In the eventual court case, twenty-three patients testified against Silver. It was widely expected that he would be imprisoned, but his sentence was handed down on the day after war was declared, and he was instead struck off the register and told by the judge to somehow redeem himself in the difficult years ahead.

When he looked back from the window, Crowley was watching him.

'I—' Silver began.

Crowley raised a hand to stop him. 'I know,' he said.

'I never got my chance,' Silver said.

'To atone?'

'In this lot. I put my name down for everything going. I offered my services for free – you can imagine what a joke that was to most of them. I offered to swill floors, to dig latrines. I applied for a job burning medical waste at Saint Thomas's. I wasn't even considered trustworthy enough for that.'

'I know,' Crowley said. 'I know. We are both, in our own ways, wasted men.'

'"Wasted"?'

'Our potential, our capabilities, the challenges we might once have met, the desires and ambitions we might once have pursued and fulfilled.'

Silver smiled and shook his head at the melodramatic words, but at the same time acknowledging the kindness they contained. 'And so here we are,' he said. '"A wrack line of Humanity washed up on the shores of History".'

'Haw Haw again?' Crowley said.

'Churchill.'

'That bare-faced liar? Wait until the elections.'

'They'd make him King if they could,' Silver said.

Crowley shook his head. 'You just wait.'

'But the man on the street—'

Crowley laughed at the phrase. 'The man on the street? The man on the street? You forget, my dear doctor, that I, too, have had countless encounters with that so-called man on the street, and let me tell you, that so-called good, honest, God-fearing, decent, salt-of-the-earth man on the street is as petty, as prejudiced, as self-serving and as greedy as the rest of us.'

'You and I included?' Silver said.

'I'm afraid so. I'm afraid so.'

Silver finally put down his undrunk tea and dropped his stethoscope back into his bag. He still carried this with him everywhere he went. When, occasionally, people asked him if he was a doctor, he would laugh and joke with them and tell them that he had retired only a few weeks earlier and that old habits died hard. Sometimes he added one or two darker remarks – the things he had recently endured, the things he had seen, things he had been called upon to do that had once been unimaginable to him – and people would tell him that they understood him perfectly and would wish him a happy retirement. What was it, a cottage in the country somewhere, a village green, a garden full of flowers and vegetables and a clutch of grandchildren and grateful ex-patients forever filling his days? Something like that, he would say, something like that, and then he would edge away from them back into that surrounding emptiness he now inhabited.

'Are you leaving?' Crowley asked him.

Silver looked at his watch. 'I have other – I mean – things to do, people to see, all that.'

'Of course,' Crowley said. 'However – my scheme. Surely I mentioned it to you before you insisted on listening to the music of my dying heart.'

'Your arrhythmia,' Silver said. 'Not entirely uncommon in men of—'

'My abused and ravaged state?'

'Your age.'

'But I'm immortal,' Crowley said, laughing. 'Don't you read the papers? Don't you listen to me?'

Silver put his bag back on the table.

'Are you not drinking your tea?' Crowley asked him, reaching for the cup, his small, ringed finger already raised in expectation.

3

LAURA FELT THE MAN'S LEG PRESS SLOWLY BUT DELIBER-
ately against her own. On the other side of her, the
second man moved away from her slightly, but then stayed
firmly where he sat. The plush of the seat felt warm against
Laura's skin.

'You seem a friendly enough sort of girl,' the man with the
pressing, testing leg said to her.

'That's me,' Laura said to him. 'Friendly enough.'

The man seized on the remark, which he mistook for
more than the practised encouragement it was.

'Is that friendly enough, or *more* than friendly enough?'
he said.

Laura caught the glance he exchanged with the second
man.

'Depends,' she said. She picked up her glass and waited for
both men to do the same. 'A toast,' she said. 'To friendly people
everywhere. A proper toast, down in one.' She possessed a
whole array of similar ploys and techniques. *Drink, drink,
drink,* Tommy Fowler always said. *That's where the money is.*

'To friendly people,' the first man said.

Laura's glass had already been filled when it arrived on the
tray, and the young waitress who had put it in front of her

had kept her finger on the slender stem until Laura picked it up. Water. Then the champagne bottle filled with a mixture of cheap sweet wine and soda water had been put down and the waitress had filled the other two glasses by pouring from a foot above them in an effort to create at least the semblance of celebratory bubbles. Besides, who remembered what real champagne actually tasted like? Who had even been able to afford that champagne when it *had* been available? And who *wouldn't* want champagne now that everybody was ready and waiting and desperate to celebrate? It sometimes felt, Laura had said only the previous day to Frankie Doll, as though the whole world was holding its breath, bursting to let it out and to shout. And Frankie Doll had said that he supposed so.

'It's already opened,' one of the men had complained as the drink was poured.

'Club policy,' Laura said.

'Policy?'

'Put your eye out, a cork like that.' They must surely have known that it wasn't real champagne – real anything – and that they were as trapped and as complicit in the deceit as she and the waitress were.

'That's right,' the waitress said. 'We can't go popping our corks left, right and centre, now can we?'

Both men laughed at the remark and picked up their glasses. A single sip, whatever their response, and the bottle was paid for. No argument.

They drained their glasses, both clearly disappointed with what they had been given. They shared another glance. The man who sat with his leg against Laura's lightly touched her thigh and then motioned for her to refill the two empty glasses.

34

'Down in one, you said.' He tapped the rim of his glass against Laura's, which remained almost full.

'It's two in the morning,' Laura said. 'I'm already half-cut. You don't want me passing out on you, do you?'

'Half-cut?' the second man said anxiously.

Laura understood him perfectly and smiled at him. 'But still friendly,' she said. She winked at him. 'If you catch my drift.'

The waitress refilled the two empty glasses. Another reason for the bottle already being opened was that it had never been properly sealed in the first place, and to disguise the fact that it had only ever been two-thirds full as it approached the table. If anyone complained at this – and few did, not now that the bottle was standing there and the bubbles rapidly flattening – then either some of the drink had been lost when opened, or the waitress had helped herself to a sip – and surely they didn't begrudge a hardworking girl like herself a tiny little drink to keep her going at the end of a long, hard night, did they? – or a glass had already been poured for Laura here. To add further to all this uncertainty, the waitress might even then pretend to swig from the bottle herself, immediately offering the lipstick-covered rim to whoever had protested the most loudly and uselessly at the swindle.

Laura looked to the bar, where two of Tommy Fowler's men stood and looked back at her. They knew as well as she did where to focus their attention. Newcomers, people finding seats, men looking lost, men being approached by the girls, drinks being served. A second bottle ordered and everyone could relax. The compact was made and everybody was in profit. Or, more accurately, Tommy Fowler was in profit, and everybody else could just get on with keeping it that way.

She looked around the darkened room hoping to see Frankie Doll, but he wasn't there. Upstairs with Fowler, most likely. Being told what to do next. And then what to do after that. Perhaps reporting on the night so far. It might have been two in the morning, but everything in that place, including the dawn and early morning, counted as night.

The place was mostly filled, not too many Americans, fifty-fifty forces and others, so many bottles sold, so many girls working, the names of the girls already come and gone, familiar faces, people who owed Tommy Fowler money or favours – and there were always plenty of those – people who didn't owe him enough, and people Tommy Fowler wanted to see.

'So,' the man to Laura's left said, drawing her back to the pair of them.

Laura instinctively raised her glass. 'To the end of the war,' she said. You needed to pick a toast no one would refuse to drink to. To the end of the war. To loved ones, absent friends. To the days ahead and the months and years beyond. Avoid anything more specific than loved ones. No mention of wives or sweethearts, for instance. Men were there to forget – another of Tommy Fowler's – and the girls were there to help them do just that. It was a simple enough equation, simple enough to remember and simple enough to forever be a part of.

This time, neither of the men emptied their glass, both stopping after a single sip. If there was one thing Tommy Fowler hated, it was a sipper.

At the bar, Tommy Fowler's two men turned their backs on Laura and started talking to the barman.

'What's your name?' the second man asked her.

'Laura.' None of Tommy Fowler's suggested alternatives had ever appealed or stuck. 'And you are?' Whatever he told her, she would forget the instant he left her. She knew after only a minute which of the new customers would return and become regulars, and which she would never see again.

The man hesitated, and she wanted to laugh at him and ask him what he thought he would achieve by the lie he was struggling to concoct.

'Jim,' he said eventually. 'Jim Smith.'

'Then pleased to meet you, Jim,' Laura said. She held out her hand to him, her fingers horizontal and folded slightly, and the man took it and kissed it. Another suppressed laugh.

'You, likewise,' he said. 'Laura.'

You, likewise.

He had a broken nose, and so for the rest of her time with him she would think of him as 'Nose'.

'And you?' she said to the other man.

And he too gave her a false name. He had a double chin. 'Chin'.

'Jim and John and Laura,' Nose said.

The young waitress came back to them. Ten minutes would be counted out after the last of the first bottle, twenty after the second. Two people drinking, add five minutes; four people, deduct five. 'Do we need another bottle here?' she said.

Laura immediately finished her water. 'Do my gentlemen friends look like cheapskates?' she said to the girl. She picked up the empty bottle and let the last of its frothy dregs drip out.

'More of the same?' the waitress said.

Neither of the men spoke. Chin tapped his jacket to feel

the outline of his wallet. 'Might as well,' he said. 'Why not?' Next he might say that the night was still young, or that they only lived once, or that they might as well get it while they still could, or that nothing good lasted for ever, or that . . .

Laura stopped listening to him and resumed looking around her.

Beyond the waitress, a man crossed the room and nodded once in Laura's direction. Deserter Sweeney. Another of Fowler's lackeys. A new arrival at the club, even further down the pecking order than Frankie Doll. Sweeney wore a hat and kept this low over his eyes as he walked.

Everything about the boy looked furtive. Laura held his eyes for an instant and then Sweeney turned away and continued on his course across the room.

The waitress tapped Laura's foot with her own and Laura looked back up at her.

'Lucky old you,' the girl said. 'Two handsome men all to yourself.' It was another prompt, a suggestion that a second girl be sent to the table. Two men, two wallets.

Laura looked at her more closely. Perhaps she wanted the work herself. The girl had been drinking, that much was obvious. In which case, Tommy Fowler had better stay upstairs; even the two men standing at the bar had better not look too closely at the girl.

'Luckier than she knows,' Nose said, winking at Laura and sharing a glance with Chin.

'You need to pay her,' Laura said to Chin. 'For the second bottle.'

Chin took out his wallet and slowly unfolded and handed over the notes.

'We've got stronger stuff,' the waitress said. 'But I'm only supposed to offer it to special customers, to the privileged few, so to speak.'

'Of course they're special,' Laura said. 'They're with me.' It always amazed her how little these men actually heard and saw.

'And that makes us special, does it?' Nose said. There was a sudden, harsher note in his voice.

'Of course it does.' Laura felt his hand tighten on her leg.

The waitress took the notes Chin offered her and tucked them into her cleavage, shaking her breasts as she did this. Tommy Fowler said it added value to the transaction at no extra cost to anyone. Now both men watched her.

'So,' she said. 'The hard stuff or more of this?' A single bottle of the diluted wine was usually enough. 'A proper drink it is, then,' she said, growing exasperated by the two men's lack of response to her calculated prompting.

'What about Laura here?' Chin said.

Laura pretended to laugh. 'Treat yourselves to the good stuff,' she said. 'Too much more of anything and I'll be good for nothing.'

'And we wouldn't want that, now would we?' Nose said to her. 'Not after everything else.' He finally lifted his hand from her leg and took out his own wallet, holding out more notes and waiting for the waitress to lean forward so that he could tuck the money between her breasts. The girl did this, giggling as he pushed in and then patted the notes.

'You'll get me into trouble, you will,' the girl said. 'I'm only here to fetch and carry. What do you take me for? Honestly.'

Save it, Laura thought, but said nothing. *You're already on the treadmill; just be patient.* It was rare that any of Tommy Fowler's investments failed to pay off one way or another.

'You saying you're not as friendly as our Laura here?' Chin said to the girl.

'I'm on duty,' the waitress said. 'I'm not saying that I *can't* be as friendly as the next girl, just that right now I'm supposed to be working.'

Laura looked at the other girls sitting at other tables, at the girls coming and going, some leaving with customers, others returning to the club alone. She wished Fowler would finish with Frankie Doll and that he would come back downstairs. She would feel better having Frankie Doll in the room instead of Fowler's other men. Not safer, exactly, but he would be *there*, and he would know that *she* was there, and it would make a difference.

'Don't go away,' the waitress said. She turned her back on them and pulled the notes from her cleavage. Once received, all money was to be carried only in the club's purses. And all purses were to be carried only in the pockets sewn into the front of the club's own tunics. And any employee found in possession of any money except in those purses in those tunic pockets . . . it seldom needed to be said; there were always stories of dishonest employees and what had happened to them.

'So,' Nose said, both his hands now on the table, his leg still against Laura's.

'So,' Laura said.

'I meant, so what now?' Nose said.

Chin took out a cigarette case, opened it and laid it on the table.

'We wait for the drink to arrive and then enjoy it when it comes?' Laura said.

'And after that?' Nose said, smiling.

'That all depends,' Laura said.

'What, on how much of this watered-down piss you're going to go on conning us into drinking?'

Laura started to speak.

'And don't act all surprised or offended,' Chin said, also smiling.

Nose lit two cigarettes and gave one to Laura. She took it and drew hard on it.

'You knew the rules the minute you came into the place,' she said to Nose, causing Chin to laugh. 'So, what are you?' she said. 'War Office or Secret Service on a well-earned night off?'

Chin laughed again. 'She's got us,' he said to Nose. 'Got us bang to rights.'

Nose, however, was less amused by this sudden turn of events.

'Or perhaps you're General Staff, already planning what happens next,' Laura said.

'If you think—' Nose said.

'Options, you see,' Laura said. 'That's what all this is really about. Options. Your options, mine, what happens next, what doesn't happen next.'

'She's right,' Chin said, still amused by everything Laura was revealing to them, the curtain she had so swiftly and un-expectedly pulled aside.

'She's a working girl, that's all,' Nose said.

'Steady on,' Chin said.

They were back on level ground, back at a starting point, and, to Laura at least, the way ahead was again reassuringly clear.

'I am what I am,' she told Nose. 'The same as those two men at the bar are what *they* are.'

Both Chin and Nose turned to look, and at the bar Tommy Fowler's men looked back. The waitress was standing beside them, ordering the new drinks. One of the men pointed at the table and slowly shook his head.

'There's no need for that kind of thing,' Chin said to Laura, his voice dry.

'If you say so,' Laura said, watching. And she pointed back at the two men, raised her empty glass an inch from the table and then set it back down again. At the bar, the men nodded once and turned away from her. 'See?' she said. 'Do you see now how simple and straightforward and obvious it all is?'

'Oh, we see,' Chin said, smiling again.

The waitress came back to them, this time carrying a tray with two glasses and a jug on it. Two small blended, un-branded whiskies, to which she immediately added water.

At the far side of the room a door opened and Sweeney reappeared, closely followed by Tommy Fowler himself. They moved through the tables, Tommy Fowler gesturing and talking briefly to his regular customers. The two men at the bar went to him, adding to this entourage, always a few paces behind Fowler as he leaned over shoulders, shook hands, kissed cheeks and lifted and drank from glasses.

'He looks like he owns the place,' Nose said.

'There's a good reason for that,' Laura said. She kept her own eyes on the door from which Fowler and Sweeney had emerged, and a moment later it swung open again and Frankie Doll finally came into the room.

4

PRISON OFFICER ARTHUR BONE LET HIMSELF INTO THE CELL where Peter Thomas Lester Tait sat waiting for him. Punctuality, that was Bone. Rules and regulations, order and precision were night and day, sun and moon to the man.

At Bone's first rap on the door – always this professional courtesy – Tait leaped to his feet and stood at the opposite wall, the back of his head resting against the sloping window ledge. He could feel the rising sun on his scalp, imagine the shadows of the six upright bars on his skull. The sun was coming in now with the spring – Tait's last – and tipping an inch further over the ledge with each passing day. And just as Prison Officer Bone's life was grounded and governed by those reassuring regulations, so were Peter Thomas Lester Tait's few remaining weeks of life taken up more and more by these observed and measurable minutiae.

The door opened and Bone removed his key before coming inside. The key was one of dozens on the chain at his belt.

'You up, then?' he said to Tait.

'Up and waiting,' Tait answered him.

'Good boy. That's what we like to see.'

'You know me,' Tait said.

'I do that,' Bone said. 'I do that. What is it now?'

Tait didn't understand him.

'I mean how long have you been here?' Bone said. 'Me and you, all this.'

'Four months exactly,' Tait said.

'You should have said.' Bone looked quickly around the cell. Everything present and everything in its proper place. Good lad.

'Said what?' Tait said.

'The four months thing. We could have – I don't know – something.' Bone held out the key he still held, pointing around the small space with it.

'Marked it, you mean?' Tait said uncertainly.

'Something like that.' Bone came fully into the room, careful to leave the door open behind him, measuring the gap with his polished boot.

Tait was glad to see him. It was never the same when Bone was off duty. The others treated him like a murderer.

'Long night?' he said to Bone.

Bone waited before answering. 'Speak when spoken to, lad.' Then he smiled, dismissing the small transgression.

Bone was in the ARP. 'Longish,' he said. 'I thought all that was well behind us, but they want us standing ready until' – he shook his head – '"the Cessation of Hostilities".' He breathed in deeply and patted his chest. 'I wasn't on. Not last night. Not rostered, see? But I heard fast enough. Ear-to-the-ground man, that's me. I came round past Hillmarton Road on my way in. That's where it fetched up. Professional curiosity. See if there was anything I could do.'

Tait half turned his face to the sun on the window ledge, feeling it against his cheek, closing his eyes against its sudden glare.

Bone saw this. 'Feel good, does it? East-facing, see? The opposite side won't get the proper benefit until the height of summer. You want to thank your lucky stars you got this allocation.'

'No good to me, the height of summer,' Tait said.

'No, well . . .'

There was a moment of awkward silence between the two men, and then Bone said, 'Still, you never know – your appeal and all that.'

'I suppose so,' Tait said.

'That's the spirit,' Bone said quickly, as keen as Tait himself was to move on. He came further into the cell and stood beside Tait at the window. He pulled a face at the smell of the bucket at Tait's feet.

'Tuck it under the bunk, lad,' he said.

'It's against—'

'This is *me* telling you – Arthur Bone. Go on – tuck it under until slop call.'

Tait pushed the enamelled bucket beneath the lower bunk.

'Still sleeping up top?' Bone said.

'I can see the sky better,' Tait said. 'The moon, stars, all that.'

Outside, along the raised walkway, other doors were opened, and shouting, echoing voices filled the space. There were footsteps. Men called to each other, doors were slammed shut.

'When will they move me out of here?' Tait said.

Bone, unprepared for the question, said, 'Oh, that? Plenty of time yet. Not until – well – not for a while yet. And who knows . . . ?'

'Right,' Tait said, again regretting having forced the pair of them into this awkwardness.

When his appeal was heard and either dismissed, or taken under consideration or allowed to proceed, *then* a decision would be made on where Tait was moved to next in the prison.

'So, what was it?' he said to Bone.

At first, Bone didn't understand him. And then he said, 'Oh, the bang? A rocket. Doodlebug. V-1. They heard it coming from miles off. Observer Corps telephoned it in ten minutes before it landed. Fat lot of good they are. Telephones? What's wrong with a proper field radio set? Word is, the ack-ack boys have been told not to do any more shooting. Bad for morale. Makes people jumpy, makes them think things are turning bad again, if you get my meaning.'

'What about the fly-boys?' Tait said.

Bone shook his head. 'Them? What good have they been recently as far as we're concerned? They should put the lot of them on bombers. Bomb the launch sites, problem solved. All this kind of thing should be long over by now; people should be looking forwards, not backwards. Talk at the ARP station is that it was an accident.'

'What was?'

'The rocket. One of the new lads I talked to on my way in said someone had told him that he thought *we*'d fired the thing off by way of a test.'

'A test? What sort of a test?'

'You tell me,' Bone said. 'You know what these boffins are like. Everything for the Greater Good, and all that. You tell me.'

'Were there any fatalities?' Tait asked him.

'Good lad,' Bone said. 'You remembered. First thing they drilled into us, that – "fatalities". Supposed to sound better

46

than "deaths". Material damage on a scale of one to ten. Fatalities and lesser injuries. That used to be the big joke – what would be greater than fatality? Death's death, whichever way you look at it, whatever fancy name you try and give it.'

'You don't need to tell me that,' Tait said. And this time there was no awkwardness, but even a kind of knowing and shared reassurance in the remark.

'No, I suppose not,' Bone said. 'And in answer to your question, I can't give you any figures. Nothing released yet. Even the blokes on the ground didn't have a proper grip on what was happening. Some of these new blokes – sloppy, no other word for it. All wide-eyed and excited. Never seen a day's proper action in their lives, and then all of a sudden – whoosh – this. Some of them younger than you, it looked to me. Kids, some of them.'

Tait was nineteen, convicted of murder and expected to hang. No date had yet been confirmed for his execution.

Thirteen months earlier, the previous March, Tait and three others had attempted to rob a club in Globe Town. There had been a fight, during which Tait had been struck on the head and knocked unconscious for several minutes. At some point in the failed robbery, a man in the club, a customer, had been shot and killed. The first Peter Tait had known of this was when he had regained consciousness on the back seat of the car in which he and the others were escaping, and when he was told what had happened and what *he* had done.

In court, Tait's lawyer, unable to dismiss a great deal of the material evidence and witness testimony against his client, had attempted to defend Tait on the grounds that his accomplices had concocted their story about Tait being the killer while he was unconscious to save their own skins. Two of the other men had been arrested alongside Tait; a fourth man remained at large. There was gun oil and powder residue on Tait's hand and sleeve, and his fingerprints alone were on the gun. Both of the other arrested men pointed to Tait as the killer, and both of them now awaited sentencing on lesser charges, gained largely in exchange for their testimony against Tait.

It was an age ago now, and the world had turned. A single, accidental killing set against all those millions and millions of cruel and deliberate other murders. But, as the judge had told Tait during his summing-up, Humanity dwelled in the details of circumstance, and those details, there and then, and in that particular court and on that particular date, had convicted Peter Tait of the murder of a man he had never known.

After the trial, his lawyer had made it clear to Tait that he had no appetite or hope for a successful appeal. And so another man, a stranger to Tait, had been appointed to represent him in this. Over the past nine months, Tait had seen the man only twice – in total for less than an hour – and had heard from him on only three other occasions, and then only to remind him of the slowly moving machinery into which his life – or what now remained of it – had fallen.

'Where does guessing get you?' Bone said. 'You search, you dig, you count. You look in directories, you find out who was living in the bombed house. Every station has a directory. By rights, they should know exactly who everybody is and exactly where they are living. Or not, as the case might be. Rules and procedure, see? You know where you are – no room for all this . . . this . . . what is it?'

'Speculation?' Tait said.

'That's the one. Speculation. And what's that when it's at home except guessing? What the world needs now is certainty, proper order, a way ahead. Not guessing and speculation. That's a man panning for gold in a river, that is, speculation.'

'My father was a pawnbroker,' Tait said unexpectedly, interrupting this flow.

'Oh?' Bone said.

'Whitechapel. Nothing official, you understand. More of a money-lender, I suppose.'

'But with security,' Bone said.

'Clothes and pieces of furniture, mostly. None of it worth anything.'

'You're wrong there,' Bone said. 'I've seen people who've lost their wives and husbands and kids searching through the smoking wreckage of their homes looking for a hat or a book or a special teapot. Searching for them like they were family jewels. Kids, neighbours, all sorts lying dead under tarpaulins, and there they are, digging in the bricks and what-not looking for a teapot. You'd laugh if it didn't make you want to cry for them.'

'I suppose so,' Tait said.

'I'm serious,' Bone said. 'First step on the road to the nut house for some of them.' He tapped a finger to his temple. 'And I'll tell you something else that's not common knowledge' – and here he looked behind him as though there might be someone stood at the door eager to overhear what he was about to say – 'there's things they're turning up over there that's sending some of our lads in the same direction. And I know that for a fact.' He moved the finger from his temple to tap the side of his bulbous nose.

Bone was fifty-seven. He had worked in the prison service since he was eighteen, after four years of working as a labourer alongside his father. He had married at twenty, and his wife had died of cancer of the stomach, bowel and womb seven years previously, after an illness of two years. It had been a long, slow and painful death, and Bone had cared for his dying wife and done everything possible for her. There had been no children. The pair of them had prayed to God, but their prayers had gone unanswered. Like every one of Bone's prayers ever since.

At the outbreak of war, Bone had been turned away from the recruitment office set up in Camden Town Hall because he was too old. He had joined the ARP four days later and had made this his surrogate military life. He had few friends, mostly workmates and casual acquaintances, and most of these avoided Bone as assiduously as he avoided them. When the doctor had finally drawn up the sheet over his wife's face in the bedroom of the only home they had ever lived in, Bone had shaken the man's hand, sent a message to the undertaker, and then set off for his shift at Pentonville an hour later.

'You do things properly, see?' he said to Tait. 'You do things properly or they're not worth doing in the first place.'

Tait was still thinking of his pawnbroker father, caught off-guard by the vividness of the unexpected memory.

'Right,' Bone said loudly. 'That's me and you done for the time being. I'll say you was alive and well and that you'd had a good night's sleep.'

'I suppose so,' Tait said. And, in truth, he was alive and well and he had had a good night's sleep.

'You got that detective coming back in next week,' Bone

said. 'Someone marked it up on the visitor list. He's a bit keen.'

'He's not happy with all the uncertainty, and things,' Tait said.

'There you go, then. What you worrying about? You got a lawyer, an appeal hearing coming up, and a copper with doubts. What more do you want?'

'I suppose so,' Tait said.

The rising sun was hidden briefly by a solitary passing cloud, casting a shadow over Tait's face, chilling him and causing him to turn away from the window.

'Believe me,' Bone said, 'I've seen it all. In here, I mean. "Reasonable doubt" – that's what you've got. In spades. Your first judge should have directed the jury better.'

It was what the second lawyer had told Tait, and what Tait had told Bone. More hope born of nothing substantial, another barely marked path into the dimly lit future.

'He should have made more of me being knocked out,' Tait said. He'd said the same thing fifty times afterwards to the lawyer as they'd sat together in the court cell following his conviction.

Uncomfortable at hearing Tait say this, Bone said, 'Of course he should,' and took a step back towards the door.

'Are you going?' Tait said.

'You ask me that every single morning,' Bone said.

Tait laughed.

'That's the spirit. I got some real criminals, some real hard nuts along here to go and read the Riot Act to. You, you're a good lad, no bother to anyone, you keep it that way and things will all turn out for the best.' He stuck his thumb up, and Tait did the same. 'Back later.'

Bone left the cell and pulled the door shut behind him, locking it and then opening and securing its inspection panel.

Back in the cell, he saw, the sun had reappeared over the window sill, and Tait was now standing with his back to the door and again basking in its warmth.

5

A T THE SOUND OF SWEENEY'S RETURN, VERONICA MAR-
guerite Tulley (christened Vera Margaret) – 'Veronica'
after that woman in the Bible who wiped Jesus's brow on
his journey to be crucified – opened her door and waited on
the landing, watching as he climbed the final uncarpeted
staircase in the darkness, his progress revealed only by the
glow of his cigarette and by the rasp of his laboured breathing
in the cold air. She waited for the boy's head to draw level
with her slippered feet before speaking to him.

'That you?' she said.

Sweeney paused in his climbing and wiped his mouth on
his sleeve. 'Jesus Christ, what you doing standing there in the
dark like that?'

'I heard you coming in,' Veronica said. 'That's all. I thought
you might like some company. Everybody needs a bit of company now and then.'

'It's five o'clock in the morning,' Sweeney said.

'You know me,' Veronica said. 'Light sleeper, always have
been. Dead to the world one minute, wide awake and raring
to go the next.'

'You could still stay put,' Sweeney told her. 'In bed, I mean.

Who else you think's going to come panting all this way up here?'

'I suppose so,' Veronica said. She waited for him to finish climbing the stairs.

'Still, I don't suppose you can be too careful,' Sweeney said to her, finally arriving on the landing beside her. It was an apology of sorts, and Veronica understood this. She reached out and rubbed his arm.

'You're freezing,' she said. She was old enough to be his mother, and Sweeney was young enough to be the son she had never had.

'Walked,' Sweeney said.

'All that way? From the Regency?'

'I've walked further.'

'Busy night?'

'So-so. Bit of business for Fowler, an hour at Archer Street, bit of time round Mayfair.'

'The man takes advantage of you,' Veronica said. 'And worse than that, you let him.'

Sweeney said nothing.

'I worry for you, that's all.' She continued rubbing his arm.

'It's what I'm there for,' Sweeney said. 'He's not all that bad. We get on.'

'I can see that,' she said. 'Let's talk about something else.'

Sweeney pinched out the last of his cigarette, watching as the few sparks that fell to the floor died before they hit it.

'I've got the kettle on,' Veronica said hopefully.

'I'm fagged out,' Sweeney said.

Veronica pushed her door further open. 'Gas is lit.' She doubted if Sweeney lit his own small gas fire one day in ten. Even during that last cold winter and spring.

'Ten minutes, then,' Sweeney said. It was never ten minutes; but even that would have been enough for Veronica. He followed her into her room.

Sweeney had been born with a cleft palate and a harelip, which a clumsy operation when he was eighteen months old had done little to rectify. It was why he spoke as little as possible now, why he spoke with a lisp, and why he spoke in short, fractured sentences. It was why he usually kept his head bowed, and why he often lifted his hand to cover his mouth when he spoke; it was why his lips were forever wet, and why he frequently wiped them. It was why he was shy around most women, especially those his own age, and why, though increasingly aware of their attractions as he entered his twentieth year, he avoided them whenever possible.

Sweeney had never known his father – even his teenaged mother had been uncertain of the man's identity – and at the time of the operation on his palate he had been handed over by his mother to the first of a succession of orphanages and other homes.

Two years ago, at seventeen, he had applied to join the fighting Army and had been rejected because of his mouth. He had been sent instead to work for the Ordnance Corps at Colchester, where he had been bullied and scapegoated and regularly beaten and put on orders. After three months of this, he had absconded from the depot and returned to London. He was listed as Absent Without Leave, sought out and then returned to detention in the military prison adjacent to the Ordnance depot. Upon his release after five months, he had done the same thing again, and this pattern had been repeated until the previous autumn, when the Army had finally tired of him and given him a dishonourable discharge. The two men deputed to escort Sweeney to the lorry compound en route back to London had waited until the three of them were alone, told him to sign his release documents, and had then beaten him unconscious.

Sweeney's first memory – or so he had long since convinced himself – was of his young mother screaming at the sight of his wet and gaping mouth.

He had returned to the city and offered his services to Tommy Fowler, who had heard him out in the company of a dozen others, and who had then laughed just as loudly as his mother had screamed. But Sweeney had stayed, and after a month of running errands – 'making himself useful' – Tommy Fowler had pushed a handful of screwed-up notes into his pocket, grabbed and held his face and told Sweeney that he wanted 'none of this mouth stuff' – meaning his mumbling and turning aside in his own presence – and that the job was his. Errand boy promoted to lackey promoted to wait-and-see. Then Fowler had asked him if he was related to Sweeney Todd, and because Sweeney had no idea who Sweeney Todd was, he said that of course he was. 'Then you'll do for me,' Tommy Fowler had told him.

The first thing Sweeney had done upon his return home that particular morning was to ask his new neighbour what she knew of Sweeney Todd, and Veronica – having a theatrical background herself – told him all she knew, and whatever she could concoct, about the demon barber, prolonging Sweeney's simple enquiry into the first of his hour-long visits to her room. And everything she told him, Sweeney committed to memory, ready to repeat to Tommy Fowler when the connection was next mentioned.

In her room now, Sweeney sat close to the small fire. It was clear to him that it had not been burning long, that Veronica had most likely lit it only when she'd heard him coming in.

There were four floors to the house, eight landings, four long and four short staircases. All the tenants came and went at all hours. It was that sort of house. Veronica said it was a house that had lost its way because of the war. And she should know; she had lived in enough of them over the past forty years. Sometimes the place was filled, and all of the dozen rooms were occupied; and sometimes it seemed to Sweeney that he and Veronica were the last two people living there, completely alone up in their attic rooms.

More often than not, all Sweeney ever knew of these other faceless tenants further down were the lights beneath their doors, the music from their radios and gramophones, an occasional raised voice or crying child, and the smell of their cooking which lingered in the unventilated stairwell.

The house was part of a block, which included five others, and where, three years earlier, a bomb had sliced off the end wall, leaving the pattern of rooms, stairs and fireplaces revealed to the passing world. A timber buttress had been put up against the lower walls, but no other attempt at repair had ever been made. The land at the side and the rear of the house was filled with mounded rubble, upon which strangers endlessly scavenged. The supply of gas, water and electricity to the house was as intermittent and as unreliable as its tenants.

'You want sugar in your tea?' Veronica asked him.

'They're asking fourteen bob a pound on Brewer Street,' Sweeney told her.

'That a yes or a no?'

He knew how little sugar she would possess. 'Not for me, ta.'

'That because you're sweet enough already, is it?' Veronica said, regretting the words immediately when she saw how they embarrassed him. Old enough to be his mother? Who was she kidding? She was fifty-four, old enough to be his grandmother, if you thought about it, and if you stretched a point.

There wasn't a single photograph of Veronica in her room – framed photograph, mind, *professionally* framed – that showed her older than thirty. Go on, then, stretch another point – thirty-five. Professional studio, lighting, make-up, the lot.

She'd been a real beauty, once; a proper beauty, not like some of these girls today – skin deep with most of *them*. No – a proper beauty, and with a genuine gift.

It was a sign of something, she had once said to Sweeney during another of their encounters on the landing. His divided lip – something special. Trust her; she knew. She told fortunes, she looked into the future, she foretold what had yet to happen, of lives yet to come. This was her gift, the gift passed on to her by her mother, and which had been possessed by her grandmother and great-grandmother before her. Her mother had never once lived in a house, only a succession of caravans. She, herself, Veronica, had waited until she was fifteen years old before she'd slept in a proper bed, which, coincidentally, had been on her first wedding night. Travelling people, circuses, fairgrounds. Her first husband had been forty-eight and had broken two of her ribs on that first night. The man had died six years later. No great loss. Good riddance to bad rubbish.

Her second husband had been five years younger than herself, nineteen. Joined up. Last lot. Dead. France. Or Belgium. Much of a sameness, those two.

That was the last of her husbands, and Sweeney had learned all of this within an hour of meeting her.

Sweeney cradled the tea in his hands. 'Busy night yourself?' he asked her.

'Went up Walthamstow. The dogs are back on. Always a soldier and his sweetheart ready to stake a bit of money to find out what lies in store for them. Not as profitable lately, of course, not now the skies are finally clearing and everything's starting to look rosy again, but the first thing I tell them is that there will always be uncertain times ahead, and hard times, too.'

'The Japs?' Sweeney said.

Veronica shrugged. 'I don't talk about anything too . . . Name of the game, see? All *I* need to do is to suggest, to infer, make a few pointers in the right direction. Mostly I do it with the women, the girls. Right little tarts, some of them.' She saw him look up at the word. 'You know the sort, must do, working for Tommy Fowler and everything.'

'I suppose so,' Sweeney said.

'"Keep the girl happy, keep the boy happy,"' Veronica said. She reached out to him as though about to put her hand on his leg, but then she thought better of the gesture and withdrew without touching him.

A superintendent in one of the orphanages had told Sweeney that he had the Mark of Cain on him. But Sweeney knew this was wrong. He had befriended a boy with a birthmark covering half his face, who had been told the same thing, and who, or so Sweeney later heard, had afterwards blinded himself in one eye during an attempt to remove the blemish with soda crystals.

'Always easy to know what people want,' Veronica said. 'Bit

of peace, bit of stability, a little bit of a helping hand forwards. You think about it – who's going to *not* want to be looking forwards after all this lot is over and done with? The future – that's where everybody wants to live now. No future in the past.' She stopped, repeated the words, and then laughed. 'You hear that? "No future in the past." I should have that as a slogan. Everybody has a slogan, these days. That could be mine.'

Sweeney acknowledged the tired saying with a smile.

'If they want a nice little house somewhere, kids, garden, all that, then it's what I see. You check for a wedding ring or a pale band on a man's finger and you tell them that there's good times ahead, but that there's trouble coming sooner than that. I tell them they've got a future that will be all the better and brighter for being forged in adversity. People like that – a bit of hardship, a bit of a struggle. "Adversity" – that's a good word to use. Gives the thing a bit of dignity, don't you think? No need with the Yanks, of course. They're all going to be back off home soon enough. One blow of the trumpet and that lot will be gone before you can blink. Gone faster than they came, that's for certain. The girls are more often than not blind to it all. Blind and stupid. Some of *them* are living their lives now as though all of this is going to last for ever. You hear Churchill sounding off again? The war is won and now we've got to fight for the peace. How can that be right? Are *you* going to fight for the peace? Of course you aren't, nobody is. What does he think we are? Where's *he* going to do his fighting when all this is over – one of his castles or country houses? No, thought not.' She was suddenly out of breath, and stopped talking. She came closer to him and sat beside him, holding her free hand to the small blue flames of the fire. 'Listen to me,' she said. 'Never know when to stop, that's my problem.'

A fortnight after they'd met, she'd taken Sweeney's hand in both her own and had turned it palm up. At first, he hadn't realized what she was doing, but as she'd started to caress him with her thumbs, tracing the lines across his skin, he had finally understood what was happening and had pulled sharply away from her.

'Nothing to be afraid of,' she'd told him, surprised by his reaction. 'Only a bit of harmless fun.'

'And if you saw something there?' Sweeney had asked her.

'Then I'd tell you.'

Sweeney had clamped his hands into his armpits.

'You look done in,' she said to him now.

'No rest for the wicked,' Sweeney said.

The small blue flames grew even smaller and started to flicker. Then the gas began making a familiar popping noise and some of the flames died completely.

'Got a shilling?' Veronica said to him.

'Cross your palm with silver, you mean?' Sweeney said, and she finally reached out and patted his hand.

6

'S AY SOMETHING,' CROWLEY SAID TO HIS SILENT, DISBELIEV-
ing companion.

Outside, the nearby factory whistle sounded. Eight o'clock.

'Ah, "The Toilers in the Dawn",' Crowley said. His eyes
never left Joshua Silver.

'But it's a man's life,' Silver said eventually. He knew
there was nothing he might say that Crowley hadn't already
long considered, and for which he would not have prepared at least two answers. Whatever his objections to the
plan Crowley had just revealed to him, the argument was
already lost.

'A life already squandered and, to all intents and purposes,
already over and forgotten,' Crowley said calmly.

Silver looked again at the newspaper Crowley had given
him. He looked at the photograph of the condemned man, an
old photograph, fixing the man somewhere in his late, blinking adolescence.

Crowley poured sherry from a decanter into a pair of
ornate, embossed glasses, and handed one to Silver, who took
it and drained it in a single motion.

'Clearing with crows,' Crowley said.

'What?' Silver said, wondering if he had misheard.

'Crowley. The name. From the Old English. A clearing with crows.' Crowley sipped his own drink.

Silver wanted to shout at his friend, to tell him to stop being ridiculous, but, like a great deal else where Crowley was concerned, this too was beyond him.

'I never believed it, of course,' Crowley said, smiling to himself. 'But others did. Possibly, the crow connection.'

'He's only nineteen years old,' Silver said. He waved the paper at Crowley.

'What does the age matter? Like I said – a life already thrown away, a life made forfeit. Read it again. He killed a man. In, as they never tire of saying, cold blood. He's been tried and found guilty by a good, honest, decent, tax-paying, God-fearing jury of his peers. And now he'll—'

'His lawyer is applying for the right to appeal,' Silver said.

'His *appointed* lawyer,' Crowley said. 'And we all know what that means. It's a formality. *Of course* he's applied for the right to appeal. It's what lawyers do to keep their bills topped up. On what grounds?'

'It doesn't say.'

'Because it *can't* say. Because there *are* no grounds. It's murder: he'll hang; it's how our wonderful justice system operates. The judge has spoken. Justice will now be done, be seen to be done, and everyone will sleep that little bit safer in their beds at night knowing one less mindless murderer is stalking the streets. And after that, no one will give him a second's thought ever again.'

'His family might,' Silver said.

'Read it again. There *is* no family.'

'He'd never agree to what you're suggesting,' Silver said. 'To your . . . your . . .'

Crowley waited for Silver to find the right word, but Silver finally abandoned the struggle and fell silent.

'I can see that nothing I say will alter your course,' Silver said eventually.

Crowley nodded once. 'All my life I have searched for a means of freeing the human soul, releasing it from its corporeal body and giving it everlasting life.'

'There must be other ways,' Silver said.

'None that *I* have ever found. And tell me, have you ever known or ever even heard of anyone as assiduous or as determined in the quest as *I* have been my entire life? Look at me. I'm seventy. My time is ebbing. Even you can't deny that I might drop down dead tomorrow of any one of a dozen causes.'

'Not if you took better care of yourself,' Silver said, but without conviction.

'My habituations, you mean?'

'Your addictions, yes.'

Crowley laughed at the correction and all it implied, after which neither of the men spoke for a moment.

Silver held out his glass for more sherry. 'I assume there's a procedure,' he said. 'I imagine all this is already arranged and – what? – calculated in your own mind.'

Crowley remained silent.

'And if I choose to have nothing to do with it?' Silver said. But that, too, he already knew, was beyond him.

'Then I shall regret your absence,' Crowley said. 'It's as honest an answer as I can give you.' He smiled at his friend.

'What convinces you you can achieve this *now*, after a lifetime of failure?'

'Oh, not failure. A lifetime of striving, questing. A lifetime

of boundary-pushing and eliminating false avenues, surely?'
Crowley paused. 'Do I forever sound ridiculous to you?'

Silver shook his head.

'Desperate, then?' Crowley said.

'Perhaps.'

Crowley considered this. 'Then tell me, Joshua, do you
honestly believe – knowing me as you do – that I would have
persisted in my striving and brought upon myself the scorn,
ridicule, loathing, fear and hatred of almost all of my fellow
men if I *hadn't* been convinced that there was a way of achieving—'

'Immortality?'

'Something. Immortality, hopefully. But how can even *I*
say that for certain? For decades, I imagined – *believed* – that
I would move forward in stages, that whatever was one day
going to be revealed to *me* would be presented in a kind of
sequence, that the rewards to begin with would be small, but
that they would grow as I progressed along the continuum of
revelation and self-awareness.'

'Culminating in this?' Silver said. He was accustomed
to this convoluted, antiquated-sounding language from
Crowley. Language which flowed slowly and steadily and
with deceptive strength and endless meaning in its turbulent
depths. He'd read some of the countless books and tracts
Crowley had written and published – given to him by
Crowley himself to keep the allegedly priceless volumes out
of the hands of his creditors – and this same deep brown river
of language flowed there too.

'I don't know,' Crowley said. 'All I know is that I am
seventy, failing fast, and that my time in *this* old and worn-
out body is limited.'

'Whatever I say, you'll—'

'It embarrasses you,' Crowley said. '*I* embarrass you. I can't apologize for that. You worship your god and *I* worship mine.'

'My *god*?' Silver said angrily. 'I don't see much sign of his benign or protective presence of late.' He shook the paper he still held.

'No,' Crowley said. 'But your faith will remain. Some of it, a deep root.'

Silver refused to either deny or concede the point.

'It will,' Crowley insisted. 'Believe me. I daresay countless further horrors are about to be revealed; but something will remain unshakeable.'

Silver was uncomfortable with this diversion from their argument, and he shook the paper again. 'And if the man is actually innocent?' he said.

Crowley considered his answer. 'I won't lie to you – an innocent man would serve my plan and purpose even better. Innocence – even if only in this instance a point of legal technicality – is still such a rare and precious commodity. Besides, it isn't for us to say.'

'Do you have no sympathy for the man, no pity whatsoever?'

Crowley shrugged. 'No one else appears to believe him innocent.'

'There was *doubt*,' Silver said. 'At his trial. His lawyer made a great deal of the fact. Otherwise why the appeal application now?'

'His lawyer made a mess of his defence, that's all. The man was guilty and destined to hang the minute some policeman or other put his hand on his shoulder.'

'And none of this is of even the slightest concern to you now? Now – when all *you* can see is your own—'

'My own final opportunity, yes,' Crowley said. 'A lifetime of experiment and preparation, and now this final opportunity to put everything into action.'

'But why? To reap your reward? Because you persevered? Because you were right all those years, decades, and everybody else was wrong?'

'I possessed the strength of my convictions,' Crowley said, his voice still even and low. 'I had the courage of my convictions, and once I had the wherewithal to indulge my enthusiasms. All I ever truly lacked was that final part of the process, that final insight or understanding.' He closed his eyes and smiled to himself.

'And what about this man' – Silver looked again at the photograph – 'Tait. What is there in any of this for him? Why would he be willing to accede to even the smallest part of what you're proposing?'

'Accede?'

'You no longer possess that "wherewithal", remember? Your fortune – fortunes – are all long gone. You only need to look around you to see that much.'

'Granted,' Crowley said. 'And to see also that I am reduced to the charity of others, to the kindness of strangers, my benefactors.'

Silver laughed at the word. 'There haven't been too many of those of late.'

'Ah,' Crowley said. 'Alas not.'

'*Do* you have anything to offer him?'

'Perhaps,' Crowley said. 'I haven't given that part of the matter much thought yet.'

And this sudden, uncharacteristic evasiveness made Silver suspicious. 'What?' he said. 'Tell me.'

Crowley shook his head. 'I can't tell you anything for certain. At least not yet. Not until the thing is underway, and perhaps not even then.'

And so Silver started guessing, hoping to provoke Crowley into giving him an honest answer.

'Are you going to promise him the same? Will there be some kind of reciprocal pact between you? He does this – whatever it is – for you, and in return you somehow achieve the same for him? He, too, gains everlasting—'

'I don't know,' Crowley shouted. 'Don't make me lie to you.'

'And is this what you'll tell him, how you'll persuade him? I assume none of this will be possible without at least *some* degree of knowledge on his part, or contact between you. Knowledge, belief, commitment, acceptance, what?'

'Some of those things,' Crowley said absently.

'And it might still all be one big lie, and you the sole beneficiary? Perhaps it would all be more straightforward if there *was* some surviving family. At least then you might have used your new-found immortality and everything it afforded you to do *them* some good.'

Crowley heard the mockery in Silver's voice. 'You're right,' he said. 'All my life I've been made to see how material, and never spiritual, wealth is a far greater force in the world.' It was a clumsy way of making the point and Crowley signalled this with a wave of his hand.

'One of the first things you told me when we met all those years ago was that the suppression of natural instincts—'

'Sexual urges, primarily.'

'That the suppression of natural instincts was an insult to nature.'

'Man's nature,' Crowley said.

'And, if I remember rightly, a short cut to moral deformity.'

'I probably said exactly the same to a thousand others,' Crowley said.

'I remember I was treating you for gonorrhoea at the time.'

'Ah.'

'You were sixty-three. There was a woman less than a third your age.'

'Details, conventions, niceties.'

'A woman as addicted as you were at the time.'

'Her name was Scarlet,' Crowley said.

'No, it wasn't. You called them all that.'

'She followed me everywhere. They all did. Everywhere I went, they appeared. Fodder for the press, most of them.'

'You're missing my point,' Silver said.

'No, I'm not,' Crowley said. 'You want to tell me that, despite all my excuses, all my righteous indignation, I am the most morally deformed man you have ever encountered. Please, this is not a criticism of you; I daresay most would say the same. No – not most: all. Or perhaps only now do I have some competition truly worthy of the name.'

Crowley flicked the paper Silver still held. The front page was filled with a report of the forthcoming peace and its trials and tribunals. The news and picture of Peter Tait took up only half a column at the bottom right-hand corner of the page.

Silver went back to the window and looked down at the people outside. 'Do you know how to go about getting every-thing – I don't know – started, in place?'

'I believe so,' Crowley said.

'How to contact this Tait?'

'The article mentions his newly appointed appeal lawyer, something of his crime,' Crowley said. 'It won't be difficult. And certainly not impossible.'

Silver remained standing with his back to the room, this simple degree of detachment and separation helping him to talk. It was clearer than ever to him that Crowley was set on his course. The street below was already filling with people walking to work. There was a slight haziness in the air as the day started to warm up following a cold night.

After several minutes, Crowley said, 'Eighteen ninety-three,' and Silver turned back to him.

'What about it?'

'My very first case of gonorrhoea. I was eighteen.'

'The treatments have hardly changed. The Americans have new drugs. Antibiotics. The thinking is that they can be adapted to cure anything.'

'It seems an impossible hope.'

'It is,' Silver said. 'This other matter – do you require my help, my assistance, in any way?'

For a moment, Crowley didn't understand him, and then he said, 'I need you for the guidance you have always offered me.'

'And which you have hardly ever listened to, let alone followed.' It seemed a true and concise summary of the nature of the bond between the two men.

'I need to be strong,' Crowley said.

'In what way, strong?'

'Even when I was young and in my physical prime, every ritual and procedure I attempted was an exhausting experience, the rigours of which few other men could have endured, let alone repeated.'

'And now you're old and frail and—'

'And now I'm old and frail and, if the truth be known, apprehensive. This, as you rightly surmise, may be the greatest challenge of my life, and, like the old and worn-out fool that I've become, I've left it until now to attempt. Just imagine if I'd known at twenty or thirty – or forty, even – what I know now, and a similar opportunity had presented itself to me *then*.'

'Bottomley says your only aim in life – even now – is to sell your soul to the Devil in exchange for your own immortality.'

'Bottomley says whatever sells his tawdry rags. The Devil?'

'So was it always mostly a question of self-gratification?' Silver said. 'The rituals, the women, all your . . . your . . .'

'My unnatural practices? Yes, I suppose it was. Though in fairness to myself, I never made excuses for any of those things at the time.'

'Exercising your natural instincts?' Silver said. 'And is that what you believe you're doing now?'

'If I said yes, you'd accuse me of making excuses for myself. You only have to look at the ocean of words, libel and slander dear old Horatio Bottomley and his ilk have tried to drown me beneath, to see what tides and currents of conjecture, scorn and disgust I have endlessly swum against.' Crowley made a swimming motion with his arms, spilling the remains of his sherry on his sleeve.

'You laugh at *him* harder than *he* prods at you,' Silver said.

'Once, perhaps. But not now. Now I can see that beckoning, wide-open grave and hear that ticking clock. Forgive the melodrama, but it's true.'

After this, neither man spoke for several minutes.

'Is there a timetable for all of this, an order?' Silver said eventually.

'For the ritual?' Crowley said. 'Twenty-one days, preferably. A few days either side wouldn't be a problem. There are recitals, incantations and lesser sacrifices that need to be made at specified intervals before the moment of final exchange.'

'And do you already know what these recitals and sacrifices are – what they involve?'

'I've known them all my life,' Crowley said. He raised his wet sleeve to his lips and sucked at the slowly spreading dampness there.

7

A WEEK HAD PASSED SINCE FRANKIE DOLL HAD STOOD AND watched the flying bomb splutter along its dying course over Archer Street. And now here he was again, standing in the same doorway in the same dawn light, adjusting to the same early-morning chill after the warmth and smoke-filled air of the club.

He still looked instinctively up at the sky – they all did – but, the flying bomb apart, all he ever saw up there these days were the scribbled, melting vapour trails of the departing and returning bombers; American, mostly, he guessed. There was the occasional low aircraft, a late return, off course, missing an engine perhaps, or a small part of a wing. And each time Frankie Doll saw one of these lonely, desperate stragglers, he imagined himself up there with the men inside, keen only to sight their distant base and land safely and survive and be as far away as possible from the war as it approached its end. After all, who wanted to die in those final few weeks after all that time spent fighting? Or supposing the Germans actually went against their nature and did the decent thing and surrendered suddenly, what then? What if a man was suddenly made to understand that the very last hour of the war had finally arrived? What if, like in the last lot, a man knew to the exact second when that time would come? How then would he go on fighting and putting his life at risk?

This tangle of thoughts filled Frankie Doll's mind as he stood in the doorway and looked up at the empty sky.

'You look in a thoughtful mood. Never had you marked down as a thinker.'

The voice gave Frankie Doll a start, but he quickly composed himself.

Ruby Nolan.

'You on the lookout for another rocket?' she said. 'You think there's still one up there with your name on it?' She came out of the club and the two of them went together to the centre of the empty street.

Frankie Doll hadn't known she was in the club. Laura had left at three and hadn't returned. She had waved to him on her way out, blown him a kiss with her left hand, another of their signals. The man trailing after her was short and fat and twice her age, and Frankie Doll recognized him as a regular. No trouble there. He held up the fingers of one hand, followed by a V sign, letting Laura know that he'd be home by seven. Leave the club at five, home by seven, two hours of running the usual errands for Tommy Fowler in between.

As he rose through the ranks, hopefully all this errand-running would decrease until eventually Frankie Doll himself would be telling others what to do, where to go, who to see, how much debt to collect, what messages and threats to deliver, how forcibly to press those messages home. Soon, Frankie Doll hoped, very soon, with a bit of luck, the Sweeney boy would be running the longer errands, along with the gamut of abuse and threatened violence *he* now endured on Tommy Fowler's behalf. In fact, to Frankie Doll, Sweeney was the perfect messenger boy for Tommy Fowler – one of life's natural victims, a man who attracted ridicule and violence, something to which he was probably long accustomed, and perhaps even immune.

'They still reckon it was a freak – the bomb,' Ruby Nolan said. 'Something gone wrong. One of the papers called it a "monster". Scientists or something. Killed a baby. Hillmarton Road, wherever that is.'

Or if not a baby, then a pregnant woman, or a group of schoolchildren, or an old man, or a mother protecting her own frightened children in a cellar, under a table, in a shelter, in her arms.

As though reading these thoughts of Frankie Doll's, Ruby Nolan then said, 'What's that then – another "innocent victim"?' She gave each syllable equal emphasis and repeated the word 'innocent'.

'Search me,' Frankie Doll told her. He lowered his gaze from the sky to the gutter. He felt awkward at having been seen like that. 'Good night?' he asked her.

'Three punters, two in-and-outs and one a little bit . . . special.' She grinned as she said this, waiting for Frankie Doll to ask her to tell him more.

But Frankie Doll said nothing.

'Aren't you going to ask me?' she said after only a few seconds.

'Go on, then – what kind of little bit special?' He already knew everything there was to know about the punters' 'specialities' from Laura.

'He wanted me to pretend to be a schoolgirl. Asked me if I had anything I could wear. Never even took his trousers off. Ministry of Defence.'

Frankie Doll resisted laughing.

'Something high up. I told him I believed him. We went through all that – you know – all that pretending everything was secret, that he was doing his little bit and I was doing mine. I put on a skirt and some brown socks and he gave me his tie to put on over my blouse. I went to sit on his knee and tell him what a naughty girl I'd been and next thing I knew he was struggling up out of the chair and telling me it had all been a big mistake.' She laughed.

'He'll say exactly the same next time round,' Frankie Doll told her.

'I know that,' she said, now with a note of anger in her voice.

'What?' Frankie Doll said. 'I only meant—'

'I know what you meant. I was just saying. Easy money, that's all. It beats getting crushed underneath them all the time. And some of these older ones . . .' She left the sentence unfinished. 'What time did Laura go?' she said.

None of her business. 'Not sure.'

'Thought you were meant to be keeping an eye on her.'

'I am,' Frankie Doll said. 'I do.'

'She thinks a lot of you,' Ruby Nolan said.

'I know. And likewise.'

Tommy Fowler controlled the girls who used the club, and he occasionally called on them for favours when the need arose. He had once used Laura like that, sending her to the tables of his associates and clients, discharging his own small debts. But not any longer. And the reason Tommy Fowler no longer used her like this, and the reason he tolerated Frankie Doll's relationship with her – or so Frankie Doll liked to believe – was because he had too much respect for Frankie

Doll now that he had proved himself to be such a valuable and trusted employee.

'You don't sound very certain of that,' Ruby Nolan said to him.

'Of what?' He knew exactly what she was saying to him.

She yawned. 'Forget it,' she said. 'Keep your nose out, Ruby. You got any more of them pictures?'

'Which ones?'

'Does it matter? The last lot went quick enough.'

Tommy Fowler owned a photographer's business in Holywell Street – a respectable enough concern when he'd 'acquired' it, but now turning out the pornography that had elevated it into a considerably more profitable business. Frankie Doll knew the men who took the pictures and who then endlessly reproduced them for Tommy Fowler's girls to sell to their customers on commission. In addition to which, the girls themselves often posed for the photographers, thereby adding to the allure of the pictures and allowing them to charge premium prices for the shots. Some of the girls were happy to do this – though Laura never had been, despite Frankie Doll's own urging and promises – and some had then gone on to other, more adventurous work with the photographers, creating further lucrative sidelines for themselves and Tommy Fowler. It was all business, and it was all money, and round and round and round it all went. And, recently, the more he thought about it, the more it seemed to Frankie Doll that he was standing off to one side of that spinning circle of profit and more profit – standing to one side and watching all this wealth spin off into the pockets and wallets of other men, and not into his own, where – surely? – at least *some* of it belonged. He had worked hard for Tommy

Fowler and had been running his errands and delivering his threats and messages for over three years now.

'You tell Fowler,' Ruby Nolan said to him. 'About the pictures.'

'That you're interested?'

'More than interested.'

'I can put in a word,' he said. 'It's not everybody gets to move into that side of the business.' As though she would need his say-so before Tommy Fowler agreed to the proposition.

Ruby Nolan shook her head at this. 'Not what I heard. The Maltese use their mothers and sisters if it turns a profit for them.'

'They're evil, that lot. My advice to you is to steer well clear of the greasy, conniving bastards.'

Tommy Fowler swore blind to anybody who would listen that they – the Maltese – would be his – everybody's – biggest problem when this lovely little war was over and the Defence Regulations were relaxed and then finally scrapped in favour of going back to proper, enforceable laws. Few doubted him.

'Aren't you going to ask me?' Ruby Nolan said.

Now what was she talking about?

'I'm due at the Monaco,' Frankie Doll said. 'And after that, up at Frascati's. And after *that* – and I'm *walking* all this, remember – I've still got to carry the bag to the Lagoon at the back of Regent Street and then trot on to the Panama down in fucking Chelsea.' The 'Lagoon' was the Blue Lagoon, and 'carrying the bag' meant gathering in the night's takings for Tommy Fowler. It was another job entrusted only to Fowler's most reliable employees. And this was something else Frankie Doll frequently reminded himself of as he walked through the dark streets and alleyways with all that money in his hand, imagining himself watched and followed at every corner, every shadowy figure and passing stranger preparing to rob him, or worse. And a large part of that 'worse', and forever uppermost in Frankie Doll's mind as he plotted his night's secretive courses through the city, was how Tommy Fowler himself would react to learning that he'd been robbed. There was no doubt in Frankie Doll's mind who suspect number one would be. It was another reason for wanting to move up the hierarchy and let someone like Sweeney take his place.

'I applied for a job in the statics at the Windmill,' Ruby Nolan said to him, again distracting Frankie Doll from his thoughts.

Frankie Doll looked her up and down. 'You've not got the height for it,' he told her. 'Nor the build. If you're not going to move, then you've at least got to have something worth looking at. Besides, the Epsoms tried to burn the place down a few weeks back.'

'"Epsoms"?'

'Epsom Salts. Malts. They prefer to run things at the bottom end of the market. They think the Windmill's costing them money. Cheap and fast and always ready and willing, that's their motto. Turnover.' It was all business talk; she probably wouldn't understand the half of it.

'Is that me, then – cheap and fast and always ready and willing?' Ruby Nolan said, but with more amusement than either anger or denial in her voice. 'Is that me, then – turnover?'

'I didn't say that,' Frankie Doll said.

'No, but it's what you meant. I can see it in your face.'

'All I meant to say was—'

'That I wasn't tall enough.'

'Right.'

'I'll believe you,' she said. 'Millions wouldn't.'

She was laughing at him, Frankie Doll understood that – probably too sharp for her own good – and he seized this opportunity to change the subject. 'Shall I tell you what Tommy Fowler said to me when the Yanks started turning up in numbers? Shall I tell you how he said he knew our fortunes were made?'

'If you must. And by "our", I assume you mean "his".'

'You want to know or not?'

'Fire away.'

'He said it was because the Yanks had a habit of wanting to sit at the bar instead of at the tables, and because – and this is the clever bit –'

'If you say so.'

'– because of their habit of taking out their wallets and –'

'Billfolds,' Ruby Nolan said suddenly.

'– and leaving them on the bar counter.'

'Prey to the dips?' Ruby Nolan said.

'You'd think so. Tommy's stroke of genius was to tell all his staff to look out for this and then to warn the Yank customers against having their wallets snatched.'

'And that he'd break all the fingers of any member of staff who helped themselves?'

'Probably,' Frankie Doll said. His own bag-carrying predecessor at the Craven Club in Paddington had been found with every single bone in both his hands broken – fingers, palms, wrists, even one arm-bone for good measure – shattered and largely unmendable except as stiff claws. The man now wore two black gloves at all times and lived and worked somewhere a long, long way from Tommy Fowler. In summer, his hands were reputed to swell to twice their normal size, and in winter they became completely numb and useless to him. The last Frankie Doll had heard – and there were always these stories, these everlasting straws blowing and settling in the wind – was that the man was telling anybody who would listen to him that he'd been injured in the Italian campaign. And perhaps in time it was something he would come to believe himself.

'So that was his great secret?' Ruby Nolan said, clearly un-impressed.

Perhaps she hadn't understood him.

'He *could* have stolen the wallets, but he *didn't*?' she said.

'And so when the Yanks saw what a close call they'd had, they passed the word and more and more of them started turning up at Tommy's bars and clubs. Tommy treats them to a glass of bona fide Scotch, and after that they come again and again and Tommy Fowler recoups his investment a hundred times over.'

'I can see *you*'re impressed,' Ruby Nolan said, her interest fading even further.

After walking all the way to Paddington, Frankie Doll would return via the Edgware Road and see how much the pink petrol was selling for that morning. The price changed almost daily now, usually downwards, and Tommy Fowler always told Frankie Doll what level of bid to leave. Soon it wouldn't be worth anyone's while buying the stuff. Fowler had recently told Frankie Doll that his regular customers were now buying the petrol from a dozen other sources. No loyalty. Besides, what did they think; did they think that the minute the war was over every petrol station in London was going to be overflowing with the stuff? Didn't anybody read the papers past the front-page news? Didn't they know what had happened to all those oil wells and fields, and – what was it? – refineries? Hadn't they seen all that thick, black smoke pouring up into the sky over the past six years like ink spilled in water? No – if anything, the stuff was only going to get *more* scarce and valuable. Rationing – that was another thing. Did people honestly believe that it would all end at the same time the war ended? Well, if that's what they thought, then some people were in for a big shock. The fucking farmers were already shouting for more than their fair share of the petrol. Though, in fairness to those farmers already approached by Tommy Fowler, they did sell on their own Ministry allocations to him at a profit to them both.

'I was going to go up the Cumberland,' Ruby said.

'Oh?' Ten minutes had passed since Frankie Doll had come out of the club; he needed to move.

'An arrangement with a customer.'

'Nice spot, Marble Arch. Even with all that damage. Nice view of the park.'

'You could put a word in with Fowler,' Ruby said. 'The photographs. You could tell him I've got specialities.' It was more speculation than fact.

And he'll know what they are without even looking, Frankie Doll thought to himself. *In fact, he'll tell* you *what they are.* 'The schoolgirl thing?' he said.

'And more. But definitely that. I'm not long after being one, after all.'

'Back in Ireland?' If she'd expected him to laugh at the remark, then she'd have to try harder than that.

'Where else?' she said.

'Probably adds to the thrill,' Frankie Doll said. 'Your accent.'

'I'm sure it does. That and the baby talk.'

'You wouldn't hear it on a photo,' Frankie Doll said.

'There is that.'

Or perhaps recommending Ruby Nolan to Tommy Fowler would be another inch up the ladder, and perhaps *then* split-lip Sweeney would definitely get to take over some of the more distant drops and pick-ups.

'Never been to the Cumberland before,' Ruby Nolan said.

Why was she still talking to him? What did she want him to say? With Laura it would be reassurance, but not with this one.

'The boys on the door know Tommy,' he told her, wondering if this was the kind of thing she wanted to hear. 'I mean, you won't get stopped at the door. The law won't ever get called, not to the Cumberland, not where Tommy Fowler's concerned. Always best to have a name or room number, though. Or if—'

'Why don't you come with me?' she said suddenly.

Frankie Doll shook his head. 'Already told you – places to go, people to see. Besides, it's a different direction completely. Just wait around outside. They'll see you fast enough. Nobody's going to stop you walking in on an arm full of gold braid. They do like all their ornaments and fancy dress, the Yanks.'

'I suppose so,' she said. She stood to attention and saluted him. Perhaps if she was lucky, the customer with whom she'd already made her loose arrangement would even be waiting and looking out for her.

'Or you could just go home and get some sleep,' Frankie

Doll suggested. He knew she'd been in the club since at least ten the previous night, and very likely in others – Fowler's Early-Bird bars – before that.

'Fat chance,' she said. 'I'm broke. Rent day tomorrow. I know – tell you a sob story you *haven't* heard.'

Most of the girls, Ruby Nolan and Laura included, rented their rooms from Tommy Fowler at the usual extortionate prices.

'Besides, I was talking to some of the other girls . . .'

'And?'

'Some of *them* were saying that this age of so-called plenty and golden opportunity was all about to come to an end, all going to come crashing down, and that if anything was going to happen to improve *our* lot, then it needed to happen fast.'

'Happen?' Frankie Doll said.

'You know – *happen*. I need to make something of myself; at least make something *for* myself while the opportunity still exists.'

Such as? What opportunity?

Frankie Doll wondered if she was talking about finding a wealthy husband, but guessed she wasn't looking that far ahead. At least not yet. Some of the other girls were already talking about returning to America with their so-called boyfriends. When those so-called boyfriends were shipped back here from Germany, that is. When they were shipped back here – to Archer Street, in London – before being put on a boat and taken all the way home to California, that is. If they weren't all about to be gathered up and then shipped straight to Japan to sort out that little lot over there. If all of that, and if their whispered words had ever been anything but lies and empty promises, and if they even remembered saying a single, solitary word of any of this in the first place.

Frankie Doll kept his mouth shut on all of this.

'That's all I need myself,' Ruby Nolan said. 'One chance. One golden opportunity.'

Golden?

'Tommy Fowler usually makes sure all those opportunities find their way directly to him without making any stops along the way,' Frankie Doll said.

She laughed again at this. 'Then perhaps I've got to do a little diverting of my own,' she said.

The suggestion alarmed Frankie Doll – not for what it might mean with regard to her, but because of his own involvement now that she had confessed the thing to him – and he was unable to disguise this.

'Don't worry,' she said. 'I'm not stupid. Let's stick with the photos, shall we? No harm in that.'

Afterwards, she turned and walked away from him. It had rained in the night and water still lay between the cobbles in the street. Her heels clicked on the paving.

And having made a note of how much petrol was up for grabs, and at what price, Frankie Doll would make his usual call on Billy Leach's in Paddington to see how much the bookies' gangs were creaming. Billy Leach – talk to him personally. Tommy Fowler had been very particular about that little get-together. Visit Billy Leach, Paddington, make sure everything's all right. He'll know what I'm talking about.

Frankie Doll watched Ruby Nolan continue to the end of the street and then turn the corner. He wondered if Laura was still awake and waiting for him. Some days, especially recently, he'd started to wish she wasn't.

8

DETECTIVE INSPECTOR ERNEST PYE WAS DIRECTED TO A metal chair and told to wait. He went, he sat, he waited. Younger men – and he was more often than not accompanied by such on these visits – would baulk at being told what to do by the warders. They would ask how *long* they were expected to wait, why wasn't there somewhere more *comfortable* for them to wait, why wasn't the prisoner prepared and ready and waiting for *them*. But not Pye, who settled himself in the uncomfortable metal chair, who arranged the hat and coat he carried on the empty seat beside him, and who then locked his fingers together, leaned forward slightly, resting on the balls of his aching feet, and waited.

After a while, another prison officer, an older man – similar age to himself – came into the room where Pye waited and sat opposite him. Each man acknowledged the other with a nod and then remained silent.

A minute later, the warder said, 'They're bringing him to the interview room for you now.'

'No rush,' Pye said. More time for him to question and doubt his motives for being there.

'I'm the attending officer. Bone. I'll take you to him.'

And then he would stand rigidly and silently beside the

door, his back against the wall, while Pye and the boy spoke to each other.

'Shouldn't be too long now,' Bone said. 'He knew you were coming, just not when, exactly. Probably thinks you're his new lawyer.'

Pye noted the cold edge with which the man invested the word, but said nothing. 'Not entirely certain why I'm here myself,' Pye said. He'd already questioned Peter Tait on half a dozen occasions before his trial, and had then attended the trial itself. The last he'd seen of the boy was when Tait had been led out of the dock and down the narrow staircase to the holding cells. Pye had attempted to see him there, too, but Tait's trial lawyer had denied him this. Pye had overheard the man talking to Tait, telling him to be patient and steadfast and not to worry. A short time later, he'd heard Tait crying alone in his cell. *Steadfast?* The man was living in a different world. Tait probably didn't even know the meaning of the word, let alone how to *be* it.

'Waiting,' Bone said. Everything had a faint echo in the empty room.

'Sorry?'

'Waiting. All this. Forever waiting for someone to come or go or something to happen. Half the job, some days.'

'All part of the game,' Pye said.

'Thirty-nine years,' Bone said. 'Me. This job. Man and boy.'

Then you must enjoy it, Pye thought. Perhaps the man expected a compliment. 'They'll give you a long-service medal,' he said. They would give him one, too. Thirty-four years. Man and boy.

'I suppose so. Forty-year mark, and all sorts of fireworks will be going off.'

Pye saw immediately how lost and directionless that would leave the man.

'ARP.' Bone said then. 'You?'

'The same.' Pye said it without thinking. He had last patrolled two weeks earlier. He was down to one night a fortnight.

'A regular?' Bone asked him.

'City commission. May '40,' Pye said. 'Bit of a johnny-come-lately, if the truth be known.' It was a joke among the old hands. 'You?'

'September '39,' Bone said.

Pye might have guessed. 'One of the first.'

'I saw what was coming. Last lot?'

Pye nodded. 'You?'

Bone nodded.

'You'll have seen some things,' Pye said.

Bone nodded again. 'Enough to be going on with.' He held out his hand to Pye. 'Arthur. Arthur Bone.'

'Unusual name,' Pye said.

Bone smiled. 'Only one I've got. My mother – God rest her soul – always said it came from the French – Bon. Apparently it means "good". When we were kids we always thought it had something to do with Marylebone. Just one of those things. My father always used to upset her and say it was bone pure and simple and nothing wrong with that.'

'I can imagine,' Pye said.

'And you are?'

'Ernest Pye,' Pye said. 'Detective Inspector. I was Tait's interviewing officer.'

'Right,' Bone said.

After that, the two men fell silent for a minute. All around them, footsteps came and went in the corridors outside; doors were rattled open and then slammed shut again. There was no quiet way to open or close a prison door.

After a further minute, Pye said, 'You know him, then – Peter Tait?'

'You might say I keep an eye on him.'

It was a telling remark. 'Is he still in one of the regular cells?'

'For the time being,' Bone said, and then, unable to resist, added, 'Has something turned up?'

It was what Ernest Pye had been waiting to hear. He shrugged. 'Not really. Just all those loose ends and unanswered questions forever flapping in the wind. Said anything to you, has he?'

But Bone – perhaps because of the small indiscretion he knew he had just committed – anything to give the boy hope – became suddenly wary. 'Such as?' he said.

Pye shrugged again. He'd have to watch that. 'Whatever it is they do,' he said. 'Protested his innocence, bemoaned the fact that his defence let him down and that the judge should have been picked up on a couple of things.'

'They all do that,' Bone said. 'One way or another. Until they work out how much is left of their lives beyond the sentence.'

'Or, in Tait's case—'

'Exactly,' Bone said.

There was an even longer silence after that, following which the door beside Pye was noisily unlocked and pushed open. A second warder entered, and Bone, Pye noted, was on his feet and standing upright before the man had taken a step into the room.

'Bone,' the man said. 'Thought it'd be you.' Turning to Pye, he said, 'And you are?'

Pye took out his warrant card and held it for the man to read.

The man looked at the clipboard he held. 'Pye,' he said. 'DI, Tottenham Court Road. That's the one. I need you to sign the docket.'

Pye did this as the man looked on.

Then Pye and Bone were let out of the room and the door was locked behind them.

They walked along a succession of corridors and through other unlocked and locked doors for a further five minutes. Everywhere smelled of watery disinfectant and cooking vegetables.

'They're getting hungry,' the second warder said to Bone. 'Feeding time at the zoo.'

'No need for that,' Bone said, but the man only laughed at him.

Eventually, and after signing a second sheet of paper, Pye was asked to wait for a few minutes while a final door was unlocked from the far side.

The second warder finally left them.

'Friend of yours?' Pye asked Bone.

'Just arrived from Durham. Three years in and he knows it all. Full of Jerry officers, by all accounts, Durham. Ask me . . .' He fell silent as the door in front of them was pushed open.

Pye and Bone went into the room; Peter Tait sat at a small table and looked up at them.

'No talking until the door's locked,' Bone said quickly to the boy.

Pye wondered if he was sending a signal to Tait, who had smiled the instant Bone had appeared behind him.

Pye then went to the table and sat opposite Tait, while Bone waited beside the door. 'Remember me, Peter?' he said.

'You did all my interviews. You were in court.'

Pye turned to Bone. 'You can sit, if you'd prefer,' he said, indicating the third chair in the room. 'Please.'

Bone took the chair to the door and sat there, a compromise of sorts.

Then Pye took out a packet of cigarettes, opened it and gave one to each man. He placed the packet at the centre of the table.

'Do you know why I'm here?' he said to Tait.

Tait shook his head. 'Mister Bone said you were due in this week some time, that's all.'

'During our interviews—' Pye began to say.

'You did right by me,' Tait said suddenly. 'In the station *and* in the court. I know that much.'

'Let the officer finish what he's saying,' Bone said to Tait.

'Sorry,' Tait said, the apology directed more at Bone than Pye.

Everything the boy did and said reminded Pye what a child he still was. There had even been a suggestion at his trial – something else his lawyer had refused to consider – that Tait might be retarded in some way; nothing too obvious – he clearly wasn't an imbecile or whatever they were called these days – but *something*, and perhaps that something might have been enough somewhere down to line to finally spare him from the noose.

'You do know what's happening to you, don't you, Peter?' Pye said to him.

'Happening?'

'To you. Here, now, out there, what's happening concerning the likelihood of your appeal.'

'My lawyer says everything will take place in due course. He says I should just sit patient and bide my time. It's how these things work. He's a specialist. He specializes in appeals.' He turned and grinned again at Bone. 'Isn't that right, Mister Bone? That's what he told us – a specialist, and that all I had to do now was to sit tight, bide my time and wait for something to turn up that would—'

'Settle down, lad,' Bone said quietly but firmly, immediately silencing Tait.

'I'm sorry,' Tait said.

And again, it was as much as Pye needed to see and hear, and he waited a moment before saying, 'And what exactly do you think is going to turn up?'

Tait looked puzzled.

'The fourth man, for instance?' Pye prompted him.

'They never found him,' Tait said. 'I never even knew who he was. I didn't know who any of them were until I was persuaded into going along with them to make up the numbers.'

'*Who* persuaded you?' Pye said. He had asked him the same question a hundred times before.

'It was all in the trial,' Tait said. 'I don't know.'

'You don't know who recruited you; you don't know who the other men were; you didn't know what you were going to do, what was expected of you. And now here you are – and you alone, effectively – carrying the can for everything that should be landing on all those other shoulders.' Pye cast a glance at Bone, who was doing his best not to nod along in agreement with everything he was suggesting. 'Does all that not strike you as just a little bit odd or suspicious, Peter?'

'The others are still waiting to be sentenced,' Tait said.

'Perhaps. But they'll not be sentenced to hang. And soon their own clever lawyers will put in appeals saying that justice has been served by you being hanged and that *their* clients deserve greater leniency and, perhaps, forgiveness.' Surely the boy could see how his own execution would have at least some bearing on those other cases? Bone, Pye guessed, understood all this as clearly as he did.

And as though to confirm this point, Bone said, 'I hope you're listening to all this, Peter.'

'You were left holding the smoking gun,' Pye said to Tait. 'In this instance, literally. Everybody else can see that. The real problem now is that the louder either you or your lawyers go on shouting your innocence, the more desperate and less believable you all sound. I think that jury convicted you – against all odds, I might add, for murder – because they didn't trust the fact that you and your legal team weren't screaming out the obvious right from the very start. You let too much doubt seep in. All this mysterious concussion and unconsciousness. "A gun went off and then I blacked out." You made life hard – impossible – for yourself. In my experience, there was enough reasonable doubt floating around that crime scene for a dozen men to get off. And yet here you are now, looking for all the world like the dupe you were all too clearly hand-picked to be, waiting to be—' Pye stopped talking, his meaning as clear now to Peter Tait as it had always been to Bone.

'Listen to him,' Bone said again from the door.

'The fourth man,' Pye said. 'It sounds like the title of a gangster film. Is that what you are, Peter, a gangster?'

'They never found him,' Tait said absently.

'My whole point,' Pye said. 'My whole point. They never caught him, and he certainly didn't put up his hands and turn himself in when he found out what was happening to you. I'm not necessarily saying you were deliberately taken along to Globe Town as some kind of – what? – planned sacrifice. But what I *am* still saying loud and clear is that you were at least taken as some kind of insurance in case anything *did* go wrong and somebody more important needed to be protected. And as far as I can tell from what we learned from the others, all four of you were relative amateurs, out of your depth and flexing too much muscle, and so the chances of something *not* going to plan – if much of a plan ever existed in the first place – were pretty high. *That*'s what your lawyer should have been saying over and over to the jury. It's certainly what the prosecution briefs were careful not to let slip.' He wondered if all this was too much for Tait to take in, and so he stopped talking. Anything he hadn't just made clear to the boy, Bone would explain later.

Pye handed round more cigarettes. The room's high ceiling was already marbled with smoke. There were no windows.

'So have you heard nothing whatsoever about my appeal?' Tait said hesitantly.

'Still under consideration,' Pye said, again making his meaning clear to Bone if not to Tait himself.

'At least that's good,' Tait said.

'And, for the record, we've stopped looking for the so-called fourth man. We'll keep the usual notices posted, keep the port alerts flagged up – for what good that'll do while

94

they're still under regulations. But no one's actually *looking* any more. Not like in the beginning, before the trial. All he's got to do now, this fugitive from the law, is to keep his head down and his mouth shut and wait.'

'And once I'm—'

'Exactly,' Pye said. 'Once you're hanged, everything will just go away. A nasty smell might hang around for a few months, but after that . . .'

Pye had said what he'd come to say. He had seen Tait and now he had seen Bone, and he better understood the lie of the land. He was at the end of the rope being played out to him by his own superiors. They themselves may not have been entirely convinced that the evidence against Tait was strong enough to hang him, but they certainly didn't share Pye's sense of outrage at what had happened to the boy. All in all, Pye knew, they would be content to see Tait hanged, and afterwards to convince themselves that, one way or another, justice had been served.

'So why are you here?' Tait said eventually, again hesitantly. It was the first real question he had asked.

Ernest Pye pushed himself back from the small table. 'Because, and like I was saying to Mister Bone earlier' – he paused for a second to allow this to register with both men – 'there are too many loose ends, and loose ends are one of the many things I don't like. Mister Bone and I both serve in the ARP and we've both seen a lot of those loose ends over the past few years. You might not think that's what a bomb does, but that's invariably the result of every bomb that falls – loose ends. They're a different kind of loose end, but that's what they are all the same. I sometimes wonder if that isn't part of why I do the ARP work.'

Beside the door, Bone nodded again.

'I don't get you,' Tait said.

'Because I can convince myself that the people responsible for all those loose ends will one day be made to account and pay for them.' It seemed an inadequate explanation, especially to Pye, but it was something of which he had long been convinced.

Another nod from Bone.

'But what can I tell you?' Tait said. He slumped forward in his seat and let his palms fall on the table.

'Hands,' Bone said to him, and Tait immediately pulled them back to his sides. 'Good lad.'

'I don't know,' Pye said. 'I don't know *what* you can tell me. But there must be something.'

'Listen to the officer,' Bone said. 'Listen to him.'

You'll disappear, Pye wanted to say to Tait. *In fact you've always been invisible, especially before your arrest. In all likelihood, it's why they chose you in the first place. And now you'll disappear for good, for all eternity, and no one will either notice you've gone or miss you. You'll vanish and nobody will even remember you once existed.*

At the door, Arthur Bone looked at his watch.

'Time?' Pye asked him.

'Near enough.'

Turning back to Peter Tait, Pye leaned closer to him and said, 'Listen, Peter, listen.' He waited until Tait was looking directly at him. Even Bone leaned forward in his seat. 'Suppose, just suppose, that I had my suspicions. And that's all they are – suspicions. But suppose I had my suspicions. Two and two and all that.'

'Two and two?'

'I come up with something – even a hunch – and you come up with something – a memory, a tiny and otherwise inconsequential detail – a word, a mannerism, a throwaway remark you overheard and then forgot about – anything – and we put them together.' He looked back and forth between Tait and Bone as he said all this.

'I'll try,' Tait said. He had tried fifty times before and nothing had come to him that his lawyer had been able to make any use of.

'That's all I ask,' Pye said. Just as he had asked before and had had nothing revealed to him.

Before Pye could say any more, there was a rap on the door and it was unlocked and opened. The same warder appeared. He waved his hands at the smoke which flowed out of the room around him.

'Jesus Christ,' he said, coughing. 'It's like Dover Street baths in here. And you know what that makes you lot, don't you?'

No one answered him.

'Bone, I said: you know what that makes you lot, don't you?'

'I heard you the first time,' Bone said. He rose to his feet and blew out the last of his own smoke.

'Suit yourself,' the warder said.

At the table, Ernest Pye pushed the packet of cigarettes to Peter Tait, and Tait took this and slid it quickly into his pocket.

9

LAURA WOKE WITH A START AND SAT UPRIGHT ON THE BED where she had fallen asleep fully clothed. Her hair had come loose and lay across her face. The thin curtains were drawn, and at first she thought it was still night, but then she heard the daytime noises of the street outside and guessed that it was already closer to midday. The sky was dark. It had been raining when she'd walked the short distance home from Archer Street, and it was still raining now.

There was a sudden flash of light at the window, followed a few seconds later by a distant peal of thunder. This was what had woken her. There was too long a gap between the flash and the noise for it to be anything other than thunder and lightning, and she felt reassured by this.

She looked around the room for any sign of the man who had accompanied her there from the club, but there was nothing. She remembered his complaints when she'd told him she lived on the third floor. She saw him surreptitiously looking at all the other doors on the way up, perhaps imagining what lay beyond. He'd been drunk and almost broke by the time he'd summoned up the courage to approach her in the Regency. He'd showed her how much money remained, and she'd taken this from him, promising to keep it safe for him.

He, in turn, had told her that he had better stick close to her to safeguard his investment, and thus their contract was made: nothing explicit, everything suggested, nothing incriminating revealed, nothing vital left unsaid.

After that, he'd followed her around the club, from the bar to a booth and then to the cloakroom, as the place slowly emptied. And then Laura had waited for him outside and he'd followed her to Warwick Street and all those stairs. He'd wanted her to walk with her arm through his, but she'd warned him against this, telling him instead to follow her at a reasonable distance. Despite his drunkenness, he'd understood what she was telling him. Laura had kept a careful eye on the streets as she'd walked, leaving Archer Street via a narrow alleyway which led past the rear of the Apollo to Brewer Street.

At the corner of Warwick Street, she paused, raised her leg and took off her shoe, ostensibly to shake out a stone, in reality to send a signal to the girl standing opposite her. She showed the top of her stocking and her thigh to the man following her – anything to heighten his excitement and thereby, hopefully, make their eventual encounter as brief as possible. The girl standing opposite clicked a small torch on and off and Laura put her shoe back on and lowered her leg. Her own torch lay in her bag. 'Looking for my keys, looking for my lipstick, looking for my purse,' the girls would tell the men who approached them. And the men would offer to help and the girls would walk slowly away and the men would follow them.

Years ago, in the seemingly never-ending depths of the full blackout, a High Court judge had announced in his court that it seemed eminently sensible to him for women to carry torches to keep themselves safe and to allow them to identify any strange men who might approach them in the darkness intending them harm. Tommy Fowler, conscientious and concerned citizen that he was, had afterwards gone to the trouble of buying a gross of the torches and then of having the names of his clubs stencilled on them. On more than one occasion since, he had pointed out this altruistic act to many a lesser magistrate and to countless reluctant licensing clerks.

The man's money still lay on the table a few feet from Laura's bed. She remembered taking it from her purse after he'd gone. He'd been with her less than half an hour, and most of that time had been spent talking to him and cajoling him, encouraging him to become even braver and to start to undress. His reluctance, inebriation and incapability were all inseparably intertwined. It was a common enough equation, and, like all the other girls, Laura was practised in its solution.

After the half-hour, the man had looked down at her, his trousers still around his ankles, and said, 'Is that it?'

Laura had waited before answering him, and had then said, 'Unless there's more.' At which, like all of them, he had struggled to his feet and gathered together his other clothes. He had told her he couldn't stay, that he appreciated every-thing she'd done for him, that he might see her again, that he would *like* to see her again, that he would *definitely* see her again. She told him she'd like that and that he knew where to find her. She wondered if he was about to ask her her name again, but his embarrassment and rising sense of shame drew its boundary somewhere and so he remained silent.

A second flash of lightning was followed by a quicker peal of thunder. She counted the seconds and guessed the distance, something she had done since she was a young girl. A lifetime ago. Everyone spoke of Before the War and During the War, but to Laura, they truly did feel like two separate ages, two completely different countries almost: an age of accepting, unsuspecting childhood – she had been fourteen when the first bombs had fallen – and an age of accommodating, adapting adulthood. She had been fourteen then and she was nineteen now, and it sometimes seemed to her that the whole of her life had already passed in those few years, and that, whatever came afterwards, nothing would match what had happened during that time. It sometimes seemed to her that she was no longer even the same person, and this was both a regret to her and a source of uncertain pride.

At fourteen she had been a child playing in the streets, helping her mother around the house, running errands for her father and looking after her two baby sisters, six-year-old twins.

And now, five years later, she was this.

Three seconds. Meaning that the storm was three miles distant. It was all to do with the difference between the speed of light and the slower speed of sound. One mile in one second. Light travelled fastest, sound lagged behind. It took eight minutes for the light of the sun to reach the earth each morning. Frankie Doll had told her that shortly after the two of them had met. Eight minutes. And she had told him that she'd had some relationships that hadn't lasted as long as that, and Frankie Doll had laughed and told her he believed her.

Then he had told her that she could look up and see stars in the sky every night – perhaps dozens, perhaps hundreds of stars – that no longer actually existed up there. Stars that had either exploded, burned out or spun off into too-distant orbits to be any longer visible. Some of those stars, he told her, had vanished before either of them – him and her – had even been born, but would also remain visible to people down here looking up for a hundred years after the pair of them were dead. That was how far away they were. That was how long it took the light they had already given off to complete its journey.

She had been more sceptical about this, but he had insisted it was true. And so she had started to speculate that, in theory, you could be looking up at the sky one night, at one particular star, and it could actually disappear right in front of your eyes. That's exactly what could happen, Frankie Doll told her. And no one else would see it? No one else would know what catastrophic or momentous thing had just happened? And no one would ever believe you, Frankie Doll said. So, Laura continued to speculate, it might be a cataclysm in outer space, but down here on, say, Archer Street, or Warwick Street, it would be an event of a single second, less, and no one would ever know the difference? Got it in one, Frankie Doll told her. He told her that he'd once looked up the word 'cataclysm' and that it fitted the bill exactly. He told her he looked up lots of words, that it was the only real way to learn anything. He told her that knowledge was power – and much bigger names than Frankie Doll had come to that particular conclusion – and that power, of any sort, was always a thing worth having. Then he told her that he was going places. His name was Frankie Doll and he was going places. That was his plan in life, his aim and his goal, and she had listened closely then to every word he'd said to her and had believed every single one of them.

She had never seen that vanishing star. But she had since read books on the galaxies and constellations and she had learned some of their names. On clear nights she still occasionally went to the broad corner of Glasshouse Street and sought out above her the stars she could identify. She knew others prayed for cloudy nights and thin, fading moons, but not her. Some stars brought her luck; others were portents of misfortune. Some stars would keep her safe; some would expose her to danger.

She even started calling herself Stella in the club. Until Tommy Fowler told her it was the name of his dead mother and to go back to Laura. Perhaps she could even lose the 'u'. It sounded more American. She'd started to explain what 'Stella' meant, and Tommy Fowler had slapped her hard across her face and asked her if she hadn't heard him the first time. Then he had squeezed her cheeks and told her how sorry he was for what he'd just done, but that he felt they now understood each other better. She had nodded, his hand still tight around her face.

She remembered Frankie Doll standing close behind Fowler at the time, and giving her no indication whatsoever that he might intervene or even object on her behalf. Later, after Fowler had left the club, he had asked her if the slap had hurt and she had told him to mind his own business. Where Tommy Fowler was concerned, Frankie Doll was a coward, and she had seen this in a single glance into his eyes. She might afterwards grow fond of him – she might even convince herself that she actually loved him – but she would always know that, at heart, he was a coward; and she would know, too, where *she* fitted into this great unfolding plan of Frankie Doll's life.

She rose from the bed and went to the window. It was raining more heavily now, and the water was already gathering along the inside sill and dripping to the linoleum beneath.

Another peal. Four seconds. The storm was either wavering or it was already moving away.

Frankie Doll had said he'd be back there by mid-morning at the latest.

At fifteen, she'd been evacuated to near Lavenham, in Suffolk. To a farm where she was turned into a servant and labourer. Her two sisters had gone to the West Midlands with her mother. She had never understood the reason for this separation. Her father had gone all the way to Africa and had disappeared there. First he was missing, then he was believed dead, then he was truly dead.

The man she was staying with in Suffolk told her all this. She had cried, and he had comforted her, and after comforting her, he had raped her. It was finished before she had fully understood what was happening to her, and afterwards he had given her an apple, promised her extra meat on her plate that night, and said that the same again, but worse, would happen to her if she shouted her head off about what *she* had done. She might even be sent back to London in disgrace. Back to London, where people were being bombed from the air and burned to death in their beds.

And so she had stayed in Lavenham until she was sixteen, and the same thing had gone on happening to her once or twice a week, usually depending on when the man's old wife was away from the house. He had shown her things; he had told her she loved him. He would protect her, he said. And later, when she was properly grown up and she understood all that he had done for her, she would realize that everything had happened for the best.

A hundred times since her return, she had imagined telling

Frankie Doll what had happened to her and pointing him to the man's door.

Her mother and two sisters had been killed during the first raid on Coventry. Dead, identified and buried before Laura was even told. People were very sorry for her loss. For all her losses. They said it to her all the time. It was the times in which they lived. There was terrible evil in the world and that evil needed stamping out. Good and justice would one day prevail, and it was all, they insisted, simply a matter of waiting.

But where did any of that sympathy or understanding get her?

And so at sixteen she had run away from Lavenham and come back to London, where she had changed her appearance, lied about her age, and afterwards concocted a thousand other lies about her past.

The giant drops of rain looked metallic as they fell from the dark sky above her. Mercury, like mercury. There was no wind to scatter them and they fell heavily, and she could see the individual explosions where they hit the canopies and awnings beneath her. The drains and gutters already streamed. Spouts overflowed and cascaded to the street, and people walked in new patterns to avoid the worst of the water. Yesterday they had been taking off their jackets and their ties and unfastening their collars and holding up their faces to the sun; and now this.

She waited for the next flash of lightning and peal of thunder, but neither came. The storm was spent, fading away across the distant rooftops.

Thunder was the noise of the Devil beating his wife, her vanished father used to say to his three frightened daughters.

Beating her with a stick, or a broom perhaps, or perhaps even a garden spade. They had squealed with excitement at each violent addition to the list following each clap of thunder. The lightning, he said, was the sound of the woman's screaming.

Perhaps it was all part of that same pattern of good and evil in the world.

Frankie Doll would surely be back soon. She had long since learned that he wasn't exactly what you'd call a man of his word.

Laura drew back the curtain, but this did little to illuminate the room. The rain was slackening off now, and soon the Devil would grow tired or stop for another drink and his wife would escape her beating. And when that happened, Laura knew, the woman's tears would stop falling, the clouds would part and quickly vanish, and then the golden, glowing sun of her smile would once again appear. It was what always happened – as unchangeable and as predictable as those distant, dying stars of Frankie Doll's which came and went in the heavens high above.

10

A T Crowley's appearance, Tommy Fowler remained
pointedly seated at his desk. A revolver lay open to view
at the centre of the empty surface, its barrel pointed directly
away from Tommy Fowler. As intended, Crowley saw this
immediately upon entering the small office, what Tommy
Fowler referred to these days as his Centre of Operations. But
even before Crowley's eyes were accustomed to the dim light
of the room, his acute sense of smell had detected the gun
oil with which the barrel and drum mechanism had recently
been lubricated and cleaned.

Joshua Silver followed Crowley in and then stood to one
side as Frankie Doll closed the door and turned the key.
Crowley inclined his head an inch to register the solid click
of the lock. He knew about locks, and the lock which had
originally held this door had been replaced with something
considerably more robust. A time-buyer. Something sturdy,
and supplemented by two equally solid bolts at the door's top
and bottom edges, which Frankie Doll also slid into place
once Crowley and Silver were in the room and facing Tommy
Fowler.

All these unnecessary safeguards amused Crowley. He
waited where he stood for a moment, closed his eyes, breathed

deeply, and then approached closer to where Tommy Fowler awaited him.

In response to this, Tommy Fowler raised his hand from his lap and laid it on the edge of the desk close to the gun.

Crowley grinned and held up his hands in surrender. 'Please, don't shoot me,' he said. 'Not now, not after such a long and terrible life, and especially not after all those cruel stairs. Spare yourself the notoriety.'

Uncertain how to take this, Tommy Fowler said, 'Nobody's shooting nobody.' He opened the desk drawer and slid the revolver into it.

'Noted,' Crowley said. He held his palm flat to his chest as his breathing slowed.

'What is?' Tommy Fowler said.

'That you still have the thing to hand and that whatever evil spell I choose to cast upon you must do its work within the two or three seconds it would take you to snatch it back out, point it at me and pull the nice clean trigger.'

Tommy Fowler laughed at the remark. 'And you can still do all that, can you – cast evil spells?'

'Oh, assuredly,' Crowley said with a flourish.

Silver came to stand beside him. 'May Aleister sit down?' he asked Tommy Fowler, who motioned for Frankie Doll to position two chairs in front of the desk.

Crowley lowered himself slowly and awkwardly into his seat, letting out a succession of small, involuntary gasps and a solitary satisfied grunt when he was finally settled and comfortable.

'Is he in pain?' Tommy Fowler asked Silver.

'A body my age, and having endured the rigours of a life lived as mine has been lived, is prey to a multitude of pains and a host of aches and ancillary failures, fraying edges and wearing outs,' Crowley said. 'Perhaps something to help ease all these irritations is at hand?'

Silver heard all these false and melodramatic high notes and once again he regretted them. He doubted if Tommy Fowler would be taken in as easily as most of Crowley's other, more willing victims had been.

'You want dope?' Tommy Fowler said, uncertain what Crowley was suggesting.

'He means a drink,' Silver said quickly. 'Brandy, for preference.'

'All the papers call him a "dope-fiend",' Tommy Fowler said.

'Not all, surely?' Crowley said, still smiling. He held Tommy Fowler's gaze for a moment, and in that instant something of an understanding passed between the two men. 'Besides, I imagine you yourself also attract their opprobrium on a somewhat regular basis.'

'Not really,' Tommy Fowler said, though again not entirely certain what Crowley had just suggested. He looked to Frankie Doll, who shrugged.

'Get Mister Crowley a drink, Frankie,' Fowler said, motioning for Doll to take a bottle and glasses from a nearby cabinet.

'I must warn you,' Crowley said, 'I cannot tolerate the sewage that usually passes for fine spirits these days.'

'Me neither,' Tommy Fowler said. He indicated for Frankie Doll to show the bottle to Crowley. 'Pre-war, that. French. Picture of a castle on the label and everything. What more could you ask?'

'Then I shall accept your kind offer of the libation and

afterwards remain eternally grateful to you. Though perhaps I ought also to warn you that I am a man of no small appetites.'

Silver shook his head and tutted loudly at the words, and Tommy Fowler laughed.

Frankie Doll filled the large glasses half full, put Tommy Fowler's on his desk and then held out Crowley's to him at arm's length.

'What is it?' Crowley asked him.

'He's frightened to touch you,' Tommy Fowler said. 'We all are. Ever since he knew you were on your way in. You might say that your reputation precedes you and does you no favours. No favours whatsoever.'

'It was always thus,' Crowley said. 'A scabby, vicious, unpredictable little dog running ahead of me along a narrow, dirty, dimly lit street.'

'If you say so,' Tommy Fowler said. 'How about your friend here?'

'My name is Silver,' Joshua Silver said.

'My personal physician and much-valued companion,' Crowley added.

'So I see,' Tommy Fowler said. 'I have a few personal physicians of my own on the books, if you know what I mean.'

'Oh, I understand you perfectly,' Crowley said, draining most of his drink and then waiting for a moment with his eyes closed before smacking his lips.

'Told you,' Fowler said to him.

'So you did.'

'Mister Silver?' Fowler said. 'Something for—'

'I endeavour to remain sober and responsible at all times while attending to Aleister,' Silver said.

'I can imagine,' Fowler said, looking between the two men.

'As, I imagine, do your own faithful employees,' Crowley said to Fowler, smiling at Frankie Doll. 'Especially when employed in an emporium of illicit nocturnal delights such as this one. Easy to fall prey to temptation in a place such as this, I should imagine. Especially for a weak or greedy or easily corrupted man.'

'Weak?' Frankie Doll said. 'Who are you calling—?'

'You endeavoured not to even touch me on the basis of ridiculous tittle-tattle already fifty years old,' Crowley said without looking at Frankie Doll. He drank the last of his brandy and held out his glass.

Frankie Doll waited for the nod from Tommy Fowler before refilling it.

'Ah,' Crowley said the instant Frankie Doll withdrew the bottle from the rim of his glass.

'What?'

'Just then. You felt it.'

'Felt what?' There was a dry, anxious note in Frankie Doll's voice.

'See?' Crowley said to Fowler. 'Perhaps our fingertips touched, perhaps they didn't. It hardly matters; what matters is the power of suggestion.'

'What's that when it's at home?' Tommy Fowler said.

'I didn't touch him,' Frankie Doll said. 'The bottle touched his glass, that's all.'

'And you wouldn't consider that contact enough?' Crowley asked him.

Beside Crowley, Silver raised his eyes and then closed them.

'He's tired of your games,' Tommy Fowler said.

Crowley laid a hand on his friend's shoulder. 'I disappoint

and embarrass him on an almost daily basis these days,' he said.

'At least daily,' Silver said.

Turning back to Frankie Doll, Crowley said, 'My apologies, Mister Doll. My supposedly satanic powers were always much exaggerated, always made more of than they warranted, depending on my persecutors. I don't deny that I possess them – powers, that is, and of many kinds and to varying degrees – but the description and, usually, condemnation of those powers was always of greater profit to others than to myself. So you have nothing to fear. Besides, I could touch you again and revoke anything I might have transferred with my first touch.'

'You know my name?' Frankie Doll said.

'I do,' Crowley said. 'You told it to me at the foot of the stairs. In fact, you made a point of telling it to me, in full, and of afterwards telling me what part you played in all of this.'

'I only—' Frankie Doll began to say.

Tommy Fowler slapped his palms on the desk. 'You're here for a reason, Mister Crowley.' He positioned his own un-touched drink exactly where the revolver had been.

'I most certainly am,' Crowley said.

They were there because of Crowley's scheme, and because the newspaper reports of Peter Tait's trial and its outcome had repeatedly mentioned the 'shadowy underworld' in which Tait and those countless others like him lived and operated. Tommy Fowler had been mentioned as a major figure in that underworld, and the Regency club on Archer Street had been mentioned as the hub of his so-called empire. It was simple enough for a man like Crowley to confirm all this, and for him then to arrange a meeting with Fowler. All Crowley needed now was for Fowler to arrange and guarantee the safe delivery of something to Tait.

In truth, Crowley had been surprised by the speed with which Fowler had agreed to meet him, especially if it meant Fowler exposing some part of his own involvement – even if only by implication – in what had happened to Peter Tait, and he remained wary of the man's motives now. Or perhaps, as so often before, Tommy Fowler was simply intrigued by Crowley's own notoriety and this was why he had agreed to see him so soon after being approached.

But whatever the reason for Fowler indulging him, and whatever the outcome of all this, Crowley knew that he had little to lose by any payment the man might eventually demand in exchange for providing this vital contact with Tait. And it was equally clear to Crowley that he himself – the all too obvious benefits of a successful attempt at gaining immortality aside – had little except that notoriety, those hinted-at powers, with which to bargain now.

'You mentioned a boy called Tait,' Tommy Fowler said hesitantly, as though he might never have heard the name before. It was a mistake on his part, and both Crowley and Silver saw this.

'A common murderer, apparently,' Crowley said, his own apparent lack of concern better manufactured and presented. 'He's going to hang – and good riddance – for killing a man during a robbery. You may have read about him in the press. His lawyer – for what good it will do him – is hoping to appeal his sentence.'

'I heard of him before,' Tommy Fowler said.

'Before his arrest?'

'There's hundreds of them, these know-it-all youngsters.'

'Such was my understanding, too,' Crowley said. 'My interest in the man is purely personal. I'm not after any kind of revenge or retribution, if that's your concern.'

'Personal, how?'

'Because he is condemned, and because he will know, when his appeal application fails and his sentence is confirmed, the precise date and time of his early demise. His character and history are of no concern or interest whatsoever to me.'

Tommy Fowler shook his head, confused. He had agreed to meet Aleister Crowley – *the* Aleister Crowley – because he'd imagined the man might have known something of the details of the robbery and of Tait's part in it, and now here he was spinning him a different line completely. But whatever story he was spinning, he was still Aleister Crowley and you could never be one hundred per cent certain with men like that. Either way, Tommy Fowler had needed to see him and to know. And now, listening to Crowley's assurances, he was even more intrigued, and already starting to consider what there might be in the arrangement for himself. And from what he read in the papers, this Crowley still attracted bad publicity like a corpse attracted flies, and so perhaps that might work to his advantage, too.

He watched as Crowley drained his second large brandy and then flicked a fingernail against the bowl of the glass to attract Doll's attention.

'And him being sentenced to hang means what exactly?' Tommy Fowler said.

'I've already told you,' Crowley said, impatient with Doll and his pouring. 'It means that at some point in the hopefully not-too-distant future, our friend Tait will know the exact moment of his death. Believe me, it is the rarest of gifts and the greatest of privileges, a kind of knowledge that eludes all other men. Just imagine if the same could be said of everyone living – that we were all, by whatever means, to learn of the exact moment of our own deaths. What would our lives be worth then? How would we live those lives? What would or wouldn't we do to prolong them, knowing we had so short a time remaining to us? What wouldn't we do to learn the secret of altering those unalterable facts? And what power would the holder of *that* particular secret not then possess?' Crowley was panting and Silver put a hand on his arm to restrain him. 'Forgive me,' Crowley said after a few seconds.

'And you honestly think that because this Tait character will know the exact time of his own death,' Tommy Fowler began to say, his faltering words and reasoning coming together only as he spoke, 'then he might have something of this power?' He smiled at what he had suggested. 'I'm beginning to remember the man – boy, really – and I doubt he possesses the gumption to fasten his own shoelaces most days.' He looked at Frankie Doll. 'Can you bring him to mind, Frankie? Little runt with a few slates loose.' He tapped his temple. 'Ask me, he's likely to have confessed to everything because he couldn't lie fast enough. Besides which, according to the papers, the law had him bang to rights from the very start.' He laughed again, and this time Crowley joined him.

'You sound a good judge of character, Mister Fowler,' Crowley said. 'From what I read, he's practically an imbecile, and a vicious little one at that. And one, moreover, who will be neither missed nor mourned by a single living soul.'

'Making him—'

'All the more valuable and vital to my enterprise, yes,' Crowley said.

Tommy Fowler picked up his own glass and drank from it for the first time. 'And so what, exactly, do you want from me?' he said, sitting back in his chair.

'Oh, I daresay nothing,' Crowley said. 'That is to say, next to nothing. I merely wish to indulge another of my experiments and, to that end, for you to guarantee the delivery of something from me to the boy.'

'From what I've heard, you've blighted more lives with all your comings and goings and experiments than old Adolf himself.'

Crowley laughed at the remark. 'I sincerely doubt that.' It was enough that the man remained intrigued and compliant.

'National enemy number one, you was, at one time. Like Al Capone.'

'"Was" being the operative tense.'

'The what?' Frankie Doll said.

Crowley ignored him. 'And now here I am, forgotten and anonymous in a crowd of growing millions,' he said. 'Though thinned out soon enough, no doubt. "War Criminals". What a strange concept, don't you agree?'

'You've lost me,' Tommy Fowler said. 'Besides, it won't be *that* soon – not if the old Koblenz Comedian has got it right and we're all about to start fighting Uncle Joe alongside the Jerries.'

'Haw Haw?' Crowley said. 'Hardly a man renowned for his grasp on the truth.'

'No, I suppose not,' Tommy Fowler said. He rubbed a hand over his face. 'So what is it you want me to get to Tait?'

'Merely—'

'And, more importantly, would *he* need to know about it,

this connection between you and him. Because if he gets even the slightest—'

'Absolutely not,' Crowley said. 'Absolutely not. In fact, the last thing I want to do is to add to the poor wretch's woes by having him associated with *me* in any way.'

'That's good,' Tommy Fowler said.

'Besides . . .' Crowley said and then paused.

'Besides, what?'

Like a fish rising to a perfectly presented fly.

'I was merely going to add that once I have made this connection, it is highly unlikely that any appeal regarding Tait's commutation would succeed. It is my belief that once contact is established between us, Tait will definitely be hanged.'

'And you can do that – make sure he hangs just by getting in touch with him?' Tommy Fowler licked his lips and drank more of his brandy.

'Ensure he pays his full and proper debt to society for the brutal slaying of an innocent man, yes,' Crowley said. 'Innocent man, father, son and husband.' He was guessing now, but judging by the look in Tommy Fowler's eyes, and by his tongue running back and forth across his lips, it didn't really matter.

'And what would it be?' Tommy Fowler asked him.

'What would what be?' Lift up the rod and pull the line tight.

'This thing you want delivering to him.'

'Oh, that?' Crowley made a show of patting his pockets. 'Merely this. A book. A Bible.'

'Last thing I'd have expected *you* to want to give to anybody.'

'The press again,' Crowley said. He took the small book

from the case inside his inner pocket and slid it on to Fowler's desk. There was more to Doll's suspicions than the man would ever know.

Tommy Fowler picked the book up and rifled its gilt-edged pages. 'It's too small to read,' he said. 'Send a man blind trying to make head or tail of that. Besides, prison light's not the best – trust me – and I doubt if reading comes high on Tait's list of priorities.' He laughed again, and again Crowley joined him.

'Whatever his interests and predilections to date,' Crowley said, 'the book will serve its purpose.' And the prison authorities would certainly not prevent it from being delivered to the condemned man, himself awaiting God's own grace. And even if they searched it using a magnifying glass, they would not find even the imprint of the words Crowley had transcribed on to its pages and then meticulously erased. Words which had come and gone, but which would permanently remain. And words which, in the possession – unwitting or otherwise – of the right man, were the first part of that potent equation known only to Crowley himself. And besides, what man ever refused a Bible, let alone a man waiting to die?

'We're very grateful,' Silver said. He started to stand up. It was four in the afternoon, the dead heart of the club's day, and the journey home would be a long one for the two of them.

'Which brings me to my next point,' Tommy Fowler said, motioning for Silver to sit back down.

'Sorry?' Silver said.

Crowley laughed at his friend's naivety. 'Perhaps you and I might discuss that alone, in private, later, once the thing is safely delivered,' he said to Tommy Fowler, quickly touching a finger to his lips.

'Receiving you loud and clear,' Tommy Fowler said.

'Of course you are,' Crowley said. 'I'm sure you understand me perfectly. And I'm certain that at the proper time I shall be able to convince you even further of the benefits to yourself and your . . . your . . .' He waved a hand at the room around him.

'My little empire,' Tommy Fowler said proudly.

'Precisely.'

Joshua Silver finally rose from his seat and helped Crowley up from his.

The four men then went back down the steep stairs and into the club.

Women with dustpans and brushes moved among the tables. A barman restocked his shelves from a stack of crates and poured drink from a jug into bottles using a funnel. A second man stood to one side of the room, his face hidden. He turned even further away at the appearance of Crowley, Silver, Fowler and Doll. A few girls sat at one of the tables, drinking tea, smoking and talking among themselves. They lowered their voices when Tommy Fowler entered the room.

Something about the man at the side of the room attracted Crowley's attention, and turning to Tommy Fowler, he said, 'May I?'

Tommy Fowler didn't understand him.

'May I speak to him?'

'Him?' Tommy Fowler said. 'Who is it?' he asked Frankie Doll, who had been on his way towards the table of girls, having seen both Laura and Ruby Nolan sitting there.

'Sweeney,' Frankie Doll said over his shoulder.

"Course it is,' Tommy Fowler said, and he called Sweeney over to them.

It was clear to Crowley that the man was reluctant to come. Tommy Fowler shouted again and Sweeney came to him, his hat low and his head still down as he came.

'Mister Crowley here would like a word,' Tommy Fowler said.

Turning to Crowley, Sweeney raised a hand to his mouth.

Crowley looked closely at the boy's lips. 'My apologies,' he said. 'Please, lower your hand.'

Sweeney looked over Crowley's shoulder to Tommy Fowler, who nodded once, and Sweeney took away his hand.

'I thought so,' Crowley said. He held the boy's arm. 'I myself was born with a condition known as *frenulum linguae*. The doctor had to cut a flap of skin which fastened my tongue to the floor of my mouth. I was tongue tied.'

The boy relaxed slightly. Behind Crowley, Tommy Fowler and Frankie Doll moved away to hold a whispered conversation.

'You have my sympathy,' Crowley said to Sweeney. 'I can see that you were considerably less fortunate in your own family doctor.'

Sweeney laughed at the words. 'Make that family, full stop,' he said.

'I see,' Crowley said. 'Again, forgive me if I've caused you any embarrassment in front of these others.'

'Not really,' Sweeney said. He licked his lips to catch the saliva.

'Good,' Crowley said. 'Good.' He turned to where Tommy Fowler and Frankie Doll stood together. 'This man Sweeney,' he called out. 'I trust him. And I am nothing if not a good judge of human nature and character. Is that noted, Mister Fowler?'

Tommy Fowler, unaccustomed to being spoken to like this, and certainly not in front of his employees, was nevertheless amused by Crowley's continuing imperiousness, and he saluted him and called back, 'Duly noted, Mister C, Sir,' and only when he laughed at himself did Frankie Doll and the girls at the table afford themselves a short, awkward outburst.

Crowley went back to Tommy Fowler, and when only Fowler could hear him, he said in a whisper, 'Both our advantages, remember?' And then he turned and signalled to Silver that it was time for them to leave.

11

SWEENEY HAD HEARD FROM VERONICA THE STORY OF THE man who had been completely vaporized by an explosion. The story had its usual variations, but, essentially, the man had been struck – actually, physically struck – by a bomb. A big bomb, one of the biggest, a five-hundred-pounder at least. 'Vaporized,' Veronica said, meant that the man had been turned to vapour – bones, flesh, blood, everything. Another report she'd read had used the term 'atomized'. But she had no idea what that meant. Atomized – a man turned to atoms, presumably, the tiniest pieces of his being, smaller even than a single drop of blood or flake of his skin. Smaller than any-thing there had ever been. And because he'd been 'atomized', he had vanished completely. There had even been speculation, Veronica had gone on, her voice by now reduced to its usual stage whisper even though the two of them were alone, that these millions and millions and millions – because, believe her, that was how many there were – that all these millions of individual atoms might then somehow recombine into a completely new shape of something living. Another man, say, a dog, a fish, a flower, anything. This was where she had lost Sweeney – as fully as she herself was already lost – and when he had asked her to speculate more precisely on what form this new shape might take, she had refused even to guess. The stuff of nightmares, she had told him.

He was reminded of all this now by the blocked road ahead of him. An unexploded bomb had been found. A man in the small crowd said it had fallen over three years previously and had only just been discovered. A dozen homes had been destroyed by another bomb near by. Four whole and eight half-families had been wiped out, almost two dozen people. Sweeney wondered if any of *them* had been atomized or vaporized. He had seen the dust-covered survivors pulled from ruins night after night at the height of the bombing. Men, women and children turned white or black or grey from head to foot, standing like marble statues, streaked by either the falling rain or the water from the hoses played back and forth over the smoking ruins of their lost homes.

He wondered how many corpses lay waiting yet to be discovered. There were still-unfilled mass graves on Clapham Common and in Battersea Park, dug out by mechanical excavators at the start of the war when the fatalities were expected to be ten times higher. Sweeney had seen the pit in Battersea Park, already crumbling at the edges and long since filled with water.

He tried to get closer to see, and as he did so, someone pulled at his arm, and he turned to see one of the girls from the club. He recognized her, but didn't know her name. She was a newcomer, younger than most, popular with the customers, always busy.

'London's full of them,' she said to him. She looked directly at him. 'Everywhere. One in five never exploded, that's what they say. They say you should count the craters, six in a row, ten in a row, something like that. Look for gaps, holes in roofs, that kind of thing, but no craters.' She stopped talking and waited for him to answer her.

'You're from the Regency,' he said.

She held out her hand to him, pushing it into his before he could respond. She told him her name – Ruby Nolan – said that she already knew who he was, and that she'd seen him at the Regency with Tommy Fowler earlier. She looked from his eyes to his mouth and then put the tips of her fingers on his chin.

'You don't have to hide it,' she said. 'What's the point?' She put her arm through his and pushed herself closer to him. 'That was a queer affair,' she said. She turned back to the ruined houses and the men working there.

'What was?'

'Fowler with that strange-looking man and his funny little friend, the Jew.'

She had followed him, she must have done. He had been walking for half an hour since leaving Archer Street, and at his usual pace.

'You followed me,' he said, immediately regretting the words and all they implied, and she withdrew her hand and then stood back from him.

'Most men wouldn't complain,' she said. She pointed along the cordoned-off street. 'Look.'

A warden was walking along the centre of the street, carrying a piece of clothing in one hand and a shoe in the other.

'Perhaps they found somebody,' she said. 'After all this time. A skeleton, perhaps.' She turned back to him. 'Who was he?'

'A man called Crowley,' Sweeney said.

Her eyes opened wide at the name. 'Aleister Crowley?'

Sweeney shrugged. 'The other was a man called Silver.'

'And he was actually *there*, in the club? Aleister Crowley?' She was unable now to suppress or disguise the excitement in her voice. 'No wonder.'

'No wonder what?'

'Didn't you feel it? The place felt like a grave when he appeared. All the warmth just went out of the room.'

He didn't understand her. She was starting to sound like Veronica. The club was in a cellar; it was always cold.

'Who is he?' he asked her.

'Who is he? Are you serious? Aleister Crowley? According to the papers, he's the wickedest man in England.' She returned to him and put her arm back through his. 'So tell me,' she said. 'Tell me what he wanted with Fowler, what the two of them were up to.' She clasped her hands together.

Anyone looking at them, Sweeney thought, might think they were sweethearts, a young married couple even. He wondered how much he dared reveal to her.

'I can't tell you,' he said. But instead of disappointing or dissuading her, this seemed only to excite her further.

'Sounds intriguing,' she said. '"Sweeney – Man of Intrigue".' Her face was closer to him now, her cheek practically pressed into his chest. 'Something private, is it? You just said you never heard of him before. Aleister Crowley? Does it not ring even a distant bell?'

'Perhaps Veronica would know him,' Sweeney said. 'It's more her line. She tells fortunes. Among other things.'

He felt her stiffen at the name and then draw slightly away from him.

'Veronica?'

125

'I live with her,' he said. 'Not *with* her. In the same house. Rented rooms. The room next door. She was there when I arrived. She's old. Old enough to be my mother – older. It's not as though . . . I mean . . .'

Ruby Nolan tightened her grip on his arm again and laughed. 'What are you trying to tell me? Trying to scare me off, are you?'

'I just thought . . .'

'And you know what thought did, don't you?'

He wondered if the remark was intended to mock him or if it was something flirtatious, almost affectionate. Besides, it was curiosity, not thought, that killed the cat. The girls in the club often teased him like this, but there he was always better able to judge their true intent. This felt different to him. She was still holding him and her cheek was still almost pressed against his chest.

'So you're not going to tell me,' she said. She feigned disappointment and then pouted.

'I don't know what I *can* tell you,' Sweeney said. It was the truth.

The warden came closer to the watching crowd and told them all to go home. The bomb was dead and there was nobody beneath the rubble. He asked them what they were waiting for, what they expected to see, if they hadn't all had a bellyful of this kind of thing already. If they didn't disperse soon, he said, then he'd be obliged to start taking names and afterwards to make a report to the police.

'We ought to go,' Ruby said.

'Go where?' Did she mean together?

'Wherever you like,' she said, as though it were of no consequence or interest whatsoever to her. 'Unless you're too busy running errands for Tommy Fowler and the wickedest man in England. Unless you want shot of me, that is. Perhaps you're embarrassed to be seen with me this far from Archer Street.' She looked around them. 'I doubt if anybody here knows what I am.'

'I didn't mean that,' Sweeney said.

She pulled him away from the barrier and then drew him along the street beside her.

'The papers called Crowley the wickedest man in the *world* at one time,' she said. 'Some people even said he was the Devil in human form. Everybody knows who Aleister Crowley is.'

Sweeney faltered in his step. 'I didn't,' he said.

'Millionaire, once. He's supposed to have spent a fortune trying to conjure up evil spirits and then to get himself possessed by them. Haven't you even heard of all that other stuff? It's been in the papers for years.'

'I'm not much of a reader. Veronica – she's more of a one for the papers and magazines.'

'Then I'll bet *she* knows everything there is to know about him. You should ask her. How far is it?'

'Far?'

'To where you and this old-enough-to-be-your-mother Veronica live.'

'Five minutes,' Sweeney said. He pointed in the direction of Beaufort Street.

'Not far at all, then. We could go back there now. Perhaps *then* you'll let me in on whatever big secret it is you're keeping.'

'What did you mean – about "all that other stuff" in the papers?'

'About Crowley? Oh, you mean the sex stuff. It was mostly

127

what they all went on about. Crowley and his virgins. Young women, his followers. Young women, old women, poor women and rich women. Men, even. *Animals*, even, if you believe all you read. Goats, sheep, that sort of thing. Abroad. According to the papers, he got up to all manner of things with them. Things they didn't see fit to print, things they said no decent man or woman should ever have to be confronted with.'

'What sort of things?' Sweeney said. Did he sound as though he doubted what she was telling him?

'*Things*,' she said. 'Just *things*. You have to use your imagination. Covens, sects. Black magic practices, sacrifices, secret rituals and—'

'Sacrifices?'

'That's what they said. According to them, there wasn't *anything* he wouldn't do in trying to conjure up the Devil or whatever.'

'I thought you just said he *was* the Devil?'

'That's what the papers called him. I didn't even know he was in London. I didn't even know if he was still alive or not. He's lived all over the world. He was somewhere on a Greek island for years, surrounded by his followers. You must at least have seen a *picture* of him.'

Was that because she knew he couldn't read? Veronica had started teaching him, but progress so far was slow and intermittent. He could identify and spell out all the signs of the zodiac. He didn't know what they were, exactly, or what they were intended to suggest or represent, but he could spell them all out in large, childish capitals. It was an achievement of sorts, a start.

'Left or right?' Ruby said. They were standing at a junction.

'Left,' he said, already wondering what Veronica would say when he and the girl turned up together. The people in the crowd might not have known her, but Veronica would see her immediately for what she was. He patted the small Bible again.

'What is it? A letter? Is that your errand?'

'It's a Bible,' he said, already knowing that soon, in the confines of his room perhaps, he would take it out and show it to her.

'A Bible? Oh my God. And Aleister Crowley gave it to you?'

'To Fowler. Crowley wants it delivering to somebody Tommy Fowler knows.'

'Who?'

'Fowler said I was to keep schtum. A word to anybody, and he said he'd . . . he'd . . .' He touched his mouth again.

'I can imagine,' Ruby said. 'Don't worry – I won't make you tell me.'

'*Make* me?'

'It was a joke. My womanly wiles and feminine charms and all that. Or perhaps you think I don't possess any.'

'It's not that. It's just that—'

'Don't worry,' she said. 'I know what you mean – Fowler.'

Sweeney nodded.

'Last night a customer told me he was a wholesale butcher. Told me he could get me all the quality meat I wanted, steaks, everything. Meat jokes – you can imagine. He said that eating red meat was the only reliable cure for nerves.'

'What sort of nerves?' Veronica was forever telling him she lived on her nerves.

'Bomb nerves. War nerves. He was talking about that

rocket that landed. He had a theory that we should cut off the Jerries' meat supply and stop eating so many vegetables ourselves. He said too many vegetables were turning men into women.'

'Women?'

'Not women, exactly, but you know what I mean.'

He finally understood her. 'I see,' he said.

'It's because of what I am,' she said. 'What they're paying for. They say things. They think it gives them rights and privileges. Things they wouldn't dream of saying to anybody else.'

'Their wives, you mean?'

'And others. One man asked me if I knew any words of German. He wanted me to look at pictures and tell him what I thought. I thought he was talking about – you know – but instead he wanted me to look at those pictures of all those dead bodies. I couldn't make head or tail of what I was look-ing at at first. And all the time, there he was – you know – and watching me like a hawk.'

'Don't,' Sweeney said.

'Sorry. I know. It's just these times. Each man to his own, I suppose.'

Sweeney stopped walking and she stumbled and almost fell.

'This is it,' he said. He indicated the high house.

'You and the fortune-teller?' she said. She seemed disap-pointed, suddenly uncertain of why she was there.

For his part, Sweeney imagined she was about to leave him, to tell him she should never have come, say goodbye and then carry on walking along the Fulham Road. The thought of this happening was suddenly unbearable to him.

'I could show it you,' he said. 'The Bible.'

Ruby Nolan looked again at the house. 'I suppose so.'

Sweeney went up the steps and waited for her between the chipped and blistered stucco pillars of the porch.

'All very grand,' Ruby said, coming to stand beside him. She looked both ways along the ruined and dilapidated street and then followed him inside.

The hallway was cold and dark. Sheets of newspaper lay scattered over the tiled floor.

'I live at the top,' he told her.

'Penthouse suite?'

'Not exactly.'

'Don't worry,' she said. 'Next thing, you'll be telling me you're not really one of those millionaire playboys we're always reading about.'

Not like this Crowley once was?

Sweeney wondered when he'd last possessed ten quid to call his own.

They climbed the stairs together, neither of them speaking, their breath clouding in the cold air.

At the top, a door opened and Veronica appeared.

'Thought I heard you coming up,' she said to Sweeney. 'I said to myself, I said—' She stopped abruptly at the sight of Ruby Nolan a few feet behind Sweeney.

Ruby held the woman's gaze until Veronica turned away, pulling together the loose front of the gown she wore over her skirt and blouse.

'This is Ruby,' Sweeney said. 'She works at the Regency.'

'Oh, does she indeed?' Veronica said, looking back at Ruby.

'I'm a waitress there,' Ruby said, smiling her best smile.

'I can imagine,' Veronica said. 'And a very popular one at that, I should think.'

'Oh, very,' Ruby said, still smiling.

'She walked home with me,' Sweeney said to Veronica.

'Live in this neck of the woods, does she?'

'Brewer Street,' Ruby said.

'Bit out of your way, then.'

'I fancied some fresh air,' Ruby said. 'I bumped into Sweeney here' – she remembered his name just in time – 'and so we decided to walk together. They found an unexploded bomb on Pavilion Road.'

'I could have told them all along where it was,' Veronica said.

'Sweeney said you did a bit of crystal-ball gazing.'

'Everybody round here's known where it was since the night it fell,' Veronica said. She turned to Sweeney. 'You coming in for a nice warm drink?'

'We were thinking of having a little talk,' Ruby said to her. 'We've got a bit of club business to discuss. Confidential business.'

'I doubt that very much,' Veronica said. 'Sweeney?'

But Sweeney had come too far to turn the girl back now. 'She's right,' he said to Veronica, mumbling again. 'I'll come round later.'

'I might not be here later,' Veronica said.

'Going somewhere nice?' Ruby asked her.

'Wherever I'm going, it's none of yours,' Veronica said.

'Perhaps some nice gentleman's coming round to take you up the West End.'

Sweeney blushed at hearing the words, knowing what they signified in the Regency.

'Once again, none of yours,' Veronica said. Turning back to Sweeney, she said, 'Right, I can see I'm not wanted here. Surplus to requirements. I know when to make myself scarce. You two lovebirds got something a lot more important on your minds, so I'll make myself scarce and leave you to it.'

'It's not like that,' Sweeney said to her.

'I know exactly what it's like,' Veronica said. 'I've got eyes in my head. But, like I said – don't mind me. I've never been one to get in the way of anybody else's bit of fun.'

'Glad to hear it,' Ruby said. She came closer to Sweeney and put her arm back through his.

'Just so long as you know what you're doing,' Veronica said to Sweeney.

'Just talking,' Sweeney said.

'That's right – we're just talking,' Ruby said. 'Here, I hope you're not letting your imagination run away with you. I know what you're like, you fairground types. I've got some in my own family.'

'Along with the tinkers and gypsies, I should imagine,' Veronica said.

'Then you'd imagine right. Gypsies and tinkers and thieves.'

'Goes without saying,' Veronica said.

'Feel free to keep your big mouth shut, then,' Ruby said. She pulled herself even closer to Sweeney.

Veronica turned sharply and went back into her room, slamming the door behind her and sending the echo of this all the way down the stairwell.

Sweeney opened the door to his own room.

'It's colder in here than out there,' Ruby said as Sweeney switched on the only lamp and lit the gas fire. 'And that's saying something.'

'Drink?' Sweeney said to her.

'What have you got?'

He looked uncertainly around him. A solitary bottle of English sherry stood on the sideboard, left over from Veronica's appearance the previous night.

'What's that?' Ruby said.

'English sherry.'

'Nothing but the best. You sure you're not a socialite?'

Sweeney brought the bottle and two small glasses to the low table beside the settee.

They sat and talked for half an hour, mostly about Fowler and the club and the other girls they both knew.

Then Ruby finally said, 'Go on, then, show me.'

Sweeney fetched the Bible from his coat pocket and carefully unwrapped it before giving it to her.

She took the book in both hands, pressed her palms to its covers and then sniffed at it. There was nothing.

'And all you have to do now is give it to somebody else?' she said. 'That's all there is to it?'

'That's all,' Sweeney said.

'Can I look inside it?'

'I've already looked; there's nothing there. Not even an inscription or whatever it is they're called.'

'What did you think – money, dope?'

Sweeney shrugged. 'Something like that.'

'It wouldn't hold much.'

'Enough for a man about to be—' He stopped abruptly, aware of what he'd been about to reveal, of the little he already knew, of the few sparse details with which he'd already been entrusted on the threat of death by Tommy Fowler.

'About to be what?' Ruby said, already guessing.

'I can't say.'

'Not really much point me being here then, is there? I might as well . . .' She started to get up.

'I'm supposed to take it to a man in Pentonville,' Sweeney said.

'And that's it? That's the big secret?' She knew, of course, that there was much more to the errand, but that it was time now to stop pushing the boy. Besides, all that mattered to her was that it was Aleister Crowley's Bible. She ran her fingers over the book, traced them along the gilt-edged pages and then felt the lightly embossed lettering of its title. She held it to her cheeks, her lips. She sniffed at it again, opening it and burying her nose in its centre. There was still nothing.

'Like I said,' Sweeney said, watching all this, 'there's nothing there. It's a Bible, that's all.'

After that, neither of them spoke for several minutes.

Then Ruby said, 'I could write you down my address, if you'd like.'

'Just tell me the number,' Sweeney said. 'I know Brewer Street. I've got a memory for things like that.'

'You saying you don't want me to write it down for you? I don't give it away to just anybody, you know.'

'No, right,' Sweeney said.

'You got a pen, then, a pencil or something?'

There was a pencil in the sideboard drawer. A pencil and a notepad filled with the names and the signs of the zodiac. 'I keep one in the drawer,' he said, rising to get it for her.

'Paper?'

'In the kitchen,' he said. 'Perhaps.' And he went to look, searching through the cupboard and drawer there for a piece of paper or card large enough for the address he probably already knew.

When he finally found a piece and took it back in to her, she was sitting back on the sofa with the Bible on the low table beside her.

'Did you find anything?' he said to her.

'In that? Like you said, it's just a Bible. Perhaps Crowley intends it for an old friend, an anonymous gift.'

'It—' This time Sweeney stopped himself after the single word.

'You don't have to tell me,' she said. She patted the settee beside her. 'Not if it's another big secret. Not if it's something you can't tell even to little old me.' She held out her hand to him and he took it. 'I meant for the paper,' she said. 'My address. Have you forgotten already?'

'Right,' Sweeney said, giving her the paper.

She wrote down the address on Brewer Street. Another of Tommy Fowler's rented rooms.

'All Fowler told me was that I was to deliver it to someone and not to say a word of how it had come to him,' Sweeney said.

'No mention of the great Aleister Crowley, you mean?'

'I didn't even know who he was until—'

'Until *I* opened my big mouth. Perhaps that was why Fowler trusted you – you, specifically – with the errand.'

'No – it was Crowley who insisted on it being me.'

'Oh?' This time she managed to hide her interest.

He watched her fold the paper into a small square.

'How do you mean he insisted on you?' she asked him. 'Like you just said, you didn't even know who the man was.'

And so he told her the story of Crowley's tongue – he

wished he could remember the term Crowley had used – and the connection Crowley believed this created between the two of them.

'You should make something of that,' she told him, leaving him uncertain what she meant.

'My lip?'

'No – Crowley. Him thinking you and him have got something in common.'

'Why should I want to do that? Especially if everything you've just told me is true.'

'There is that, I suppose,' she said. 'But he's an old man now, ancient. Perhaps all his powers have either withered away or dried up. It's what happens to old men; believe me, I know.'

Sweeney didn't want to hear her saying things like this. 'Have you finished with it?'

'The Bible? I only really wanted to hold it, that's all. So that I could tell people I'd held Aleister Crowley's Bible.'

'And that would count for something, would it?' He took the book from the table, wrapped it in its sheet of tissue and returned it to his coat pocket. Then he went back and sat beside her. Their glasses were empty.

'Any more drink?' she said, spinning her glass.

If they finished the bottle, then he would have to replace it before Veronica came to retrieve it, which is what she usually did. He refilled their glasses.

'Ten to one she's got her own glass to the wall,' Ruby said.

'Her own glass?'

'Listening. To us – you. Though judging by these walls, she probably wouldn't even need one.'

It was true; they were thin walls, and Sweeney could often

hear Veronica in her own room, moving around, laying out crockery, singing, talking to herself.

'I'll bet she listens to you all the time,' Ruby said. 'She looks like that kind of woman.'

'Can't we talk about something else?' Sweeney said.

'Anything you like,' she told him. 'The price of nylons, the margarine ration, next season's Paris fashions, you just name it.'

12

'GERMAN, SEE? HAMBURG, BERLIN, WHAT'S LEFT OF THEM. Strong stuff. Stronger than anybody over here was turning out. You wouldn't get anything as explicit or as obvious as this from any of our lot. None of our boys would touch this kind of work with a barge pole. Not even the Morgan brothers up Kilburn, and you know what they're like.'

Frankie Doll wasn't listening to the man. He was there in Holywell Street to order magazines, photos and postcards, sent by Tommy Fowler with Tommy Fowler's list in his pocket.

'See her?' the man said. 'Look at how they've worked that pose. Five blokes. You're looking at six infringements minimum in that one shot. That's your so-called Aryan superman, that is. They'd get my vote. We couldn't put a shot like that on the market in a hundred years. We're still marking it up "Dutch", right?'

The photographer – a man called Julian Beazley – finally stopped talking and waved a hand in front of Frankie Doll's face. 'You've hardly listened to half of what I've just said.'

'Less than that,' Frankie Doll told him. He dropped the cigarette he had just sucked to its final half-inch to the floor and rubbed it out with his foot.

'Watch what you're doing,' Beazley shouted at him. 'You know the sort of stuff we keep in here, all the developing chemicals. One spark and—'

'You tell me every time,' Frankie Doll said.

'I'm just saying.' Beazley pulled a box from a low shelf and broke its seal.

'I've got something on my mind, that's all,' Frankie Doll said. It was an apology, of sorts, and Beazley, who saw Frankie Doll on an almost weekly basis, and who himself occupied an equally lowly position in Tommy Fowler's hierarchy, understood this.

Beazley opened the box and took out the packets of postcards it held, examining these and laying out the packs on the table.

'You want a drink?' he said to Frankie Doll.

'Might as well.'

Beazley opened two bottles and gave one to Frankie Doll. 'From the Watney's blaze. No bombs within a mile of the place for three years and then the place goes up like a bonfire. They logged two thousand barrels lost. Fowler took delivery of exactly the same four days later. Burned all night, that gaff.'

'I'll bet,' Frankie Doll said. 'Lucky old Fowler.'

'You sound like he's—'

'You know what he's like,' Frankie Doll said.

'You and him had words, then?' As though people – especially people like Frankie Doll or Julian Beazley – ever 'had words' with Tommy Fowler.

'He should have asked me to do something for him, that's all,' Frankie Doll said. 'But instead he gave the job to somebody else, a nobody – worse than a nobody, a *recognizable* nobody. Three years I've been with him now. Three years.'

'You and me alike,' Beazley said. 'Was it something big, then?'

Frankie Doll shrugged, uncertain how much to say to the man, how much of what he said might find its way back to Archer Street. It hardly mattered how important or not Crowley's errand was; what *mattered* was that it should have been entrusted to *him*, to Frankie Doll; and if not to him, then to anybody other than Sweeney.

'An errand, that's all,' Frankie Doll said.

Beazley sat beside him on another pile of unopened boxes. 'Want to know something?' he said, nudging Frankie Doll with his elbow, touching their bottles together, and then looking all around the empty room for effect.

'What?' Frankie Doll said. It was how Beazley operated.

'Fowler. The way I hear it, his days are numbered.'

'Meaning?' Frankie Doll had heard the same rumour, or another like it, or something similar, something better, something worse, a hundred times before in those three years.

'The way he operates, I mean. All his little scams and rackets, his bits and pieces. How long do you think *that* particular way of doing business will last once this lot is over?'

'I don't get you,' Frankie Doll said.

'Yes, you do. Fowler. He only gets away with what he does because of all this, the war. Working girls, illegal drink, black-market food and petrol and tobacco; his dirty books and pictures, all this strong-arm stuff. How long is all that going to last once all the wartime restrictions are lifted and the authorities need people to get back to their real lives and start cleaning everything up? They're already talking about bulldozing half of Soho and the top of the street. I've seen the plans. They stuck them up in the Marylebone library.

They've got plans to rebuild half the country after this lot.'

And again, Frankie Doll had heard it all before. 'You're wrong,' he said. 'There's always going to be a demand for what Tommy Fowler provides. So what if drink and smokes go off ration? There's always the girls and all of this. Besides, do you honestly think everything's going to come back on tap again just because somebody blows a whistle and waves a flag and shouts out that it's all over? What about the Japs?'

Beazley was disappointed by this response, by Frankie Doll's lack of enthusiasm for the coming changes. 'You're missing my point,' he said. He waved at the stacked cases of pornography and at the photographs already spread across the table. 'What I'm saying is that it's all going to go somewhere *else*.'

'Go somewhere else? What are you talking about?'

'I mean it's all going to go respectable, half respectable at least. It's all going to go legit and respectable. That's where the real money's going to be in the years to come. You been up the refurbished Windmill yet?'

'It's a joke,' Frankie Doll said. 'They stand there perfectly still with their tits out and half a second of you-know-what behind an ostrich feather and that's your lot. Good luck and good night, Vienna.'

'Exactly. That's what I'm saying, that's what I'm telling you. And not a proper tart or working girl among the lot of them. House rules. And yet the punters still pay a small fortune just to sit and look. They cancelled their regular order for the magazines and pictures months ago. Too down-market. They were half our business at one time, the Windmill. Now they want something classier. No more cards or picture sets. Magazines. *Proper* magazines. With stories and articles as well as pictures. And nothing too obvious, if you catch my drift.'

Frankie Doll was beginning to. 'Not really,' he said.

'The girls. Nothing too obvious. Good-quality pictures, more colour – all colour for some, in fact – before too long. And believe me, the Mill's going to be the first of many. All looking and no touching. At least not on the premises, and not with *those* girls. Legit magazines. I'm telling you – it's the way ahead.'

'The law won't tolerate it,' Frankie Doll said, his interest slowly growing in what Beazley was telling him.

'The law will change,' Beazley said. 'People have had enough of all this restriction and regulation stuff. And that's not just me talking; that's people in the know – politicians, people like that.'

'You don't say.'

'The law will change and everything will rise above board. The law will tell you what you can and can't have, and in return there'll be no more prosecutions for indulging in all those things that turn people like Tommy Fowler a good profit now. Speciality' – he said the word slowly, emphasizing each of its syllables, as though by this alone everything would become clear and convincing to Frankie Doll – 'that's the name of the game from now on.'

'And the girls?' Frankie Doll said.

'What about them?'

'It's why the punters come into the Regency, what they come looking for while Tommy Fowler milks them dry with his watered-down drink.'

Beazley laughed. 'And puts money into your pocket as well as his own. How is Laura, by the way? Long time no see.'

'Leave her out of this,' Frankie Doll said sharply.

Beazley held up his hands. 'You know what I'm saying. You know it makes sense, even if you don't know *why* yet, even if *you* don't see it. To begin with, the Maltese are going to get stronger. There are already gangs south of the river saying that they want a bigger share of things. When did Tommy Fowler last do any real business in Clapham, say, or Camberwell? In Lewisham, Bermondsey, out that way? They're half an hour away most days, and Tommy Fowler acts as though they're foreign countries. Everything is being stitched up, Frankie boy. Everything's up for grabs, and it's because everything's going to change with the end of the war that this whole business is unsettled and getting ready to jump. How long since Tommy Fowler last sent you to Clerkenwell to collect his debts? Little Italy, they're calling that place. Billy Leach has been recruiting up in Kentish Town for the past six months. Six months. Him and Jewish Johnson had a Christmas party together up the Golders Green Empire. What's Tommy Fowler going to do if either of them two decides to come further into town to do their business?'

Frankie Doll sipped his beer. '*You*'d still make a living,' he said. He picked up a stack of the postcards and looked through them.

'Probably. But not with cheap rubbish like this. Four for a nicker, most of this lot. Sixty for a quid wholesale.'

'Tommy Fowler charges a guinea each in the Regency,' Frankie Doll said, beginning to make his own calculations.

'That's the other thing I'm telling you,' Beazley said. 'All profit, not much risk. Only thing wrong with that little equation is that the profit all goes to Tommy Fowler and the risk stays ours – yours and mine.'

'You got that right,' Frankie Doll said.

'And when all those changes come, all that deregulation – because that's what they're calling it – then that profit will be squeezed like the proverbial lemon. Not that anyone's seen any of them for a long time now.'

'He'll still have the girls,' Frankie Doll said.

'Of course he will. But that's as far as men like Tommy Fowler can see. He'll still have the girls and he'll still have the pictures and he'll still have his overpriced coloured water. And *you*'re still not listening to what I'm telling you, Frankie.'

'Which is?' Frankie Doll understood perfectly what Julian Beazley was telling him. What he didn't yet fully understand was *why* he was telling him all this. But he was starting to guess.

Beazley let out an exaggerated sigh and offered Frankie Doll another cigarette.

'Aren't you scared the place will burn down?' Frankie Doll asked him.

'According to the fire certificate, the place is a fur store. We picked up the dockets from that ice-house over in Deptford for a song. The furs exist, the insurance policy exists. If the place *did* burn down, then—'

'Tommy Fowler would stand to make another small fortune.'

'Got it in one.'

'So what could possibly go wrong?' Frankie Doll said.

'I know,' Beazley said, seeming to deflate. 'But what *does* go wrong, what goes wrong every single fucking time, is that the people like you and me, we never make a single extra penny out of it all. Everything else changes and we stay exactly the same, down at the bottom of the pile. Little people like you and me, we just go on running our errands and doing what we're told to do. All this change, all this opportunity lands at our feet and we're the ones in no position whatsoever to do anything about it.'

'So what do you suggest?' Frankie Doll said, already wondering how much more Beazley was going to reveal to him. They were on dangerous ground, the pair of them. He wondered, too, at the man's new-found bravery. Perhaps Billy Leach or Jewish Johnson had already been to see him and make him their own offers. Or perhaps Beazley's bravery had finally stretched to seizing the initiative, and perhaps *he* had been to see *them*. It was all uncertain terrain to Frankie Doll and it kept him cautious.

'None of this gets back to Fowler, right?' Beazley said.

Frankie Doll crossed his heart. 'Scout's honour.'

'Funnily enough, I was in the scouts,' Beazley said, surprised by the sudden, unexpected memory. 'When I was a boy.'

'And there's me thinking you'd joined up as a mucky photographer. Go on.'

'Sex,' Beazley said dramatically.

It sounded like the start of a spiel to Frankie Doll. 'Apparently, it's what makes the world go round,' he said.

'That's money,' Beazley said. 'Let me finish. Sex – it's all up here.' He touched a finger to the centre of his forehead.

'Not necessarily,' Frankie Doll said. 'I know a few girls who would point that finger somewhere else completely.'

'Then they're wrong,' Beazley said. 'Because it's mostly up here. Or there's enough of it up here enough of the time to make it a profitable proposition.'

'Are we back among the tits and feathered fanny in the Windmill?' Frankie Doll said.

146

'You can laugh, but those girls earn ten times what Laura and all the rest of Fowler's girls make working out of the Regency, and none of it on their backs or on their knees or up against a wall somewhere off Shaftesbury Avenue.'

'And you know this for a fact, do you?' Frankie Doll said after a few seconds of silence.

Beazley nodded. 'I know it for a fact because it's true.' He rose from the crate he was sitting on and went to the table, where he split open another of the packages. He took out a magazine and brought it back to Frankie Doll.

Frankie Doll took it and looked at its cover. A woman wearing only a pair of slender panties was kneeling on a beach with both her hands on an inflatable beach ball. It was like a thousand others he had seen.

'Open it,' Beazley said, sitting back beside him.

Frankie Doll flicked through the pages. Writing, adverts, smaller pictures, cartoons, pictures of people fully clothed, cars, caravans, horses.

'Page twenty,' Beazley said.

Frankie Doll searched. A four-page spread of the same woman on the same beach, this time with the ball in the air above her head, at her feet, held to her side.

'Is that it?' Frankie Doll said.

'Cover price five bob,' Beazley said. 'Five bob.'

'For this watered-down rubbish?'

'Last month we shifted fourteen thousand copies. Fourteen thousand. Not one thousand, not two thousand, not even five thousand. Fourteen thousand.'

'It's pathetic,' Frankie Doll said. 'There's nothing to see.'

'You're wrong. There's just enough to see. Once again, you seem to be missing my point, Frankie.'

'Go on. I'm listening.' *Frankie?*

Beazley took the magazine back from him and rolled it into a baton. 'It's *legal*, legit and above board. You can sell this *anywhere*. No risk. No chance whatsoever of prosecution. Guess how much it cost to produce?'

'Surprise me,' Frankie Doll said.

'Pennies,' Beazley said. 'By my reckoning there's a thousand per cent mark up on that so-called watered-down rubbish. Guaranteed sales, payment by subscription – so you make your money up front – and delivered direct to your door through the post and nobody any the wiser.'

'But what's the point of it?' Frankie Doll said, impressed by the margins but still doubtful about the magazine's true appeal, or what part it might now play in the collapse of Tommy Fowler's empire.

'The point, Frankie, is fourteen thousand punters – and set to double every three months – at five bob a pop, including postage. And that's *before* advertising income – and, believe me, that's where the *real* money's going to come from – advertising. Places turn legit and then they can advertise themselves. People still smoke and drink, they still want entertaining and a bit of how's-your-father every now and again, none of that's going to stop.' He shook the magazine. 'And this is where it all comes together. This is what they buy to find out about – and then hopefully buy – all that other stuff.'

'Is this the first edition?' Frankie Doll said. He was starting to be impressed by the figures and by everything else Beazley was telling him.

'Fifth,' Beazley said. 'Half of everything until now has gone directly overseas. Armed forces. Germany, mostly. The Yanks have got their own stuff. Remember all the material we were expecting to get out of Paris once the place was liberated? What a let-down that turned out to be. All that arty hands-over-tits and can-can-dancer stuff? They can keep it.'

Frankie Doll looked again at the woman on the beach. 'Tommy Fowler would burn you down tonight if he knew the half of this,' he said to Beazley.

'I know. But only after he'd made sure I was in here with both my legs broken, tied to a chair and with my tongue cut out.'

Both men laughed again at this, and then neither of them spoke for several minutes.

As far as Frankie Doll knew, Tommy Fowler had never once cut out a man's tongue.

Beazley was the first to resume. 'The Messinas were here the other day,' he said hesitantly. 'They're looking to organize the girls on a more solid footing. According to them, Tommy Fowler's going to find himself squeezed on all sides, north, south, east and backside.'

'Meaning people like you and me should start planning ahead?' Frankie Doll said.

Beazley shrugged. 'You were the one who said you weren't being properly appreciated. They shut the Ninety club on Clapham High Street last week. Big raid. Contravening the nudity laws. They only pull *that* one out when everything else fails. No great loss; most of their money came from the Yanks, and those days are numbered.'

'Tommy Fowler thinks they'll be back when it's over.'

'Not according to Tony Messina, they won't. After Germany, they'll all be sent straight out to sort out the Japs. Makes sense. You ever seen a naked Nip?'

149

Frankie Doll shook his head. 'You?'

'We've got a few titles on order. Apparently, it's all sitting in a warehouse in Hong Kong somewhere.'

'More specialities?' Frankie Doll said.

'You're learning.' Beazley took out two more bottles and opened them. 'What I said about not breathing any of this to Tommy Fowler . . .'

'I'm not stupid,' Frankie Doll said. 'But speaking of Fowler, how do you imagine any of this is ever going to happen *without* him getting wind of it?' Or, worse still, getting wind of Frankie Doll's part in it all.

Beazley admitted that he didn't know. 'I suppose we have to somehow go our separate ways,' he said.

'And how do you suggest we even begin to do that?'

Beazley shrugged again. 'You do believe me, though, don't you? I can tell.'

'That everything's going to change?' Frankie Doll said. 'One way or another. I suppose so.'

Beazley went back to the stack of packages. 'You got any new girls might be interested? We need some new faces.'

'One or two started at the Regency recently.' Ruby Nolan for one. 'I'll have a word.'

'Don't show them the German stuff,' Beazley said. 'Put anyone off, that would. Show them the beach-ball shots. Tell them it's a new direction.'

'I doubt they'd believe me,' Frankie Doll said.

'Then tell them it's the future,' Beazley said absently. 'Everybody wants to believe in the future. It's all most people have got going for them.' He raised his bottle. 'To the future,' he said, and waited for Frankie Doll to do the same.

13

'So, the blessed runes are definitely cast,' Silver said, helping Crowley into his chair and then standing beside him as he regained his breath.

They had been prevented from boarding a succession of overcrowded buses, and the journey from Soho to Coleherne Road had taken almost two hours, with Crowley needing to rest every few hundred yards. He had told Silver to go on ahead of him, but Silver had insisted on staying with him. They had taken the Underground from Piccadilly Circus to Hyde Park Corner, but the line had been closed after that, and so little had been gained for the loss of their sparse pooled change.

Crowley heard the scepticism in Silver's words. 'Is that what you imagine I've done?' he said. 'Cast the ridiculous runes? Is that what you truly think of me?'

'What, then?' Silver said. He pulled Crowley's coat from his back and took off his own. He then unfastened and slid off Crowley's shoes and briefly massaged his feet before pulling on his worn leather slippers.

'You should have left me at Hyde Park Corner,' Crowley said, patting his chest. 'I could have slouched slowly homewards under my own failing steam.'

'I daresay,' Silver said. He filled the kettle and balanced it on the small cooker. 'And you still don't think Fowler agreed a little too quickly to what you asked of him?' He had raised the same point several times on their journey, but Crowley had been in no fit state to argue with him.

'Of course I know he agreed too quickly. And before you say it, yes, he will almost certainly insist on making some ridiculous or excessive future demand upon me.'

'Either that, or it suits *him* as well as it may benefit you to see the man hanged. You leave yourself very open, Aleister, very vulnerable, that's all I'm saying.'

'And you believe him – Fowler – capable of *greater* evils, of even greater cruelties and depravities than those of which *I* am endlessly accused? Perhaps you *over*estimate him and *under*estimate me.'

Silver sighed. 'I merely believe him capable of demanding back from you tenfold what you have already asked of him. What I'm also saying is that there might have been another way to the man in Pentonville.'

Crowley considered this, but only briefly, and then shook his head at the suggestion. 'Each of these connections possesses a potency,' he said. 'And there is something to be gained by that potency.' He paused. 'Or perhaps it is simply a question of Fowler having more faith in me, in what I am about to attempt and, hopefully, achieve, than you yourself possess.'

'Meaning what, exactly?'

'Meaning, perhaps, that he is already working out my worth to him once I achieve immortality. An extremely valuable commodity, I'd say, especially to a man like Fowler.'

Silver sighed again and shook his head at the suggestion.

'No – it needed to be done precisely the way I did it,'

Crowley said flatly. 'Besides, and as you have already so crudely suggested, the process is already started and the thing in motion. Unstoppable motion, I might add.'

'By simply having handed over the Bible?'

'The Bible containing my invisible inscription, yes. That, and all my whispered, mumbled imprecations and incantations – call them what you will, but *runes*? – on our journey home.'

'I merely thought you were struggling for breath as usual.'

Crowley smiled. 'Mostly it was that. But I also needed to say what needed to be said within an hour of the contract between myself and Fowler being agreed. Now a further forty-eight hours may pass before the condemned man himself – our unsuspecting but very necessary third partner, you might say – need take possession of the thing.'

Silver remembered Crowley standing holding on to the railings outside the Brompton Road Public Baths, looking over a fireweed-covered bomb site, mumbling to himself.

'Did I tell you my mother wanted me to be a solicitor when I was a boy?' Crowley said unexpectedly. Changing the subject. Another of his over-used ploys. 'Among other things.'

Silver occupied himself with making the tea.

'A solicitor, a doctor, any kind of respectable businessman; a stockbroker or banker, even. My father, of course, would have been happier had I followed in his own evangelizing footsteps. Plymouth Brethren. How I loathed, hated and despised that wretched excuse for a woman.'

'She was still your mother,' Silver said, lifting the whistling kettle from the flames.

'Loathed, hated and despised her, just as she loathed, hated

153

and despised me. She was twenty-five years younger than her husband. I still have no idea what she saw in him.'

'They shared beliefs, strong beliefs,' Silver said. 'You know exactly what his attraction was.' He had been devoted to his own parents, and they to him. His father had been a glove manufacturer, and both his parents had lived to see his early success in his own profession.

'The only belief they truly shared was their conviction that Christ was imminently to return to earth and establish His new kingdom here. Not *too* much to ask of the poor man, surely? And especially not considering the vast amount of money my deluded father spent in promoting and advertising this glorious, much-anticipated and yet never-to-be Second Coming.'

'He died when you were young,' Silver said. 'You can hardly have known him.' These stories and remembrances came in a constant angry stream of variations.

'I was twelve,' Crowley said. 'A grown boy. Old enough. And if he had lived any longer I would no doubt have been drawn by the pair of them into that same small, obsessive, overheated, claustrophobic and self-regarding world, instead of—'

'Instead of the small, obsessive, overheated, claustrophobic and self-regarding world entirely of your own making?'

Crowley laughed at this. He watched Silver rinse out the cups. The cold water spluttered noisily from its tap, causing the pipe to rattle and then tick somewhere inside the wall.

'He dragged me with him everywhere he went to carry out his preaching and pamphleteering. He was a wealthy man, he could have been driven, could have taken the train, but instead he insisted on walking everywhere, over all the roughest roads and tracks, and dragging me alongside him. Warwickshire and Surrey were always his most profitable hunting grounds. He would preach to an audience of two, and both of *them* would heckle him or ask him for money. Cancer of the tongue. I wondered afterwards if my natal complication might not have been a sign of the same thing about to be inflicted upon my own earthly body.'

'The boy with the harelip,' Silver said. 'Another of those potent connections?'

'*You* may not believe it to be of any consequence, but these things count. For months before his speechless, rasping death, my father paid out another small fortune to a charlatan who administered electro-homeopathic treatments guaranteed to cure him. And all that time, ever since his diagnosis, my mother had implored him to accept and embrace what was happening to him, telling him that he would be the first of them to return to Christ's One True Kingdom. I remember her once telling him to stop complaining of his pain – and most of *that* was caused by this costly quackery – and to be grateful for what had been visited upon him. I daresay *she* saw no contradiction between Christ's new kingdom on Earth and the one for which her own husband was shortly bound. I remember I once imagined that the two of them might pass each other – my father and Christ, one ascending, the other descending. I could even imagine the look on my father's face as he saw Christ passing him by on His way down to my mother and her coven of hymn-singers, beckoning Him ever Earthwards with the brilliant, warming glow of their own overblown piety.'

'He left the pair of you well enough provided for,' Silver

said. He brought a cup and saucer to Crowley and put them on the table beside him.

'Money,' Crowley said. 'That's all. A brewing fortune made by the family of a man who spent his life railing against the evils of drink and extolling the virtues of every form of abstinence imaginable.'

'Perhaps it explains something of your own contradictory nature,' Silver said. In the past, he might have countered these stories with ones of his own. But the journey back to Coleherne Road had wearied him, too – and his own onward journey would take another half an hour – and so he said little.

Crowley ignored the remark and whatever gentle criticism it contained. 'She was the first person to call me a beast, an animal, and truly mean it,' he said. 'Imagine that.'

Unlike much of what Crowley had just said, it was the first time Silver had heard this. 'I imagine all parents might say the same of their children at some point,' he said.

'Not in the way she intended it,' Crowley said.

Silver didn't pursue the point, and Crowley went on talking.

'My father was once confronted by a man at one of his roadside pulpits who showed him the remains of his vestigial tail. He called my father Soapy Joe, and said that the only part of the Bible *he* ever paid any attention to was the Book of Revelations.'

'Your own mainstay,' Silver said, and the pair of them laughed together at the old joke.

'A surgeon had cut off most of the tail when the man was born. He told my father that he still had it at home, preserved in a jar of alcohol. He offered to fetch it and show it to him, offered to hold it to the stump which still protruded from the base of his spine.'

'What did your father say to that?'

'He told the man to go home and to stay there. He told him to get rid of the tail and then to smash the jar and pour away the alcohol. The man asked him how much he'd pay him to do all that, and my father said five pounds. He then took this from his wallet, and the man snatched it from his hand and ran away laughing, followed by half of the rest of the small audience.'

'I imagine he ran only as far as the nearest public house,' Silver said.

'Of course he did.'

'And you saw all that?'

Crowley nodded. 'The same thing, in one shape or another, happened to my father everywhere he went. I once accompanied my parents to a funeral – an old aunt – and because of their beliefs it was beyond them to enter the church where the service was being held, even for the minute or two it would have taken them to pay their last respects, and so instead the three of us stood outside in the pouring rain. We stood for an hour and almost drowned. Torrential. His cancer was diagnosed not long afterwards and I was never able to consider the two things separately. It started in his throat and then moved to his tongue and his face. I imagine that the descending Christ would have covered His eyes or looked away in pity when the two of them passed.' He sipped his tea, closing his eyes as the cup reached his lips.

'So . . . what comes next?' Silver asked him.

Crowley waited a moment before answering. 'Now I wait to hear that the Bible has been safely delivered and accepted.

After which, I make my further necessary calculations and resume the prescribed process.'

'I see,' Silver said.

'Don't worry – I'll keep you informed of my progress,' Crowley told him, opening his eyes. 'I'm not deliberately excluding you.'

'Yes, you are,' Silver said.

'But only for your own good. I know from all-too-painful past experience that the rituals ahead are exhausting ones. Even as a young and healthy man I would often require days to fully recover my health and my—' He stopped abruptly.

'Your sanity?' Silver suggested.

'If you like. I prefer to think of it as my equilibrium.'

'How many times have you attempted this thing?'

'In the manner in which I am attempting it now? Never. I have never before been able to depend upon the exact moment of a man's death, only his extreme suffering, or, in a few instances, that man's *belief* that he was about to die.'

'You promised me you knew exactly what you were doing,' Silver said, knowing as he spoke how useless this feeble protest was.

'I know I did,' Crowley said. 'And I was being as honest as I could be. I *can't* know for certain what will happen, what further degree of success I will attain, or what might be the physical or mental cost of the attempt. If all of that could be known in advance, then others would surely have succeeded for themselves by now.'

'Then why do *you*—'

'Why do *I* believe myself capable of success where others can only look on and decry everything? Because *I* have devoted my entire life to being prepared for this moment.

And, yes, I do realize how fatuous and self-regarding I make that sound.' Crowley started coughing and put down his cup and saucer until this subsided and he regained his breath. 'But believe me, I do know what I'm attempting. It may – it almost certainly *will* – sound harsh to you – ungrateful, cruel even – but nothing of what I am aiming to achieve depends in the slightest on your own belief or conviction – or that of any other living man or woman, come to that. Only my own. I have sometimes felt as though the whole world was against me in the past.'

'Only sometimes?'

'Often, then. Always. But my point is that I have *endured*. My beliefs and convictions remain intact, stronger today than they have ever been. I retain my rank, my position. Only my physical body is weakening and failing. Of course I regret that it is no longer able to relish and satisfy my old appetites – of course I do – but *this*, what I am attempting *now*, is the purpose and point of all that earlier preparation and failure. You may have little faith in my chances of success, even in my reasoning or sanity in attempting what I am about to undertake, but you, of all people, must surely understand that I have no other choice but to seize this opportunity and make this one final attempt at something to which I have already devoted so much time, money and energy.'

'Of course I understand,' Silver said.

'Then if it makes you feel any easier, you can keep an eye on my physical health as the thing proceeds,' Crowley said. 'Perhaps you alone know that I have a heart like any other man and that it still beats.'

'That it beats irregularly and at times too weakly, yes,' Silver said.

'And I was such a healthy and vigorous young man,' Crowley said. 'All that walking and open-air preaching. All my mountaineering and other exploits. You see before you a shadow of a husk. The energy I have expended in my lifetime would have driven and sustained a dozen lesser men.'

'Perhaps,' Silver said.

'No – for certain.'

'Only if you hadn't also abused yourself at an equal and opposite rate.'

Crowley laughed at this. 'Ah, that. Perhaps. But it was all part of the same thing, don't you see? Freeing the mind alongside the body, freeing the will to attain a new and higher level of consciousness.'

Silver held up his hands. 'Please, not another of your lectures, Aleister.' He looked around them. 'Any drink?'

'You should have accepted the gangster's brandy.'

'One of us needed to keep a clear head.'

'There you go again,' Crowley said. 'Why?'

'In case he let slip what he expected of you in return for delivering the Bible.'

'That? Let him ask. Who knows – perhaps by then I'll be in a position to do whatever it is he wants. Perhaps he even imagines that, should I be successful – and as far as I know, he hasn't the faintest idea of what I am attempting – then it will be within my power to grant the same to him.'

'I hardly—'

'Whatever he expects of me, there is nothing he can do now to either compromise or jeopardize what I have already set in motion and sent along its straight and unwavering course.'

'And there is nothing anyone might say to prevent you from going ahead?' Another pointless question.

'Far too late for that,' Crowley said. 'Besides—' And again he stopped abruptly.

'What?' Silver said.

'To even attempt to stop the process once commenced would be a dangerous thing. Just as breathing the oath of the Golden Dawn would be punishable by a lightning bolt.' He smiled as he said it.

'I wish you'd told me that before you started all this.'

'Of course you do. But, believe me, the end result would have been exactly the same.'

'But there are still so many intangibles, so many un-certainties. The condemned man may yet be reprieved, for instance. What then? What if the ritual is broken by that?'

'Then I daresay we'll find out the hard way,' Crowley said. 'Or at least, *I* will.' He was amused by the suggestion, but conscious too of his friend's unshakeable concern.

'Meaning what?' Silver said.

'Please, stop worrying. What do I have to lose? And as for Fowler – perhaps he already imagines I'm doing him a bigger favour than the condemned man is unwittingly doing me.'

'A mutually beneficial arrangement?' Silver said coldly.

'Exactly,' Crowley said.

'From which the only person to be excluded – the only person not to actually benefit, that is – is the condemned man himself.'

'The judge and jury are the ones hanging him,' Crowley said. 'Not you or I.' He sipped his tea again. The cup and saucer and spoon, which before had betrayed his constant slight tremor, were now perfectly steady and silent in his hand.

14

DETECTIVE INSPECTOR ERNEST PYE WAS SITTING IN THE canteen at the Tottenham Court Road station when the duty sergeant called in to tell him that there was a man downstairs asking for him. The sergeant left before Pye could swallow the mouthful of food he was chewing and ask him who the man was or what he wanted. He was tired. It was seven in the evening and he'd been at the station since late the previous day.

He went down to the entrance. The duty sergeant was back at his post, and as Pye appeared he pointed his pen at a man sitting on the bench opposite. It was a warm evening and the sun still shone into the building, but the man was wearing a heavy overcoat and a bowler, which hid his eyes. At Pye's arrival, he immediately rose and took off his hat and Pye recognized the prison warder.

'Bone,' Pye said. 'Arthur.'

Arthur Bone held out his hand.

'You wanted to see me. About Peter Tait?'

'I was hoping . . .' Bone looked around them. 'Nothing official,' he said. 'Just . . .'

'A talk?'

'That's it, just a talk. Off the record.'

'Wait.' Pye looked at his watch. 'You're in luck – I'm officially off duty as of now.'

'Just come off myself,' Bone said.

'Name of the game,' Pye said, starting to wonder what the man wanted. 'Shall we?' He held the door for Bone and the pair of them left the station.

For a minute, neither man spoke; they walked briskly, marching almost, crossing the busy thoroughfare into the calm of Percy Street.

'I have to warn you,' Pye said, 'the Tait inquiry is closed, out of bounds, until the appeal lawyer gets his ruling. I can't discuss it – not officially, that is – and certainly not with you.' He hoped his true meaning was clear to Bone.

'Message received and understood,' Bone said. 'I imagine that's why we're putting a bit of distance between ourselves and the station, is it?'

'Some days I'm just glad to see the back of the place.' Pye indicated the Endeavour public house ahead of them and they went inside.

They sat in a corner booth, surrounded by high leather seating and frosted glass.

'But you're still interested, right?' Bone said as Pye put down their glasses. He took off his coat and hat.

'Has something happened?' Pye said. It was five days since he'd visited Peter Tait in Pentonville.

Bone looked around them before answering him. 'We had incendiaries all down this street. December '40. All these small green fires everywhere you looked. We thought at first that they were gas bombs. I lost a good friend that Christmas. Some politicians – warmongers, then – were saying the bombing would last for years to come. It was on the next street over, Stephen Street, that I saw a dead child being dragged out from the wreckage by its legs. I couldn't see if it was a boy or a girl, just that it was a child – turned out to be a girl, eight years old. Anyhow, I stepped in and told the two men pulling her out to do it properly, to hold the poor little bugger by her arms. No decorum, see? No sense of . . . of . . .'

'Right and wrong,' Pye said. He licked the froth from his lips. 'If I remember rightly, there was a booklet issued on how to go about clearing the rubble and pulling out the injured and the corpses.'

'There was,' Bone said. 'Issue Document AR, '47. We all had one. I've read the rights and wrongs from that one on many an occasion.'

Pye waited patiently. There was always this mulch of shared recent history. Sometimes it was the history of yesterday, but more often than not, like now, it was the history of the past six years, which sometimes seemed to Ernest Pye to be more distant, and fading more rapidly, than the history of the Ancient Greeks and Romans in which he also had an interest.

'How did you lose your friend?' he asked Bone. 'In a raid?'

'In a manner of speaking. It was over in St Pancras, Judd Street. Man called Harrison. A few weeks beforehand, he took a busload of stranded passengers from the bus to a nearby shelter when the alarm sounded. Dropped them off and then went back on patrol. Two pregnant women among them. The shelter took a direct hit, everybody killed. When Charlie Harrison went back there he couldn't believe his eyes. Rubble everywhere, flames, smoke, the lot. And yet not a single window of that stranded bus was even cracked. Not a crack, not a scratch, not a dent. Driver, conductor and all the passengers gone, but the bus itself could be put right with a minute and a duster. He took that hard, Charlie Harrison.'

'What happened?'

'Inquiry,' Bone said sourly. 'For what *that* was worth in those days. Charlie Harrison was exonerated, of course, but it was still an inquiry, and he still blamed himself for what had happened. Never the same after that. He used to say that it was the loss of those two unborn lives that affected him the most. Make of that what you will. People said he got sloppy. He just lost heart – that was the truth of it. Some of the other lads – "lads", they were old enough to be his father, most of them – complained at being put on the same shift as him.'

'Sloppy, how?' Pye said, hoping to shorten this lengthening tale.

'A few weeks later, he went out before the all-clear looking for people to help. A weakened wall, three storeys, warehouse off the Farringdon Road.'

'He was under it?'

'Crushed flat, by all accounts. They wouldn't even let me say a few words at his funeral. Finsbury Park cemetery. Dereliction of duty, some of them started to whisper.'

'Some kind of atonement?' Pye said. These stories haunted the city like endlessly wandering ghosts.

'I suppose so,' Bone said. 'One misjudgement – not even that – and he was blighted and finished with himself from that moment on.' He finally took a sip from his own glass.

Pye waited, hoping that these preliminaries were now over.

'He had a visitor,' Bone said. 'Yesterday.'

'Tait?'

'Out of the blue. A boy. Not what you'd call a looker. Split

lip.' Bone touched a finger to his upper lip. 'Put it this way –
you wouldn't miss him in a crowd.'

'What colour hair?' Pye said.

'Ginger. Cut short. Jug ears. Come to think of it, he doesn't
have much going for him at all in the face stakes. You know
him?'

'No. But I will do now if I see him in the future,' Pye said.
He sensed that Bone didn't completely believe him. 'Do you
know what he wanted? With Tait?'

Bone shook his head. 'Visiting Order came through. No
contention. No grounds. Tait can see who he wants, especially
now. Funny, that – I'd have thought his brief would have been
forever there, sorting out the appeal.'

'And?'

'Him? Not a dicky bird. Apparently, he sent word to Tait
telling him that it was all being done on technicalities. And I
think we all know what *that* means.'

'Perhaps it is,' Pye said.

'If you say so.'

'Were you with Tait when this man arrived?'

'I made sure I had a look in. I wasn't the attending officer,
and when I asked, nobody remembered the boy's name.
Besides, I wouldn't be at liberty to repeat anything I might
have seen or overheard.'

'I understand that,' Pye said. *So why are you here now?* Or
perhaps Bone had already told him all he needed to know.
Split lip, ginger hair, jug ears. They were simple enough
details. It narrowed the field. In fact, it narrowed the field
to one. All he had to do now was find out who that one was.
He needed Arthur Bone to tell him more about the visit,
and the best way to keep him talking, Pye decided, was to

166

return the pair of them to that shared history. 'We arrested an evacuation mob in Bermondsey. Summer '41. Emptying houses, pretending they'd been sent by the council or by the relocated families themselves.'

'There was a lot of that sort of thing going on back then,' Bone said.

'Looting?' Pye said.

'I doubt most of them would have called it that.'

'It's what it was,' Pye said.

'I know. I reported one lad myself. Helped himself to a pantry full of tins, saying he was taking them for his mother.'

'What happened?'

'Magistrate gave him the opportunity to sign up. I sometimes wonder what happened to him. Tins of fruit and condensed milk, mostly. But I daresay there was much worse.'

'And none of it helped by the evacuees pinning their own notices to the door, announcing to the world that the house had been abandoned and leaving their FAs, eh?'

Forwarding addresses. Another bond, another old joke worn thin.

Bone smiled. 'We were told to take them down and hand them in at the depot when we came across them,' he said. 'You can't blame people. I doubt if *any* of us were seeing or thinking straight at the beginning.'

'Tait is connected in some way to a man called Tommy Fowler,' Pye said suddenly.

Bone smiled. 'Tell me something I *don't* already know.'

And now, via this visitor, Tommy Fowler might be back in touch with him. Why? Under the circumstances, it was the last thing Tommy Fowler would want; in all likelihood, the last thing Peter Tait would want, too.

'And so you think this ugly-looking character was sent by Fowler?'

'It's a possibility,' Pye said.

Bone smiled again. 'Oh, is that what it is – a possibility?'

The two men touched glasses. They were still talking the same language, still on the same wavelength, still moving in the same direction.

'There was a consignment of ten thousand tins of fruit stolen from a warehouse in Hackney,' Pye said. 'Pineapple from the West Indies. You ever tasted *fresh* pineapple?'

'I doubt I would even if I had the chance,' Bone said. 'You know how I spent most of last year when I was on AR duty, because there were so few raids?'

'Go on,' Pye said.

'Checking permits. Permits for everything under the sun. One day it was permits for cameras, the next it was wheeled carts – one axle and two – the day after that it was for dogs, and the one after that for pigeons. Is that how we're winning this bloody mess – checking permits for keeping pigeons? Checking permits and then sitting through talks about the Defence of the Realm Act?'

'Under which looting was made a capital offence,' Pye said.

'Old Pierrepoint and his boys would have been working twenty-four hours a day if *that* particular piece of legislation had ever been put properly into practice,' Bone said.

'That little mob are going to be kept busy for long enough into the foreseeable,' Pye said, meaning the hangmen.

Knowing that he had earlier underestimated Bone and his understanding of Tait and the journey he had taken to his cell, he decided to take a further chance. 'Three years ago,' he said, 'my partner, a man called Andrew Clark, good man, thirty-five, DS, wife, two kids – daughters – went on a raid. We'd been tipped off about a store room in Wembley. By all accounts, Tommy Fowler had organized it. Ministry of Food stuff. Filled to the roof with sugar, butter, meat, you name it. Everything was ready and waiting; all *we* needed was for Fowler's men to turn up and start loading their lorries – who knew, perhaps even Tommy Fowler himself might put in an appearance.'

'What happened?' Bone asked.

'Nothing. No show. Somebody tipped Fowler off that we were waiting for him. Two days later, Andrew Clark went missing – he was found a week after that on a bombsite half a mile from the Wembley store with a full outline of our plans for the raid in his pocket. As far as we were concerned, there was nothing whatsoever down in writing.'

'It sounds like—'

'It sounds like exactly what it was,' Pye said.

'What did Fowler have to say for himself?'

'Tommy Fowler threw up his hands in shock and surprise, and then made sure there was nothing whatsoever we could do to connect him to the raid which never happened. We arrested his brother on another job not much more than a week after that. *His* lawyer said we were victimizing him because he was Tommy Fowler's brother and because we'd been left with egg on our faces at Wembley.'

'What was in the second store?'

'You name it. And all of it off the books and traceable to a Ports Provost scam that Tommy Fowler's brother had been running for the duration. He's still in Wandsworth. Another three years minimum to do.'

Arthur Bone considered everything Ernest Pye had just

told him. 'How does any of that connect to Tait?' he said.

'Perhaps it doesn't,' Pye conceded.

'Except *you* still bear a grudge against Fowler for what happened to your partner.'

'"Accidental Death by Enemy Action in the Pursuance of his Duty",' Pye said. 'Apparently, he was killed by a stray bomb on his way home in the early hours of the morning.'

'A long way from home, presumably?'

'A very long way. His wife couldn't cope with his death. The two girls were taken into care. You'd be surprised how many bodies turn up where nobody ever expects them to be.'

'No, I wouldn't,' Bone said. He picked up their empty glasses and went to the bar, returning with four bottles and the same glasses. 'Nothing left in the barrel,' he said. 'These are our last drinks, unless you know how to pull rank.' He poured out two of the bottles of dark ale.

'So tell me,' Pye said. 'Why do *you* think Peter Tait is innocent?'

Bone, perhaps sensing that the question was another of Pye's tests, remained silent for a moment, and then said, 'The word in the prison is that the lawyers of the other two rounded up with Tait—'

'Mulcahy and Colquhoun,' Pye said.

'Them's the ones. The word is that their lawyers are unhappy about the possibility of Tait's appeal being given the go-ahead, because if that happens then everything's back up in the air as far as their own clients are concerned. And these are proper lawyers, mind, paid for and working hard; not like the joker Tait got stuck with. With Tait guilty and hanged, then at least someone's been judged and punished. I suppose the lawyers' reasoning is that if *he*'s guilty – Tait – then it stands to reason that their own clients can't be.'

'Them or the fourth man,' Pye said. 'And there's only Tait still insisting that there actually *was* a fourth man on the raid. Mulcahy and Colquhoun are adamant it was just the three of them.'

'What about the other witnesses?' Bone said.

'Confused and contradictory stories all round. Too much uncertainty, too much room for doubt.'

'And Tait having been found guilty and then eventually being hanged removes the last of all that inconvenient doubt?'

'It certainly looks that way as things stand,' Pye said.

'What about the Tommy Fowler angle?' Bone said. 'Can't you push him a bit harder to see what gives?'

'I've been told in no uncertain terms to stay well clear of Fowler. He's got the best solicitors of all. Same solicitor he bought for his brother to reduce the charge and sentence. I only have to say hello to Tommy Fowler for him to allege harassment. Even my own superiors are telling me that I'm sailing too close as it is to perverting the course of justice. They certainly weren't happy about my visit to see Tait while his appeal application was still pending.'

'And the convenient knock on the head and the smoking gun in his hand was what?' Bone said.

'Your guess is as good as mine,' Pye told him. It was clear to Pye that Bone doubted this, but he remained silent.

They were interrupted by the arrival of a group of a dozen soldiers, who bought their drinks and then stood nearby in the open doorway.

'I've met him,' Bone said eventually.

'Who?'

'Pierrepoint. He was in on an earlier job, telling me about everything he'd got coming up.'

'The war trials?'

'There's talk they could last for up to five years.'

Pye shook his head. 'No, they won't. They'll want everything cleaned up and brushed under the carpet a lot faster than that. Months, a year at the most.'

'If you say so,' Bone said.

Suspecting he'd offended the man with this vague rebuttal, Pye said, 'Can you remember anything else about the boy with the lip?' He expected Bone to be reluctant to say more, but Bone – almost as though everything that had just passed between them had been some kind of test – said, 'He gave Tait a Bible. A small Bible. Said he'd brought it for him special.'

'For what reason? From Tommy Fowler, do you think?'

'The boy never said. Just that he'd brought it for him special. You see a lot of that kind of thing. Bibles, rosaries, lucky charms, photographs.'

'For Tait to prepare himself in some way?'

'For the Great Hereafter? Perhaps. Who knows?'

'Did you look through it?'

'I did. Nothing whatsoever in it – no pages missing, no contraband, no writing even, nothing. Thinnest paper you ever saw.'

'How long were the two of them together?'

'Not long. They didn't strike me as being great friends or anything like that.'

'So Harelip was definitely only a messenger, a delivery boy?'

'I'd say so.'

'Did he say anything to you? To you personally?'

'Not a word. My impression was that he didn't much like talking. Understandable, I suppose – his lip and everything. Forever holding his hand over his mouth. I was due off and offered to see him out, to save somebody else the walk.'

'Was anyone waiting for him?'

'Was Tommy Fowler there, you mean? No such luck. Just a girl. Waiting on the corner of Wheelwright Street. I walked on the opposite side of the road. I doubt he even saw me. He just kept his head down and walked. She was waiting for him, and the minute she saw him she shouted to him and waved. They were definitely together.'

'Did you recognize her?'

Bone shook his head. 'To my mind, she looked a bit of a tart. Hard to say, though, these days. A short skirt, knees, and a jacket. Heels and make-up. Not a bad looker, if you like that sort of thing. Redhead. Might have been Irish. Whoever she was, she was happy to see laddo coming back towards her. She could hardly wait to get to him. All over him, she was, arm through his, rubbing up against him, that sort of stuff.'

'Did she kiss him?'

Bone thought about this. 'On his cheek, perhaps. All excited, she was, asking him what had happened, pushing him to tell her everything he'd done.'

'And how did he react to all this?' Pye said.

Bone considered his answer. 'Like he wasn't used to it. He was hardly pushing her away – I don't know what red-blooded young man would, these days – but you could tell he wasn't accustomed to that kind of thing.'

Pye asked Bone to describe the girl in more detail, and he

did this. But even with everything Bone told him, she could still have been one of thousands.

Then Bone smiled.

'What?' Pye said.

'How does "Ruby Nolan" sound?'

The name meant nothing to Pye. 'Why do you say that?'

'Because I lied about finding nothing in the Bible. It was there, on the first page, written in pencil. By rights, it should have been rubbed out – regulations – but nobody had bothered. It was still there when I asked Tait to give me a butcher's.'

'So could the Bible have been from her, do you think?'

'It's possible. Then again, most Bibles have got a few names written in them. I rubbed it out when the boy wasn't looking.'

'Did he make any comment on it?'

'I dropped the name into a conversation with him earlier today. Nothing. Not a flicker. I doubt if he even noticed it. You can still see the imprint if you know where to look. Name mean anything to you?'

'Not yet,' Pye said. 'I'll ask around.' If she was on their books, then he'd find out who she was.

There was a further long silence between the two men.

Bone watched the soldiers in the doorway. 'They say the Russians are fighting from room to room through the buildings in Berlin,' he said. 'Is it a big city, do you know?'

'However big it is – was, once – I can't imagine there's much of it left standing now,' Pye said. 'In fact, I can't imagine there's much left of any of them.'

'They're calling them savages,' Bone said. 'The Russians. Some of the papers, at least. The women – that sort of thing.'

'They've had it hard enough themselves, I suppose,' Pye said.

'I suppose so,' Bone echoed. 'Still, it makes you wonder how on earth it can all just stop – I mean, how it can all ever just come to an end and be over and done with.'

'I doubt that's what will happen,' Pye said. 'At least not in any simple or straightforward way. No regulations or directives for that sort of thing.'

'Long shadows, all that?' Bone said.

'Something similar,' Pye said.

In the doorway, the soldiers burst into laughter and then parted in silence to let a woman and her sailor boyfriend come into the bar.

15

THE MAN OPPOSITE VERONICA – GEORGE SOMETHING OR other – had started crying the moment he sat down, and had afterwards been unable to restrain himself during their time together.

His first near-convulsive and unstoppable outburst had come when Veronica had taken his hand into both her own, as she had leaned closer to him, their foreheads almost touching, her sweet scent filling his nose, and as her elevated and carefully moulded cleavage had finally been revealed to him.

It was a private sitting, the man's own home, a personal recommendation; another sad and lonely widower bereft and unsure of himself in the sudden absence of his wife of forty years.

'You can cry,' Veronica had told him. 'No harm in that, especially not these days.' Knowing that this would help both to quieten him and to put him further in her debt. Quieten him so that he would at least be able to hear her telling him that it was necessary for him to pay her before they started.

He fumbled for his wallet, reaching into the jacket he wore.

'How much?' he said.

'You must decide that yourself,' she told him, as though the money were of no consequence to her. She would, however, expect a minimum of five pounds for the full hour, perhaps more at the end. And perhaps something extra to recompense her for the greater effort she would undoubtedly be called upon to make on his behalf.

She already knew that the man's wife had died of heart failure while visiting their grandchildren, who lived in the countryside somewhere. On a farm, she imagined. She knew the pair of them had been married forty years – a ruby anniversary had already been mentioned – and that he had been almost wholly dependent on the woman.

'You've suffered a great loss,' she told him, watching his hand push into his pocket. 'I can see that.' She closed her eyes, breathing deeply, panting almost. Her exposed shoulder was only inches from the man's hand. The man's wife's name was Ann. He probably called her Annie; he looked the type. The woman would have been devoted to him. Child bride, in all likelihood. He must have been at least sixty-five, perhaps nearer seventy.

His wallet was finally on the table.

Veronica had arrived at the house just before the man himself had shown up. Briefcase, umbrella, rolled newspaper. His wife's own coat, hat and scarf were still hanging on the elaborate coat stand in the hallway. Her outline, in his mind at least, was still imprinted on the mattress they had shared for forty years and upon which he now slept alone. Veronica knew this man better than he knew himself.

She tried to remember more precisely how long ago the woman had died. The man's grief and disorientation still seemed profitably raw to her, something over which she would perhaps be able to run her soothing, reassuring hand for many more sessions to come. But grief was a funny thing; with some of them you never could tell. Some men got it out of their system as quickly as possible, while others nursed and encouraged and endlessly reshaped it to suit themselves. Some men put it on. Some men tried to impress her with their grief. To some, their grief was almost an achievement, something necessary, something to be nurtured and protected. There were thousands of women, of course – women bereaved, women suddenly alone – but these lonely, wandering men were Veronica's speciality; the widowed women sometimes seemed a different species entirely to Veronica.

She watched through her half-closed eyes as he took out the five notes and laid them beside her hand. A real production; a single fiver would have been more straightforward.

'I sense a great bond of affection,' she said. 'A loving connection. So strong.'

'Does it still show?' he asked her, wiping his eyes and blowing his nose.

'They only make contact who want to make contact. You'd be surprised how easy it is for them to simply slip away and make no effort whatsoever to return to us.' She half turned and cocked her head. 'What's that?'

'What?' he said, turning to look.

'I'm conversing with the spirits,' Veronica told him. Some of her old and familiar sitters occasionally made a joke out of this and laid empty glasses between them. And who was she to say no?

But not George.

'She's calling you "Georgie",' she said. Even if he denied that his wife had ever called him this, she might easily insist that this was how Ann had always affectionately *thought* of him and that it was what she was calling him now. After all, who in their right mind – and who, recently bereaved, *was* in their right mind? – was going to argue with the dead?

'That was what she sometimes called me when we were alone, when we – you know – in our younger days,' he said, smiling.

Smiling. A good start. 'She was a very loving woman,' Veronica said, cupping a hand to her ear. 'She's growing faint.'

'No,' George said involuntarily.

Veronica waited a few seconds, a pained look on her face. 'No – she's coming back to me. Someone else on the other side interrupted her, that's all.'

'Who? I mean—'

'Another restless spirit. Oh, believe me, they can get very jealous.'

'Jealous?'

'Of the bonds that still exist between the living and those already wandering on the far side. You're a lucky man, George, I can tell that much. She's insisting on coming back to me, anxious for me not to let her slip away again. Not to let Annie slip away. I only hope I'm strong enough for you, for the pair of you.'

'Annie,' he said, and gasped for air.

'That's what she's telling me – to stay strong and to do right by you.'

For the first time, she released her hold on his hand, feeling his own grip tighten slightly as he tried to hold on to her. She waited a few seconds and then held him again. It was worth a pound at least, that particular little move.

'She's telling me to hold on to you,' she said. 'She wants you to know that these are *her* hands, that *she*'s holding you.'

179

She pretended to pull away again, but this time his grip was secure.

'What's happening?' he asked her.

'I'm not sure,' she said, feigning concern. 'It doesn't often happen, not like this. The wandering spirits are sometimes frightened of coming too close, of causing anguish or' – what was the word? – 'consternation. And besides . . .' It was important to keep hope and despair mixed in exactly the right proportions. It was a thin line, sometimes a very thin line.

'Go on,' he urged her.

'It's difficult for me. Harder to be possessed in that way. It exhausts me.' She moved her fingers slightly inside his own. 'The last time I contacted a holder – that's what we call them, "holders" – I was left exhausted for days afterwards; I had to cancel all my other appointments. It wouldn't have been fair, you see – not fair to the other sitters waiting to see me.'

'I'll pay extra,' George said.

'It isn't a question of money,' she told him.

'Then what?'

'It's a question of what I – me, myself – it's a question of what *I* can bear. It's a hard thing, possession. Strenuous. Exhausting.' She fanned her face with her hand. Her breasts shook beneath the tasselled shawl she wore.

'Please,' he said.

She could feel his eyes on her. She flicked her own eyes from side to side beneath her closed eyelids, fluttering her mascaraed lashes. Waiting until she had his full attention, she smiled, opened her eyes and then parted her lips and nodded.

'What?' he said, his voice low now, a whisper almost.

'She's in the countryside,' Veronica said. 'Fields, trees.

There's a blue sky, hedgerows. I can hear birds singing.' She'd leave the actual animals out for the time being.

'She died in Devon,' he said.

'I can see that. I can hear a river, flowing water. Cornfields.'

'She died in hospital,' he said. 'Exeter. She collapsed, lived for an hour and then died. I didn't know anything about it until the next day.'

'You knew at exactly the moment it happened,' she said.

'No one—'

'You *knew*,' she said. 'You think back – you knew.'

He considered this. 'Well, come to think of it, I did get a sense of *something* being not quite right at just about the time she—'

'That was Annie saying goodbye,' Veronica said. His wife's death – something not quite right.

'A chill. Just for a few seconds, something unsettling. I thought I was going to break out in a sweat, as though I was coming down with something. I'd forgotten all about it until now. It was two months ago.'

Two months. 'There was snow,' Veronica said. But no cornfields. 'On the hills, in the distance. And the corn was only just beginning to show, tiny green shoots in the earth. She was among people she loved, that was the main thing.'

'Our daughter and grandchildren,' he said.

'And your son-in-law?'

'*Him?*' he said. 'I doubt if he even—'

'No,' she said suddenly, a note of alarm in her voice.

'What is it?'

'She's telling me not to mention his name, not to even think of it.'

'Geoffrey,' he said. 'He always told people to call him Geoff.'

'That's right. "Leave Geoffrey out of it," she's saying. Concentrate on your daughter and your grandchildren.'

'So-called reserved occupation,' he said.

'The land. He—'

'Mechanic servicing farm machinery. A shirker from the day he was born.'

'Don't,' she said. 'She's telling me again to tell you not to talk about him. She wants you to think about the little ones instead.'

'Annie and Peter,' he said.

Perfect. 'That's right – Annie and Peter. So small. And such a terrible thing for them to have to endure.' Veronica stopped talking. No good running when you could still walk. She took a deep breath and started mumbling to herself.

'I can't hear you,' George said.

She pretended not to have heard him. 'I'll tell him,' she said.

'Tell me what?'

'She says she was thinking of you during that last hour.' Speaking of which, she glanced over his shoulder at the clock on the wall. Twenty minutes left.

'She was unconscious,' he said.

Veronica smiled at him. 'That was how she *appeared* to everyone around her.'

'They all said—'

'Just as those same people would all now insist she was dead and gone and lost to you for ever?'

'I suppose so.'

'You sound . . .'

'What? I sound what?' he said.

Veronica shrugged. *Doubt me*, she wanted him to understand, *and you doubt her, your own dear departed wife, your own dear departed Annie.*

She waited until he got the message before going on.

'Now she's wondering if your own heart isn't fully in this,' she said. She finally pulled her hand from his.

'That's not true.'

'She's wondering if . . .' She trailed off, pretending to strain to hear someone whispering to her. Then she laughed and held his hand again. 'She's telling you to drop the mask, George. You're not in your stuffy old office now. You're in your house, your little palace – yours and Annie's. She's telling you to lose the stiff upper lip. It's just you and her now, George. Just you and Annie.'

And me, of course.

The notes on the table had started to unfold of their own volition and she watched this.

After that, she remained silent for a few minutes.

The clock on the wall struck the hour. Six o'clock on a dull day that already felt like evening.

Then she looked down at George's hands, both of them now flat on the table. Perhaps he was inviting her to hold him again. *Well, keep hoping, George.* All of that would have to wait until next time. When she looked up at him, she saw that he was watching her closely. She saw the tracks of his tears on his cheek, the wetness in his moustache.

'You seemed in a kind of – I don't know – a kind of trance,' he said.

'It's what happens,' she said. It helped to pass the last part of that long hour. 'I was trying to keep Annie within reach.'

'Has she gone, then?'

She nodded. 'For now. Sometimes, a few minutes is all they can manage.'

'I see.'

'She told me she wants to watch over you, to make sure you're taking care of yourself, that you come to no harm now that you've not got her to keep an eye on things.'

He looked around the room. 'I've let things go a bit,' he said.

'She can see that. It's the last thing she'd have wanted for you.' House-proud Annie, and George sitting in his mausoleum.

'You're right,' he said.

She was always right. She was talking to the dead; all the sitters had to do was to sit and listen and believe.

'Is she gone, then?' George said again.

Veronica nodded. Ten minutes to go. 'For the time being. But, like I said, it's a strong connection. She'll come back.'

She rose from the table and put her hand on his shoulder. What did ten minutes matter? But she knew that her charms had been wasted on George. Some of them suggested a drink to finish with, something to help her recover from her exertions. Some of them even insisted on paying for a second hour simply for her to stay and talk to them about other things. They almost all made arrangements for her next visit.

But not today, not George. She wondered if he'd even wanted to be convinced of his dead wife's efforts on his behalf in the first place.

'I have to go,' she said. 'I'm a busy girl, not one to disappoint. Shall I come back?'

He struggled to answer her.

'You could tell me more about her,' she said.

'Just talk, you mean?'

'You and her, yes.'

'Oh.' He looked away. It wasn't what he'd meant.

Veronica put on her coat and gloves and scarf.

'Stay where you are,' she told him. *Live in confusion and uncertainty and misery with your memories and fears.* 'I'll let myself out.'

George came with her into the hallway. He thanked her and told her he'd get in touch. He said the sitting had taken a lot out of him, given him a lot to think about. Excuses.

Veronica left him and then turned back and waved at him from the front gate. A cherry tree was coming into blossom in the front garden, its flowers vivid in the dull light.

'*She* planted that,' George called to her.

Veronica looked at the tree and nodded. Good for her. And now the tree was like flowers on a grave.

She walked to the end of the undamaged street and looked back. George was standing close to the tree, sniffing its blossom.

Reaching the main road, Gloucester Road, Veronica took the money from her pocket and put it in her purse.

A few minutes later, she was waiting to cross the road to reach the Fox and Grapes, immediately beyond the Underground station, when she saw Sweeney walking in the same direction on the far side of the road. She was about to call out to him when she saw that he was with that girl again, the nasty little tart who had come back to the house with him four days earlier. They drew clear of a group of other pedestrians and she put her arm through his. *He doesn't want it*, Veronica thought to herself, but then saw by the way Sweeney folded

185

his own arm over the girl's hand that he was doing nothing to shake her off. The girl was talking excitedly, tugging at him, turning back and forth as they walked. They passed the Fox and turned off the main road. They were walking in the direction of the house. He was taking her back there with him again.

Careful to avoid being seen by the pair of them, Veronica crossed the road and walked past the Fox, watching Sweeney and the girl fifty yards ahead of her.

She began to imagine what the little tart might be saying to him, and how easily he would allow himself to be manipulated and led by her. Sometimes, it seemed to Veronica, the world was full of people whose only purpose and point and pleasure in life was to get one over on everybody else around them.

16

LAURA SAT AT THE WINDOW, HER FACE CLOSE TO THE GLASS, looking down at the people below. At Frankie Doll's arrival, she acknowledged his presence with a glance and then went on looking.

'Anything interesting?' he said. It was three days since he'd last seen her, and he immediately sensed her hostility at this long and unexplained absence.

'Your money's on the table,' she said. 'I expected you before this. You've obviously found something more interesting to do.'

Frankie Doll went to the table and sat down. 'Don't be like that,' he said. 'I tried to get here yesterday, day before. You know how it is. I've had things to do.'

'Of course you have – you're a busy man,' she said. 'For a messenger boy.'

'Don't,' he said. He slapped his palm on the table.

'And don't tell me Fowler sent you off on a longer errand than usual, because he was the one asking me where you'd got to. And believe me, he wasn't well pleased.'

'I'm not at his beck and call,' Frankie Doll said.

'Of course you aren't. You're Frankie Doll – your own man. Are *you* going to tell him that, or do you want me to go on doing your dirty work for you?'

'I'll go and see him,' Frankie Doll said. 'Sort everything out.'

'He told me to tell you to make it sooner rather than later. Like I said, he's not a happy man. Asking me what you were up to, and everything.'

'Then you should have made up some excuse for me,' Frankie Doll said. 'Told him—'

'He won't listen to whatever I might have to say.'

There was a catch in her voice and Frankie Doll heard this. 'Oh?' he said. 'Has something happened?' He'd been about to tell her of the plans he and Julian Beazley might soon be making, about how soon he would be exactly what she had just accused him of not being – his own man. But now he held back. Something was wrong. He had already started to consider what part *she* might play in those plans.

'Such as?' Laura said.

'You tell me.' It sometimes seemed to Frankie Doll that the two of them drew an uncrossable line between themselves and then spent their time batting back and forth across that line. It never used to be like this, and he wanted to tell her that he was tired of all her complaints and evasions, all this unnecessary hostility for no good reason that he could see.

Eventually, Laura turned to face him, and he saw by the light of the window that she had a bruise on her cheek.

'Satisfied?' she said.

'Was it' – Frankie Doll stopped himself from saying 'Fowler' – 'a man?'

'A mark, you mean? A punter? A customer? Of course it was a man.'

'You know what I'm saying.'

She turned back to the window and sat with her eyes closed for a moment.

Perhaps when he and Beazley were up and running and in demand and successful and making their own small fortunes, then perhaps Laura could take care of the clerical side of things for them – typing, answering the telephone, taking orders, making out lists, that sort of thing.

'I'm sorry,' he said. 'I know I should have been back sooner. Do you know who it was?'

'I don't have his name or address or his service number, if that's what you're asking.'

'You should have gone to Fowler, told him. Perhaps he could have sent—'

'The only person he would have sent is me – packing,' she said. 'Forget about it. You're here now. For what that's worth.' Everything she said to him felt like a blow or a jab or a push of one sort or another.

'Was it somebody you picked up at the Regency?' he said. He expected her to shout at him again, but instead she nodded.

'Just a kid,' she said.

'In the Regency? What sort of kid? Tommy Fowler would never—'

'What I said – a kid. Can't have been much older than sixteen or seventeen. He even looked as though he was wearing his father's suit.'

'Fowler would have shown him the door,' Frankie Doll said.

'That's what I thought, too. But, instead, he pointed him in my direction. Funny, that, don't you think?'

'Fowler sent him to you? A kid?'

'Told me to take care of him, to get him into a corner, keep

189

him quiet and out of sight and trouble, and then to get him out of the Regency as soon as he'd had a skinful or was showing signs of wanting to make a move.'

'So Fowler knew him?'

She applauded him slowly. 'And then to add injury to insult, Fowler said that if the Nolan girl turned up before he went, then I was to stick him with her. More his age, he said. Said she'd have more *appeal* for him.'

'So why didn't you?'

'Because she didn't show. I asked around. One of the girls said she'd seen her talking to Sweeney a couple of days earlier, but since then nothing. Thick as thieves they were, apparently.'

'Did you tell Fowler?'

'I covered for her and told him she'd already left with a customer. Fowler said not to worry, the kid would have to make do with me. He gave me some of the kosher whisky to give him. Told me to keep my wits about me and to let him know if the boy started shooting his mouth off or looking for trouble of any kind. If you ask me, the kid was there to prove a point, and there was something about him being there that kept Fowler on his toes.'

'Meaning what?' Frankie Doll was already making his own uncertain calculations.

'Meaning he had something on Fowler, and knew that he could waltz in and act the big man and that there was nothing Fowler could do about it. At least not in the Regency, in a room full of people.'

'Fowler knew he could trust you to keep everything to yourself,' Frankie Doll said.

'Big of him. Still, that's me – good old dependable little Laura.'

'I didn't mean it like that.'

'No? Oh, perhaps you meant to ask me if the punch I got for all my dependability hurt me, if there was any blood, if the bruising was sore, or even if it had started going down yet.'

Frankie Doll waited a few seconds. 'Does it?' he said. 'Hurt?'

Laura considered this. 'I could do without the bruising – it hardly adds to my irresistible good looks – but the slap was nothing new.'

'And the boy did it?'

'In the club. He was drunk inside of an hour. Fowler sent Sammy the Glass to sit nearby and help me keep an eye on things. But the boy saw this and told Sammy to get lost. When Fowler came back to sort things out, the boy told him to get lost, too.'

'What did Fowler say to that?'

'Not much. And certainly not what he'd have said to you or me if we'd told him the same. He just warned the boy to watch his mouth. For all their sakes, he said. Then he told *me* to forget everything I was hearing and seeing. And then he went.'

'Leaving you alone again with the boy?'

'Leaving me alone again with the boy. I don't suppose *you* know where the Nolan girl might have been?'

'Me?'

'You're good at that – coming the innocent.'

Frankie Doll hadn't seen Ruby Nolan since the morning she'd left him to go to the Cumberland, three days earlier. What interested him now was the connection between her and Sweeney. To the best of his knowledge, she'd never paid him a moment's attention before.

'Cross my heart,' he said. 'On my mother's death.'

Laura laughed at this.

'I wonder who he was,' he said. 'The boy. He must have said something, let something slip.'

At the window, Laura turned back to face him, deliberately angling her bruised cheek at him, and then smiling.

'What?' Frankie Doll said. 'You know something?'

'Tommy Fowler must think I'm stupid,' she said. 'Perhaps you think the same.'

'No, I don't,' he said.

'Then tell me that you haven't been wanting to ask me that ever since you saw my face.'

There was nothing Frankie Doll could say to this.

'And you see that?' Laura said, indicating a pile of money on the nearby dresser.

'What about it?'

'Most of it was from Fowler himself. For me taking care of the boy. He actually showed up here, in this dump, Tommy Fowler, Mister high and mighty himself, an hour after the kid had thrown up on the carpet and then run off. He saw me like this, asked me what had happened, and then he actually said he was sorry for everything.'

'Tommy Fowler said sorry?'

'See – you're all ears now, a lot more interested in that side of things than in what happened to me.' She pushed a finger into her cheek and then flinched at the pain this caused her. 'He took out the money, said he appreciated everything I'd done, asked me what the boy had said about anything, half believed most of what little I told him, and then went. Ask me, he was as happy as I was that the little bastard had disappeared. I even told him that the boy hadn't been able to . . . you know . . .'

'And Fowler left the money anyway?'

'Now, why do you think that was? What do you think *that* was payment for?'

Blood money, Frankie Doll thought to himself. The boy had something on Fowler. But what? And if the boy worried Fowler this much, then it would be something big. What wouldn't it be worth to another man to know what that was? Especially a man who might be looking for favours from Fowler in the very near future. Or if not favours, exactly . . .

'And he believed you? About the boy not having given anything away that would have explained anything about Fowler's own back being up?'

'Next you'll be telling me to keep all the money for myself,' Laura said. 'Buy myself some good foundation and a nice pair of dark glasses.'

'You earned it,' Frankie Doll said, knowing immediately that it was the wrong thing to say. But he still wasn't thinking straight: all those calculations going round and round and round inside his head. 'And if the boy did say anything . . .' he said, prompting her. Round and round and round. All he knew for certain was that there was *something* to be gained from all of this, something that might give him something on Tommy Fowler.

'What, you think that if the boy *had* said something to give the game away, then I'd have been better off telling Fowler? Give me some credit. Fowler said that when Ruby Nolan did finally show her face, she'd be getting a taste of what I'd just had, only *she* wouldn't be getting paid for hers.'

'From Fowler?' *Had* the boy told her anything or hadn't he? 'When did *he* last get his hands dirty?'

Frankie Doll went to the cooker and lit the ring beneath

the kettle. He made tea using the leaves always sitting in the pot. He picked up a bottle of milk from the table and sniffed it.

'Off,' Laura said.

Frankie Doll saw the bottle of brandy on the drainer amid the unwashed crockery there.

'Fowler told me to put it in my bag. In the Regency. I think he came round here hoping to find the boy blotto. I think Fowler expected to just pick him up and carry him off and put him back in the box he'd managed to escape from.'

'And from where he'd gone straight to the Regency,' Frankie Doll said.

'It can't have been a coincidence.'

'He was there to prove a point.'

'Give the man a coconut. Fowler asked me if I needed a doctor, said he'd get one to me.'

'And?'

She shook her head. 'When Fowler asks questions like that, the answer's usually plain from the off.'

'You got that right,' Frankie Doll said. 'Do you think he was serious – about the Nolan girl?'

Laura shrugged. She rose from beside the window and yawned. Then she came to sit with Frankie Doll at the table, close enough to reach out and hold his hand, close enough for him to do the same.

'He'll probably just tell her to get lost,' she said. 'The gravy train's running out of steam. She's baggage, that's all.'

Just like you and me, Frankie Doll thought, but again he said nothing. He finally reached out and held her hand for a moment.

'He was one of Billy Leach's,' Laura said. 'The boy.'

'What makes you say that?' He was listening carefully.

'He talked about him a lot. It's what you all do.'

'Right.'

'He might even have been Billy Leach's son, for all the airs and graces he gave himself,' she said. She reached for the bottle and stood it between them on the table.

Not very likely. As far as Frankie Doll knew, Billy Leach didn't have a son. And besides, Billy Leach and Tommy Fowler went back a long way. The last thing either of them would want would be somebody in either family rocking that particular boat.

'In the Regency, the boy called Fowler "Mister" Fowler,' Laura said. 'Said it like he was spitting at him.'

'Sounds a right little bastard and trouble-maker. I'll keep my eyes and ears peeled.'

'And do what?'

Frankie Doll shrugged.

'Exactly. The biggest surprise to me – to everyone – was that Fowler let him talk like that – just stood there and listened to the boy and took it all on the chin. Fowler told me when he turned up here that he'd already sent word to Billy Leach to come and find the boy and take him home. So there's definitely some connection to Leach. In the Regency—' She stopped talking and closed her eyes.

'What is it?' Frankie Doll said.

'Fowler – he said a funny thing. He told the boy to stop and think what his father would make of it all if he ever learned about what he'd done.'

Which would definitely rule out Billy Leach. 'And what did the boy say to that?'

'That was another funny thing. The boy stood with his

face only inches from Fowler's and said, "Perhaps he'll send me to Billericay." Just like that. And then he made his fingers into a gun, pretended to shoot Fowler and then laughed in Fowler's face.'

'Billericay? Why Billericay?'

'Search me.'

'What did Fowler say to that?'

'It was as close as he came to grabbing hold of the boy all night. He told me straight off that the boy was drunk, that he didn't know what he was saying. It was fairly obvious what he was telling me.'

'To forget what you'd heard.'

'I thought it might have been some kind of code word or something – slang.'

'Not to my knowledge,' Frankie Doll said. *Beyond the authority of the Metropolitan Police.* 'It's Essex. Smuggling country. All that water and stuff, camps and depots, military surplus.'

'If you say so.'

'And there was nothing else?' Nothing to connect the boy to Frankie Doll's pointless little errand to see Billy Leach three days earlier?

Laura pretended to consider this. 'Apart from this, you mean?'

Frankie Doll reached out and held his fingers a few inches from her face.

'I'm having a few more days off,' she said. 'Get myself looking beautiful for when the big day finally arrives. He had a little moustache, the kid, a line across his top lip. I touched it and most of it came off on my finger. That was how I got this, not the other.'

196

After that, neither of them spoke for a few minutes, both of them listening to the noise of the street outside. A car sounded its horn and was joined by several others. There were blockages twenty times a day. Traders set up their stalls most days of the week.

'What will you do?' Frankie Doll finally asked her.

'About what?'

'When Fowler comes back and asks you again what the boy might have let slip to you.'

'Tell him the same old story. Like I already said, I doubt if changing my tune will make things any better for me.'

'Do you think he believed you?'

'What I think is that he was just relieved to see the back of the boy. He told me that in all likelihood I'd never see the little bastard again for a long time to come.'

'He's good at making promises like that,' Frankie Doll said, and again he regretted the words. 'I went to see Beazley,' he said. 'That's where I've been.' Not for three days, but it was a start.

'Said he, changing the subject.'

'We've been talking about setting up our own little business. He says things are going to change. Laws, regulations, stuff like that.'

'Once the war's over?' It sometimes seemed as though the phrase contained the whole of the knowable and unknowable future in its entirety.

'According to Beazley, everything will go through the post. Pictures, cards, magazines; films, even.'

'Films?'

'Why not?'

'How will people watch them?'

'It's all in the future,' Frankie Doll said. '*Everything*'s going to change.'

'Fair enough. What kind of films – stags?'

'I suppose so.'

'And you believe him?' Her own scepticism was clear.

'Why not? He knows what he's talking about. The world's definitely going to change and people like me and Beazley – people like you – we have to be ready for when that change comes. And according to Beazley, that change is coming a lot sooner than anybody thinks.'

'And you've whispered even a word of this to Tommy Fowler, have you? About you and Beazley being the coming men, and how people like him – Fowler – are the ones about to get left behind?'

'Not exactly,' Frankie Doll said. 'Besides, Fowler can make his own arrangements. Beazley says that people will want more of everything and that they'll want whatever that is to be better than before. He says that being a soldier – going off and fighting for queen and whatsit – that it changes a man.'

'You're beginning to sound like a newsreel,' Laura said. And again it was something approaching a small, uncertain affection between them.

'And you look like a mug shot,' he said.

Laura turned her face one way and then the other. 'That's me,' she said. 'Laura the Desperado. Wanted dead or alive.' She made her own fingers into a gun and fired them at Frankie Doll.

'You got me,' he said. 'Every shot bang on target.'

'Good,' Laura said. She blew on her fingers and then slowly spread them apart as far as they would go.

17

Ruby Nolan stood opposite the house on Coleherne Road and looked up at its windows, wondering which of the rooms might belong to Aleister Crowley. She had already established that the house contained sixteen separate flats over four floors and a half-cellar. This latter was reached via the rear of the building and was occupied by a solitary old woman. The narrow garden, also to the rear, was overgrown and made dark by two lines of trees which had been allowed to grow high.

She held the page of a newspaper containing a photograph of the house. The paper was a month old and the headline under the picture said that this was 'The Lair of the Beast'. The word Beast was spelled out in dark capitals. The short accompanying article gave the address, followed by a warning to all its other residents and nearby neighbours. Aleister Crowley, the Great Beast, the self-proclaimed Antichrist, occultist, so-called sage and pompous windbag seer, convicted liar, bankrupt and fraudster, charlatan and con-man, lived there. Devil-worshipper, evil incarnate, fake, opportunist, necromancer, sexual deviant.

It made Ruby Nolan smile to see how many of these names and other accusations were fitted into the small piece – the thrust of which was simply that Crowley had recently moved back to London from Aylesbury. He had disappeared for a while – no doubt chased away by his multitude of creditors – and now, magically, like the fetid stink he was, he had reappeared. Come back to blight the lives of all those who fell under his devious spell and corrupting charm.

In addition to which, Crowley had made yet another preposterous application to be buried in Westminster Abbey. Apparently, Crowley was approaching the end of his life – and Good Riddance – and wanted all the loose ends of his miserable existence neatly tied up. London, he had announced, was a stop-gap. He would no doubt have preferred another house in leafy Richmond or back in urbane Jermyn Street, but these were now way beyond his means and so here he was in dusty Earl's Court. But anywhere, Crowley had allegedly announced, would be better than the living graveyard of Torquay, where he had gone to avoid his good friend Hitler's Blitz.

Ruby had been to the dilapidated porch and read the nameplates there. No Crowley, but plenty of empty spaces where the flimsy, handwritten pieces of card and paper had been pushed into place. Another house of shifting, restless occupancy, tenants coming and going unknown and hardly ever seen.

One name, though: an Edward Alexander written in fancy lettering, dark, well-formed and carefully transcribed, and preceded and followed by two small symbols – circles filled with dots and strange letters which meant nothing to her, but which she knew were more than mere decorations.

The article concluded with the remarks that England, in its hour of need, had absolutely no need whatsoever of

Crowley, and that London would be glad to see him once again depart for somewhere else. The anonymous writer suggested somewhere in Germany, perhaps; anywhere in Germany.

Beneath the picture of the house was an old photograph of Crowley himself. He was middle-aged, overweight, and shaved bald except for a tuft of hair growing at the centre of his forehead. Mister Crowley in all his so-called Satanic glory, the article sneered. She imagined the picture to be at least twenty years old, perhaps more. The man she had seen in the Regency looked at least forty years older.

Drug Fiend, the article remembered in its closing paragraph. Drug Fiend, sado-masochistic, misogynistic and capricious. It seemed a flippant, almost apologetic way to conclude such a tirade. Capricious. It meant goat-like, she knew that much. Capricorn. Like herself.

She watched the house closely, moving up and down, left to right, from one window to the next. The outlines of the road's trees were reflected in the glass, making it hard to see anything inside.

Just as she was beginning to wonder how much longer she might have to wait there – it was already late afternoon – a figure appeared at the road's end. It was an old man in a heavy overcoat and wearing a hat. It looked like the man in the Regency. He walked with a cane, striking this loudly on the pavement as he came. And after every half a dozen paces or so, he stopped and rested for a minute, leaning on the ball-topped gate-posts of the houses.

Ruby crossed the road and walked towards the figure, pretending not to notice him, and as she approached within a few feet of him, she slowed. The man ahead of her leaned against a pillar and coughed. He took out a handkerchief and held it to his mouth.

Arriving where he stood, and as he turned slightly to let her pass on the narrow pavement, she looked more closely at him. He kept his own face turned away from her, the handkerchief still to his mouth.

'Are you all right?' she said to him. She stopped walking.

At first, he seemed uncertain who had spoken, or even if the words had been directed at him.

'My chest,' he said.

She went closer to him and put a hand on his upper arm.

He turned to her at feeling this and looked directly at her.

'Let me help you,' she said. 'Where do you live? Is it far? I'm in no hurry.'

The newspaper article was folded into a small square in her pocket.

Crowley looked from her face to where her hand still rested on his arm, and from there to her pocket.

'I just need to recover my breath,' he said. 'That's all.' He looked back and forth along the empty street.

'Have you been walking far?' she asked him.

'You're Irish,' he said.

'Belfast.'

'I would have guessed as much. You and your countrymen are in for troubled times.'

'It sometimes seems to me that we can't live without trouble of one kind or another,' she said.

Crowley smiled at this. 'I've known a great many Irishmen in my time, and I daresay you're right.'

'I'm Ruby,' she said. 'Ruby Nolan.'

He hesitated before responding to this. The he took off one

of the gloves he wore and held out his hand to her. 'Edward,' he said. 'Edward Alexander.'

'Pleased to meet you,' she said.

Perhaps she was imagining it, but his hand felt cold to her. His grip, too, was stronger than she had anticipated.

'You're cold,' she said to him.

This time he laughed at the remark.

She withdrew her hand and asked him again where he lived.

Crowley raised his cane and pointed.

'Here?' she said. 'So close? That's lucky.'

The tip of the cane was sheathed in silver. Its head, too, had a silver and ebony handle, and she found herself wondering if it contained a sword.

'I could at least walk to the door with you,' she said. 'See you safely home.'

'I'd appreciate that,' Crowley said. 'It's been a long time since such an attractive young woman offered her services to me.'

The remark hung between them for a moment, and then Ruby said, 'You sound like a man who's been around a bit, seen something of the world.' But it was obvious flattery and she sensed that it put Crowley on his guard. 'I'm sorry,' she said. 'I didn't mean anything by it.'

'Not at all,' he said, appearing to think better of his response. 'Would it surprise you to know that I was once a close associate of Yeats?'

'Yeats?'

'William Butler, of course. Not his mud-flinging artist of a brother.'

'The poet?'

'If you say so. A man much given to his own self-importance, cloaked in his own high opinion of himself and his dreary work, and perfumed by his own rank self-regard.'

'You didn't see eye to eye, then?' she said.

'Eye to eye? The man would never deign to lower his gaze *this* far.' He tapped the head of his cane against his chest.

'Careful,' Ruby said. She held his arm as he resumed walking. 'Which one?' she asked him as they arrived at the steps to the house in the picture, the Lair of the Beast.

'Here,' Crowley said. 'I'm on the first floor.'

'I'll say goodbye, then,' she said. 'It was good to meet you. My father used to recite Yeats to us when we were children and he was drunk.' Her father had never recited so much as a limerick in his entire life. 'I never much liked it. It all seemed a bit . . . too much.'

Crowley smiled at this. 'Everything about the man was a bit too much. W. B. Yeats? Wind Bag Yeats, I used to call him.'

She laughed. *Exactly the same name the paper called you.* 'I'll let you get in,' she said. 'Your wife might be worrying about you.'

'Sadly not,' he said, clearly amused by the suggestion.

'Is she . . . ?' She wondered what she might add.

'A long time gone, I'm afraid. She wanders in another realm. The old story. Once you get to a certain age, not only do you outlive everyone else, but you soon enough start to outlive yourself.'

'I'm sorry,' she said. 'I didn't mean to intrude.'

'Please, don't apologize. I've lived a life of intrusions – my own and others. Did you know that Wind Bag Yeats never once in his entire life knocked upon a door before entering a room or a house? Never once. He imagined his own presence in that room or house – regardless of its inhabitants or how their own small, dreary, insignificant lives were playing out there – was of such great and welcome importance that knocking was completely unnecessary. Those poor, small people, he imagined, would always be so overjoyed to see him, to have him among them – a great glowing sun to their own cold orbits – that anything so banal or tedious as knocking to announce that presence was completely unnecessary.'

'Why spoil the happy surprise, you mean?' she said.

'Exactly.' He looked at the key he held an inch from the lock. 'And how about yourself?' he said.

'Me?'

'Do you not have someone waiting for you, eagerly listening out for your own approach and tender knock? A young man, say, or even a lucky fiancé, perhaps?' He had seen her ringless fingers.

Ruby shook her head. 'No one. I'm not long over here. Besides, I doubt he'd consider himself lucky to be kept waiting by me.'

Crowley unlocked the door and pushed it open. He stood to one side so that she might precede him into the hallway. 'Two flights,' he said, indicating the stairway.

She took his arm again and helped him up the stairs.

They stopped finally at a door on the first-floor landing, and she saw the card pinned to it bearing the same symbols she had seen in the porch.

'What's that, then?' she said. 'A good-luck charm or something?'

'Why do you say that?' Crowley said, hesitating in unlocking the door.

She feigned nonchalance. 'I just assumed, that's all.'

'It's a sign of the *qabala*,' he said.

'And what's that when it's at home?'

He spelled out the word for her.

'Still never heard of it. What is it — some secret society or something? You a mason?'

Crowley smiled at her ignorance. 'It is something to which I was once attached.' He unlocked the door and let it swing open.

The room beyond was in near darkness. The afternoon sun was at the rear of the house. Here, at the front, above the tree-lined street, there was only dying light and lengthening shadow.

Crowley went in ahead of her and switched on the lamp beside a chair. She followed him in and looked around her. The door closed behind her of its own volition.

'Very cosy,' she said.

'It's pitiful,' Crowley said immediately. There was neither apology nor offence in his voice. 'Believe me, I've lived in what most would consider to be palaces and mansions. You might say I am here following a succession of misfortunes and reverses. All soon to be put right, hopefully, but not quite yet. Fortunately, I have never been defeated by my circumstances and surroundings, and though often cast upon the mercy and charity of others — especially and increasingly of late, it seems — I have never truly suffered as a consequence of the withholding of that mercy or charity.'

Ruby only half understood what he was saying to her. 'Were you in business, then?' she said. 'Something professional?'

'No, not business, not trade, if that's what you mean.'

Crowley started to take off his heavy coat and she went to help him. She hung it on a hook behind the door, adding his scarf and hat, and propping his silver-headed cane against the wall. Then she helped him to the armchair in front of the dying fire and he asked her if she could put something on this. The small hearth was filled with wood ash, spent matches and the pinched ends of cigarettes.

Everything about the room disappointed her. Lair? She had anticipated paintings, exotic rugs, great ornaments, a touch of the East, perhaps, the Orient. But apart from a solitary bookcase containing three shelves of books, there was nothing. A mirror above the fire with an ornate frame, a heavy-looking clock on the mantel, a few photographs scattered around the other surfaces; but apart from that, nothing.

She went to one of the photographs – a woman and a child – and picked it up.

'Rose and Lola,' Crowley said. 'My wife and only living – perhaps I should say only acknowledged living – daughter.'

She was caught unawares by the word.

'I had another,' Crowley said. 'Another daughter. Lilith. Jezebel Lilith. She was a baby. I was in Shanghai when she died. It was all a very long time ago, the turn of the century.'

'Still . . .' Ruby said. She looked more closely at the picture.

'Yes, still . . .' Crowley said. He looked around him. 'There's a bottle of cheap whisky somewhere,' he said.

Ruby searched and found it behind Crowley's chair.

He motioned to a cabinet. 'Glasses. You'll join me?'

Ruby opened the cabinet. It was filled with other books, an assortment of glasses and several pieces of silverware, bowls and cups.

'Were you to return to burgle me,' Crowley told her, 'then that's the only place to look. There and the clock.' He indicated the clock on the mantel. 'Ormolu. Malachite and gilt. A symbol, token and reminder of those past glories. But I daresay the silverware is currently of greater value. Believe me, devoted collectors would pay good money just to *see* some of those pieces. Ceremonial ware. Chalices.'

Ruby closed the door with a loud click. 'Chalices? You make it sound – I don't know – religious or something.'

'That cabinet once stood in our headquarters and was used to store our records and minutes.'

'Headquarters?'

Crowley gestured for her to pour the drink and then tapped a finger against his glass to indicate for her to add more.

'I'm not much of a drinker myself,' Ruby said.

'Oh? I thought all the Irish sucked it down like mother's milk.'

'My father was all for it,' she said.

'Is he no longer living?'

'Collapsed and died. Froze to death in the Harland and Wolff shipyard. He'd gone there for work. When they found him his eyes were open – they said he looked surprised – and there was a frozen drink in his hand.'

'Surprised?'

'The men who found him made a joke of it and said that perhaps in his dying seconds he'd seen the Devil coming to fetch him home.'

Crowley laughed at this. 'Then he saw what I myself have spent a lifetime hoping to see. And who knows – perhaps that's exactly what he did see.'

It was a true story – the men's remarks – and one she had

repeated many times. Ever since she was a girl of six, she had prayed for her father's death, and so far it was the only one of her prayers ever to have been answered. The supposed appearance of the Devil had been an unexpected, though much appreciated, detail.

'You believe in all that, then?' she said. 'Is that what the thing on the door and the stuff in the cabinet is all about?' She wondered if she'd said too much, leaped too far forward. The tale of her father's death had come without her having considered what she was saying, let alone to whom she was saying it.

'Gewgaws,' Crowley said. 'Trappings, incidentals, gaudy distractions.'

'I don't follow you,' she said. She drew the room's only other chair away from the table and closer to the struggling fire. 'What sort of distractions?'

'From this,' Crowley said, his voice suddenly solemn, and simultaneously pressing his palm into his chest and closing his eyes.

She waited without speaking, holding her breath. She drank half her own whisky while his eyes were closed.

And then, just as suddenly and as unexpectedly as it had arrived, Crowley's mood changed again and he opened his eyes, lowered his hand and drained his own glass. 'What was I saying?' he asked her.

'Not much,' she said. 'Something about the stuff in the cabinet.'

'I have a tendency to drift,' he said. He turned his hand palm up and looked closely at its scored surface. Then he looked at her glass. 'You've not finished,' he said. 'Humour me.'

She finished her drink and licked her lips.

'I have an associate who does his best to keep me supplied with the stuff gratis,' Crowley said.

'Gratis?'

'Free of charge. Buckshee.'

She knew what gratis meant. 'Oh, right. It's the drink,' she said. 'It always goes straight to my head. I'll need to watch myself. Still, better than some of the places it could have gone to, eh?' The men in the Regency always appreciated that one.

'I suppose so,' Crowley said.

Ruby looked at the clock on the mantel. 'I ought to be making tracks,' she said.

'Do you have far to go?'

'Beaufort Street,' she said, remembering Sweeney's address. Not that she'd be rushing back to that place while the gyppo was still keeping watch over things and staking her claim on the boy. Besides, all Sweeney had ever been to *her* was a means to an end, and as far as she was concerned that end had now been reached. If ever she did go back there, then it would only be to fill in any missing gaps, and perhaps to have another go at the fortune-teller.

'To your family?'

'They're all back in Belfast. What's left of them. I'm here all on my lonesome, in a rented room. Nothing much to write home about, but it'll do until things look up.' She wondered how much more bait she would need to lay before him.

'And will things?'

'Will things what?'

'Look up. It seems a common affliction of late, all this hopefulness.'

'I hope so,' she said. 'As far as I'm concerned, it's doubtful

if things could get any worse. Who knows, once the hostilities
are—'

'Hostilities,' Crowley said. 'I wonder who thought that
one up. They've been marauding like savage animals and
burning people in pits – men, women, children and babies.
Hostilities?'

'Marauding? You mean the Russians?'

'All of them,' Crowley said. 'All of them.'

'If you say so,' she said. She rose and put her empty glass on
the table beside him. 'Thanks for the drink,' she said.

'My pleasure entirely,' Crowley said. He struggled to rise
from his own chair.

'Don't get up,' she told him. She leaned over him and kissed
him quickly on his cheek.

'Another distant memory,' he said.

She stood back from him and waited. 'I've enjoyed our
little chat,' she said.

'Will you . . .' he said.

'Will I what?'

'I was going to ask if you'd come back, if you'd do something for me.'

'You hardly know me,' she said.

'What difference do you imagine that makes?'

She pretended to think about what he'd said. 'Go on, then,'
she said. 'In for a penny, in for a pound. And God knows we
could all use a few more of those these days.'

18

THE PRISON GOVERNOR SENT FOR ARTHUR BONE.
Bone had been on the point of leaving and was sitting in his coat in the cloakroom, delaying his departure until the rain outside stopped falling. It was another excuse – rain, sleet, snow, wind, anything to keep him away from his empty home.

'What is it?' Bone asked the man who delivered the Governor's message, already guessing what he was about to have confirmed. News of Peter Tait's right of appeal should have been delivered two days earlier, but hadn't come. When Tait had asked him about this, all Bone could do was tell him that no news was good news. It was another prison lie, another cold seed lying on stony ground and waiting for a warm rain that never came.

'Search me,' the man told Bone. 'I'm due off in five. Make your own way.' He looked at Bone sitting in his coat. 'You should have been long gone yourself by now. If you like, I can send word back that you've already left.' He waited for Bone to say something. 'Suit yourself,' he said eventually, and then went.

Bone heard him whistling as he walked along the corridor in the direction of the prison gates.

It had been a week since he'd had a drink with Pye, and the detective had neither returned to the prison nor contacted him in that time.

He took off his coat and checked his tie, collar and jacket before making his way to the Governor's office.

He knocked on the door and the Governor shouted, 'Enter.' Bone went in.

The man was sitting at his desk, signing a succession of sheets of paper. He motioned for Bone to sit down and said he wouldn't be a minute. It was all part of that same, practised order: an unshakeable structure, and every single part of that structure fixed firmly in place.

Five minutes later, the Governor closed a file and said, 'Right. Bone.' He seemed momentarily not to know why Bone was there.

'You sent for me,' Bone said.

'Ah. Yes.' He searched through the papers he had just finished stacking. 'Our man Tait,' he said.

'His appeal.'

'Denied, I'm afraid.' The Governor read silently from the confirmation order. 'No more or less than we expected, eh?' He looked up and waited for Bone to agree with him.

'Twenty-one days, then?' Bone said.

'Fourteen, I'm afraid. We're still under special provision.' He waved the sheet of paper. 'According to this, there were no additional considerations whatsoever to be taken into account that were ever going to allow the appeal to proceed. No new evidence, no additional contest of prosecution testimony, no new police . . . You know the score. How is the boy?'

Bone had seen Tait an hour earlier. 'He seems well enough.

He still doesn't know for certain what happened, and I doubt if—'

'There you go, then – hardly helping himself, is he?'

'No,' Bone said. And all those other men who had shouted and screamed their innocence on the way to the gallows, how exactly had *they* been helping themselves?

'Besides . . .' the Governor said. 'All that part of things is a long way behind us – him – now. Best all round if we start to prepare for what happens next.'

'Right. Of course,' Bone said.

'There was another note,' the Governor said, again searching the pile of papers.

'To do with Tait?'

'Indirectly. Lord Chancellor's office. Asking us to clear the decks.'

'Clear the decks?'

'Unfinished business. Thing is, they might decide to prosecute some of the higher-ranking POWs we've been holding over here, though nobody seems certain at this stage. We just need to be ready, that's all.'

'I imagined the majority of them would be packed straight off home,' Bone said. 'Plenty for them to be getting on with over there, I should imagine.'

'You're not wrong there,' the Governor said. 'Again, not really any of our concern. All I've been asked to do is to ensure my day-to-day paperwork is up to date and that our capacity and availability is as healthy as I can make it. The same instructions will no doubt have gone out to every other Governor in the country. We're all still doing our bit, see?'

Bone saw. 'Do you want me to tell Tait?' he said.

'I'm afraid that's *my* responsibility,' the Governor said. 'As well you know. But I would certainly appreciate you being with me. I thought first thing in the morning. Give him another decent night's sleep, at least.'

'He doesn't seem unduly distressed either way,' Bone said.

'So I'm led to understand. Perhaps that should tell us something.'

'Perhaps,' Bone said, wondering again what he was agreeing to.

'Any visitors. I mean, apart from his—'

'One,' Bone said. 'A friend.'

'Presumably his lawyer will want to see him now that the execution order's been signed.'

Bone doubted this. The book was all but closed on Peter Tait, and everything now could be allowed to settle. 'I suppose so,' he said.

'Everything possible has been done for the man,' the Governor said.

This time Bone said nothing and the Governor looked uncomfortable.

'Don't let me keep you,' he said.

Bone rose from his seat.

'Ten o'clock?' the Governor said. 'I've already spoken to Charles Simpson.' Simpson was the prison chaplain. 'Perhaps you can go to Tait earlier, get him ready, so to speak. I've put you and Lynch down for the watch duties. I imagined it's what you'd want.'

'It is,' Bone said.

'By rights, I ought to have picked a pair of newcomers. Better for Tait. But I knew you'd appreciate the opportunity.'

'Thank you,' Bone said.

'No need for that. We're all human. Guilty or not, he's still some mother's son.'

Not that you'd know it, Bone thought.

'Still no family showed up?'

'None,' Bone said.

'How will he take it, do you think? The news?'

It was a difficult question for Bone to answer. He had undertaken the same duty a dozen times before. 'He seems resigned to his lot,' he said.

'Glad to hear it.'

'He reads his Bible most of the time.'

'There you go, then. Perhaps he's preparing himself. I always say that's half the trick – acceptance.' The man slapped both his palms on his desk and rose from his seat. It was the signal for Bone to leave. 'I appreciate this, Bone,' he said, walking with him to the door.

Arthur, Bone thought. 'Me, too,' he said. 'I'll come in early and make sure everything's ready.'

'No word until I deliver the order,' the Governor said.

'Of course.'

'I see they're decreasing the petrol ration again.' The Governor motioned to his desk.

The remark caught Bone off-guard. 'Sorry, what?'

'The petrol allowance. Ninety miles a month. Bloody ridiculous. Neither use nor ornament to most drivers.'

Bone had never driven a car in his life. 'I don't drive,' he said. The Governor, he knew, had been given a Ministry car for the duration with an additional allowance for his personal use.

'Wise man,' the Governor said. They were at the door. 'Until tomorrow, then.'

Bone left the prison and walked along the Caledonian Road towards the city centre.

Arriving at the Tottenham Court Road station, he asked the desk sergeant if Pye was there, and the man went to find him, returning a few minutes later with Pye beside him.

And just as Bone had immediately understood the exact nature of the Governor's summons an hour earlier, so Ernest Pye understood why Bone was there to see him now.

The two men went outside.

'Drink?' Bone said. Before their brief excursion a week earlier, it had been four years since Bone had last been in a public house.

'Sorry,' Pye said. 'I'm on until midnight.' It was almost seven. 'Has the lad's appeal been thrown out?'

'And the execution notice delivered. I don't suppose . . .'

'This end? Nothing whatsoever. Mulcahy and Colquhoun are sticking to their stories and that's all they need to do.'

'And loosening their own collars, no doubt,' Bone said. 'What about the boy who brought the Bible?'

'It's hardly evidence,' Pye said.

The day after their last meeting, Pye had asked around about the boy with the harelip and had quickly learned his identity and the fact that he worked for Tommy Fowler. It was a connection to Tait, but that was all, nothing unexpected, and certainly evidence of nothing, proof of nothing. He had gone to Archer Street and waited outside the Regency for two hours in the hope of seeing Sweeney, but the boy hadn't shown. A dozen working girls fitting Pye's description of Ruby Nolan had come and gone during that time, but to have approached any of them with his questions would have lost Pye a great deal more than he would ever have gained.

'How long?' he asked Bone.

'Fourteen days. Thirteen, perhaps. The Governor's reading him the notice tomorrow morning. I doubt if anything's going to stop it now.'

'No. Me, too,' Pye said.

'Harelip never came back,' Bone said. 'Though I think I saw the girl again.'

'Oh?' Pye did his best to conceal his interest.

'Yesterday, it was. I saw her standing on the same corner when I came out on my way home.'

'Do you still think she's a working girl?'

Bone shrugged. 'I thought at first that the boy might have returned to see Tait, but I went back in and checked, and he hadn't. She was still there when I came out again.'

'So do you think she might know Tait herself?'

'It was the only conclusion I could come to.'

'Perhaps she was plucking up some kind of courage.'

'By just standing there? Besides, after tomorrow everything changes for Tait. They'll move him to the waiting cells and his visiting orders will be extended. Anybody who wants to see him will get the chance. I'm covering half the watch on him. If anything happens, I'll be the first to know.'

'Perhaps when the girl hears what's about to happen, she'll finally get brave and go in to him. There's no mention of anyone – no girlfriend or even working girl – on his sheets. Still not much of anything, in fact.'

Sensing that Pye was getting ready to leave him and return inside, Bone said, 'It's doing him some good.'

'What is?'

'The Bible he was given.'

'Oh? In what way? There's nothing remotely religious in any of the court papers.'

'He reads it. All the time. Every few minutes, forever picking it up, putting it down, picking it back up again. He's even started quoting to me from it. At first he read from the thing, but now he can quote from it without even looking. I don't know, it all seems somehow a bit too . . .'

'A bit too what?'

'I was going to say that it all seems a bit excessive. He gets over-excited by it.'

'Excited?'

'That's probably the wrong word. But you know what I mean.'

'I think so,' Pye said.

'Perhaps "dependent" would be better.'

'He's not got much else going for him,' Pye said. 'What sort of quotes?'

'All the fire-and-brimstone stuff, the end-of-the-world rubbish, death, plague, doom and destruction, demons and harlots on horseback, all that.'

'Perhaps he already knows what's coming to him and considers it more appropriate,' Pye said.

'That's what I thought at first,' Bone said. 'I told him he ought to be more careful, to start thinking a bit more clearly about what he was doing.'

'You think he should – what? – be praying for forgiveness, searching for some kind of redemption, even?'

'I doubt he even knows what that is,' Bone said. 'Besides, he's still not put his hands up and confessed his guilt.'

'It's why he'll hang,' Pye said.

'I know,' Bone said. 'I've seen the same before, all this

religious stuff – last-minute conversions, proper confessions – but this is – I don't know – this is something different.'

'In what way?'

'I'm not an educated man. But it strikes me he's doing it for something *inside* himself. He doesn't want others to change the way they look at him and think about him. It's more something to do with how *he* looks at things. Does that make any sense to you?'

'I suppose so,' Pye said. 'But perhaps only because he has no family weeping and wailing at his feet. The wife of the man he was convicted of killing wrote to my superiors. She sent a photograph of him and her together with their children. She wanted us to make sure that Tait didn't somehow escape the noose. She rounded off by saying that if justice wasn't done to Tait, then what had the last six years been for?'

'I can understand that,' Bone said.

'Her brother died six months ago in Belgium, and her mother a few years before that in a raid. She wrote that it hardly seemed fair to her for her children to lose their father to a murderer when there were so many other men losing their lives for such a just and noble cause.'

'I can see that, too,' Bone said.

The two of them stood without speaking for a moment. The rain had finally stopped, but water still ran in the gutters.

'I appreciate you telling me all this,' Pye said.

'For what it's worth, what good it'll do him,' Bone said.

'I asked around,' Pye said, feeling the need to reciprocate.

'And?' Bone said.

'I think our harelip boy is called Sweeney.'

'Have you talked to him?'

'He's a messenger boy, that's all. For Tommy Fowler. One

220

word to Sweeney – or the girl, for that matter – and Fowler will hear about it ten minutes later, and that won't be to anyone's benefit.'

Bone resisted saying, 'Including yours?' and said instead, 'I'll tell you one thing – you and your lot are going to have your hands full keeping the lid on that mob – Fowler and all his sort – when this lot is over and done with. A lot of other things might go away, but men like that won't.'

'Tell me something I don't already know,' Pye said. 'All identifying Sweeney really means is that there's a connection between Tait and Fowler.'

'But what you're really saying is "Case closed".'

'Not necessarily,' Pye said, but without conviction. 'But it's a safe bet that Fowler will already know of everything that's happening to Tait.'

'And so all everybody else has to do now is to wait those few days, watch Tait hang, heave a big sigh of relief, and then they can all come out from wherever it is they're hiding and holding their breath. Like I said, "Case closed".'

'Perhaps when Fowler hears about the failed appeal he might send Sweeney back to see Tait,' Pye said.

Bone shook his head. 'Tait said he hardly knew the boy, that he'd seen him around, that's all.'

'And the girl?'

'Never seen her, never even heard of her. According to Tait, it's widely known that's how Fowler makes a big part of his living. I doubt if I have to spell it out for you.'

'They're decent enough girls, some of them,' Pye said.

'If you say so,' Bone said. 'Though I'd hardly use the word "decent".'

Pye knew he had disappointed the man, that Bone had

expected much more from him. And if not in any practical sense so late in the day, then the man had at least expected Pye to share a measure of hope with him.

'You must have known that it was likely to come to this all along,' he said.

'I suppose I did,' Bone admitted. 'I could probably tell you with my hand on my heart that ninety-nine out of a hundred convicted and condemned killers get exactly what they deserve – less, in some cases.'

'They'll repeal the death penalty one day,' Pye said.

'I very much doubt that,' Bone said. 'After all this blood-letting and with everything that's yet to come? Not in our lifetime, they won't.'

'And that other man, the hundredth?' Pye said.

'Exactly,' Bone said. 'What about *him*?'

'What time was the girl there?' Pye said.

'Same time she was waiting there for this Sweeney character. End of afternoon visiting. Why? Do you think she'll be back?'

Pye shrugged. Even if she did return to stand outside the prison, it still wouldn't mean anything. And at the slightest suggestion that she was being watched, she would probably disappear faster than Sweeney already appeared to have done.

'I could look out for her,' Bone suggested.

'And then what?'

'I could let you know.'

'And then the pair of us could go round and round in circles forever afterwards,' Pye said.

'Or for the next thirteen days, at least,' Bone said, immediately indicating to Pye that he regretted the remark and all it implied concerning Pye's involvement now.

'Whatever happens, you certainly wouldn't be doing Tait much good by raising his hopes without good reason,' Pye said. 'There won't be any reprieve, not now; we both know that.'

'If you say so.'

And again it seemed an uncharacteristically cold rebuke for Bone to make, leaving Pye feeling uncomfortable in the man's presence.

'I mean it,' Pye said. 'Even if you do see the girl again, leave her well alone. Perhaps she was looking for Sweeney. Perhaps she doesn't even have the first idea who Tait is.'

'Perhaps,' Bone said.

Both men stepped to one side to let a horse and cart pass them by.

'I ought to be getting back in,' Pye said, motioning to the doorway. 'Like I said, I appreciate you telling me all this.' He held out his hand to Bone and Bone did the same.

'Funny thing,' Bone said absently as they shook. 'Listening to the lad reading like that – all that death-and-destruction, Sodom-and-Gomorrah stuff – it made me dig my own Bible out. My wife's, really. She used to keep it in the wardrobe. Her mother's before her, and *her* mother's before that. They all wrote their names in it. I needed a magnifying glass to read the thing. I found the same pages and passages Tait was reading and then memorizing. I'd never been much of a man for church and all that – especially not after my wife – well – but it seems to me now as though there's a lot of sense in it. If you know where to look, that is. A lot of sense. Especially in light of all our own recent revelations and discoveries.'

'I can't say I've ever . . .' Pye began to say.

'As you know, we imagined at first that somebody was trying to send some sort of message or threat in to Tait.'

'And what – you think now that the Bible itself is the message?'

'I do,' Bone said confidently. 'And if you'd heard Tait reading and reciting the thing, then you'd begin to see that it was what *he* believed, too.'

Pye didn't know how to respond to this, and so he simply said, 'I see,' and then turned and went back into the station.

19

SILVER LET HIMSELF INTO CROWLEY'S ROOM. HE HAD knocked and there had been no answer. It was already late morning, and it was unusual for the near-nocturnal Crowley not to be at home at this time. He was most likely still asleep, drugged and unresponsive beneath the blankets and eiderdowns he piled on his bed. It always amused Silver to see how many of these there now were, giving Crowley's bedroom the appearance of some kind of woodland-dwelling creature's den, mounded and cushioned. The scatter of clothes, books and other paraphernalia around the high, solid bed only added to this impression. Some days, especially in the room's perpetual gloom, it was impossible to tell if the bed was occupied or not. Often, the only indication of this would be the sound of Crowley snoring from beneath the mound. That, and the room's usual brew of endlessly replenished odours.

Now the first thing Silver saw as he came into the room was Crowley slumped in his chair, fully clothed and completely silent and unmoving. Silver's immediate response at seeing this was to remain completely silent himself and to stay where he stood. He pulled the door quietly shut behind him and continued watching.

Unusually, the curtains were open and the room was filled with light. It was more common for Crowley to leave them drawn until at least the early afternoon, even when he himself was up and moving around. It was how he had always lived, Crowley insisted. The half-light, he said, was more conducive to thought and contemplation.

Silver looked closely at Crowley's chest, searching for the slightest of movements through the layers of clothing. He knew that Crowley had not been out the previous evening, and that he had said he was coming directly home when the two of them had parted earlier in the afternoon.

Silver coughed slightly and said Crowley's name.

There was no answer.

He went closer to the chair and saw the bottle and two glasses there. He looked around for Crowley's pill boxes. There were a dozen of these – each with its specific contents, and each with some small ritual or other attached to its use – scattered amid the room's other detritus. Some were full and some were empty, and there were many in between. Although he had once tried to keep up with Crowley's current medication – prescribed and otherwise – Silver had found this increasingly difficult. There were pills and medicines for Crowley's heart, his lungs and his liver; for his gout and his diabetes and his various digestive complaints. In the few years he had known him, Silver himself had diagnosed Crowley's bronchitis, pleurisy and myocardial degeneration. He knew that Crowley was again injecting a solution of heroin – he admitted to using ten grains a day – and that his preferred way of taking this was with alcohol, brandy for preference, followed by buttered biscuits and warm milk. And it was knowing this that caused Silver to look more closely at the bottle on the table beside Crowley now. He had frequently watched Crowley heat up his powders in the glasses and then draw them into a syringe, watching with growing excitement as his own blood coloured the solution.

Four months earlier, during a month spent in Hastings, Crowley had sworn that the heroin was finally behind him – that he was finished with all the drugs to which he had 'attuned' himself over his long life – the heroin, cocaine, morphine, opium, hashish, ether, sparteine and an even greater variety of hallucinogens. A combination of morphine, opium and sparteine had long been Crowley's favourite mixture – his 'tincture mirabilis' – and the closest he himself believed he had ever come to freeing his soul by pharmaceutical means alone.

The two glasses were empty. Silver moved silently closer, picked them up and sniffed at them. A visitor? Unlikely. More likely that Crowley had used both glasses. The same way he always insisted on being given a clean glass or cup in the few remaining cafés and restaurants where he and Silver could still afford to eat, and where, as they ate, Silver surreptitiously checked his own thin wallet as the bill came ever closer.

Then Silver looked elsewhere in the room. The fire was long out. In other rooms, in other houses, where the heating had been by gas fire, Crowley had frequently fallen asleep and left the gas on until the meter had run out. Silver had warned him of the poisonous fumes which sometimes filled the unventilated rooms when this happened, but Crowley had never listened to him. Or had listened and then laughed at his friend's concern. And when this happened, Silver invariably heard the coming mockery of the hostile press, the collective, well-honed scorn of the waiting obituary-writers.

He went past Crowley to the window and looked out. The late spring was finally here and people were moving about again. The year was being reborn – the world in its entirety was being reborn – and people understood this and seized whatever benefit or pleasure it brought them. Silver considered opening the window and letting some of that same warm, invigorating air into the stale room.

When he turned back, he saw that Crowley's eyes were now open and that Crowley was watching him closely. There was a smile on his lips.

'Did you imagine this poor, worn-out body passed over, or whatever it is they insist on saying these over-mawkish days?' Crowley said to him. He picked up the two empty glasses and tipped them one at a time to his lips.

'They're empty,' Silver said, careful to conceal his relief that Crowley was still alive. 'I checked.'

'I imagine you did,' Crowley said. He held the bowl of the second glass to his face and breathed deeply.

'What is it?' Silver asked him, wondering now if Crowley's immobility and silence hadn't all been part of a deliberate deceit on his part.

'I had a visitor,' Crowley said.

'Oh? I didn't—'

'Followed by a dream of my lost sister.'

'Sister?' Silver said. In addition to the faint smell of the cheap whisky, Silver now detected that the room held something of another scent, and at first he imagined this to be the remnants of the Egyptian incense that Crowley sometimes burned when the occasion warranted it. He had acquired several years' supply of this before the war started and the Mediterranean had become its sunny battleground.

A tarnished copper pot beside his bed contained the last of his stock.

Crowley breathed deeply again. 'My sister, Grace Mary Elizabeth. She died when she was five hours old. She might have been my one true companion through life. I myself was five years old. She and I might have grown up and then old together.'

'I had no idea,' Silver said, wondering why Crowley had never mentioned the short-lived child before.

'Five hours. A short life, but a life nonetheless. A life into which there was sufficient time to arrive, and from which to depart.'

It struck Silver as a strange and convoluted remark to make, but he was used to this by now, and so he said nothing. 'You said you had a visitor.'

'So I did. Strangest thing. A strange young woman who approached me in the street. And do you know, for an instant I was reminded of a parlour maid – parlour maid, chamber maid; they all came and went – in Herne Hill when I was sixteen. She cannot have been much more than five feet tall – she looked like a girl of ten, but with everything in proportion and with full, ripe breasts and the darkest nipples.'

'I don't wish to hear it,' Silver said. He knew the story was unlikely to be another of Crowley's concoctions; sometimes he remembered perfectly.

'No?' Crowley said. 'Then I shall wring all the pleasure from the distant memory solely for myself.'

'Who was she? The girl yesterday.'

'My physicians always told me that I myself had large breasts. For a man, that is. Even in my slender and vigorous prime. Large breasts. I hoped at first that what they meant was muscles, but what they meant was breasts. Shrunken somewhat now.' He cupped his hands to his chest.

'The girl,' Silver said, sensing evasion in all this diversion, and becoming suspicious of what Crowley was keeping from him.

Crowley closed his eyes for a moment before answering, perhaps trying to bring the girl more clearly to mind.

'She approached me under the guise of offering to support me. The slightest suggestion from me and she followed me in here and shared a drink with me.'

'The two glasses,' Silver said.

'I wasted nothing of any value on her.'

As though there had been anything of any value to have given her in the first place. 'Did you imagine she was a tart, a thief perhaps?'

'At first – no, not even then. She approached me and asked me if I needed help. I exaggerated my breathlessness at seeing her watching me.'

'Of course you did,' Silver said, relaxing a little. 'Along with your stiffness and exhaustion and racing heart.'

The two men shared a smile at this. The women always miscalculated their appeal or overestimated their charms, and Crowley did likewise with his own faded appeal and current capabilities.

'I'm nothing if not the consummate performer,' Crowley said.

'Go on,' Silver said. The man was like an old and unreliable actor, alone on the stage and with no one watching, but still constrained to continue going through the motions because he could not do otherwise.

'From the instant she approached me, I felt a certain

connection, a frisson – I can put it no more succinctly or accurately than that.'

'A frisson?' It was a new one on Silver.

'Something – something I used to feel all those years ago when I was exercising the full extent of my powers. In the Golden Dawn and in Cefalu. Especially in Cefalu.'

'*Don't,*' Silver said sharply. He had heard too many lurid tales of Cefalu.

'Oh, especially in Cefalu, when Jane and Leah were both there with me. Those two and all the other, lesser followers.'

'Please,' Silver said.

Crowley stopped talking. 'Forgive me.'

'Talk of the Golden Dawn, if you must,' Silver said. 'But let's give that place and everything that happened there a miss, for pity's sake.'

'Most of which was fabricated by Horatio Bottomley and his scapegoating bully-boys.'

'I don't care,' Silver said. 'I'd just prefer not to have to hear you going over that same old ground again. For your own sake as much as mine. It was Cefalu that led you to where you are today.'

Crowley heard the honest nature of this plea and acceded to it. 'I felt she *knew* me,' he said, looking as surprised by the remark as Silver was.

'Perhaps she did,' Silver suggested. 'A lot of young women read those kinds of stories these days. Perhaps she's seen your picture in one of her magazines.'

'And she recognized me looking like this?' Crowley said. 'Looking like what I have allowed myself to become? Hardly.'

There was nothing Silver could say to this. 'Or perhaps she simply had a kind heart and took pity on you.'

231

Crowley doubted this. 'I felt it when she held my arm,' he said. 'And then when she helped me up the stairs and into this chair.'

'All of which you are perfectly capable of achieving un-assisted.' *Or with my help.*

Crowley smiled at this. 'It would have been ungallant of me to have refused her offer of assistance.'

Silver shook his head. *Ungallant?* 'Then perhaps you reminded her of her grandfather,' he said. 'Or her great-grandfather.'

'Perhaps you're right,' Crowley said. 'But whatever it was, I still *felt* it. You know well enough by now that I'm a man governed by instinct, and—'

'And unresisted impulses.'

'And that I trust that instinct above all else.'

'And so your instinct told you what?'

Crowley shrugged. 'Merely that there was *something.*'

'You'll be telling me next that you believe she was *sent* to you.' He hoped Crowley might laugh at the suggestion.

But all Crowley said was, 'And would that be so ridiculous, so out of the question or unbelievable?'

'I give up,' Silver said.

'You think I'm going to embarrass you further with more talk of my various other scarlet women,' Crowley said.

'It had occurred to me,' Silver said. 'Besides, how can this one—'

'With talk of Lady Babalon, the Consort of the Beast? Or perhaps in her incarnation as Shakti, partner of Shiva, the pair of them locked in the eternal embrace of everlasting physical and spiritual orgasm?'

Silver shook his head at the words. 'You no longer shock

me,' he said. 'But what *would* surprise me is if you were now to ascribe even the slightest or least of those qualities – your quest for this scarlet woman to be your partner in eternity – to this chance and passing – and probably forgotten – encounter in the street. She herself will almost certainly have no intention of returning to you. I daresay *she* felt no ... no ...'

'Frisson?'

'Exactly.'

'Perhaps you're right,' Crowley said, but again he doubted this, and he left this doubt plain for Silver to see.

Then something occurred to Silver. 'I brought you this,' he said, and he took a folded newspaper from his pocket and laid it in Crowley's lap. 'Page seven.'

Crowley turned the pages until he was once again looking at the condemned man, Tait.

'His right to appeal his sentence has been denied and the date of his hanging confirmed.'

'There was never any chance of it being otherwise,' Crowley said matter-of-factly, and then read the short article beneath the doomed face. 'He killed someone. These are strange times, Joshua, and times of strange reversals. How on earth are men ever going to live with themselves, knowing what outrages they have inflicted upon each other, if they cannot point to these fine and delicate matters of morality and law and order and say to the world, "See, all this is still in its proper place and working perfectly well"? "See, look, all these checks and balances and tally sheets that we otherwise hold so dear and set such store by – these are all still working properly and being properly observed and regulated." What, say, are ten thousand lost men, women and children in a forest pit with a bullet in their skulls compared to this, compared to the machinery of the law and its carefully woven tapestries of rectitude and responsibility? This Tait is their – *our* – example. He will hang because he is a murderer, and even if there do remain doubts as to his guilt, he will still hang because his death will serve the greater good and the greater purpose of all those fine and moral men who have momentarily lost their footing.'

And hearing Crowley speak so forcibly and with such conviction, Silver was more convinced than ever that an *innocent* man – an innocent sacrifice – would far better suit his scheme now. 'I suppose you can at least schedule the remainder of whatever it is you have to do a little more precisely,' he said.

'Schedule?' Crowley smiled at the word. 'Yes, I daresay I might.'

Another thought occurred to Silver. 'Or perhaps now that the thing is already underway, perhaps you believe that that's the reason *why* his right of appeal has been refused.'

'Perhaps,' Crowley said. He looked up from the paper and directly at Silver. 'I've told you – while ever you offer your assistance in the matter, I won't lie to you.'

'Then at least keep silent in all this talk of women.' He shook his head at the scrambled words.

'My whores and tarts and thieves?'

'Your whores and tarts and thieves.'

Silver went to that part of the room that served as a kitchen and searched for the teapot and cups.

And the instant Joshua Silver's back was turned, Crowley again inhaled deeply from the glass he still held. He touched the rim of this to his lower lip and then drew back at the slightest touch of the glass and let out a small, involuntary cry.

Hearing this, Silver turned. 'What is it?'

'Cramp,' Crowley told him. 'In my leg.' He patted his thigh.

'You don't say,' Silver said. 'Perhaps it will teach you something about sleeping in a chair in the cold.'

'An old dog like me?' Crowley said. 'I doubt it.' And again waiting until Silver's attention was elsewhere, he quickly ran his tongue around the rim of the glass and then held it at arm's length, angling it into the sunlight starting to show at the window.

20

Tommy Fowler sat alone in his office. At the unexpected appearance of Frankie Doll, he slid shut his drawer and put both his hands palm down on the table.

'The Granville on Albemarle Street's been raided,' Tommy Fowler said. 'Plus four counts of immoral. That's the Piccadilly on Denman Street, the Rupert Street club and those two houses in Gloucester Place and Norfolk Square. All in the space of a fucking fortnight. I'm telling you, Frankie, somebody's got it in for us. What's this world coming to?' He stopped talking and considered Frankie Doll in the doorway. 'You want to see me? You coming in, or what?'

Frankie Doll remained where he stood. It was probably as brave as he'd ever been in the presence of Tommy Fowler.

'What is it?' Tommy Fowler said. 'You look a troubled man, Dolly. What troubles does a man like you have? None – that's what. All you've got to worry about are your girls, taking proper care of them, picking up your fees and then making sure the right percentage of those finds its way to your Uncle Tommy here. What's so troubling about any of that?' He laughed at this and then beckoned Frankie Doll into the room. 'Come in and sit down, Frankie. You're making me nervous standing there like that.'

Frankie Doll went in to him and sat down. After all those years, he knew the exact limits of Tommy Fowler's patience and humour. *He knows why I'm here*, Frankie Doll thought to himself.

'Tell me,' Tommy Fowler said.

'Somebody beat Laura up.' Each word felt drier than the last in Frankie Doll's mouth.

'Laura? Remind me.' Tommy Fowler watched him closely for a second, and then said, 'Oh, *Laura – your* Laura. Right. I always warned you about making these things personal, Frankie. Business and pleasure, and all that. Besides, I thought everything had been taken care of. Just some kid, according to her. Tell you I got word, did she? Tell you I was straight round there – in the complete and utter fucking absence of you, I might add – to help get things sorted out for her?'

'It occurred to me that you might have known who it was,' Frankie Doll said. 'All I need is a name and I can sort things out myself.'

Tommy Fowler shook his head. 'No need. Like I already told you – and like I don't really want to have to tell you again, Frankie – I already sorted it out.'

'She said you spoke to him. In here.' Frankie Doll's bravery knew no bounds now.

'I speak to a lot of people. Incidentally, and before I forget, I'm closing the knocking shops on Hereford Road and up on Warrington Crescent. Temporary measures. Maida Vale's always been a bit too far out for my liking. City boy, that's me. It should cut down on your rounds, save you money on shoe leather. And Billy Leach has let it be known that he might be interested in taking the Bayswater set-up off my hands. I'm seeing him later. Sorry, where were we?'

It was the cue for Frankie Doll to say, 'Nowhere,' and then to forget he'd ever mentioned Laura.

Instead, he said, 'Billy Leach?'

Tommy Fowler pretended to search his pockets, finally pulling out a packet of cigarettes and a box of matches. He offered one to Frankie Doll, which he took.

'Look, this Laura business – I can see you're concerned for the brass. All I'm saying is that whatever happened happened, and that now it's all over and done with. Believe me, none of us will see that little runt in here again.'

'If you say so,' Frankie Doll said.

'Oh, I do,' Tommy Fowler said. 'I definitely say so. I give you my word on that particular score. You and me still friends?'

Frankie Doll nodded.

'Good. Because I'd hate for things to get confused. There's enough confusion in the world as it is without you and me adding to it. Shake.' He held his hand across the table and Frankie Doll took it.

But Frankie Doll wasn't stupid. He knew that Billy Leach had been mentioned deliberately – most likely to let him know that Tommy Fowler had already given some thought to what Laura might have told Frankie Doll about her assailant and to all the connections he was now starting to make.

'In fact, you can do me a big favour and go and see old Billy for me as soon as. It's a nice gaff, the Bayswater house; I want to keep him keen. I need somebody I can trust.'

Another sop. 'You've trusted me so far,' Frankie Doll said, but with a cold edge, and wondering even as he said it if he was already wandering beyond the boundary of Tommy Fowler's patience.

'So I have, Frankie boy, so I have, and long may it last. But what I *don't* need is somebody turning up at Billy Leach's to transact my business whose head is filled with all sorts of other stuff. Stuff that has nothing whatsoever to do with the matter at hand.'

Frankie Doll nodded.

'All I'm saying is that it might cloud your judgement when I need you to keep a clear head and a close eye on things.'

'I hear what you're saying,' Frankie Doll said. Oh, he heard all right.

'We go back a long way, you and me, Frankie,' Tommy Fowler said.

'Three years,' Frankie Doll said. Three years, four months.

'Is that all? I could swear it was longer. I remember the day I took you in, took you on board.'

'Just after you had that thing at the Ritz in Horsham,' Frankie Doll said.

Tommy Fowler thought for a moment. 'Oh, that? That's right – you was in on that, wasn't you?'

Frankie Doll had splashed the petrol around and then thrown in the burning rags.

'Bad affair that, everything got a bit messy then, as I remember. Woman got herself badly burned. Place was supposed to be empty, and yet there she was. Lost the use of an arm, if memory serves.' It sounded exactly like the threat it was intended to sound like, and it was where the last of Frankie Doll's faltering bravery finally abandoned him.

'And after that, the Hippodrome in Rotherhithe and the two Regals in Farnham and Norwood. You were a good little worker right from the start. I do like to remember an obligation, Frankie.'

And again, Frankie Doll heard exactly what Tommy Fowler was telling him.

'But it still seems longer than three years. I suppose that's the war for you. All this sweeping-on-to-victory stuff. You ought to tell Laura to get a bit of cake on her face and to start making hay again while the sun's still shining. Summer's coming up. And after that, it's anybody's bet what will happen. According to all my sources, things are going to get cold and dark and hard again. Cold and dark and hard – and we've all got to take account of that and get ourselves ready for it. You've only got to listen to these know-it-all politicians to know that the peace is hardly going to be a picnic.' He paused and smiled. 'So – we on?'

'For . . . ?'

'For that little visit to Billy Leach.' Tommy Fowler reached into his pocket, took out his wallet and pulled a five-pound note from it. 'Give that to the girl. Don't even tell her where it came from. Tell her it's from you. And let no man say that Tommy Fowler doesn't look after his valued employees. Go on – take it. Give it to her or treat her yourself with it.'

'There's no need,' Frankie Doll said, knowing even as he picked up the note that all further discussion of what had happened to Laura was out of bounds. What mattered now, he knew, was the connection to Billy Leach.

Tommy Fowler waited. 'Like I said, it's hard days ahead. Perhaps we're all going to have to change the way we do business. Consolidation – apparently, that's the name of the game. That's why I want this little Bayswater deal to run smooth. Consolidation and specialization. Business talk. It's everywhere you look these days. Mumbo-jumbo, most of it, but it *sounds* right and it gives the right impression. You ready for the off now?'

'Off?'

'Billy Leach's place. Jesus Christ, Frankie, at least *try* to keep up.'

Frankie Doll rose from where he sat. 'I'll go now,' he said, wondering how he had allowed himself to be so swiftly and completely outmanoeuvred by Fowler and then patted back into shape.

'Bad news for the boy Tait, I see,' Tommy Fowler said to him as he approached the door.

And yet again, Frankie Doll sensed that he was being watched for his response. The condemned boy Crowley had been to see Fowler about. Apart from that, he hadn't heard anything about Tait except what he saw in the papers. And somewhere in all of that was yet another connection to what was happening now.

'Right of appeal denied,' Tommy Fowler said. 'They'll take him for a drop.'

'I never really knew him,' Frankie Doll said.

'Vicious little bugger. Good riddance all round, you ask me.'

'I suppose so,' Frankie Doll said.

'One last thing before I let you get off,' Tommy Fowler said.

'Go on.'

'That little Irish tart. According to a few of the other girls, she hasn't shown her face for a good few nights now. You wouldn't happen to have heard anything, would you?'

Frankie Doll pretended to think. 'I hardly even spoke to her,' he said. And Laura had told him she'd last seen Ruby Nolan with Sweeney. If it *was* all starting to add up to something, then Frankie Doll was still uncertain what that something was.

'I just wondered if she'd perhaps decided to take advantage of my good nature and branch out on her own. And we can't have that happening, can we? She probably thinks the world owes her a better living than she's making right now, and she's off to see what she can do about it. There's a lot of them like that these days. It just means that people like me have got to be more on our toes than usual. You see what I'm saying, Frankie? Tommy Fowler, a soft touch, losing his girls. First his girls, and then his grip. I can't have that nasty little rumour getting about, now can I? Tommy Fowler, losing his grip? It's a forest full of wolves out there, Frankie boy. One little whisper like that and you never know who's behind the next tree waiting to pounce. All I'm saying is for you to keep your eyes and your shell-likes peeled for me.'

'Will do,' Frankie Doll said.

'Right, back to the business at hand – Billy Leach. First off, tell him the Bayswater thing is still waiting for his signature. Then you can mention the Paddington house to him.'

'Norfolk Square?'

'That's the one. We've already had a sit-down so he knows the score. All I need for you to do, Frankie, is to read the signs – read the signs and let me know where I stand. Either he's serious or he isn't.'

'I'll know,' Frankie Doll said.

'It's why I'm sending you. And after all that, you can tell him that that other little bit of business out Billericay way has been sorted out and settled. He'll know what you're talking about. No need for me to go into all the ins and outs here and now.'

So, presumably, Tommy Fowler didn't know Laura had heard the place mentioned. Or that she had already told him, Frankie Doll, what she had heard.

'Just tell him to be patient,' Tommy Fowler said. 'Not long now; a couple of weeks at the outside. Tell him to keep a firm hand at his end.'

Frankie Doll waited for more. 'Is that it?'

'It's enough to be going on with,' Tommy Fowler said.

'I'll be away, then.'

'And I'd appreciate knowing it all went well,' Tommy Fowler said. 'Later, back here.'

Meaning the Billericay business, because as far as Frankie Doll could see, the Bayswater and Norfolk Square business was nothing, a cover, a smokescreen. 'A couple of hours should do it,' he said.

'No rush, take your time. You're an asset, that's what you are, Frankie, an asset. Perhaps with all these coming changes, it might be time for me to reconsider your own position in the business. Shame not to be able to capitalize on all your skills and capabilities. That's more business spiel, by the way. Like it?'

'It sounds good,' Frankie Doll said. It was three days since he'd seen Julian Beazley in Holywell Street, a week since he had seen Ruby Nolan in the street on her way to the Cumberland, and four days since Sweeney had been Fowler's golden boy and chosen ahead of him. And yet to hear Tommy Fowler talk now, you'd think it was just him and Frankie Doll running the whole shebang between them.

'You still here?' Tommy Fowler said, interrupting all these vaporous, forming thoughts and connections.

'On my way,' Frankie Doll said.

'Good boy,' Tommy Fowler said. 'I knew I could depend on you.'

It was a sharp and precisely placed blade, and Frankie Doll felt every invisible, slender inch of it.

21

ERNEST PYE WAITED FOR AN HOUR ON THREE CONSECUTIVE days opposite the prison entrance without seeing anyone resembling the girl Arthur Bone had described to him. It was a tenuous connection, he knew, and he was there on the off chance. He avoided all contact with Bone during that time, careful to avoid being seen by any of the other warders who might recognize him as they came and went from the prison. In turn, Bone had not returned to the Tottenham Court Road station.

And on the fourth day, five days after Bone himself had last seen her, Pye saw the girl fitting his description. It helped that he knew exactly where to look for her. And there she was again, on the corner of Wheelwright Street, simply standing and looking at the prison.

She was younger than Pye had expected, and certainly more innocent-looking. He had been stationed at Tottenham Court Road for twenty-four years now; he had an eye for these things.

Pye kept his distance, standing amid a group of half a dozen others, all waiting for emerging visitors. It was a common sight outside the prison, where visits were limited and journeys uncertain.

Pye had already learned from the prison that Tait had had no other visitors in those past few days, not even his lawyer, and certainly not the Sweeney boy. And so whatever the girl's reason for remaining outside, it was not due to restricted numbers.

A great deal about her intrigued Pye, but uppermost in his mind was the hope that she might somehow play a part in helping to prove Tait's innocence, and that, ultimately – somehow – the guilty man might still be found and brought to justice. And this, in due course, though in an equally uncertain and, as yet, unknowable manner, would inflict its own measure of pain on Tommy Fowler, the killer of Pye's partner.

It was another convoluted and shifting equation, and one that, as Pye understood only too well, was dependent on far too many uncertainties at each stage of its unravelling. But there was nothing else; it was all Pye had. That, and his instinct for justice. And even he knew that the legal process ticking down towards Tait's execution in ten days' time was unlikely to be interrupted or diverted without considerably more than Pye's instincts and hunches.

And as if all of this wasn't enough for Pye to have to understand and somehow manipulate to his own ends, the girl presented him with yet another dilemma. Should he approach her directly and tell her everything he knew and suspected? Or would his cause be better served by following her and seeing where she led him? Approach her directly and she might deny everything he suggested to her. Avoid confronting her now and perhaps another four days – longer – might pass before she reappeared.

As far as Pye could remember, very few men had ever

had their sentence of death commuted within the final fortnight of waiting. And then only as the result of a vigorous and committed police investigation working alongside a determined lawyer, and with everything wreathed in an equally determined and noisy public outcry on behalf of the condemned man. And Tait had none of those things, and nor was he likely to get them. As far as the waiting, watching world was concerned, it had far bigger and more important things to watch out for and wait for than the death of a man like Peter Tait.

Pye watched the girl, noting how she occasionally stepped back and forth from the wall against which she leaned. She didn't appear to be searching the emerging visitors for anyone she knew. She had come first with Sweeney, Tommy Fowler's messenger boy; and on the second occasion, as now, she had come alone. Sweeney had led her there, that was all. It surely meant something; at the very least it meant that Sweeney was not her *reason* for coming. It meant that she was there because of someone in the prison – Tait, presumably – but if that was the case, then why didn't she go in to see him? Especially now. God knows, the boy had no one else who cared anything for him. And yet here *she* was, three times in ten days, and not once even letting Tait know she was there. Was she another of Fowler's messengers who lost her nerve at the last moment and then went back to Fowler and told him she'd delivered whatever message he'd sent? There had been no more deliveries to Tait; the Bible was still the only thing. And Sweeney, presumably, having made his delivery and then disappeared, was nothing *more* than Fowler's errand boy; someone, ultimately, as disposable as Peter Tait had all too obviously now become to Fowler.

The way the girl stood, the way she held herself. Despite her looks, she was a working girl, Pye was certain of that; but she wasn't working now. And as far as Pye knew, Sweeney wasn't another of Fowler's pimps, or even running the girl under his own steam on Fowler's time. Too young and too inexperienced, and lacking every bit of the savvy and know-how he would need to operate independently and do anything other than jump every time Fowler shouted 'Jump'.

The girl lit a cigarette and walked to the kerb. She looked up at the prison wall and the roofs and high windows beyond, and then she went back to the wall, against which she sheltered from the slight wind.

Pye examined the departing visitors. Perhaps she was waiting to follow another of them, just as he was waiting to follow her.

Or perhaps – and against all Pye's instincts – Peter Tait had nothing whatsoever to do with her and her watchful presence there.

After a few minutes the emerging visitors had dispersed and the street was empty and only the girl remained. Pye felt suddenly exposed, and so he too started walking away from the entrance, hoping he was moving in the direction the girl herself would soon follow.

He walked to the nearest bus shelter and studied the timetable.

The girl followed him. At her approach, Pye asked a woman already in the shelter how long he would have to wait for a bus towards Oxford Street. She told him she didn't know, she lived in Chalk Farm – besides, the timetables were worthless these days. Pye made sure he was still talking to her as the girl passed close behind him and carried on walking. Pye told the woman he'd walk and she told him to suit himself.

He kept thirty or forty yards behind the girl, occasionally crossing the Caledonian Road to walk on the far side from her, alert to all the approaching junctions, and watching her reflection in the shop windows where he paused to feign an interest in whatever was on display.

Police work, detecting: it was what he was good at and what he enjoyed. No form-filling; no rules and regulations that couldn't be sidestepped or bent one way or another; no permissions requested, awaited, received and acted upon. Just a detective and a suspect and everything vital and predictable that bound the two of them together. All these invisible wires and currents, signals and calculations. Pye would follow her, and the girl wouldn't even know he existed. Hunter and hunted, arrow and target. Each step he took demanded another calculation from Pye, and he relished every one of them. This was the work – albeit undertaken unofficially now – that nourished and sustained Ernest Pye; it was his beating heart.

Equally, of course, he was in no doubt what would happen to him if any of this unofficial detective work was ever to come to the attention of his superiors. But here, now, following the girl simply to see where she led him, none of that mattered to Pye, and he was eager to set out along the uncertain path into the mapless terrain ahead of him.

Eventually, the girl turned back on herself and then ran to another bus stop just as a bus arrived there. Pye ran after her, and sat in a seat by the open doorway as the girl went upstairs. He showed the conductress his warrant card and, keeping his voice low, told her he was just going on duty. He was unable to hear the girl asking for her destination. Mostly, these days, people just handed over the exact fare and said nothing. It had been almost three years since the inspector riots, when Pye himself had been called out to empty a busload of fare-less travellers returning from the shelters to their lost and ruined homes in Belvedere and Charlton. After that, no one without their full fare had ever been evicted and the rules had been relaxed.

The bus made its way past King's Cross, then on towards St Giles Circus, where it turned along Oxford Street. At every stop, especially when he heard footsteps above him, Pye watched the stairs for the descending girl.

She appeared finally as the bus reached Marble Arch and then turned north again. Wherever she was going now, it had been a long journey just to stand and stare at a prison wall.

The girl stood on the platform and then stepped off while the bus was still slowly moving. No one else got off with her, and so Pye waited before standing up and getting off as the bus finally stopped at the corner of Seymour Street. He saw her waiting where she had alighted and soon caught up with her.

She caught a second bus as far as South Kensington Tube, and again Pye sat downstairs while she went up, and then alighted fifty yards further on from her.

Sweeney's address was given in his records as Beaufort Street, off the Fulham Road, so perhaps she was going to him. Wherever she was headed, she certainly wasn't returning to Tommy Fowler and Archer Street.

Pye followed her along Fulham Road. She stopped only once, going into a newsagent's and emerging with what looked like a bottle wrapped in newspaper. Pye made a note of the shop's name. Under other circumstances, he would have gone in immediately and confronted the shopkeeper. But now he didn't have time for that.

She finally turned into Beaufort Street, and Pye knew that at last he had something – again it was evidence of nothing, and it proved even less, but it was something. She might have been sent to the prison with Sweeney by Tommy Fowler, but here she was returning to Sweeney of her own accord, and after her own seemingly pointless vigil.

Pye crossed the road and followed her more closely. The trees were already in leaf and cast half the street into shadow, and walkers came and went beneath them.

Sweeney lived at number eighty-four. It was where the girl had now stopped.

Pye paused opposite her and shielded his face to light a cigarette. She was watching the house, appearing to be making up her mind about something, clearly hesitant about approaching the door any more closely, let alone knocking at it. It was clear to Pye that she did not live there herself.

It was growing noticeably cooler and she wore only a thin jacket and a skirt to her knees.

After a few minutes of this hesitation, she finally went to the door and rang one of the bells, immediately stepping back from the porch to look up at the building.

Pye looked where she looked, but saw nothing. No lights came on, no window was opened, and no one appeared and called down to her. She went back to the door and rang again.

Pye cursed his luck. It was something – she had gone from the prison to Sweeney's home, but that was all. It was some-thing, but not much, and certainly not as much as it might have been. Pye might now legitimately approach Sweeney and ask him about the girl, and, following on from that, about their shared journey to see Tait. But that was all. And even that might not get him much further along that rough and unmarked road of his as yet tenuous connections.

He watched her more closely now, certain that he could not be seen by her in the thickening shade of the trees, and just as he had convinced himself that she was about to leave and walk away, she returned to the door and rang again.

This time, an upper window opened and an older woman appeared and looked down. The girl stepped back from the porch to reveal herself. The woman called to ask who was there and the girl shouted 'Me' up to her. So the woman, whoever *she* was, definitely knew her. Pye's rope was holding by a thread.

'What do *you* want?' the woman called down, the hostility in her voice clear.

The girl shouted up that she was looking for Sweeney, and hearing the name on her lips was enough for Ernest Pye to whisper 'Bingo' to himself. It was clear to him that the woman did not want to let her in.

'He's out, at work,' the woman called down.

'Say "At the Regency",' Pye said to himself. 'Say "He's with Tommy Fowler, taking care of that Pentonville business."'

'I could wait for him,' the girl called up, but with little real hope in her voice.

The woman laughed at her. '*You?* You'd rob him blind. Besides, he never said anything about expecting you round again.'

Again.

'Apart from which, you *knew* he was at work, you must have done. He's always at work at this time. It's where you should be. *Work?* That's a laugh.'

Everything the woman said convinced Pye that his four days of waiting were finally getting him somewhere.

'You're doing this on purpose,' the girl shouted up.

'Of *course* I'm doing it on bloody purpose, you stupid tart,' the woman said, laughing.

'It's freezing down here.'

'No, it's not. It's you – you're displaying your assets and paying the price. Besides, do you think it's any warmer up here? You've been in that room, you know what it's like.' The woman started to withdraw.

'Wait,' the girl shouted.

'What now?'

'At least tell him I was here, tell him I came.'

'What, so you're finally going, are you? You've finally got the message?' The woman seemed surprised by this, disappointed almost.

'I've got somewhere a lot better than here to go,' the girl shouted.

'I'll bet. And I'll give you odds on that whatever poor bugger you're off to take advantage of won't even have remembered your name from the last time.'

Everything the pair of them continued to shout was an answer and a reward of sorts to Pye.

The girl came down the steps and back on to the street.

'That's right,' the woman shouted. 'You get along. Don't keep your sugar-daddy, or whoever it is you imagine is oh so keen to see you, waiting. And try and remember where you are next time, before you start your caterwauling in the streets and disturbing the peace of decent, hard-working people. I thought at first it was the sirens going off.' The woman laughed again at this.

The girl answered her, but only quietly.

'Can't hear you,' the woman called down triumphantly. 'Cat got your tongue, has it? Or have you suddenly got nothing to say for yourself? I saw you for what you were the instant I clapped eyes on you, lady. And don't think Sweeney himself won't be long in coming to exactly the same conclusion.'

The girl said something else, and again Pye couldn't hear her.

She started walking back in the direction she had come; keeping beneath the trees, he again followed her.

'That's right,' the woman called after her. 'You just keep walking right on back to where you belong. I might tell Sweeney you were here and I might not. I can see that *you* think you've turned his head, but what *I* know is that you're no good for him, and that you're up to no good.' She was angry now at being ignored by the girl, and she raised her voice even louder in an effort to still be heard.

When Pye looked across at the girl, he saw that she was smiling to herself, laughing almost, as though she had gained something from the fruitless and hostile encounter.

He expected that she would soon start walking back towards South Ken Tube, but instead, she turned in the opposite direction and increased her pace.

There were whole streets in that direction that had been either flattened or damaged beyond retrieval, and vast brick- and weed-filled spaces that had been there for years now, with shovelled paths through the rubble like tracks through rocky terrain.

The girl walked for a further ten minutes, along Redcliffe Gardens to Coleherne Road, and went to another house there. It looked remarkably like the house on Beaufort Street, a house divided into cheap and shabby flats. The same peeling stucco, the same small, overgrown garden, the same mosaic of nameplates and buttons in the doorway.

And here, too, she hesitated before going to the door, walking up and down the street for a few yards in each direction before finally returning to the buttons and pressing one of them.

Pye moved closer to her, standing in the shadow of a nearby boarded-up news kiosk, where he pretended to read from a board of notices, and from where he could see clearly the door she was now watching.

She pressed her face to the frosted glass, shielding her eyes with her hands, trying to see someone emerging out of the darkness.

Pye expected she would continue pressing the bell, anxious after so long a journey to be acknowledged, but instead, this time, she seemed content to wait.

Eventually, a form appeared inside, a dark shape within the darkness, and the girl stepped back. She pulled the bottle she held from its newspaper wrapper. She smoothed a hand over her flimsy jacket and skirt, brushed dust from her calves, and then held out her chest as whoever had come to the door began fumbling with its lock and latches, taking another long minute to open it and finally see her there.

'It's me,' Pye heard her say. 'Remember?' She held up the bottle.

He was an old man, cumbersome and awkward, wearing a strange kind of cap, and with a blanket or shawl over his shoulders which slowed his fumbling with the door even further.

'So it is,' Pye heard him say, surprised by both the vigour and the pleasure in his voice. 'And you've brought a friend.'

The girl laughed. 'You going to let me in then, or what? A girl could catch her death standing here like this.'

The old man looked her up and down, slowly and deliberately, and doing nothing to hide his interest or intent from her. He was smiling now, and certainly more amused than either surprised or disturbed by her sudden and unexpected appearance at his door.

Pye guessed him to be at least seventy, older perhaps – certainly old enough to be the girl's grandfather.

And then Pye felt the old man's eyes on him, and he saw that he was looking directly at him where he stood at the kiosk. This lasted for no more than a second, and then the old man dismissed him and turned his attention back to the girl.

'I was just passing,' the girl said. 'In the neighbourhood, so to speak.'

'And feeling neighbourly?' the man said, investing the word with a probing and salacious edge. Or so it seemed to Pye.

'You could say that,' the girl said.

The man then stood back from the doorway and waved a hand for her to go in.

'Missed me, have you?' she said as she passed close by him.

The man laughed at the remark and all it might imply, and then the door slammed shut on the pair of them and Pye was left with the impenetrable inner darkness framed by the entrance.

Only then did it strike him that there was something familiar about the man – something *recognizable*, that he was perhaps someone Pye had encountered before, or seen, or at least seen pictures of. But it was that line of work, and it was that sort of world these days, that sort of time.

22

'PRICE'S CONTINENTAL SHOW. EVERY SUMMER. HAMPSTEAD Heath, two months minimum, four or five in the years just before all this carry-on. I had a booth. The first that was properly mine. I used to winter it in Deptford each year and then find some accommodating strong young man to give me a lift with it over to the Heath.' Veronica held Sweeney's forearm, gripping him tighter at the slightest indication that he was about to pull away from her.

'Fan dancers,' he said. 'Price's Continental. Outdoors. They could move.'

For a moment, Veronica seemed uncertain of what he was saying to her. She picked up her glass of sherry, saw the liquid tremble at its rim, and then put it back down again. She'd been drinking gin and water before Sweeney had come back. The girl had left her feeling anxious; she'd needed something to calm herself. And now it was the usual sweet English sherry with the word Madeira on the label. Something more civilized – what was the word? – something more *decorous*.

'Fans – that's right. Black fans for the late Saturday show. There was always an accommodating boy to help a lady before the war. And that was a proper booth, not one of these gimcrack paste-and-board jobs you see these days. "The

Touch of a Vanished Hand" – that was me. Famous advert, that was . . . in its time.'

Sweeney breathed in the odours of the airless room. She'd come out to him the moment he'd arrived home. Important news. Something he needed to go back into her room with her to hear. It sometimes seemed to Sweeney that there had been a thousand other nights just like it. It was probably closer to a hundred, but it felt like a thousand.

'"The Touch of a Vanished Hand",' Veronica repeated, smiling.

'They're finally getting round to clearing Pavilion Road,' Sweeney said.

'What? Pavilion Road?'

Sweeney wiped the saliva from his lips.

'You're not drinking your drink. You've got to have a little drink with me. Everybody needs to have a little drink now and again.' Veronica held out the glass to him and he took it.

In the past twelve hours, Sweeney had been from the Regency to the home of the man in Clapham who had washed the money from the Hove greyhound stadium robbery; from there to Stockwell, to Tommy Fowler's jeweller, who was taking care of the North Audley Street job; and from there to Swiss Cottage to see the head of the laughingly named 'Girl Protection Patrol' – a man called Swindles; another fucking laugh, if you asked Tommy Fowler – who was also a senior member of the Public Morality Council, and whose job as head of the Protection Patrol was to examine all those public air raid shelters where strangers – men and women – were still occasionally spending their nights together. The warning calls were rare these days, but the shelters were still there, still mostly available for use, and still sought out by wandering men and licentious women.

At the house of the jeweller, Sweeney had anticipated meeting one of the men who had actually carried out the robbery, only to discover that the man breaking down the jewels and settings for resale was almost ninety. He had stayed with the man for an hour, watching him work and then checking his own tally of gems and metal against the one entrusted to him by Tommy Fowler.

It was all part of Sweeney's continuing education, and although Sweeney understood and welcomed this, it had still surprised him to have been given so much responsibility so quickly. He wondered if someone else further up the hierarchy had either been similarly promoted or was about to be dispensed with by Fowler. Tommy Fowler had been particularly keen to impress upon him the significance of the Stockwell visit. A clever and devious breaker could pocket any number of the gems and pieces of gold and silver. After all, who was to know for certain how many pieces of jewellery had actually been handed over to him in the first place? Sweeney himself, Tommy Fowler told him, would have to determine whether or not the old man was telling the truth about his rendering and its value. And if he isn't? Sweeney had asked him. And Fowler had simply smiled and said that that wasn't Sweeney's problem.

Sometimes, Sweeney now understood, life was much simpler, much more knowable and much more predictable than most people – for whatever reason – made it out to be. It was a good lesson to learn, and something else Sweeney appreciated knowing.

Following the visit to Swindles, Sweeney had then gone to

one of Fowler's doctors with an envelope of money. Sweeney had found the man precisely where Fowler had said he would be – in a cellar casino in Mayfair. Sweeney had found the address, knocked on the door and whispered Tommy Fowler's name. The door had been ceremoniously unlocked and opened and he had been beckoned inside. He was Tommy Fowler's man, and Tommy Fowler's name in his mouth unlocked these otherwise impregnable doors. Everywhere he went, it now seemed to him, with everyone he spoke to, he learned something new and important. It had been a long night, but a good one, and he had felt more awake at the end of it than he had done twelve hours earlier when he'd started.

He was drawn back from all these thoughts – this reverie almost – by the drunken Veronica saying, 'I saw it – that warehouse, Churchill's warehouse.'

He wondered how long it would be before she got to the point of what was so important it couldn't wait until he'd had a few hours' sleep.

'Churchill's warehouse?' He'd smelled the gin on her breath the moment she'd spoken to him on the landing.

'His warehouse full of coffins. Churchill's coffins. Up east, in the docks somewhere. A warehouse full of coffins.'

Everybody had heard the tale of the warehouse supposedly filled with coffins stockpiled in readiness for the coming bombing campaign. Old Hitler and Goering between them were going to bomb every English city off the face of the earth.

'A hundred and fifty thousand boxes, there were. A hundred and fifty thousand. Imagine that.'

Sweeney had heard the number elevated to half a million. He couldn't even imagine what half a million people looked

260

like, let alone half a million corpses, laid out and boxed and ready for burial somewhere. Come to think of it, he didn't even know what half a million *was*.

'A hundred and fifty thousand,' Veronica said again. 'So you can forget all those other stories you might have heard.'

Sweeney wished now that he'd feigned exhaustion and avoided her entirely. 'You said you had something important to tell me,' he said.

Veronica looked momentarily puzzled at this and then rubbed a hand over her eyes.

'I'm tired,' Sweeney said. He stretched and yawned.

'*She* was here,' Veronica said.

'Who was?'

'The Irish bit.'

'Ruby. When? What did she want? To see me? What did she say?'

'Ah, *now* you're interested,' Veronica said. '*Now* you've got time for me. I waited up special just to tell you.'

'Did she leave a message?' He imagined a note lying unread on his own faded linoleum. A letter, even.

'She didn't even bother to come in,' Veronica said. She swayed slightly in her effort of remembering. 'She stood out on the street, shouting the odds like the little tart she is.'

'She isn't—' Sweeney stopped himself.

'Go on,' Veronica told him. 'She isn't what? *What* isn't she?'

'I like her,' Sweeney said. 'That's all. She's all right.'

'Hold the front page. He likes her. And what about her? Has she ever once said the same about you?'

'She doesn't need to,' Sweeney said.

'And why's that, do you reckon?'

'Because—'

'Because it's all up here as far as you're concerned.' She tapped her forehead and then thought better of the painful gesture. 'It's all up here, that's why. I don't mean to be cruel, but you've got to start seeing that, you've got to start seeing straight where she's concerned. She's using you, that's all. I don't know what for, exactly, what she's got hatching in that devious little head of hers, but that's what she's doing – using you.'

And you're jealous of that, Sweeney thought. It was plain for all to see. The only person *not* seeing that was Veronica.

She reached across to him and caressed his arm for a moment. 'Listen to me,' she said. 'Listen to me. You need looking after, that's all.'

'You could at least have insisted on her coming in,' Sweeney said. 'You could have asked her what she wanted, if she wanted to wait for me. You could have told her when I'd be back.' *You could at least have told her that there was nothing in the entire world I would have liked better than for her to have been waiting for me when I got back from my new and important job. You could at least have done that much.* It would have been the work of a minute and required an ounce of thoughtfulness, and it would have meant the earth. If Ruby Nolan *had* waited – even if she'd fallen asleep while she waited – then she would still have been there now, listening to him, Sweeney, telling her about everything he'd been entrusted with over the course of that long night. Surely she would have wanted to hear all about the jewels he had seen – actually *seen* – scattered across the baize-topped table in Stockwell. Surely she would have wanted to hear all about the casino in Mayfair – a casino he and she might soon enough be able to visit together. Surely—

'She called me all sorts of names,' Veronica said. 'That's

why I wasn't disposed to let her in. Stood in the street, bold as brass – as bold as the brass she is – and called me names.' She struggled briefly to remember if this was the truth or another of her angry embellishments.

'She stands up for herself,' Sweeney said. 'That's all. Most don't – or can't – but she does.' He knew even as he said it what a feeble defence this was.

'Stands up for herself? Stands up for herself? Until she's lying down, she does.' Veronica considered this a clever riposte and was unable to prevent herself from laughing.

Sweeney rose from where he sat and she stopped abruptly.

'I'm sorry,' she said. 'I shouldn't have said that. I'm sorry. Sit back down. Whatever I should or shouldn't have done, it's too late now. She rubbed me up the wrong way, that's all. You're right – I should have thought and tried at least to get her to come in and wait for you. But she'll be back. Her sort always are. Proverbial bad penny, that's what she is.'

'Don't,' Sweeney said, already knowing that, bad penny or not, Ruby Nolan's return was more and more unlikely. What had there ever been between them in the first place? Who was he kidding if he thought a looker like that would look twice at him? Who? He glanced at his reflection in the mirror angled down above the unlit fire. Tommy Fowler and all this new-found trust and responsibility at the start of the night and Ruby Nolan and everything she promised at its end – it seemed a dream to him, a story in a film – and something he himself would never now be entitled to properly possess.

'I'm sorry,' Veronica said. 'I'm sorry. Me and my big mouth. I know – I let it run away with me. But I had to speak my piece. I couldn't let her just . . . just . . .'

'Just what?' Sweeney said angrily. 'You couldn't let her

just want to come and see me and talk to me? You couldn't let her just want to spend some time with me? Why do you always assume everyone has to be *using* me, taking advantage of me in some way?' *Why do even* you *think you can treat me like this?*

'I can see how she might appeal,' Veronica said.

'No, you can't,' Sweeney said. *Not to me, you can't.*

'With you and your—'

'Me and my what?' Sweeney shouted at her. He pulled at his lip. '*This?* Me and *this?* Is that what you were going to say?'

Veronica looked genuinely alarmed and upset at the accusation. 'I was going to say you and all your big ideas, your ambitions for the future. Especially now that you're just starting to go somewhere. That's what I was going to say. Honestly. And let's face it – she's left it too late to find a rich Yank, and so she's probably settling—'

'For what? Second best? Not even that?'

'For what she can get, I was going to say. She's getting ready to jump. The ship's sinking, and the one thing I will give her credit for is that she's not stupid enough to go down with it like a lot of others.' It was the first time she had seen him like this, and though his anger alarmed her, she did not feel defeated by it.

'What are you talking about?' Sweeney said. 'What sinking ship? Besides, it's you who's stupid, not her.'

'Perhaps you're right,' Veronica said. 'It won't be the first time I've been told.'

After this, neither of them spoke for a few minutes.

Then Sweeney said, 'Go on, then, tell me why she came, what she said to get your back up.' His lip was sore from where he'd pulled at it. Back in the Regency, Tommy Fowler had given him the address in Stockwell and then told him that if he ever went behind Tommy Fowler's back and Tommy Fowler got to hear of it – and he always *did* get to hear of these things – then Sweeney's mouth would end up being his most attractive feature. He had laughed at Sweeney's response to this and told him he was only joking. He had squeezed Sweeney's cheeks and then given him a handkerchief to wipe his mouth.

'I don't recollect it was anything in particular,' Veronica said, surprised by this sudden failure of her imagination. She'd been doing all right so far.

'So she just turned up, found out I wasn't here, and then left?'

'Something like that,' Veronica said. 'In fact, that was it exactly.'

'What did you say to her?'

'I told her . . .' she faltered, caught somewhere between memory and calculation. 'I told her . . .'

'Don't bother,' Sweeney said. 'Whatever you say, it'll be a lie. You probably told her everything you just told me.'

'I *know* her,' Veronica said. 'At least I know her *sort*. I see her type all the time. Price's Continental was one big knocking shop. Everybody in there was a grafter of one sort or another. Nice enough girls, most of them, but that's what they were – whores. And every single one of them said that they'd jack it all in the minute they found their one good man.'

'Then perhaps that's what I am to *her*,' Sweeney said. It was the flaw in her argument, and she was too drunk to see it.

'You *are* a good boy,' she said. She caressed his arm again.

'You're wrong,' he said. 'About her. I *know* what she is,

what she does, and shall I tell you something? None of it matters to me.'

'Not now, perhaps,' she said. 'Not now. But—'

'Not *ever*. Besides, *now* is exactly what matters. It doesn't matter to me, so why should any of it matter to you? Why shouldn't the future just take care of itself? So *what* if everything's going to change? As far as I'm concerned, it can all only change for the better. Besides, what about *you*? What about the lies *you* keep telling yourself?'

'I only—'

'Sometimes, everything you say is a lie. You don't even know you're doing it most days. You drink and you make up stories and you lie about everything. And some days you must look in the mirror and hardly recognize what you see there. She's my *friend*. Where are all *your* so-called friends and admirers? Where? I don't see many of *them* beating a path to your door. You tell fortunes, you read palms, you play with tarot cards – what's so respectable about any of *that*? What? You tell people what they want to hear, that's all. They pay you and you lie to them to make sure they get their money's worth. You flatter them, tell them all what wonderful people they are – how brave they are, how strong, how interesting. So why can't you just for once do the same for me?'

The remark caught her off guard. 'You?' she said.

'Yes – me. Why can't you tell the same lies to me? About me and Ruby, about me and her and everything that the future holds for *us*, about everything *we*'ve got to look forward to?' He stopped shouting and wiped his mouth again. He realized only then that he was crying. Or if not crying, exactly, that there were tears on his cheeks.

Veronica saw these too, and she caught her breath.

'I thought—' she began to say, uncertain of what she might add. 'I thought you and me – I thought you were different from all those others. That's all some of those others ever want to hear – lies. I thought we were friends, proper friends. I would never lie to you.'

'Then perhaps you ought to start making the effort.' He regretted the words the instant he'd said them, but knew they were impossible to retract.

'I'm sorry,' she said. 'I really am.' She held her hand a few inches from his arm, and he in turn did not pull his arm away from her.

There was a further long silence.

Sweeney refilled his glass, but when he offered the bottle of sherry to Veronica she put a hand over her own glass.

'Perhaps I should have stopped earlier,' she said. 'Or at least slowed down. I never know when enough's enough, that's my problem. I should definitely have stopped earlier.'

'Not on my account,' Sweeney told her.

'On my own, then. Mind you, perhaps I should have slowed down thirty years ago if I was doing it on my own account.'

He smiled at this, accepting it for the apology it was intended to be. He moved his arm until it fitted into her cupped palm.

'You can make it all up to her,' she said. 'All she saw and heard was me shouting the odds back down at her. She knew it was nothing to do with you. You can tell her you haven't even seen me. Or you can even tell her that you heard all about it and then put me right on one or two things. I'll apologize to her, that's what I'll do. Wait until she's back round here and I'll put on my best face and tell her I'm sorry.'

'*If* she comes back,' Sweeney said.

'Invite her.'

And risk having to listen to her answer? 'Perhaps.' He already knew there was some ulterior motive to the girl's visits to see him. He might have been blind to a few things, but he wasn't *that* blind. But perhaps – and it was a big perhaps – now that he was finally starting to make something of himself, perhaps she would come to see him in a different light and things would change. Perhaps she would even—

'Two more corpses out of Pavilion Road,' Veronica said. 'Youngsters. They couldn't even pull them out from under all the rubble, they'd been there that long. Only found them when they took that unexploded bomb out. I was talking to a woman who watched it all. Thought they'd been accounted for years ago. The police went in with a kitbag, brought them out in that. Pieces, somebody said. Another woman said that the last she'd seen of the youngsters they'd told her they were off for a day at Clacton, said she thought that was where they'd been all that time. Tragic, really. *That's* what the world's come to. Not all this stuff you hear about in Germany and wherever, but that – two youngsters dead and unmissed. The authorities are going to look for relatives. God knows what that'll throw up.'

'Perhaps Churchill could give them a couple of his unused coffins,' Sweeney said, which, in its equally oblique way, was his own apology to her.

'Perhaps he will at that. The way I heard it, they had one lot of coffins for the likes of us and another lot for the nobs.'

'Always been the case,' Sweeney said.

'And thousands for children, all shapes and sizes.'

'I heard the same.'

'There you go, then – it must be true.' She smiled at him and waited for him to do the same.

'I ought to get some sleep,' he said. He felt her grip on his arm tighten again, but only slightly this time, before she released him and drew her hand back across the table. It was almost six in the morning, and already growing light.

Sweeney rose and went to the door, and Veronica remained where she sat at the table in the centre of the room. He wondered what final words he might say to her as he went, but nothing came to him and so he said nothing.

23

Ruby Nolan looked through the album Crowley had given her.

'You were a mountain climber,' she said. She tried to sound interested.

'A mountaineer, yes,' Crowley said. He sat close beside her, their two chairs drawn up to the fire.

The girl wore a short skirt and poor-quality stockings, wrinkled at her ankles and knees. She had full calves, and frequently revealed the paler flesh of her thighs when she shifted in her seat. Her blouse was flimsy, its sleeves covering only a few inches of her upper arms. It was buttoned at the front and tight enough to continually reveal the outline of her breasts to Crowley. And when she leaned forward to look more closely at a picture, he saw the pressed curve of her cleavage and the thin black strap of her brassiere. Her red hair was fastened back from her forehead, but fell over her ears and cheeks in loose curls. She was wearing a sharp, flowery scent.

'I see you appreciate a good perfume,' he had said to her as he took her coat and the bottle from her.

'It was a present,' she said.

'I can imagine.'

She laughed at the remark, adding, 'I bet you can – imagine, that is.'

In the days since she had last seen him, Ruby Nolan had sought out and read everything she could find on Aleister Edward Crowley. Magazines, mostly, and the usual array of lurid newspaper articles. A few books in which he was mentioned. Charing Cross Road and St Martin's Lane were crowded with shops full of nothing but old books. Her cheap scent and cleavage and stockinged thighs had worked there, too, and she had even been allowed to borrow some of the books she had been shown. On approval, the elderly booksellers had called it. On approval of what? A wink, a kiss on the cheek, the touch of a hand – all gratitude, all flattery – it never failed to work for girls like Ruby Nolan.

'My wife, Rose,' Crowley said. 'She used to have her scents made up by a perfumery in—'

'Paris?' Ruby said. It was where he had once lived and practised his Wicked Ways.

Crowley smiled. 'No, not Paris. Cairo, of all places. A man who said he could create for her the scents of the Ancient Egyptian queens. I suspect he was, in his own way, a charlatan, but the scents were exquisite. The spice routes – all that.'

Ruby knew the scent she was wearing was not the real thing, that the man who had given it to her a fortnight earlier frequently brought a suitcase of the stuff into the Regency. It hadn't even been in its original box, merely a small bottle with a rubber spray ball attached. He had shown the scent to her and had then sprayed her neck with it, oblivious to the significance of the gesture. Ruby had told him it was the best she had ever smelled.

'We get some of the old Cairo Brigade in the clubs now and again,' she said. 'Foreign Office, Desert Rats. Camels and pyramids and the funny little wogs and all that.'

Crowley smiled at the scatter of information. The girl had clearly been doing her homework. She wanted to engage him; she seemed eager to please; it was more than enough.

'After my time there, I'm afraid,' he said. 'Leila, too, was very particular about the scents she wore.'

'Another wife?' Ruby said. There were too many women's names for her to remember them all. She doubted if even *he* remembered all of them.

'In a sense. More of—'

'A friend?'

'A follower, perhaps. An acolyte. A believer and spiritual accomplice.'

Ruby had seen the words but hadn't fully understood what they meant. With most of the articles – and who had time to read a whole book these days? – it was implication after suggestion after implication – all dark and unmentionable deeds and shocking and unmentionable practices. It seemed to her, glutted on this sudden, steamy mound of information, that where the newspapers were concerned – whose job it was at least to *mention* things – there were a considerable number of these so-called *un*mentionables.

She leaned closer to him. 'What mountain's that?' Whoever these other women were, they were a long time past, probably even dead, most of them. Whereas she . . .

Crowley looked more closely at the small brown and white photograph. Was it the Himalayas, the Alps, somewhere in the Lake District, the Isle of Skye? He decided on Skye. The Cuillin Hills. He looked no more than a boy in the picture, and the hills were rounded and snow-free, with broken crags and vegetation growing almost to their summits.

'Skye,' he said. 'I spent a great deal of time there as a youth.'

'A youth? A kid, you mean? You look grown enough in the picture.'

'When I inherited my legacy I spent a great deal of it indulging myself.'

'I'll bet you did.'

'Mountaineering, travelling the world, collecting my libraries, publishing my books. My early passions.'

Ruby motioned to the bookcase beyond Crowley's chair. 'Some of those yours, then?' She'd already looked while Crowley was rinsing out their glasses.

'A few. Most of my more valuable publications are lost – my creditors, the vagaries of life. Only last month, Silver helped me dispose of my entire first edition of Burton for a tenth of what the volumes were worth. As you can imagine, a great many collections have been destroyed and depleted of late in the flames of moral outrage and indignation.'

Ruby didn't understand what he meant. 'The bombing, you mean?' she said.

'If I'd only been able to hold on to things, I would be sitting on another small fortune by now.'

The remark disappointed her. The men in the Regency talked forever and endlessly of the small fortunes *they* were all about to make. Small fortunes, large fortunes, fortunes beyond all their – and certainly beyond *her* – wildest dreams. *Beyond the dreams of avarice.* It was something her mother used to say to her as a girl when she asked for an uncomfortable pair of shoes or a torn and faded hand-me-down dress or skirt or cardigan to be replaced. *Beyond the dreams of avarice.* How could anything be *beyond* such dreams?

'And it's definitely all gone?' she said.

Crowley laughed. 'I'm afraid so. So if that was your purpose in bestowing your charms, gifts and attention upon me . . .'

She rubbed his arm. 'Not really,' she said. 'I think this little palace gives most of the game away, don't you?' Besides, who was Silver? The other old man who had come with Crowley to the Regency, presumably. Jewish, probably, name like that. Another yid on the make. 'Over the sea to Skye,' she said, half singing the line.

Crowley smiled at this and finished the verse as she hummed along with him.

'Where did that come from?' she said as the pair of them fell silent. 'I haven't sung that for the past ten years.'

'Thought transference, perhaps?' Crowley suggested, though not seriously.

'Seriously?' she said.

Crowley moved closer to her, their faces now only inches apart. 'You know about me,' he said. 'You've *learned* things.' He held up a finger to her. 'Please, don't disappoint me by denying it.'

Ruby stayed silent. Anybody – everybody – might know him, at least *of* him. He was a famous – infamous – man. Eventually, she said, 'I was . . .'

'Intrigued? Shall we say that?'

'That's it – intrigued. Curious. I'm a curious girl, always willing to learn, that's me. The newspapers all make you out to be some sort of – I don't know – monster.'

'Perhaps it's what I once was,' Crowley said. He appreciated the qualifying hesitation. 'What I still *am* in the eyes of some – many, even.'

Is that why Tommy Fowler had agreed so quickly to Crowley's request?

'I make devilish pacts, I control people, I exercise a malign influence over events, I indulge in operations of divination, I practise clairvoyance, have spirit visions, speak spirit languages, I tamper with the further reaches of geomancy.'

It seemed to Ruby to be a tired litany, and Crowley himself seemed to tire himself in reciting it, and perhaps disappoint himself, too. They had clearly all once been strengths that had shrunk to embarrassing and impotent weaknesses; full, firm and juicy fruits that had withered now to their desiccated skins and pips and dangling stalks. He looked into his cupped palms as he recited the list, perhaps hoping to see something there that he had not seen for a long time.

'I still keep it,' Crowley said absently.

Ruby wondered what she had missed. One minute it was mountaineering, the next his lost fortunes, the next his mouldering books. How many other men, she wondered, called a few old books in a bookcase a library?

'Keep what?' she said, realizing that the directionless, aimless wandering was all his own. She had brought half a bottle of gin with her and he had drunk two glasses of this before even pouring hers. The same glasses he'd used last time, she noticed. He sipped his drink now.

'The scents,' Cowley said. 'True scent never fades. I have owned ambergris a thousand years old – older – retrieved from Greenland bone yards. Frankincense and myrrh and the scented kidney stones of Armenian girls fed on violets for a decade and then operated upon and the stones retrieved.'

This last one didn't ring true. 'Never,' she said. Ambergree? Armenia? He might have been making up all of what he was telling her, for all she knew. But what she *did* know was that this hardly mattered; what mattered now – here, the two of them alone together – was that he was the one saying it and she was the one listening to him and feigning interest in his every word. Hers was still the name written in the Bible, and the Bible was still his, and it was still in the hands of a man preparing to meet his Maker. And even if she didn't yet properly understand the true significance of *any* of that – of any of those connections – then she knew at least that it meant *something*, and that she and her pencilled-in name were now a part of that something, and that it, too, like the pair of them alone in the room together now, *mattered*.

'Is that true about the Armenian girls?' Was it even a real place?

'I was told the story by a merchant who was himself convinced that the practice existed. He said the mothers fed the girls on the violets and other mountain flowers, along with grit to create the stones.'

'Like chickens,' she said suddenly. Her father had kept chickens.

'I believe a comparison to the pearl inside an oyster was his own particular selling point. A precious rather than a cloacal or gynaecological angle.'

'Right,' she said. 'And so the girls ate the flowers and the scented stones grew inside them?'

'That was the theory and the tale.'

'And you bought it?'

Crowley held up his hands. 'I certainly bought the so-called stones for Rose's scent, for her perfumer to perform his miracles. I doubt they were made any less precious or sought after by *not* having the story attached to them.'

'I see,' she said. He had lost her again, and again she kept a close check on her ignorance.

'Did the gangster Fowler tell you anything of my business with him?' Crowley then said unexpectedly.

The remark caught her unawares and she struggled for a few seconds to stay calm. So he had seen her in the Regency and remembered her. Had he recognized her when she'd helped him into the house and up the stairs? Had he known exactly who she was *then*? Was it all an act on his part as well as her own? Had he even connected her to messenger boy Sweeney? She knew this was impossible. Even *she* hadn't connected herself to Sweeney then. So – he recognized her, and presumably he also knew that her reappearance had been no coincidence. But so what? He was Aleister Crowley. All she had to say was that she had recognized him in the Regency and that she had been curious to find out if what all the papers said about him was true. Hence her reappearance. What else could she be? A tart on the make? So what? It must have been clear, even to him, looking around himself at the squalid backdrop to the life he now lived, that he had nothing to offer her. Or perhaps he *had* given this some consideration and was already beginning to guess at her motives for returning. Either way, it surely wasn't anything unusual for him – nothing he hadn't already experienced a hundred times before in his life, if the papers were to be believed. So, either way, what was there to worry about or deny?

'Fowler?' she said. 'Me? He never tells me anything. In fact, he doesn't waste his breath on any of the girls. Lowest of the low, me. He's barely said ten words to me in all the time

I've been at the Regency, and then it's usually only to tell me to get out of his way or to work harder or to cough up his rent. And every now and then he asks me and a few of the others to help him out – entertain his business partners, stuff like that, oiling the wheels and greasing a few palms – but that's about it. Is that why *you* were there? Perhaps you were looking for me all along and you never even knew it.' She laughed to disguise and dismiss the suggestion, and Crowley laughed with her.

He was watching her more closely now.

'I take it you're not going to tell me,' she said.

'Tell you what?'

'Your business with Fowler.'

'Nothing of any particular consequence,' Crowley said. 'Call it another indulgence.'

'He's good at indulgences, Fowler. Or at least he's good at getting other people to be good on his behalf.' She pulled together the collar of her blouse. 'If you catch my drift.'

'Your drift . . .' Crowley said. 'I believe so.'

She turned the pages of the photo album and Crowley named other places and other people for her. He told her who they were and what they had all once been to him. He pointed himself out in the pictures and she was surprised by how different he looked in many of them – only a few years older than in the picture taken on Skye and yet his appearance seemed to have changed completely – taller and thinner in some, and overweight and shapeless in others. In some he looked like a youthful man, even though he must have been in his fifties and sixties. In others he looked exhausted and drawn, even though his youth was still intact. There were many pictures of him with women, and she saw what a big part they had played in his life. All sorts of women – some young and seductive, gazing into his old man's eyes; others as old and as worn out as he was now. Some of them looked wretched, miserable, weird and intense all at once – lesbians, probably, she imagined. And some looked like wealthy High Society heiresses. He told her all their names, remembering them perfectly.

It seemed impossible to Ruby Nolan that such a vast, deep reservoir of life had flowed through the sluices of his body and left only this solitary old man behind.

'He,' Crowley said, tapping a finger on the face of a pale, bowler-hatted man – and she knew by the three precise taps he gave the distant figure that the gesture was not an idle or a wasted one – 'was a man I met while I was living in Paris. He came to me to cure him.'

'Of what?'

'Skin. He had a skin disease. His entire body flaked. He scratched at himself continuously.'

'I know a few like that nowadays,' she said.

'Heroin,' Crowley said. 'One of its more lasting and obvious afflictions.'

'So what did you do for him?'

He hesitated before answering her, causing her to listen more closely.

'There was a rite,' he said. 'I understood something of his addiction. I myself was prescribed heroin for the treatment of a bronchial disorder.'

'I've heard that, too,' Ruby said. It was a world of endless excuses.

'Then have you also heard of the Serpent's Kiss?'

She almost laughed at the theatricality of it all. It sounded like one of those comic books the other girls sometimes read, one of those films; it even sounded like one of those bottles of cheap scent in the man's shabby suitcase.

She shook her head.

'A bite,' Crowley said. 'The canine teeth alone leave puncture marks, usually on the upper arm.'

She clasped her arm, causing Crowley to smile.

He drew back his top lip to reveal his own prominent canines.

'*You* did it?'

'I undertook the rite. I was possessed of the knowledge and the powers.'

And the man's money, presumably. She looked again at the face in the photo. 'I've known girls lock themselves in their rooms and push the key back under the door,' she said. 'Known them dope themselves to get to sleep and then stuff rags into their mouths to muffle their screams.'

'I have endured the same on many occasions,' Crowley said. 'It sometimes even became a kind of ecstasy, a freeing of the caged spirit.'

'I doubt if many of the girls I'm talking about ever saw it like that.'

Six months earlier, a girl had died in the Norfolk Square house and Tommy Fowler had sent Frankie Doll to get rid of the body. That was it. The beginning of the story, the middle of the story, and the end of the story. The girl had died and Doll had disposed of her body. Nobody had missed her, nobody had come looking for her, nobody had ever mentioned her name again.

'No, I doubt they did,' Crowley said. 'But for me, you see, it was all part of that single – you might say eternal – quest.'

'An adventure – that sort of quest?'

He smiled at her naivety. 'Yes, an adventure,' he said.

'To discover what?'

'The newspapermen refer to them as the secrets of the universe, the secrets of realms beyond all earthly existence and human understanding.'

She already knew what the newspapermen called them. She'd expected something more specific; it sounded like every other kind of 'quest' she'd ever read about.

'And did you find them – these realms?' Again, she did her best to sound interested.

'They tell me that the quest is sufficient unto itself.' He paused and looked at her closely again. 'But, yes, I believe I made some discoveries, that I experienced things connected to these realms that no other man had thus far experienced.'

'Sounds interesting,' she said.

'I certainly always believed so. And there were always others prepared to support and encourage me.'

'How do you mean?'

'I mean they supported me – in my needs and practices.'

'Practices?' She knew all about those, too. Or, rather, she didn't, not exactly, not in any specific or verifiable detail.

'You must engage your imagination,' Crowley told her. 'A girl like you . . . I'm sure . . .'

'All those women, you mean?' Ruby said.

'Women, men . . .'

'I see,' Ruby said. 'And what about this Serpent's Bite?'

'Kiss. I performed it on the man and he died a month later.'

'Of the bite – kiss?'

'Not necessarily. He was a habituate, remember, and an invert.'

Neither of the words meant anything to her, but both conferred something of their meaning.

'Doomed by his own excesses from the very start,' Crowley said.

'The heroin?'

'Amid a cornucopia of other delights. The same substances, I imagine, that played a not insubstantial part in all of my own searching for—'

'Your questing,' she said, causing him to laugh.

'My questing, yes. Rose, my wife, was one of the very few who was able to restrain her own indulgences in that direction. People said I was a malign influence on her. Rose preferred to put her faith in alcohol where her own salvation was concerned. Brandy and champagne, a bottle of each – at least, a bottle of the latter – every day. *I* drove her to it, of course. *I* was the teetering pillar to which she fastened herself with no regard whatsoever for either herself or our poor child.' He sipped again at his gin and then rubbed a hand over his face. 'My apologies,' he said. 'An old man's reminiscences. They must seem . . .'

'No – I'm interested,' Ruby said. 'And do you still – you know – the questing stuff?'

'Are my own convictions and beliefs still intact, do you mean? Am I still in search of Life's one solitary, great, eternal secret?'

'I suppose so,' she said.

'Then I confess I am. The vessel may be frail and cracked and almost irretrievably broken, but the spirit it embodies – its vital fluids, so to speak – still occasionally rise to their challenge.' Crowley put his hand on her arm. 'Forgive me. You ask me a perfectly valid question and all I can manage by way of an answer are these faded, flowery wreaths which probably make no sense whatsoever to you. Here am I, an old man at the end of everything, and here *you* are, bursting with that same life and spirit and energy I once possessed, those same hopes and dreams for the future.'

Ruby remembered something else she'd read. 'Magic,' she said.

'Magic?'

'That's what you're talking about – all this searching-for-secrets stuff. All this eternal whatsit.'

'A much debased notion, I'm afraid, magic. Next you'll be expecting me to perform tricks with cards or silk flowers or fluttering doves. Endlessly sensational and profitable showmanship, I'm afraid – that's what passes for magic these days. Giving people the novelty they clamour for seems to be all that matters now.'

'So tell me,' she said. The only other thing she could remember was that he was continually ridiculed for insisting on the letter 'k' at the end of the word. Magick.

'Tell you what?' he said. 'What *I* understand by the word? What would you truly learn? Except perhaps to laugh at me and think me ridiculous?'

'It's turned midnight,' she said. 'You don't think there are a dozen other places I could be?'

It seemed like a cruel and provocative thing to say to him, but Crowley defused this by saying, 'Only a dozen? Nearer two, I should imagine.'

'Probably closer to a hundred,' she said. 'Go on – tell me what you mean. If I get bored, you'll know fast enough.'

Crowley remained silent for a moment, and then he put down his glass and touched together the fingertips of both his hands. He took several deep breaths, as though preparing himself for some exertion or other.

'Magic,' he said eventually, 'I always understood to be a possible way of establishing new levels and conditions of consciousness.' He looked at her to ensure she understood him. 'A way of communicating without obvious *means* – without a common language, say.'

'Go on,' Ruby said. He'd lost her already, but, as before, as ever, it was all still *something*.

Crowley went on: 'I believe that magic is a form of spiritual consciousness acting through pure will, and that this spiritual consciousness can bring about change – in individuals, in the world, in anything – in conformity with the will of the man who possesses those controlling powers.' He stared into his joined hands in a kind of reverie.

'And that's what you've spent your life trying to find, is it, trying to achieve? The power to do all that?' Ruby said. What he was telling her might not yet be wholly convincing, but it was at last beginning to make a kind of sense to her.

'My life,' Crowley went on, 'my energies, my fortunes, the lives and sanity of my supporters, followers and fellow searchers, yes.'

'You make yourself sound like one of those trick cyclists,' she said.

'Psychiatrists?' Crowley almost spat the word.

'I didn't mean anything by it,' she said, wondering how she had offended him. 'I just meant – all that talk about consciousness and things.'

'Psychiatrists employ their own techniques of reaching through to control the subconscious and the imagination.'

'I saw a girl hypnotized once. Private party, stag, St James's.

Completely oblivious. You wouldn't believe the things . . .' She stopped talking.

'Like I said,' Crowley said, clearly more disappointed than aroused or amused by what she'd said. 'Showmanship, novelty, tat.'

'She was knocked about something rotten, and worse, before she was finally brought out of it.' Were *they* the kind of unspeakable acts and unmentionable depravities the papers all hinted at? Was that, she wondered, why she'd even mentioned it in the first place?

'I can imagine,' Crowley said.

She knew she'd disappointed him in some way by the recollection. Ordinarily, her customers would encourage her to go on, to tell them more about the hypnotized woman and what had happened to her, to share her excited outrage with their hands already on her, their own suggestions already forming.

'I'm sorry,' she said. 'I know it's not the same thing. It's just hard to follow what you're telling me, hard to grasp.'

'I know,' Crowley said.

'Hard to see what it would all be *for*,' she said. 'Where it all might lead you, what good it will be to you after all you've been through and sacrificed.'

'The canine teeth,' Crowley said unexpectedly. 'You should always look. A sure mark of licentiousness.'

She showed him her own small, sharp teeth, pressed her thumbs into the two points and then showed him the marks this left.

'And this heroin addict – he honestly believed that you could cure him by biting him?' she said.

'I was in my prime,' Crowley said. 'In those days, I could have convinced anyone of anything.'

She laughed at the remark and then tapped the rim of her empty glass against the bottle standing beside them.

'We should drink a toast to questing,' she said, and then kissed the top of her own indented thumb.

24

'**Y**OU BUSY?'
Peter Tait looked up from the Bible.

Arthur Bone raised the two mugs he held. 'You busy?' had been a kind of joke. Sometimes it worked, sometimes it didn't; it was that kind of job, condemned-cell watch.

'Three sugars and milk. You're a lucky man. Sugar? These days? I was on the old East India when the Tate and Lyle warehouse went up. The whole of the East End smelled like toffee for days afterwards. Melted sugar like lava running out of a volcano down the streets and clogging up the drains. We had to stop women and kids from trying to scoop the stuff up. Bringing all sorts to collect it, they were.'

Bone looked quickly around the small room. The man who'd been sitting with Tait earlier – the man called Lynch, of all things – had taken a chair into the corridor outside. This was allowed, but only if the cell door was then left open and if the warder put his head round the door every ten minutes. Bone knew the man and didn't like him, considered him unsuitable for the duty.

'Thank Christ for that,' Lynch had said to him as Bone had arrived with the tea half an hour earlier than his appointed time. 'You're keen.' He had then almost run along the corridor before Bone had been able to answer him.

'You look after me,' Tait said, taking the mug, after carefully slipping the silk bookmark into the Bible and then just as carefully closing it.

Bone put his own tea on the table, noting how Tait moved the book away from the two mugs.

'And then I was on the King George Dock when that pepper warehouse went up. We had three men in hospital for a week after that with damaged lungs. Pepper, see? You wouldn't have thought it, but that stuff's lethal. Overheated air. As bad as gunpowder floating around, that muck.' He went back outside to retrieve Lynch's chair. 'So, what kind of night you had?' he said, finally sitting opposite Tait.

Tait shrugged. 'I slept well. They had fish for tea. I've never been too keen on fish.'

'You should have said,' Bone said. 'You have special privileges these days. Anything you don't like, you just need to say. After all, it's—' He stopped abruptly. There was now a conversation like this each time the two men met. 'What I meant to say was . . .'

'I know what you meant,' Tait said. He picked up the tea and sipped it. 'I was reading my Bible,' he said.

My Bible, Bone thought. He did nothing *but* read the thing. It was like he'd told Pye and the Governor – the boy was obsessed with it.

'So I see,' Bone said. 'To be honest with you, you never struck me as the sort. You can usually tell – some will take to it, others do exactly the opposite. The joke in here is that you only accept the prison-issue Bibles that old holier-than-thou Simpson hands out because their pages make the best cigarette papers.'

'I heard that,' Tait said. 'I wouldn't do that, not to a Bible. We always had a Bible somewhere in the house. Used it to keep a record of all the births, deaths and christenings, that sort of thing. Or at least my mother did until she did a bunk. I don't know what happened to it after that.'

'I bet she did. Women, eh? You never talk about her, your mother.'

Tait shook his head and sipped his tea again. 'I had a bath,' he said. 'Earlier. Every three days. I doubt I ever had a dozen proper baths in my entire life, and most of those were before the war. Scullery sink, usually. There was a doss house on Commercial Road.'

'I know it,' Bone said. 'You should have steered well clear of that particular spot.'

There was a short silence, and then Tait said, 'It's seven days now.'

'I know.'

'The eighth.'

'I know. Today's May Day. The first. Soon be the summer.'

'I suppose so. Not that I'll . . . you know . . . not now . . .'

'No, I suppose not. Sorry. Me and my size tens again.'

'Reading this helps,' Tait said, putting his hand on the Bible.

'I'm sure it does,' Bone said. He wanted to grab the boy by his lapels and shake him. He wanted to tell him to make his lawyer start doing what he was supposed to be doing. He wanted to shout at him not to act more and more resigned to his fate with each passing day. 'At least it can't hurt.' Like Pye had said – nothing to be gained by raising the boy's hopes even one per cent now, not now that the clock had started its speeded-up ticking and there was an end in sight to the days ahead.

'Helps me to see things a bit more clearly,' Tait said.

'Then good for that,' Bone said. *What things?* In seven days the boy would be dead on the end of his rope, so what was the point of seeing *anything* more clearly now?

But it was against regulations for Bone to say any of this aloud. A single complaint from Tait and Bone would be removed from the special-watch roster without a word of explanation. Rules and regulations, written and unwritten; they were still what the world needed and wanted, and what, ultimately, the world still got.

'Tell you what, boy,' Bone said.

Tait looked up and smiled at him. He wore his shirt fastened to the collar and at the cuffs. 'What's that?'

'You got old Simpson's back up by refusing to take the prison Bible from him.'

'But I already had this one,' Tait said, a sudden anxious note in his voice.

'I know,' Bone said. 'I know. And perfectly within your rights to choose. It just seldom happens, that's all. I suppose he works on the understanding that a Bible's a Bible, wherever it comes from. And speaking of Simpson, I've been told by him to tell you that he can come and sit with you if you'd like him to. Some of them see it as a bit of company, conversation, you know? Some of them like to get things off their chests – him being what he is and everything.'

'A Man of God, you mean?'

'I suppose so.' Whatever that meant these days.

'I don't much go for all that repentance and forgiveness stuff,' Tait said.

'But you've always got your head stuck in the thing.' Bone indicated the Bible.

'But not for all that – what is it they call it? – redemption, all that. I'm not reading it for any of that.'

'What, then?' Bone said. 'It must do *something* for you, give you some sort of—'

'It does,' Tait said. 'A sort of understanding of things.'

A what? It was clear to Bone that Tait didn't want to have to try and explain to him what he meant in any greater detail. Chances were, the boy himself didn't really understand what he meant, what he was saying, what it was he got from the thing, not really. He was a condemned man, it was a Bible, enough said.

'We don't have to talk about it,' he said. 'In fact, you can tell me to mind my own beeswax, if you like. You won't be the first, or the last, and I definitely won't hold it against you.'

'It's not that, Mister Bone,' Tait said. 'I appreciate everything you've done for me. I don't know where I'd be if it wasn't for you.'

Exactly the same place you are now and with the same seven terrible days coming towards you. Alone, abandoned, unnoticed, unmissed.

'Well . . .' Bone said. 'We're all only human. You being my fellow man and all that.'

Tait smiled at the words. 'We could have been friends, you and me, Mister Bone,' he said. 'Proper friends. Under different circumstances, that is.' He waved a hand around him. 'If it wasn't for all this, I mean.'

'We *are* proper friends,' Bone said. 'Present circumstances allowing.'

Tait's smile broadened at hearing this and he bowed his head.

And for a moment, Bone thought he was saying a prayer.

'Officer Lynch thinks I've got everything I deserve coming to me,' Tait said.

'Say as much to your face, did he?'

Tait nodded. 'Said it and then said he'd deny everything if I told anyone.'

'He's a real bastard, that one,' Bone said. The word hung between them for a few seconds and then both men smiled at it. 'Always has been and always will be. He's on the wrong side of this game, for a start.'

Tait didn't understand this.

'I mean he's the kind more likely to end up with the door slamming in *his* face than being the one doing the slamming.'

'Right,' Tait said. 'I get you.'

'You pay him no mind,' Bone said. 'And it won't do no good me whispering in his ear or threatening to go to the Governor, not now.'

'Don't put yourself out on my account,' Tait said. 'He was in here telling me all about some of the women he knew.'

'Oh?' Bone said. 'Go on, I'm listening.'

'The things they got up to. The things he said *I* was never going to get up to or even know about.'

'Ignore him,' Bone said. 'He's got a big mouth, that's all.'

'He said he could bring me in some magazines, books. Bring them for me to look at and then sneak them back out again, nobody any the wiser. He said he was already doing it for plenty of others in here.'

'I can imagine,' Bone said. 'But they're not you, are they? You tell Lynch you want nothing to do with him. Chances are, you'll only go upsetting yourself. Besides, that's hardly the kind of girl you would have taken up with given half the chance and if things had turned out different for you, now, is it?'

'No, I suppose not,' Tait said.

'Men like Lynch—' Bone began to say.

'I know,' Tait said. 'And I know the kind of girl he's talking about. I used to see them in the clubs and places.'

'Before you went and got yourself caught and changed your ways?' Bone said. It was another of their jokes.

'Before I saw the error of my ways,' Tait said, allowing them both to smile again.

'Seriously,' Bone said. 'You can do without all that stuff. Overrated. It's all the servicemen filling the streets. Everything out there is still seriously out of kilter.'

Tait didn't entirely understand what Bone was telling him, but said, 'I know.'

Bone finished the last of his tea. It had taken him almost ten minutes to walk there from the canteen.

'You know what they're trying to tell us now, don't you?' he said.

'No. What?'

'That there are twenty thousand deserters walking the streets of London alone. Twenty thousand. English, American, the lot. It's probably even true. We had a gang of forty brought in on remand two days ago, waiting to be sent up to Colchester to the military jail. And they'll know what's hit them when they get up there, oh yes. Picked up at an illegal still on Asylum Road in Peckham. Asylum Road, as God is my witness. Twenty gallons of whisky essence. Made a fortune, apparently. Sugar beet. They were shifting a thousand pints a week at the Trocadero down at Elephant & Castle alone. A thousand pints. Extortionate. According to the man who spilled the beans on this lot, there are similar gangs up in Whitechapel and Limehouse brewing up and then shifting ten times that amount. *Ten times*. It beggars belief. And every one of them a deserter from one unit or other.'

Tait listened to all this with interest. He wanted to tell Bone that it *didn't* beggar belief, that it was the world in which he himself had started to live.

'Plus,' Bone said. 'Plus, they're already sending POWs back over here. Sending them back and then paying them off without even a proper medical going-over. *And* they're talking about petrol rationing for at least another five years. Five years. It makes you wonder what it was we were all fighting for in the first place.' He stopped talking and looked at the boy at the table. 'It must be hard for you to get worked up about any of this,' he said. 'You should tell me to shut my cake-hole. Always putting the world to rights, that's my problem.'

'I enjoy listening to you,' Tait said. 'I mean it. It sometimes seems to me as though I've never had a proper conversation with anyone in my whole life.'

'It's a dying art, that's why,' Bone said. 'My wife used to talk, but that's all it ever was – talk. Nothing, you know, back and forth. Gossip, I suppose you'd call it, tittle-tattle, so-called news of the great and the good and the not so great or good. Took after her mother in that respect. Women tend to do that, in my experience.' She was the only woman Bone had ever truly known.

In the corridor outside, a bell sounded briefly, but it was nothing to either Bone or Tait.

'Shift change,' Bone said. 'Not me. I'm here for the duration. You're stuck with me whether you like it or not. We're short staffed again. Early lock-up on a couple of the wings.' And even as he said this, a succession of far-off doors could be heard being slammed shut and locked.

'Is it too late, do you think, Mister Bone?' Tait said as Bone was momentarily distracted by the distant noise.

Bone knew exactly what he was being asked. One way or another, every single one of them asked him the same thing. 'Too late for what?' he said. 'I'm not sure I—'

'For me, I mean. Too late for me.'

Bone considered his answer for a full minute before speaking. 'The problem is,' he said, 'that your so-called lawyer has thrown in the towel. They all have.' And even that much would have been enough to have him removed from the duty and never be allowed to return.

'I didn't mean that side of things,' Tait said, seemingly unperturbed by Bone's remark. 'I was thinking of all that other stuff – the Bible stuff.'

Bone waited for him to explain further, but again this was beyond the boy.

'There's only you can know that for certain,' Bone said eventually. 'Or at least, that's what Simpson would tell you. That, and that it's never too late to turn things around, never too late to look for that forgiveness you were talking about. Forgiveness, or some greater understanding of things as they apply. According to men like Simpson, it's never too late for anything in this world. And if you ask me, that's all part of the problem. Never too late for anything. You can see what that kind of promise or offer might do to a man. Thing is, for me it's always been more a question of what you believe in here' – he patted a hand over his heart – 'that matters most. If you can't believe it in *here*, then no amount of other people telling you what is and isn't possible at the very end is going to convince you or make you change your ways. You know that already; I can see you do. I've seen far too many so-called last-minute conversions and confessions to believe in any of that. The simple truth is, there's no easy way out for any of us.'

'But especially not for me?' Tait said.

Bone nodded at the Bible. 'And I've seen too many men put too much faith in whatever secrets that thing is supposed to hold. Sometimes a cigarette paper can seem a good, honest thing. You know where you are with a cigarette. Look at Winston. I've never smoked a cigar these past ten years, but I don't begrudge that man his. *He* smokes a cigar and it's like we're all smoking it with him.'

Tait couldn't accept this, but nor could he bring himself to disagree with Bone and create even the smallest of conflicts between them.

'And to top it all, Adolf's a bloody vegetarian,' Bone said. 'Carrots and turnips and tomatoes. Some of the papers are saying he's already dead. Apparently, no one's seen him for days. Living in a cellar, by all accounts, with everything up-stairs burning down around his ears.'

'Will that be the end, then?' Tait said.

'Of the fighting? I should imagine so. I don't know how they'd go about it – getting everyone to stop and all that – but I can't see how things could go on afterwards. It's a good point. The whisky gang rounded up at Asylum Road were all convinced that the first thing that would happen when it was all over was that good old Winston would announce an amnesty for the lot of them.'

'For all the deserters?'

'And the rest. Some of them have been walking the streets up to no good for the duration.'

Tait had met enough of them in that other life.

'I told them to dream on,' Bone said. 'Told them they'd get to serve two days for every one they'd been AWOL and some other poor bloody bugger had been catching the bombs and bullets and God-knows-what that had been meant for them.'

Tait laughed at this.

'That put a rocket up them,' Bone said.

'I would have gone to the front if they'd let me,' Tait said. 'I thought it's what the judge might tell me to do.'

'I know you did,' Bone said. But not on a murder charge, he wouldn't. 'All a bit too late for that kind of thing now, I should imagine. All a bit too late for everything, in fact.'

'I suppose so,' Tait said. 'Be good to know it was all over, though. You know . . .'

'I know,' Bone told him.

The last of the distant cell doors was pushed shut, and the dying echo rolled like a subsiding wave through the whole prison.

25

FRANKIE DOLL WAS ON HIS WAY TO SEE BILLY LEACH up in Paddington. Running Tommy Fowler's bum's rush of an errand for him. Frankie Doll believed he had started making all the right connections. Some remained uncertain, and some were unlikely, but what was definitely still missing for Frankie Doll was the connection between the boy who had hit Laura – the boy whose identity Tommy Fowler had then gone to such lengths to protect – and the secret message about Billericay he was on his way to deliver to Billy Leach now.

There was, however, something of which Frankie Doll was one hundred per cent certain, and that was that, yet again, Tommy Fowler was taking him for a fool. Well, Frankie Doll was nobody's fool, so more fool Tommy Fowler for thinking he was. And not only was Frankie Doll nobody's fool, but the more he understood of all these connections now, the less of a fool – *anybody*'s fool – he became. And that was another lesson Tommy Fowler would be learning soon enough.

Besides, whatever the outcome of all these connections – between Fowler and the boy, between Fowler and Billy Leach, between Fowler and Tait, and between Fowler and Sweeney and Crowley – there was nothing whatsoever in any of them to alert Tommy Fowler to Frankie Doll's plans with Beazley at the Holywell Street studio. So, all in all, everything seemed set fair in that particular direction at least.

Frankie Doll's world, it now seemed to him, had turned into a world of intrigue – even the word itself sounded its own dangerous and exotic note. A world of intrigue and secrets, and a reward or a profit or a further beckoning opportunity riding on the back of every single one of those secrets just waiting to be claimed by Frankie Doll. Even Julian Beazley, he guessed, didn't yet know the half of it.

Tommy Fowler and Billy Leach had worked together for twenty years, each in his own part of North London, and in the past both men had been careful to protect their individual interests by the simple expedient of avoiding too much contact with one another. But it seemed to Frankie Doll that this was all about to change, and that perhaps this Billericay business was part of that change.

Arriving at Wharf Road, Frankie Doll spotted one of Billy Leach's men standing in a doorway. He knew the man from all the previous times he had been there. The man signalled to him and Frankie Doll crossed the road to join him.

It was raining lightly, and the man stood with his collar turned up against the wet. And if it had been warm and sunny, then he would have been standing in the same doorway with his collar turned up against the sun and the heat. His name was Walsh – Welsh Walsh – and he had been a professional boxer and then a bare-knuckle fighter in the Catford and Harringay rings. After his last fight, two years ago, he had been unconscious for three days. And following that, and after Billy Leach had trousered the fortune he had made betting on the man – first to win, then to lose, then to simply be standing at the end of each bout – Billy Leach had retired him and put him on the payroll.

Welsh Walsh was a standing presence and a threat, but only to the people who didn't know his history.

'On another errand from Tommy?' he said as Frankie Doll joined him.

'Bit of trouble with that Billericay thing,' Frankie Doll said, feigning disinterest.

'Everything about *that* little charmer's been more trouble than it was ever worth,' Walsh said. 'Billy and Tommy alike will be glad to close the book on that one.'

'Still, not long now, eh?' Frankie Doll said.

'Week, tops, looks like,' Walsh said. He went on looking all around them as he spoke.

It was all the confirmation Frankie Doll needed. Whatever else there was to learn, he would learn from Billy Leach himself.

'Billy in his office, is he?' Frankie Doll said.

Walsh nodded once. 'As per.'

The office was above a vegetable warehouse, accessible through the warehouse itself and up a double flight of metal stairs, half inside and half outside the building. Plenty of notice for Billy Leach to leave the office and disappear across the rooftops in the direction of the station and its restless crowds.

'And that's *Mister* Leach to you, Frankie,' Walsh said. He kicked once on the door behind him with his heel, and a moment later a bolt was drawn. A second man appeared and looked without speaking at Frankie Doll.

'Fowler sent him,' Walsh said. 'Mister Leach knows him. He'll want to see him.'

The second man looked at Frankie Doll and then gestured over his shoulder.

Frankie Doll thanked Walsh and said he'd buy him a drink the next time he was in the Regency.

'*That* tart's parlour?' Walsh said. 'You'll have a long wait.'

Frankie Doll followed the second man into the warehouse. The smell of rotten vegetables filled the air. The place was mostly empty, with only a few sacks of potatoes stacked at the bottom of the stairs. He tried making conversation with his guide, but the man said nothing, merely leading Frankie Doll to the bottom of the metal stairs and pointing upwards. Frankie Doll had visited the place fifty times before, and this always happened. Billy Leach's tried and tested procedure.

At the top of the stairs a door led to the outside of the building – an old fire escape – and then re-entered it a floor higher. Billy Leach had once told Frankie Doll all about the pass at Thermopylae. Well, that outside staircase was his Thermopylae. Frankie Doll had shown a keen interest and had understood nothing of what Billy Leach was telling him.

Frankie Doll knocked at the door and it was opened immediately. Anyone getting that far – that close to Billy Leach – had already been vetted and searched: another lesson to learn for when Frankie Doll needed a procedure of his own.

Billy Leach himself shouted for Frankie Doll to come in to him. He already knew that it was Doll out there – a telephone call from someone downstairs, presumably. Another precaution. Nothing remotely similar at the Regency shielded Tommy Fowler from the same predatory world outside.

There were two other men besides Billy Leach in the room when Frankie Doll went in.

'Dolly, Dolly, Dolly,' Billy Leach said, causing the two men to smile. It was what Billy Leach always called Frankie Doll. 'Always a pleasure. A message from that old shyster Fowler, I imagine. Spit it out.'

Frankie Doll looked at the two others.

'What?' Billy Leach said. 'Something private?' He motioned for the two men to go outside, which they did, noisily descending the metal stairs. 'Ready when you are,' Billy Leach said.

'It's to do with this Billericay business,' Frankie Doll said, aware that he had just crossed a dangerous line. A single enquiry or remark from Billy Leach back to Tommy Fowler suggesting Frankie Doll's own interest, and perhaps everything would unravel and end even more swiftly. He would pass on the messages about the property deals later.

'I thought me and dear old Tommy had already put that little bit of business to bed. The tart playing up, is she?'

'No, not at all. Mister Fowler took good care of that. He just wanted me to make sure there were no loose ends or unfinished business this end.'

'Tell him he worries too much. The little bastard was just letting off steam, that's all. He'd been stuck out there in the sticks for months now, ever since the trial. He fancied a night on the town, that's all. He's a kid; what do you expect? You tell Tommy that what happened happened, and that it won't happen again. Besides, not long to wait now before the whole thing blows over. Believe me, neither of us needs this kind of trouble, not now.'

'That's what Mister Fowler said,' Frankie Doll said.

'Right, then, so what's the problem? You'll be telling me next that you and Tommy can't keep a steady hand on your own brasses. I doubt if Tommy would appreciate you giving people that kind of impression.'

'I didn't—'

'Don't worry, Dolly, he won't hear a word of it from me. Believe me, the sooner the poor sap in Pentonville takes his drop and the sooner the package in Billericay is off my hands, the happier we're all going to be. Christ, I only agreed to look after the little bastard in the first place as a favour to Tommy – his brother's kid and all that. He could have gone anywhere out of reach of the Metropolitans, it's just that he didn't want to go *too* far. If it had been one of mine, I'd have packed the little bastard off to Timbuktu, wherever that is. Better still, I'd have given serious consideration to getting rid of the problem completely.'

'Mister Fowler said exactly the same,' Frankie Doll said.

'There you go, then. Great minds, and all that.'

'But with it being his nephew and everything . . .'

'Exactly. Families. They have been known to complicate things somewhat.'

It was all the confirmation Frankie Doll needed. Now everything was clear to him, or as clear as anything ever was in that endlessly changing world.

'I told dear old Tommy from the off that he didn't owe his brother anything, but Tommy said there was always the Wembley job, the dead copper and his brother still doing time in Wandsworth, having kept schtum for all this time, to be taken into consideration. I can see his point. This will wipe the slate clean for Tommy, help him get ready to move on. Me and him alike, I suppose.'

'I see,' Frankie Doll said. He didn't, not completely, but he was beginning to. And for the first time, he began to wonder if Billy Leach was telling him all this for a reason. Fowler himself had certainly shared nothing of this dangerous secret with Frankie Doll. Why was that? Was he sharing it with someone else? Sweeney, perhaps? Was Billy Leach telling him everything now to somehow undermine or gain an advantage over Tommy Fowler?

'I sometimes wonder if the little bleeder didn't go to the Regency out of pure spite,' Billy Leach said. 'Looking to make trouble for me and Tommy, to put us on notice, so to speak. Because of what happened to his father. And whatever the outcome of all this, you mark my words, none of it will be properly over until he's made his own little mark on the world. Come to think of it, what was him shooting the civilian all about in the first place if it wasn't him starting to play his cards?'

Frankie Doll felt suddenly powerful and vulnerable in equal measure, and he wished he was somewhere alone and unobserved so he could begin to understand even better everything he'd just learned. What he had managed to unscramble so far was that Tommy Fowler's nephew had been the one on the Globe Town raid who had killed a man, that Fowler still owed a debt to his imprisoned brother, and that the substitution of Tait for Fowler's nephew and Tait's imminent execution would see that debt repaid.

Perhaps it all really was that simple. Perhaps Frankie Doll already knew everything there was to know. And perhaps that *did* give him something over Fowler which might come in useful when he and Beazley decided to make their move. And all through the bruise on Laura's face. It was true what they said about people seizing the moment and then making the most of every opportunity that landed in their laps. And perhaps all this was happening to Frankie Doll now because he *had* finally decided to cut the ties which bound him to Fowler and become his own man. There were still a lot of unanswered questions – the thing with Sweeney, Crowley, the Nolan girl's disappearance – but perhaps they were of no consequence whatsoever now. Perhaps Frankie Doll *himself* needed to keep things simple from here onwards, to finally be the one who decided what did and didn't matter. Perhaps that was all that had ever separated Frankie Doll from men like Tommy Fowler and Billy Leach in the first place.

Billy Leach was still talking, but Frankie Doll was only half listening to him now.

He started paying attention when Billy Leach said, 'Well?' and, 'I asked you a question.'

'Sorry,' Frankie Doll said. 'I was trying to remember everything to report back to Mister Fowler.'

'I've already told you, Dolly – there's nothing *to* report. I asked you what the world was coming to. I was saying about everybody wanting something for nothing these days, everybody wanting more than their fair share, Tommy's nephew being a case in point. Greed, that's what it is. Everybody wants something, but nobody's prepared to put in the time and the graft to get whatever that is. Yesterday's never soon enough for most people these days. Me and Tommy, we put in the time to build up what we've got. And now these vicious little bleeders like his nephew think they can just march straight in and take some of it – *all* of it, come to that – for themselves. Is that how you see it, Dolly? Is that how even you've started to think?'

'Me?' Frankie Doll said. 'Not me.'

'Glad to hear it,' Billy Leach said. 'You tell Tommy from

305

me that he's going to have to watch himself when that one's back on the prowl in a week's time. And watch himself properly, watch his back, watch everything. It's in the blood, I suppose. He might owe his brother something, but there's always a limit to every debt, and I hope Tommy knows that.'

'I think so,' Frankie Doll said.

'You're a good boy, Dolly. Faithful. Don't knock it; it's a valuable commodity these days.'

That's me, Frankie Doll thought to himself. *Faithful.*

'And I see the Bermondsey boys have been attracting a lot of unnecessary attention recently. Youngsters. They think the whole world needs to know their business. The law's not going to sit still on that mob, you tell Tommy that from me. And once they've gone, that's the bulk of Tooting, Brixton, the Castle and Bermondsey up for grabs. They might not look it now, but they're valuable prospects, they are. Me and Tommy are too long in the tooth for that kind of carve-up, but I doubt if nasty little nephew Fowler is.'

'I think Mister Fowler thinks the same,' Frankie Doll said. See – he was speaking on Tommy Fowler's behalf now. He even wondered if these were actual lies he was telling, and not merely a version of the truth that, as yet, only *he*, Frankie Doll, was aware of. It was certainly a possibility.

'You ever been to Billericay?' Billy Leach said.

'Can't say that I have.'

'Full of Army depots. All sorts. Ours, Yank, everything. Most of the stuff's been there for months. Unlikely that it's *ever* going to move now that everything's almost over. Somebody's going to make himself a small fortune on the surplus-to-requirements market.'

'Meaning you?' Frankie Doll said.

'Meaning me.' Billy Leach smiled. 'See – you're a smart boy; a lot smarter than most people give you credit for.'

Meaning Tommy Fowler?

'Just wait until Winnie gets the bill from the Yanks for that little lot,' Billy Leach said. 'He's going to be dead and buried a long time before *that* particular debt is ever going to be wiped off the slate.'

'I suppose so,' Frankie Doll said.

'Don't suppose,' Billy Leach said. '*Know*. Know it, Dolly. This is me talking, and what I'm telling you is gospel.'

'I appreciate it,' Frankie Doll said.

'I can see you do, Dolly. I can see you do.'

And once again Frankie Doll wondered if there was some ulterior motive in Billy Leach telling him all this, in having sown these seeds and then having raked over and watered the ground.

Almost as though Billy Leach had read these thoughts in Frankie Doll's head, he said, 'Gardening – that's going to be me from now on. I'll give all this another year, two tops, and then I'm off to the Home Counties somewhere, nice little house in the country with a nice big garden. I'll probably even join the local golf club. Can you see that, Dolly – me playing golf and growing cabbages and chrysanthemums?'

'I can, Mister Leach,' Frankie Doll said.

'What was that song they used to sing – "London Belongs to Me"? Well, it always belongs to somebody, Dolly, and that's a fact. And that's all well and good, as far as it goes. But when it comes to the actual change of ownership, to the handing over of the keys of the kingdom, *that*'s when things tend to get a bit messy. The trick is to know when to let go, and then on the other side when to step up and take control. You've got to know when to come and then when to go. Take my lark – the gambling – it's had its day. The world isn't going to go on turning on the odd quid bet here, a fiver or a tenner there. The dogs might be back on, the summer horses will be running soon enough, but before long everything's going to get much too respectable for its own good. After which, it's not going to be half the fun it once was. Nothing ever stays the same, Dolly, and that's another piece of good advice you can take to the bank.'

Exactly what Julian Beazley had gone to such lengths to convince him of.

'Mister Fowler says much the same,' Frankie Doll said.

'I'm sure he does. And I'm sure he looks at you and all the others like you with those same unhappy doubts in his mind, wondering when you're all going to make your moves, when you're all going to turn on him or go your own ways.'

'He's got no worries with me on that score,' Frankie Doll said. Especially now that Frankie Doll knew what he knew. Perhaps Tommy Fowler would be only too glad to see the back of him; perhaps he would even be willing to help him and Beazley make their own way in life. It was certainly another possibility. In fact, *everything* was a possibility now.

It only then occurred to Frankie Doll that for him to keep this advantage he now held, he would at some point have to actually confront Fowler with what he knew. Confront him and then threaten to go to the police. And how would Fowler react to that? Would he do everything he could to protect his nephew and repay his debt to his brother, or would he choose another way out of the problem completely?

And if Tommy Fowler was threatened with the law, didn't that also mean that the same thing would happen to

Billy Leach? Because if Tommy Fowler was ever charged with hiding the real murderer and perverting the course of justice and letting an innocent man hang, then Billy Leach was certain to be dragged down with him. Or would that, too, work to Frankie Doll's advantage? Two birds, one stone. It was an unsettling thought, and Frankie Doll felt a chill run through his entire body. How had he become such an important, powerful part of all this, and so swiftly?

'You look like somebody just walked over your grave, Dolly,' Billy Leach said to him.

If only he knew. 'It's been a long few days, that's all,' Frankie Doll said.

'I can imagine. Still, like I said, not much longer now. I know Tommy feels obliged, but if this particular problem had been of *my* making – family or no family – it would have been long gone and buried out in Hackney Marshes by now.' He made a gun with his hand and blew on his fingertips. 'And don't tell me Tommy didn't at least consider the same.'

'I suppose so,' Frankie Doll said.

'So, are we all done here? You happy to report back to Tommy?'

Frankie Doll rose from where he sat. A minute earlier he had felt that chill; now there was sweat on his brow. It was a warm room. He hadn't even mentioned the Bayswater or Norfolk Square property deals.

'Always good to see you, Dolly,' Billy Leach said.

'You, too,' Frankie Doll said. *Billy.*

26

'WHAT HAPPENED?' SILVER ASKED CROWLEY. 'DID YOU fall?'

Crowley allowed himself to be helped up from where Silver had found him on the floor. 'I was dreaming,' he said.

'Of what?' Silver looked at the yellowing flesh he held.

'Oh, nothing.'

'Was it part of the ritual?' Silver said. 'The next phase? Are things – I don't know – proceeding smoothly – what?'

'None of that,' Crowley said, smiling. 'I was dreaming of Randall Gair.'

'Your son?'

'We were swimming together.' Randall had been born eight years earlier to the twenty-two-year-old Deirdre O'Doherty, when Crowley was forty years her senior and already an old man. The Irish girl reminded him a lot of Deirdre.

'You never speak of him,' Silver said, surprised by the mention now.

'I spend my whole life mourning losses of one kind or another, along with all my lost and missed opportunities,' Crowley said. 'Hence . . .'

Silver took out his stethoscope and listened to Crowley's

heart. 'It's racing,' he said. Crowley's arm turned briefly darker where Silver held it. 'You've over-exerted yourself.'

'Once I would have said visions, not dreams,' Crowley said.

Silver looked surreptitiously around him for signs that the girl had been back there.

Crowley saw this and laughed. 'What?' he said. 'Are you imagining debauchery?'

'You're seventy,' Silver said simply.

'And that's what – a reason *not* to do something? To do it? An excuse for so-called unforgivable or unseemly behaviour?'

Silver knew better than to attempt to answer this. He went on listening to Crowley's chest, then rolled up his stethoscope and put it away. 'Tell me what happened,' he said.

Again, Crowley avoided answering him directly, brushing the dust from his legs and arms as he settled himself in his chair, the seat, back and arms of which were now moulded to his shape.

'Tell me,' Silver said. 'I've plenty of time. I have nowhere else to go, no one else to see.' It was the terrible truth, and Silver realized this only as he said it.

Crowley, too, was struck by the words and sensed his friend's sudden understanding. 'Which is why you can afford to waste your time with me,' he said. 'And yes, before you ask, the girl was here again. Of her own free will, I might add. No coercion whatsoever on my part. Well, none beyond a few spells scattered on the breeze.' He shook his head to let Silver know that he was joking.

'Is she . . . ?' Silver wondered what he was truly asking. 'I mean – is she now actually a *part* of it all?'

Crowley's brief evasive silence was all the answer he needed.

'Tell me,' Silver said. Not that he imagined Crowley

wouldn't cast those spells if he believed they would work for him.

'Let's just say – admit – that she is able to perform certain of the rites with me. Not entirely necessary, I admit, but pleasurable all the same. And she is so far proving a willing participant.'

'In addition to which, you have no intention whatsoever of turning her away,' Silver said. 'Just like all the others. Did she – the two of you, I mean – was there . . . ?'

'I hardly needed to twist her arm,' Crowley said.

'And does she *know* – I mean does she honestly understand what she's let herself in for, the purpose of all this, these rites?' He said the word as though it were a sour taste in his mouth.

'Not entirely,' Crowley said. 'And I, for one, see no need to inform her of every little detail or—'

'I can imagine,' Silver said.

'She'd heard of the Golden Dawn, of course. And of my own part within it.'

'Oh, really?' Silver doubted this. She'd read the newspapers, that was all; she'd seen the words.

'The scandal sheets. I feed her clues, of course. And each time she comes, she appears to know a little more about me. I think it excites her to be involved. In fact, I'm certain of it. Especially after last night's little—'

'Excites her in what way?'

'Joshua, use your imagination.'

Silver shook his head.

'I told her my Golden Dawn title. Perdurabo.' Crowley pronounced each syllable with equal emphasis, closing his eyes briefly as the word rolled around his mouth like a marble, and as though it were the greatest of all those losses he had just mentioned. '"He who will endure".'

'You will endure,' Silver said, 'for precisely as long as your poor struggling heart endures. Or whichever other vital organ decides to give up the ghost before it. What else did you deign to tell her?'

'Nothing of any real consequence – merely that I was the possessor of arcane truths which could be traced, like my wife's scents, back to the Ancient Egyptians.'

'*Them* again,' Silver said.

'Mock me as much as you like,' Crowley told him. 'I didn't bother with all the Rosicrucian details. It may have been too much for the poor thing. She has a much higher opinion of herself, of course, than the world at large must have of her.'

'She remains innocent of—'

'She remains innocent of nothing, believe me. And what a vice innocence all too often turns out to be. Innocent? No. And if you'd seen her last night, then you certainly wouldn't be—'

'I don't wish to hear,' Silver said.

Crowley waited a moment before going on. 'I told her of my progression through the ranks – Zelator, Theoricus, Practicus, Philosophus – and all of it meant absolutely nothing, less than nothing to her.'

'As it would mean absolutely nothing to millions of others,' Silver said. Except as something pompous, laughable and ridiculous, perhaps.

'True,' Crowley said. 'But she was still a willing listener, still afterwards willing to show her appreciation for all I had revealed. I remember a woman just like her when I was living in Chancery Lane, before I moved to Scotland to create the shrine to Abramelin. I engaged her to find me a suitable dwelling somewhere closer to the centre of civilization and then I followed her round one dreary and inappropriate property after another as she attempted to earn her all-too-generous commission.'

'Similar in what way?' Silver said, beginning to wonder where, if anywhere, the story was leading.

'Oh, the disposal of her favours,' Crowley said. 'I was a much younger man then, of course, much younger. And she too knew what she was letting herself in for. I told her why I was looking for the place, and she excited herself by the thought of our "shared" enterprise, by imagining and then actually believing herself to be a part of it all.'

'Meaning you took advantage of her,' Silver said.

Crowley shrugged at the remark. 'She knew what she was doing.'

'Just as the girl last night knows what she's doing? Just as she knows what she's getting herself into?'

'Of course. I'm still who I am. It still counts for *something*, surely? And surely you, of all people, can see that much at least?'

'You're still—' Silver began to say.

'I know – I'm still taking advantage of her,' Crowley said. 'I know. Perhaps. But, believe me, now, as then, neither of them needed much persuasion as they bent themselves to my will.'

Silver laughed at the phrase.

'Who knows?' Crowley went on. 'Perhaps they genuinely believed – believe – that some great and as-yet-unknowable advantage will be gained by allowing themselves to be joined to me.'

'As you finally gain immortality?' Silver said. 'And then

314

what? Something of that then rubs off on them?'

'It's what the gangster already half believes,' Crowley said.

Then more fool him, Silver thought. 'Is it what *you* believe might happen?'

'Perhaps,' Crowley said. He was more guarded now. 'I've been accused of exploiting the so-called fairer sex all my life, and certainly in all I've attempted to achieve.'

'Because it was true,' Silver said, wishing the remark sounded less critical.

Crowley said nothing for a moment. He shivered and pulled his jacket together. 'The young woman in Chancery Lane offered herself to me in all manner of ways if I promised to share what I knew with her. The Law of Thelema was then my overriding purpose in life.'

'More—'

'More sex, yes. It's hardly my fault that it remains the main and single most potent conduit to spiritual fulfilment. I might as well chop off my own hand as deny that.'

'I understand all of that,' Silver said. 'I merely question your . . . your . . .'

'You question my proclivities, founded as they are on blind belief.'

'I was going to say that I question your determination to continue as you do in light of your condition.'

'My condition?' Crowley seemed genuinely offended by the remark. 'I doubt if my "condition" has changed since my quest began.'

Silver rolled his eyes at this endless denial. 'You're wrong,' he said. 'And what will happen when the girl decides she wants more? Or when she finally sees that you're merely using her? Besides, how is *your* success going to be of the slightest benefit

315

to *her*? The gangster might be ultimately disappointed, but he can still make his demands of you. What will *she* have when it all comes to nothing?'

Crowley shook his head at the question. 'You're sinking in the mud,' he said. 'The Slough of Respectability.'

'And you, Aleister, as ever, as always, have your head in the clouds and the stars in your eyes.'

Crowley laughed at this. 'And when did you last make love to a woman, any woman, let alone one fifty years your junior?'

'You think I'm jealous of your – your connivances, your manipulations?'

'Perhaps not. But, equally, you haven't the slightest idea of her own connivances. You surely don't think I'm stupid enough to believe that she finds me – this – in the least attractive, do you?' Crowley patted his stomach and thighs as he said this, leaving his hands resting there, his fingers curled into his groin. 'Because I'm not that stupid, and I doubt if she's that desperate.'

'She's clearly desperate enough for something,' Silver said.

'Exactly,' Crowley said. 'I'm Aleister Crowley, the Antichrist, the Great Beast. Do you think I'm mocked and scorned and ridiculed the world over because at the back of all those mocking mouths and brains there *isn't* still a solitary dirty little seed of doubt? Do you think they all scorn me because they believe *their* conviction is greater than mine? Do you think this girl, the girl in Chancery Lane, and all the girls, men and women in between haven't harboured that same tiny, agitating seed of doubt somewhere in their own minds? Perhaps the girl last night could have been with a dozen other men on any of the occasions she's been here with me – and I daresay there are ten times that number with the money in their pockets to buy her for the evening, or hour, or however long the thing lasts for them – but do you imagine that, in her own mind, and knowing what she now knows of me, she believes that a single one of *them* might be able to offer her what *I* might – just *might*, note – one day possess?' He was breathless after the speech and stopped to regain his composure.

Silver waited, unwilling to provoke Crowley further. And besides, there was something in what he was suggesting about the girl's own motives and expectations. In all likelihood, she *was* just another thrill-seeker, another one of those men and women only too happy to associate themselves with Crowley and then to capitalize on whatever profitable notoriety this might bring them.

After a minute, Crowley said, 'The girl in Chancery Lane revealed herself to me across a table top. I told her she resembled a sacrificial virgin on an altar – as though I had ever once seen such a thing. "Then treat me as one," she said to me.' Crowley smiled and closed his eyes briefly at the memory. 'The girl last night knelt at my feet where you are sitting now. Believe me, neither of them flinched or looked too horrified at my first touch. And nor did any of those countless others.'

'I don't wish to know,' Silver said.

'Perhaps,' Crowley said. 'But if you yourself were possessed of the same powers and impulses and opportunities, I doubt you would fail to act upon them in precisely the same way.'

Silver had heard all this before from Crowley, and usually at the end of just such an argument. 'You're wrong,' he said.

'I might certainly be the age I am, but none of those things

317

– none of those beliefs, urges, tendencies – has grown any weaker with the dimming of the light.'

'"Tendencies"?' Silver said, shaking his head.

'Then look upon this current involvement of mine – this current dalliance – as merely a measure' – Crowley paused and smiled – 'of lubrication for the greater good. A small sacrifice, say, to better ensure that greater good. Surely that's something we've all become accustomed to of late – making sacrifices.'

But this deliberate provocation offended Silver further and he refused to be swayed. 'You're playing with people's lives,' he said.

'I'm playing with nothing more than that which the girl herself is offering to me,' Crowley said sharply. 'Whatever happens between us is to our mutual benefit.'

'Why? Because she "lubricates" the process?' Silver said coldly. 'The "process" seemed to me to be proceeding perfectly smoothly without her.'

'I'm simply taking what she is happy and eager to offer to me,' Crowley said. 'It really is a perfectly straightforward transaction. I haven't tied her up and kept her here and made her do things against her will. I don't keep her prisoner and insist on her indulging my every whim. Or perhaps you want to look in the cupboards or under the bed.'

'Now you're being ridiculous,' Silver said. 'All I'm saying is that you're taking advantage of her naivety, her gullibility, her desperation, or whatever it is that causes her to return here and indulge you.'

'And if she *is* able to assist me in my efforts, after which *I* am able to reward *her*? What then?'

But Silver had undergone this particular circle of an

argument a dozen times before: self-belief, self-justification and airy denial heated on supposedly superior, undisclosed knowledge and then beaten together like three metals in a forge. He rose, walked briefly around the small room and then returned to his chair.

'What, above all else, and above any incidental benefit to herself, does she imagine you will achieve?' he said to Crowley. *What have you told her? What have you promised her?*

'I believe the word "immortality" was mentioned while she was at her ministrations.' Crowley slapped his thighs again.

'You really don't need to keep on painting the same sordid picture over and over,' Silver told him.

'It's what we showmen do,' Crowley said.

'And I take it you've said nothing whatsoever to her about the part yet to be played in achieving that goal by the boy awaiting his fate in Pentonville?'

'Not a whisper. Besides, she seems far more interested in repeating to me all the stories she reads in her magazines and asking me if they're true or not.'

'And you, naturally, oblige her.'

'When memory serves, yes.'

'And when it doesn't?'

'Then I do what I've always done and elaborate according to need. Like I said, I'm a showman. I told her last night of my relationship with Diane de Rougy, that tedious, cross-dressing friend of Beardsley's. She hadn't even heard of Aubrey. Imagine that. I showed her some of his drawings, reproductions, and she pored over the things. As I said, she is nothing if not an empty vessel, eager to be filled, and even more eager to please. She offered to bring me pictures of her own – I'm not sure if she meant pictures of herself – cards, magazines. It's the world she inhabits. She said the man Fowler has his own little rackets with photographers and filmmakers. I imagine it's something else she craves. That's all it ever was with most of them – a craving for attention. *My* attention.'

'So how did it proceed?' Silver asked him.

'You mean how did she . . . ?'

'The ritual, the rite. How did it proceed, how did it go?'

Crowley seemed suddenly reluctant to answer him.

'Is it not going according to plan, to schedule?' Silver asked him.

'It's difficult to say. All I can do is follow the procedure as laid out until the final rite. I'll know only then if I've been successful or not.'

'The moment the boy is dropped through the trap, you mean?'

'The clock will be chiming in both our rooms,' Crowley said, indicating the clock on the mantel.

'But you suspect there are problems?' Silver said, sensing doubt.

Crowley fluttered his hands. 'I don't know. Perhaps something has come between myself and the spell in the boy's hands.'

'What makes you say that?'

'I can't tell you. Instinct, intuition? It's how these things work. Believe me, I wish I *could* be more specific.'

'Is there no way you can find out or remedy this – what – intervention?'

'None whatsoever. Now that the ritual is started and the first rites completed, nothing can be interrupted or revealed. The thing must run its course. The girl might guess at her own small part in the proceedings, but nothing more.'

'And the boy?'

'Vital that he remains completely innocent of the whole process.'

'Next you'll be telling me that it's as much for his own good as for yours.'

'It is,' Crowley said. 'Surely you can see that much?'

Silver nodded. 'Perhaps the appearance of the girl has somehow exerted an influence – created this intervention – in some way,' he suggested.

Crowley shook his head at this. 'I've already told you – the girl and all she happily and willingly offers to me is merely another fortifying charge helping the thing to its conclusion.'

'First she's lubrication, now she's an electrical current,' Silver said.

'And who's to say that at the moment of fruition and success the pair of us won't burst into a joyous fountain of light?' Crowley said.

'Or perhaps flames?' Silver suggested.

'Or perhaps flames.'

'Then I'll stand ready with a bucket of water,' Silver said.

'Perhaps you should have been here last night,' Crowley said.

'Perhaps I should have,' Silver said, finally smiling again.

27

Veronica read to Sweeney from her newspaper. 'He's dead,' she said. 'Hitler's dead. Old Adolf. Could have been dead a week for all anybody knows. It says the Russians have overrun whatsit – Berlin. All they're waiting for now, it says, are the peace terms to be agreed. Killed himself the day after his birthday, party and everything, imagine that. Him and that Eva bit. Even killed his dog, according to this. Apparently, there's a new Hitler. General or Admiral something or other. What sense does that make? I'll tell you what sense it makes – none at all, that's what sense it makes.'

She looked across at Sweeney, who sat on the edge of his bed, having been asleep fully clothed when she'd gone in to him.

'You listening to a word I'm saying? You haven't listened to a word of it.' She looked at him closely. He was unshaven, with dark rings around his eyes. 'You been asleep, then?'

'Working,' Sweeney said. 'Late. For Mister Fowler.'

'You do too much for that one. He takes advantage. It also says that they've arrested Hah Hah. That's what I heard a woman call him the other day. He's going to hang. I think that's a bit steep. The "Humbug of Hamburg", we used to call him when he started trying to tell us what was what.

322

"Germany calling, Germany calling." Used to send a shiver up your spine, that did.'

'Nobody will ever forget that,' Sweeney said.

It was a start, something. He still hadn't forgiven her for driving Ruby Nolan away.

'Within the year, they reckon. To hang him. They're insisting on a proper trial, the lot. Ask me, there'll be questions asked about that. It's not as though they haven't got enough to be going on with. A lot of it's got to do with him being Irish. Nicely spoken, but still Irish. "The Comic of Eau de Cologne".'

'They can hang the lot of them, for all I care,' Sweeney said.

'You don't mean that. Not the lot of them. You don't mean that.'

'Why don't I mean it? Go on – tell me. Why is it that *you* always know what's best for me?' He had been working for Fowler until five in the morning – first visiting the owners of the flapping tracks in Hendon and White City, and then accompanying Fowler himself to one of his Harringay card dens, where some money had gone missing. They were a man short when Fowler was ready to leave the Regency, and Sweeney had been the only one in there. Fowler was angry that he'd been let down by another of his employees, but had been happy for Sweeney to take the man's place.

'If she was going to come back, she knows where you are,' Veronica said, only too aware of his lingering irritation with her.

'I know,' he said.

'Besides, I doubt if *I* scared her away. Not a girl like that. Not her sort.' The little tart had been after something and now she'd found it somewhere else. So more fool him for wasting breath and worry on her.

Tommy Fowler had asked Sweeney where he lived, and Sweeney had told him. Ruby Nolan, apparently, hadn't turned up for work at the Regency for eight nights running. Tommy Fowler said that Beaufort Street sounded a bit far out and that he might be able to find Sweeney somewhere closer to the club if he wanted it. More important than ever, Tommy Fowler said, to look after his reliable employees now. How would a room on Brewer Street suit?

Sweeney was still convinced that if he'd been there when Ruby had turned up six days earlier, she would have stayed. She would have gone up to him and they would have had a drink together and they would have talked and then she just might have stayed with him. They might even have walked back to the Regency together the following day. Arm in arm, like they had walked home from Pavilion Road and the un-exploded bomb.

After the Harringay visit, Tommy Fowler had waited until the two of them were alone, asked Sweeney if he could trust him, and had then given him a loaded revolver and told him to put it somewhere safe. It was why he had asked him earlier where he lived. Nobody was actually looking for the gun, he said; it was just something Tommy Fowler liked to have around now and then. Put it somewhere safe and then keep *that* shut. Just something that helped him to get one or two little jobs done a little bit quicker than they might otherwise get done. Could Sweeney do that? Could he do that for Tommy Fowler? Because if he could, then Tommy Fowler would count it as a big favour. Hide it, keep it somewhere safe, and then when I tell you to fetch it back to me, you fetch it back to me. *Capisce?* Sweeney had slid the gun into his overcoat pocket and had then walked with his hand caressing its hard contours all the way from Harringay to Crouch End and another little bit of business Tommy Fowler had waiting for him.

Later, back in his room and dead on his feet, Sweeney had sniffed at the oil on his fingers and palm. Wipe it, Fowler had told him. Wipe it, keep it clean. Besides, you don't want your dabs on that particular pistolero. I like you; you're a good boy, dependable. Fowler had walked with his arm around Sweeney's shoulders all the way back to the waiting car, where Sweeney was no longer required. A bit of private business down Holywell Street, and the less Sweeney knew about *that*, the better. And the remark about his own fingerprints and the gun? It made sense, Sweeney supposed. After all, who, in their right mind, wanted their dabs on *any* gun?

'That was another one of Haw Haw's – telling people to steer clear of Lyons Corner Houses because they were all owned by Jews and the Luftwaffe knew exactly where they were. All that way up. Imagine believing that load of old guff for one minute. They couldn't hit a football pitch from fifty feet off the ground, most of them. Then again, I don't suppose it mattered all that much.'

Sweeney swung his legs from the bed and rubbed the cramp from his calves.

'Now that all this is over and done with, I'm thinking of going back down to Brighton. Brighton, Hove, Hastings. People will want to get back to the seaside again. That's where all the clever money will go. Who's going to want to sit around kicking their heels in this ruin once the restrictions are lifted? Ask me, this place is finished. Over and out and done with. Kaput.'

Sweeney nodded his agreement. Anything to shut her up. She didn't know what she was talking about. This place was only just beginning.

'Only, it occurred to me . . .' she said.

Sweeney waited. 'What?' What now?

'Only, it occurred to me – and tell me if I've got this all wrong – it occurred to me that you might like to come with me. Brighton. Or Eastbourne. Wherever. Get the dust out of our lungs. Get a bit of sun on our faces before it's too late.'

'It rains in Brighton, too,' Sweeney said. Besides – too late for who? Too late for what? *You're the one who's old; not me.* Ruby Nolan would never go to any of those other places. She'd already come from the back of beyond to get to London, so why would she leave the place now for another back of beyond?

'Fowler said some of the girls were starting to drift, that things were getting slack,' he said.

'There you go, then. *She*'ll have drifted away with them.'

'She wouldn't go without telling me,' Sweeney said, knowing how wrong he was.

Veronica smiled at him. 'You'll get over her fast enough. Nice young man like you. You've got your whole life ahead of you.'

'I know that much already.' Sweeney looked at the cupboard beside the door where Tommy Fowler's gun lay hidden, wrapped in newspaper behind a drawer. He'd taken it out ten times in that first hour and handled it again. And each time he'd washed his hands and then sniffed at them to ensure that nothing of the gun's distinctive smell remained.

326

'I met one of my old circus acquaintances,' Veronica said hesitantly.

Nobody called anybody an 'acquaintance' any more.

'She's got a house down there. Brighton. Evacuated when the invasion was due. Never went back. She's my age – looks older, but the years haven't been as kind to her as to yours truly. She was a contortionist in her younger days. After that, she had a dog act. Used to tell people she was on the trapeze. She wants me to go in with her. Move in together. Do up the house. She reckons I could live down there practically rent free. Big on the tarot, fortune-telling, Brighton. It's that kind of place. She reckons we'd make a killing, the two of us. Either that, or I could get back into the séance lark. Lots of people in Brighton waiting to die, according to her, and wanting to get in touch with the other side. She said she had another friend interested in setting up with her. Automatic writer. She said they made a good team, but that she'd give me first refusal.'

She finally stopped talking and Sweeney struggled to re-member what she'd been saying. Outside, a car sounded its horn, followed by another, and then silence.

Brighton. Another woman. Get her off his back. Leave him free and easy and ready to take up Tommy Fowler's offer.

'You should go,' he said. 'It might be your big chance.'

'We all need one of those.'

'There you go, then.'

'It'd mean leaving this place,' she said. She looked at the ceiling above her. 'I'm part of the fixtures and fittings.'

This was *his* room, not hers.

'It's still an opportunity,' he said.

'You hear that word a lot these days,' she said.

'There you go, then,' he said again.

'She reckons we'd be very comfortable down there. The sea air would do wonders for us. Complexion, that sort of thing.' She looked at herself in the pockmarked mirror beside Sweeney's bed. 'Too late for some, if you ask me,' she said, waiting for his denial.

Too late for you, Sweeney thought. A week ago, such a cruelty would have been beyond him.

'I suppose you could always come and visit,' Veronica said, her voice rising. 'You and . . .' She waited. 'You and whoever, I suppose. You could come as regular as you liked. You never know – London might get too much even for an enterprising young man like you one day.'

'Not very likely,' Sweeney said. And especially not now that he was on arm-around-shoulder terms with Tommy Fowler. He glanced again at the gun's hiding place. He tried to imagine himself walking along Brighton Pier with Ruby Nolan on his arm, the gulls above them, the waves beneath, visible through the boards and causing her to hold on to him. But nothing came. Brighton – it would be like being in the back of beyond in another century. Veronica was wrong on every count. All the clever money would come to London, all of it. The rest of the country – the rest of the world, for that matter – could be left to rot for all he cared.

'For a holiday, then,' Veronica said. 'Perhaps I could open a bed and breakfast and do the tarot on the side.'

She was clearly beginning to warm to the idea. That is if it hadn't all been a lie from the very start, from the instant he'd woken up and seen her sitting there beside him, watching him, ready and waiting with the excuse of Hitler's death to start talking to him.

He motioned to the newspaper now. 'How do they know?' he said.

But she was still in Brighton, surrounded by her boarders or visitors, basking in the warmth of their adulation and need. She, too, could hear the gulls out on the water, hear the waves lapping on the shingle, the noise of the crowds enjoying their long-awaited holidays.

'Know about what?' she said.

'Adolf. That he's definitely dead. He might just be pulling a fast one.'

'Apparently, the Russians found his body. Shot in the head and burned. Somebody poured petrol on him. Him *and* his' – she was careful not to give the word any emphasis – 'tart. Married, apparently. Married, happy birthday, cut the cake, and then bang bang bang, everybody's dead and over and done with. Poison, they reckon, in her case. Or it might have been poison *and* a bullet. Makes no difference, I don't suppose. According to this, it was a proper wedding, proper reception, everything. And all underground. That's where he'd been living while Uncle Joe's boys had been looking for him.'

'If he was burned, then it might not even be him,' Sweeney said. 'Might just be somebody dressed up to look like him.'

'Don't say that,' she said, genuinely alarmed by the off-hand suggestion. 'Don't say that. You've got *me* thinking now. I was all happy until you said that. You've set me thinking now. I've gone all cold. Sent another shiver down my back, that has. I'll never get to Brighton at this rate.'

There was nowhere for the conversation to go. Hitler was dead, married, shot and burned. And soon the war would be over and done with. And even if Hitler wasn't already dead, then the war would soon be over and done with anyway.

Nothing was going to alter that. History was going to resume its dependable old course soon enough either way. Everything was going to settle, and everyone was going to fall back into their rightful, ordained place. And some people would want and welcome that, and others wouldn't. And Sweeney knew better than most where *he* stood on that particular score. He knew where *he* wanted to be when everything stopped tumbling down out of those smoke-filled skies and settled back into place amid the ruins.

'So what will you do?' he said. 'Brighton, I mean.' He knew it was another of her ungraspable opportunities, another blind alley she was peering along. And he knew, too, that she preferred this kind of option to anything more likely or practical or genuine. It wasn't the going to Brighton to start a new and rewarding and fulfilling life that appealed to her, merely the *thought* of what that new life might be. It was the same kind of hopeful drift that had taken her from the circus to the fairgrounds to the variety halls and finally brought her to Beaufort Street. In all likelihood, Sweeney knew, this other woman who had made Veronica the offer was exactly the same. Veronica's life – like the lives of most people – was a string of unconsidered accidents, acceptances and barely thought-through decisions. She latched on to people – just as she had latched on to him – and she let herself be blown in *their* winds, drawn in *their* wakes.

'You've got the sea at Brighton,' she said. 'It's something to look at.'

The remark seemed to embody every degree of hopelessness Sweeney had just considered. He had visited Brighton as a boy, on an outing from one of the orphanages, and it hadn't seemed too impressive to him then. He'd spent most of the day alone, wandering on the beach. Strangers had looked at his mouth and asked him questions and he had run away from them, happy to get back on the bus for London.

'I never put much store by the sea,' he said. You could look at it, you could stand in it, you could throw pebbles into it. And then what? There was nothing there. A vast, empty horizon doing what? 'I prefer small spaces, other people.'

'That's because you're still young,' Veronica said.

He wondered what this had to do with anything, except to draw another line between them. The fortune-telling might last for a while when all the fighting was finished, but it wouldn't last for ever. She would soon be as lost and as adrift in that new world as she was in this one. What did the death of Hitler have to do with her? The nearest Hitler had come to either of them had been the wayward bomb which had fallen on the house further along the street. So what was Hitler to them, except the rubble in the street, the shortages in the shops, and the countless millions of other men and women wandering through all those other rubble-filled streets?

'There'll be proper celebrations,' she said. She was reading from the paper again. 'They're telling people to hold their horses. Old Adolf might be dead, but there are still a lot of other evil men out there waiting to—'

'"Evil men"?' He wanted to laugh.

'That's what it says. Evil men. It says we can celebrate properly when *they* decide to stop fighting and start playing fair. People will really let their hair down, then – dancing in the streets, an announcement from the King, the whole shebang. They'll give us all plenty of notice.'

'There's still Japan,' Sweeney said. 'Still the Japs. You can't talk about "evil men" and not include that little lot. We all saw what they got up to in China and Burma.' He would have added to the list, but they were the only two countries he could remember, and he doubted if he could point to either on a map. Somewhere else over that endless sea.

'I know that,' Veronica said. 'And there you go again – putting a dampener on things.'

'I'm only being realistic,' Sweeney said. Realistic. He liked the sound of that.

'I know that,' she said. 'But a girl can still dream, can't she?'

'They've already had boatloads home from the Far East. You saw the pictures, must have done. Shocking state some of them lads were in. Shocking. What your Jap is basically is an animal. He might have been civilized once, but that was in the past.'

'You've got a point there,' Veronica said. 'Funny how these things come and go – the Ancient Greeks, things like that. You make a good point.'

Of course he made a good point; he was a realist. He knew what he was talking about. His opinion was as good as the next man's, probably better.

'It's only what I heard,' he said. 'The Japs.'

'They'll soon get back on their feet,' Veronica said.

'Who will?'

'Those lads who came home.'

She had no idea. No idea at all. No idea whatsoever. Brighton? She might as well have been talking about going to live in China for all the difference it would make to him. Get back on their feet? Not in this world they wouldn't, not after what they'd been through, not after all they'd seen and suffered.

Veronica finally closed her paper and folded it into quarters, sealing tight all these contradictory and confusing visions of the future. She looked around her, as though suddenly uncertain of why she was there or what might have brought her there in the first place. She had sat for almost an hour watching Sweeney sleeping. She had made no noise, hardly moving or breathing in the dimly lit room. Even before she'd entered, she'd known he was asleep, and she had let herself in without knocking, merely mouthing his name, as though this alone gave her right of entry.

An hour, almost an hour – half an hour at least – just the two of them together, him sleeping and her watching him sleep like a mother might watch her precious sleeping child.

28

FRANKIE DOLL RETURNED TO THE HOLYWELL STREET studio. He understood better than ever that whatever power he now possessed, whatever pressure he might exert on Tommy Fowler to cut himself free from the man and set himself up with Beazley, lasted only until Peter Tait was finally executed in four days' time. After that, Tommy Fowler, Billy Leach and the boy hiding out in Billericay all went their own untouchable, separate ways. And after that, every single one of Frankie Doll's chances could go and whistle.

It was why Frankie Doll was on his way there now – to finalize arrangements with Beazley so that the man's partnership and expertise might be included in whatever hand he might soon be forced to lay down in front of Tommy Fowler. There were still a few loose ends to tie up, still a few of those airy straws blowing in the wind. For instance, Frankie Doll wasn't certain if Beazley already worked directly for Tommy Fowler or if he was his own boss at Holywell Street, working under some kind of contract – a 'gentleman's agreement' is what Tommy Fowler would call it while it suited. But regardless of the arrangement, it was still an unmissable opportunity for the pair of them. And once they were in business for themselves, then there were plenty of ways they would be able to exploit their past lives with Fowler, with the clubs and their contacts and the girls. Everything they needed was already there, ready and waiting for them, and all they really needed to do now was to sever themselves from Tommy Fowler. Which was where he, Frankie Doll, came in.

The possibilities, Frankie Doll said to himself as he walked, were endless.

Approaching Holywell Street, however, Frankie Doll knew that he hadn't yet thought everything through to its happy and profitable conclusion. Where, for instance, would he stand with Fowler once Tait was dead and gone and his brother's boy was back from Billericay and starting to demand his own slice of whatever he decided he was owed? And what would Doll and Beazley – it already sounded like a going concern in Frankie Doll's mind – do if Fowler called his bluff and told him to go to the law with what he imagined he knew? Besides, what real proof of any of this did Frankie Doll actually possess? Laura's bruises were fading, and neither Billy Leach nor Fowler's already imprisoned brother was ever going to say anything to incriminate himself. And what were the chances that the law was ever going to hold up its hands and admit to having caught, tried, convicted and then hanged the wrong man?

On the other hand, Billy Leach had already talked about retiring, taking it easy, and perhaps Tommy Fowler was thinking the same. Perhaps the pair of them might even be *grateful* for the likes of Frankie Doll and Julian Beazley stepping into the empty spaces they were leaving behind. They had reigned and then they had abdicated, and now their time was over. The whole world was crying out for change. People were sick of uncertainty and shortages and suffering and forever worrying about the times ahead; soon they would be demanding to be allowed to enjoy themselves, to look forward, to stop endlessly looking over their shoulders at a world already gone.

And if Beazley was right, then the future – *their* future, *that* future, at least – was a different place entirely from the world over which men like Tommy Fowler and Billy Leach had once ruled.

And if not 'Doll and Beazley', then 'Doll Enterprises'. Even 'Doll', for once, sounded right. 'Doll's Dolls'. He had spent hours the previous night thinking up names and titles for the various parts of his coming kingdom. Tommy Fowler had published a magazine called *White Slave*. Frankie Doll's magazines would be given names like *Sauce, Scarlet, Jezebel, Ebony, Obsession*. New names, modern names.

Nothing was decided yet, nothing fixed in stone, but everything was at last beginning to take shape and move in the right direction. Speciality tastes. Themes and variations. And on top of all this, Beazley would have ideas of his own. And every idea would lead to greater profit. Rationing would end soon enough, it stood to reason; markets would be flooded; gambling of all sorts might soon be legalized; even the clubs and brothels and independent working girls might one day be made legit and be properly regulated. And perhaps Frankie Doll and Julian Beazley alone had seen the one truly profitable path stretching ahead of them through all of this. Perhaps Tommy Fowler and Billy Leach were too slow and too set in their ways to change, and perhaps the boy in Billericay and all the other youngsters like him were either too greedy or too blind or just too stupid to work out for themselves what Frankie Doll and Beazley were already working out.

And that was another thing the few remaining days until Tait's execution afforded them – a start on all this competition. The war might not be officially over yet, but the one thing Frankie Doll and Beazley didn't intend to do now was to sit back and wait for this to happen. And knowing this bloody country and the people in charge, all those other millions of ordinary, exhausted people would go on waiting. They would wait and they would wait and they would wait. And while *they* all waited, Frankie Doll and Beazley would be getting their head start and setting themselves up very nicely indeed, thank you very much.

It was something else Frankie Doll had only half considered, but which, the more he thought about it now, the more he considered to be his due, his right, his destiny, even.

Frankie Doll started whistling as he walked. Only a few weeks had passed since he and Ruby Nolan had stood and watched the flying bomb spluttering across the London sky on its way to Hillmarton Road, and now here he was living in a completely different world, a different world completely.

Turning the corner of May Court and Holywell Street, Frankie Doll saw a small crowd ahead of him. There was an overgrown bomb site at the corner of Holywell Street, and rubble was piled against the standing carcasses there. It wasn't a particularly busy street and there had never been much traffic. The small crowd, Frankie Doll saw, included two air-raid wardens and a police constable.

Looking over the crowd, Frankie Doll saw that the windows to Beazley's studio were broken and that the wall above them had been blackened by fire and smoke. The smell of recent burning filled the street; from somewhere beyond, a line of pale smoke still rose wavering into the air.

Frankie Doll looked at all of this and felt suddenly sick. He went closer, searching the crowd for Beazley himself. And only as he finally reached the building did he see the sheeted body that had been laid out in the road beneath the shattered windows. It was beyond him to approach any closer. One of the ARP men stood watch over the body. Frankie Doll's first thought – the one he was the most desperate to believe – was that here was another old air-raid victim only just discovered, found in a recently cleared cellar perhaps, or in the rubble of the fallen walls. Most had been long since searched for and found, but there were always these isolated new discoveries, always these terrible little surprises waiting to be revealed.

But what Frankie Doll knew for certain – what he knew in his heart of hearts – was that the corpse beneath the dirty tarpaulin was that of Julian Beazley. The broken windows were his studio windows; the fire-blackened wall was the wall of his studio.

A man backing away from the constable collided with Frankie Doll and apologized to him.

'Do they know who it is?' Frankie Doll asked him. 'What it was?'

'One of the ARP men said it might have been an undiscovered incendiary. He said it happens – they fall, fail to ignite, and then just sit there on a roof or in a gutter somewhere, getting wet in the rain and heated up in the sun until . . .' He made an explosion with his hands.

'That's probably it,' Frankie Doll said, the words drying in his mouth. 'And what about the . . .' He motioned towards the covered body.

'Some poor bastard who got caught inside, apparently. They said he might even have been asleep in there. According to the

ARP man, the place was full of inflammable chemicals. Poor sod was covered in the stuff. Beyond identification, one of them said. All blackened, his face, hands, everything. That's why the coppers are here.' He nodded over his shoulder. 'The man in the grey overcoat. Detective. Ask me, they're only here to go through the motions, find out next to nothing, and then just mark it down as another air-raid death.'

'No sign that it was anything else, then?' Frankie Doll said. 'Such as?'

Frankie Doll shrugged. 'Perhaps the man started the fire himself, accidentally.'

'Then he'd be the unluckiest man in London, by my reckoning. In case you hadn't heard, it's all over, bar the shouting.' The man shook his head and walked away.

Frankie Doll still felt sick to his stomach. The blackened, unrecognizable corpse was Julian Beazley, and the fire had been anything but accidental. Tommy Fowler. What had happened? Had Beazley done or said something to show their hand too soon to Fowler? Had he jumped the gun? Had he gone behind Frankie Doll's back? Was that it? And had Tommy Fowler decided that this was one more complication he could well do without at that particular, precarious moment? After all, Fowler was more aware than any of them of the significance of the next few days. Or perhaps Billy Leach had told him about Doll's visit and the things they had discussed. Perhaps that had happened, and perhaps Tommy Fowler had put two and two together and come up with this. And perhaps Tommy Fowler had come to Holywell Street looking for *him*, Frankie Doll, and had then taken things out on the unsuspecting Beazley instead.

Without any warning, Frankie Doll burst into a sweat,

started to retch convulsively, and then threw up violently at his feet. The people standing nearby backed away from him. Frankie Doll leaned over the gutter, spitting the foul-tasting bile from his mouth.

When he finally straightened up, wiping his mouth on his sleeve, the detective was standing where the other man had been.

'You all right, son?' the man said to him.

Frankie Doll didn't know what to say.

'You'd think we'd all be used to stuff like this by now,' the detective said, watching Doll closely. 'I'm Pye, by the way. Metropolitan Police.' He deftly took his warrant card out and showed it to Frankie Doll. The name meant nothing to him.

'I've been drinking,' Frankie Doll said. 'That's all. Celebrating.'

The detective held his face over the small pool of vomit and breathed deeply. 'I was hoping you might have known the man we found in the fire. Perhaps he was an acquaintance or a friend of yours?'

'No,' Frankie Doll said, knowing immediately that it was the wrong thing to say, that he'd said it too quickly, and that no one had yet revealed the identity of the corpse to him. 'I mean, I doubt it. Somebody said he worked here. I don't even know what the place is. Chemicals, somebody said.'

The detective smiled at all this. 'Developing chemicals. It's some kind of photographic studio. Perhaps they did that aerial-reconnaissance stuff for the RAF. Bit sad, if that was the case.'

'Right,' Frankie Doll said.

The man was still watching him closely as he said all this. He was a copper – he knew exactly what kind of studio the place was. It was Holywell Street. In all likelihood, he even knew who Beazley was. What he didn't know, and what he was trying to work out now, was who Frankie Doll was and how he was connected to the dead man and the nature of his killing.

'An unexploded incendiary,' Frankie Doll said. 'That's what I heard.'

'It's always a possibility,' the detective said.

'There must be hundreds of them, thousands perhaps, just lying there, buried, waiting to go off.'

'Oh, I don't doubt it,' the detective said. 'This city must be sown from one end to the other, top to bottom, with all kinds of ordnance. And not just incendiaries – proper bombs that have buried themselves deep. Imagine what will happen in the years to come if every one of *them* goes off like this one supposedly just went off.'

Frankie Doll nodded, wondering why the man was telling him all this. They watched as part of the roof fell into the smoking building. The ARP men told the onlookers to move further away. The roof fell in pieces and settled, throwing up more smoke and dust.

'Funny thing, that,' the detective said. 'You'd think people would be sick and tired of all this sort of thing by now. You have to wonder what it is that keeps bringing them back to look and watch.'

'Perhaps they thought they could help,' Frankie Doll said.

'No, it's not just that,' the detective said. 'It's something else. People behave as though they have a *right* to stand and look.'

'And don't they?' Frankie Doll said.

'Perhaps they do. Perhaps you're right. Where were you going?'

The question caught Frankie Doll off-guard. 'Going?' he said.

'To bring you here. At this time of day.' It was not yet seven in the morning.

'I was on my way home,' Frankie Doll said.

'From?'

'Work.'

'You work nights?'

'Lots of us do. Night shifts. The war effort and all that?'

'Right. And you work where, exactly?'

Frankie Doll could think of no good lie to tell, and so he said, 'I work on Archer Street, the Regency.'

'That's interesting,' the detective said. 'I know the Regency on Archer Street. In fact, I know Archer Street very well. Like the back of my hand.' He held up his palm to show Frankie Doll.

'A lot of people do,' Frankie Doll said. 'It's a popular place.'

'Especially now, I should imagine,' the detective said.

'People want to enjoy themselves,' Frankie Doll said.

'They certainly do. And so you yourself – you're in the entertainment business, are you?'

But before Frankie Doll could answer him, one of the ARP men called to the detective and then came towards him.

'I have to go,' the detective said to Frankie Doll. 'Duty calls.'

'Don't let me stop you,' Frankie Doll said to him, suddenly brave in the face of the departing man.

The detective started to go, but then turned back to him. 'I never got your name,' he said.

'Doll,' Frankie Doll said. 'Frankie Doll.'

'Nice to have met you, Frankie Doll.'

342

Frankie Doll felt unexpectedly sick again and breathed deeply in an effort to clear the taste from his mouth.

The detective watched all this, and then said, 'Doll as in . . . ?'

'Doll as in Doll,' Frankie Doll said.

'Perhaps you ought to sit down,' the detective suggested, smiling. 'I can see that all this has come as a bit of a shock to you. Is that where I'll find you, then – the Regency on Archer Street? If I need to speak to you again, that is.'

'And why would you need to do that?' Frankie Doll said.

The detective shrugged. 'Just in case we turn up anything here that casts any light in that direction.'

As intended, the remark unsettled Frankie Doll even further, and he remained silent.

The detective finally went to the ARP man, leaving Frankie Doll alone.

Frankie Doll could taste the chemicals in the air. They filled his mouth and nose and eyes. It was the bitter taste, he knew, of a suddenly shattered dream, broken into a thousand pieces and scattered irretrievably into a suddenly rising and unstoppable wind.

29

THIS TIME THE GIRL STAYED WITH HIM. IT WAS THE THIRD act – of five – in the quickening process of the ceremony. The fire – or so Crowley now assumed – had slowly taken hold and the flames were at last starting to rise. There was no harm in her staying. The line of contact between himself and the condemned boy was made and strong and fixed, and the first few impulses had already run their course along that line. She could witness everything that now happened. She might even, if the need arose, participate further. There had been plenty of others in the past, writhing in those same fierce, all-consuming flames; plenty of others joined to his will and his flesh in their own small storms of abandonment, fulfilling unspoken fantasies and forbidden desires of their own as adjuncts to his own excesses.

There was still some doubt in Crowley's mind concerning the girl's true motives and the extent of her commitment – just as there was a lingering doubt about something having contaminated the purity and strength of the connection between himself and the boy – but he was prepared to dismiss all doubt now as an acceptable uncertainty. After all, he had never before attempted this particular ritual with such a perfect subject, and so, he reasoned, why *wouldn't* these small uncertainties exist? Silver, he knew, would not dismiss all this so readily. But Silver, too, had never before witnessed or participated in anything of this nature. So, for every doubt there was reassurance, and for every uncertainty a far greater reward waiting to be claimed. It was ever thus, ever thus.

She was kneeling at his feet now, her hands splayed on the thin rug, her knees apart. She wore another blouse with a low neckline, and from where he sat Crowley was once again able to see her breasts where they rested in her flimsy white brassiere. He knew – as he had known on the previous occasion – that this was no accident on the girl's part. Knowingly or unknowingly, she was presenting herself to him, offering herself. She had learned about him; she *knew*; she was participating on her own terms, and this, Crowley decided, was something to be embraced and enjoyed.

'What do you do?' she said, distracting him from all these thoughts.

'Do?' he said, wishing she'd remained silent where she knelt.

'The ceremony. Now. What do you actually do?' She looked up at him, closing and opening her eyes several times, though to what end – if any – Crowley was at a loss to understand.

'Do you not already know?' he said to her. Of course she didn't know. She might *think* she did, but how could she?

She shrugged her shoulders, causing her breasts to shake. She tugged at the near-transparent material of her blouse. Everything deliberate, everything perfectly judged and executed, and everything just as carefully observed and considered by Crowley.

'Only what I read,' she said. 'Everything sounded the same. All ... all ...'

'Magic, witchcraft, death and sex?' he said, causing her to smile and look up at him again. 'And what if it were all true, and not merely another greedy journalist rattling his stick in the swill bin?'

She was lost for an answer. Because there was no answer.

'I wouldn't mind,' she said eventually.

'Mind what?' Crowley said.

'If you told me. The truth. The papers said—'

'That I indulged in unnatural practices. *Of course* they were unnatural practices. I was attempting what no other man on Earth had attempted before me.' Mostly true. He could count those earlier seekers on the fingers of one hand – two, if pushed – but, as ever, this grandstanding and self-regard – this *self-belief* – were a vital part of the process now and were little more than breathing in and out to Crowley. 'What would be *natural* about any of that?'

'And is it the same now – this ritual?' she said. She licked her lips, accentuating their colour.

'It is,' Crowley said solemnly. 'All my life I have sought to extend these corporeal limits and to expand the boundaries of human consciousness, when all around me, my ever-fearful, ever-obedient fellow man has been committed and determined – honour-bound, I might almost say – to do precisely the opposite. Of course I was accused of unnatural practices. Accused, condemned, ridiculed, cast out, mocked, scorned, pilloried and re-cast as the social pariah that most presently consider me to be.' He was disappointed at the ease with which this list had come.

'I see,' she said.

She had brought another half-bottle of gin with her and it stood half full on the floor beside her.

She put a finger to her lips and screwed up her face in an effort of thought.

'You wish to know about the sexual element of my rituals?' he said, knowing by her quick smile that he had guessed correctly, and that this was a vital part of her own interest and involvement, even if only for the tales she might forever afterwards tell – or sell, as Silver would no doubt insist.

'It's what the papers always shout loudest about,' she said.

One moment she seemed completely innocent to him, the next all-knowing. One moment she seemed a child at his feet, the next another of those voracious, insatiable women – another Leila, perhaps, another Leah, another Jane Wolfe, even – desperate to warm themselves in his heat. Desperate to hold their hands and faces as close to those rising flames as they dared.

'It's what sells their papers, that's all,' he said.

'So was it all lies?'

He closed his eyes and took a deep breath. 'I have always been a sexual creature,' he said. 'I have always enjoyed and nurtured and afterwards cherished my . . . encounters.'

'The papers call it a "never-ending stream".'

Crowley laughed at the phrase. 'It sometimes seemed like that. What did they call them – poor deluded and desperate fools who had fallen under my spell?'

He imagined she only looked at the headlines and then at the photographs.

'Something like that,' she said.

'Some were, I suppose,' Crowley said. 'But not my true devotees.'

She held his gaze as he said this.

'But most, I daresay, were little more than curious thrill-seekers who let either their curiosity or their boredom get the better of them. And in between there were the true and honest seekers after the same solitary great truth, happy to believe in everything I attempted and undertook alongside them.'

'Eternal life,' she said. '*That* solitary, great truth?'

'I suppose so, though to concentrate upon the acquisition of that alone is to ignore a great deal else.'

'What, then?'

Questions, questions, questions. Just like Maria Teresa, just like Pearl Brooksmith, just like Frieda Harris. And always this excessive interest in the Life Eternal.

'I suppose the more intelligent or understanding among my followers might call it a kind of transubstantiation or transmutation, a transference of the soul or spirit. Simply to call it Eternal Life suggests something too . . . too . . .'

'Obvious?' she said.

'Precisely,' he said. It wasn't the word, but he was growing tired of having to explain his every evasive remark. She had been kneeling at his feet for half an hour now. He could smell the gin on her breath, taste it on his own.

And then, almost as though in response to these thoughts, the girl finally rose from where she knelt and sat beside him on the shabby, sprouting settee. She picked up the bottle and filled their glasses.

'If you want me to leave . . .' she said. 'For the ritual . . .'

'An invocation,' he said. 'Nothing more. 'I don't even have to actually say the words out loud, just imagine them, let them whisper themselves silently in my head. A minute, two at the most.' A matter of only four days now until the boy's pre-ordained and certain death, an arrow flying silently and surely to its target. He had been intoning the words all his life, pulling back the bowstring and firing all those other arrows into those other darknesses. 'You could hold my hand,' he said. Completely unnecessary, but he knew she would appreciate even this small degree of involvement. Appreciate and then reward. It had been over five years since he'd last indulged himself in this particular ritual with a woman in attendance – the blessed Marjorie Fleetham down in Torquay – after which he had passed out, bled from his ears, nose and anus, and then been laid up for a month, able to swallow only liquids.

'Really?' she said.

Crowley put down the glass he held and presented his hands to her, clasping both her own and then letting them rest on his thighs.

'Do I need to do anything?' she said.

'Close your eyes and remain silent for the duration. No movement, no interruption.'

She nodded once and closed her eyes.

He'd been about to explain more to her, to add to the drama of the moment, to heighten the tension and her expectations, but there seemed little point now.

Her hands felt suddenly taut in his own. He relaxed his grip on her slightly and began murmuring.

He continued this for a minute or two and then stopped abruptly. He clasped her more tightly for a few seconds and then released her completely, withdrawing his hands so that her own rested directly on his thighs, where she kept them.

Crowley opened his eyes and cleared his throat.

She opened her own eyes and watched him closely. 'Is it over?' she asked him.

He nodded.

'I felt something,' she said absently.

'I would be surprised if you hadn't,' Crowley said, but surprised that she had.

She spread her fingers slightly, raised her hands and then let them fall back to his legs. 'The women . . .' she said.

'Were never the deluded fools everybody else wanted them to be.'

'Did you sleep with them all?'

Sleep? He wanted to shout at her. 'We indulged ourselves. "Sleep" sounds so . . .'

She understood him and nodded. 'Because sex – the climax – was all a part of your rituals?'

'It's a simple enough thing to grasp,' he said. He sipped his gin, wondering how close she was to making her point. Besides, *what* had she felt? *How?*

'The papers made it sound as though you made most of it up,' she said. 'The sex, all that side of things – for your own . . . own . . .'

'Gratification?' Sometimes it was painful even listening to her.

'That was it. "Personal gratification".'

He knew exactly how the papers made it sound: taking advantage, forcing women against their will, debauching them, demeaning them, leaving them soiled and wretched and abandoned and wishing they'd never heard of Aleister Edward Crowley in the first place.

'Who knows?' Crowley said. 'Perhaps there was an element of that. I was convinced from the very start that all of my serious attempts demanded at least *some* sexual component. I promise you, there was never any pleading or coercion on my part.'

'That's not what—' She stopped abruptly.

'Not what the papers say? Of course it isn't.'

He saw that she regretted the remark, that she believed she had offended him by her insistence.

'I didn't mean anything by it,' she said.

Pathetic. Everything she now said and did betrayed her reason for being with him. Was she already considering her own fate as the latest of that long line of spent and used-up women?

'No?' He half turned from her, moving his leg slightly, playing to his advantage. The wounded soul. He felt her grip tighten. She leaned forward, urging him to turn back to her, which he did, but without looking directly at her.

'I don't mind,' she said eventually.

Mind what? What was there for her to mind? 'Mind what?'

She seemed uncertain of what she was saying to him. 'Hearing about it,' she said.

'I imagined we at least had an understanding, you and I,' Crowley said. 'A bond of some sort.'

'We do,' she said. She moved closer to him. 'We do.' She surreptitiously unfastened another button on her blouse, and Crowley pretended not to notice this, or the further small piece of pale, quivering flesh it exposed.

'What did you imagine?' he asked her. 'Altars, daggers, decapitated chickens, sodomized goats?' It was certainly what she would have read about. Especially after Cefalu. 'Do you want me to shout out loud to you that it's true what they say – that I believe that the successful culmination of my rites, of all I hold dear, of everything I have devoted my life to achieving' – he began to wonder if even he wasn't overdoing it – 'that the successful culmination of a rite should always include the death of the passive partner, or at the very least the sacrifice of some living thing?'

She shook her head at hearing him say all this. Shook her head, and yet at the same time flicked her eyes back and forth. She was excited. The words had excited her. The drama had had its desired effect.

Seizing this advantage, Crowley said, '*Do* you want me to tell you all that? And perhaps to add that I *do* believe that the way to heighten the impact and potency of that sacrifice even further is for either the practitioner or the victim to experience orgasm at the point of death. Is that what you want to hear me say?' He was shouting again, and fell suddenly silent. He began to wonder if he hadn't revealed too much to her, but knew this was unlikely.

Her hands were still on his thighs, and she, too, was panting slightly, her breasts rising and falling close to him.

'Don't say anything,' he said to her.

She shook her head.

'Forgive me,' he said.

She opened her mouth and breathed more deeply, licking her lips again, and again leaving them wet and shining, the tip of her tongue remaining exposed as her breathing subsided.

She would have read in the papers that in Greece he had sacrificed chickens, cats, dogs and goats, and that these killings were one of the Greek Government's weapons against him when finally expelling him and his entourage of devotees.

After a few minutes of silence, she said, 'Can I speak now?'

'Of course,' he said. 'My apologies. The ritual always

demands a great deal of me, and, increasingly, more than I myself am ever prepared for.'

'I can see that,' she said. 'That's why I'd like to help.'

'Your being here . . .' Crowley said. 'Your physical presence . . .'

'I meant more,' she said.

He remembered the last time.

'I once knew a girl who worked as a magician's assistant,' she said. 'She told me that it was all about the sex thing. Him sawing her in half and all that, pushing his swords into her. She had a costume that would have got her arrested if she'd worn it outside. She worked with a knife-thrower in a circus before that. When the magic bookings were slow, she started doing the stags. That's where I met her. You could say we had a kind of double act.'

'I can imagine,' Crowley said.

'Don't knock it. They were good little earners. I'm telling you all this to let you know that I understand – about the sex stuff, what it means, how big a part it can be of something. Everything one minute, nothing the next – like men in general, I suppose. Well, like the men *I* get to meet. I knew another girl who made a small fortune performing acts – you know, cruelties and such like – on her clients.'

'Masochism,' Crowley said.

'That's the one – masochism. Sadie, she called herself. Always very popular, always in demand. Whips, canes, the lot, you name it.'

He wondered why she was telling him all this. Her hands were still on his legs. He was an old man, getting older.

'You wouldn't believe some of the things they paid her to do to them.'

'I probably would,' Crowley said.

'Oh, yes, right.' She laughed. 'So, you catch my drift, then?' she said. 'I'm not as easily shocked as you might think.' She sat upright and pulled her shoulders back.

'I *used* to have altars,' Crowley said. 'Real altars, all the usual paraphernalia.'

'Parapher – what?'

'For the rituals, sacrifices. The robes, the daggers, chalices. Everywhere I lived. Beginning in Scotland.'

'You had an estate,' she said. 'You were a baron, or a lord, or something.'

'I was all those things. In fact, I still am.' He wondered whether she would point out to him that the papers had said all these titles and other claims had been self-proclaimed and bogus to begin with.

But she said nothing. She was still participating, still playing her part.

He turned away briefly, and when he turned back to her his face was only inches from her breasts. Her hands were no longer on his legs, but were now somewhere behind her back, as though bound.

'We all have to make sacrifices in life,' she said to him.

He watched as she shook her shoulders and then as her suddenly released breasts were revealed to him whole, the nipples already swollen and dark.

'My wife Rose . . .' he began to say. *My wife Rose put rouge on her nipples and played with them with her fingers before feeding them into my mouth. When Lola was born I drank milk from her. I still remember its richness, and the way the heavy, creamy drops clung to those nipples, offered up to me and tempting me.*

'Well?' she said.

He regretted the word. Next she might ask him what he was waiting for.

He felt confident that this third part of the ritual had been safely and successfully concluded.

He raised his hands slowly and cupped both of her breasts, feeling them at once pliant and resistant in his palms. They were softer than he had anticipated, but full for their size. There was no slack in the flesh or in the skin.

She moaned slightly – a little too practised for his taste – and he moved closer to her, licking his lips and lowering his head to everything she too was now offering him.

30

'SOMEBODY HERE TO SEE YOU, PETER.' ARTHUR BONE STOOD to one side as Ernest Pye came into the room. It was twice the size of a normal cell, with a bed, a full-size table, a toilet and three chairs.

Peter Tait was sitting at the table, in the middle of which was placed his Bible. A mesh-encased light sat above this calm centre; the room's only other light lay across the sill of the high window.

Tait stood up as Pye entered. There had been a succession of visitors these past few days, all of them accompanied by Bone.

'Regular Piccadilly Circus, this place,' Bone said to Pye. To Tait, he said, 'Say hello, Peter. We might be – well, you know – but we can still be polite. "Manners maketh the man" and that's a fact.'

'Hello,' Tait said to Pye.

Pye looked closely at the boy. He wanted there to be no misunderstanding, no raising of hopes or waiting for impossible miracles. He held out his hand and Tait took it. 'No news, I'm afraid,' he said.

'No – well . . .' Bone said. 'I don't think any of us—'

'I wish it were otherwise,' Pye said.

Tait sat back at the table and put his hand over the Bible.

'Still,' Bone said. 'Good of him to come like this, eh?'

'It is,' Tait said. 'Good of you to come, Mister Pye.'

And even in that brief and fractured exchange, Pye understood how things had changed between himself and the pair of them, Bone especially. It was something he regretted, but, equally, it was something he could now do nothing about. Tait would be hanged in three days' time and this would be the last time he saw either of the two men. Loose ends. The Holywell Street fire and the death of the man called Beazley, the man called Doll working at the Regency club, and the boy called Sweeney, who also worked there and who had delivered to Tait the Bible an inch beneath his hand now. All loose ends. All connections of a sort, perhaps, but nothing strong or conclusive, and all connections which were now rapidly evaporating and which would soon no longer exist.

'Sit down,' Bone said to him.

Tait pulled a chair from the wall and set it beside his own at the table. Bone brought a third and sat opposite the condemned boy.

Pye nodded to the scattered pages of a newspaper on the floor of the room. 'Been keeping up?' he said to Tait.

'Mister Bone reads to me,' Tait said, his voice low, his eyes never leaving the Bible sitting beneath his raised palm like a shadow.

Pye glanced at Bone and saw that the man was uneasy about something. He felt bad about how the two of them had last parted. Each, in his own way, had let the other down.

Pye had come to the prison intending to ask Tait what he knew about Doll and Beazley and the Holywell Street studio and the Regency club. But now that he was there he knew that there was nothing to be gained by the questions, that it was beyond him to fan even this dim and solitary ember into life. In all likelihood, Holywell Street was something completely separate. And he certainly knew how desperate he would sound if he were to mention it now to either Tait or Bone, let alone to Tait's worse-than-useless lawyer. The tide of the law went in and out, in and out, and here they were, the three of them, abandoned on its wrack.

Now that Tait had entered these final days there were few restrictions on the number of his visitors or the duration of their visits. When the final thirty-six hours arrived, they would be stopped completely, but until then . . .

'Been reading up on old Adolf, haven't we?' Bone said. 'What a mess. They should at least have made sure of that one. They'd have been queuing up to put a bullet in his black heart.'

Tait looked up at this, watching Bone like an affectionate son might watch a good and caring father. 'Mister Bone thinks they should shoot the lot of them,' he said to Pye.

'It's not just me thinks it,' Bone said awkwardly.

'I daresay,' Pye said. A conversation about mass executions with an innocent man about to be executed himself?

'I tell him he needs to look into his heart and find some forgiveness there,' Tait said.

'That's right,' Bone said. 'Him, telling *me*. Him and that Bible. I ask you.'

Tait finally let his hand fall on to the book. 'It makes a lot of sense,' he said. 'At least to me, it does. Especially now.'

'Like I said – you're not the first,' Bone said flatly.

Pye wondered how much the boy was able to read, and how much of what he managed he actually understood.

'Tell him what you told me,' Bone prompted Tait. 'About the Great Hereafter.'

'Oh?' Pye said.

'He reckons he'll meet his mother up there,' Bone said. 'In Heaven.' He raised his eyes to the ceiling.

'It's a possibility,' Tait said.

'Of course it is, of course it is. I'm not saying it isn't.'

'I hardly knew her in this world,' Tait said.

'Of course you might see her, of course you might. Nice thing for a lot of us, to know we had that much coming to us, to know that—' He stopped abruptly and looked down at his hands.

Pye waited for a moment and then took a chance. 'Heaven?' he said. 'I don't mean to speak out of turn, but you're a convicted murderer, Peter.' He again watched Tait closely as he said this and saw the quick, sly smile and then the look of utter calm and conviction which crossed the boy's face.

Tait closed his eyes briefly, and when he opened them he was looking directly at Pye. 'Then I shall be a sinner redeemed,' he said.

Bone tutted loudly at the words.

'Either that, or you've finally managed to convince yourself that you're *not*,' Pye said.

'Not what?' A second smile.

It was clear to Pye that the boy understood perfectly what he was saying to him. 'Not a guilty man, not a murderer, not a sinner.'

'That was always in the hands of others,' Tait said calmly.

'You got that right,' Bone said, sharing a look of exaggerated exasperation with Pye.

'I don't mean just the judge and jury,' Tait said. 'A life for a life.' He tapped the Bible. 'It's all in here.'

'What isn't?' Bone said.

But Pye had seen and heard enough in the seemingly inconsequential exchange to convince him that something had changed – something fundamental – and that Tait, though still unwilling to act on his own behalf, now possessed a completely different understanding of his situation. It was something he wanted to probe further, and for the first time during his visits to the boy, he regretted Arthur Bone's stifling presence.

'If you know so little of your mother,' he said to Tait, 'how, for one minute, do you imagine you'll even recognize her, or her you?'

Tait smiled again. 'Faith,' he said. 'Belief. Everything comes right in the end.'

'Not for poor old Adolf, it didn't,' Bone said. 'And not for all those Poles and gypsies and everybody else he sent to meet *their* makers. You think *he*'s going to be welcomed up at the Pearly Gates with open arms?'

Pye saw how Tait kept his calm throughout this small and predictable assault; his smile was now the merest line on his lips.

'Mister Bone wants everything put right,' he said to Pye.

'I just want the world turning properly again on its – whatsit – its axis, that's all. That's not too much to ask for after all this lot, is it?' Bone said.

Pye wanted to tell the man to shut up. 'What else?' he said to Tait.

Tait waited for him to explain.

'Your alleged sins – crimes – will they all be forgiven? Is Heaven a second chance for you?'

'I suppose it is,' Tait said.

It was clear to Pye that nothing he might say would breach these defences. 'Then good luck to you,' he said.

'I shall ask for forgiveness and be granted it,' Tait said.

Pye shook his head. 'No, you won't. Because you've nothing to be forgiven for. There's something else in all of this. Something the rest of us have yet to see.'

Tait smiled again, looking back and forth between the two men.

'Oh, I see,' Pye said. It was clear to him that he had been right in his assumption that there was something Tait was keeping to himself, and that the boy was now playing a kind of game with the pair of them. 'You've had nothing in this world, you've been badly treated here, and so everything you deserve on that account will be waiting for you in the next, is that it? Along with the supposedly loving mother who threw you away like a piece of rubbish and who never afterwards gave you even a second thought?'

Another man might have lunged at him across the table, tried to grab him, sworn at him at least.

'You sound like Mister Bone here,' Tait said to him. 'And, like I said to him, I know why you're doing all this, I understand you. But you're wrong. I know Mister Bone cares for me, I know that.'

Bone looked down at the floor at hearing this.

'But I've understood and learned a lot these past weeks,' Tait went on. 'I've found something inside me that I never even knew was there.'

'It's that bloody book again,' Bone said. 'That's when all this forgiveness-and-living-happily-ever-after-up-in-Heaven malarkey started.'

'Of course it was,' Tait told him. 'You know what kind of man I was, Mister Bone. You might not have known me, but you know my *kind*. And you, Mister Pye, you know what kind of man I would have turned into. You can't deny it, either of you. Neither of you can honestly say otherwise.'

'What, and now, at the eleventh hour, you've been shown an alternative?' Pye said. 'Somebody else you might become?'

'I don't know,' Tait said, a sudden note of uncertainty in his voice. 'I don't know. But what I *do* know is that there's something else, something important waiting for me. Why not? Why is what *I* believe any more or less likely than what either of you believe?' He looked back and forth between the two men and neither dared answer him. In three days he would hang, and when that happened the strength of his convictions would be his alone to test and bear.

Bone was the first to speak. 'I believe you, Peter,' he said. He reached out to hold Tait's arm.

'Me, too,' Pye finally conceded, but only because he could do nothing else in the face of Tait's conviction, and more aware than ever of his own complete failure where the boy was concerned.

After this, the three men sat without speaking for a moment. They were interrupted by a knock on the door, which was pushed open by warder Lynch, who carried in a tray of tea.

'Room service,' he said as he put the tray down.

Only Tait smiled at the feeble joke.

'That's it,' Lynch said. 'Laugh or cry.' He looked at the scattered newspaper. 'And look at the state of this place. I'll have to send the cleaners in.' He tapped the sugar bowl. 'Sugar, Taity boy. I found some in the Governor's secret supply.' He tapped his nose and exchanged a glance with Bone, who was doing his best to ignore the man. War or no war, there would always be sugar for a condemned man. Sugar and cigarettes. 'He won't miss it.'

'I appreciate that,' Tait told Lynch, and to Pye it sounded like a completely different man speaking. Tait's hand was back on the Bible, keeping it secure as the tray of rattling crockery was put down and then unloaded.

'Right, well,' Lynch said, already withdrawing from them and from this room in which a dead man was sitting. 'Just give me a shout if there's anything else you require. We aim to please.'

Again, only Tait smiled at the words.

'I'll leave the door,' Lynch said on his way out.

Waiting until the man's footsteps had faded along the corridor, Bone said, 'His brother copped a packet over the Rhine. Transport plane. Missing, presumed.'

Pye looked at the open door. All these ghosts. All these other dead men still walking around.

Bone poured the tea and added Tait's milk. He and Pye drank theirs black.

'I went to see a man called Julian Beazley,' Pye said the instant the rim of the cup touched the boy's lips, watching for Tait's reaction to the name.

'Who's he when he's at home?' Bone said. 'Cups *and* saucers. We are honoured.'

'He worked for Fowler,' Pye said, still watching.

'A lot of us did, one way or another,' Tait said.

Pye saw that despite Tait's lack of obvious concern or interest, he was now waiting for Pye to say more.

'A photographer. You can imagine the sort of thing.'

'Filth?' Bone said. 'Women?'

'Filth and more filth,' Pye said.

'What about him?'

'He died in a fire at his studio.' He looked back at Tait. Still nothing. 'The ARP boys were making noises about an unexploded incendiary.'

'After all this time?' Bone said. 'Not very likely, I shouldn't have thought. I could write the book on unexploded incendiaries.'

Pye shrugged. 'Still, no witnesses, Beazley's body badly burned, and any evidence lost in the blaze.'

'You think he fell out with Fowler over something?' Bone asked him.

'He certainly fell out with somebody, and somewhere down that line of falling-out was Tommy Fowler.'

'This city will be like a minefield for years to come,' Bone said.

'Julian Beazley,' Pye said directly to Tait. 'You sure you never heard of him?'

Tait picked up the Bible, kissed it and held it a few inches from his mouth. 'The name means nothing to me. Tommy Fowler's got his fingers in every pie going. He must know dozens of photographers.'

'Pornographers,' Pye said. 'You're right. Them, and the girls they use. Supply and demand, I suppose.'

'*That* never changes,' Bone said. 'What else was the ARP mob saying?' He pronounced it 'arp'.

'Not much. All the usual.'

'Probably all a bit excited at finally having another call-out after all this time,' Bone said.

'Probably,' Pye said.

All three men sipped their tea again.

'This will be my last visit,' Pye said to Tait. 'You do know that?'

Tait nodded. 'I appreciate your coming.' That voice again. 'And all you've endeavoured to undertake on my behalf.'

All you've endeavoured to undertake on my behalf?

Even Bone looked up at the words. He smiled. 'If it's done nothing else, that thing, then it's taught him how to speak a bit better, mind his p's and q's.'

'I was going to ask you about that, Mister Pye,' Tait said the instant Bone had finished.

'About what?' Pye said.

'Oh,' Bone said. 'That's right.'

'About you coming one more time,' Tait said.

'There's really no point if you insist on—'

'He means as one of his witnesses,' Bone said. He looked away as he said it. 'He's allowed to choose—'

'I know,' Pye said. 'I see.'

'I'd appreciate it, I really would,' Tait said.

'They normally want a close family member or their parish priest or vicar,' Bone said.

'I don't know,' Pye said.

'I understand,' Tait said.

'What if I believed I was watching an innocent man hang?' Pye said. It was an unforgivable final prod and he regretted the words even as he said them.

'I imagined that might be your reason,' Tait told him.

'He asked me,' Bone said. 'But I told him I'd be there anyway. Waste of a choice, see?'

And I was the only other person he could think of, Pye

thought, but said nothing. He held Tait's gaze for a moment. 'Of course,' he said.

'It's on the—' Tait began to say.

'He knows when it is, Peter,' Bone said. 'No need for you to tell him that.'

'No,' Tait said. He put the Bible back to his mouth and held it there.

Pye finished his tea and stood up. 'Time I was off,' he said. 'This Holywell Street business. The war has to stop being an excuse for everything that happens sometime soon, I suppose.'

'You got that right,' Bone said.

Then Bone rose and said to Tait, 'I'm just going to walk Mister Pye here to the gate. You be all right on your lonesome?' It was almost another joke, and all three men smiled at it.

Tait rose and held out his hand to Pye. They shook, neither man speaking, Pye nodding once, and Tait closing his eyes briefly. It was enough, a bargain accepted, honoured and sealed.

'Five minutes,' Bone said to Tait as he went.

He motioned for Pye to look back at the boy, and Pye saw that Tait was already hunched over the Bible, his arms laid around it as though it were a vessel safe in harbour and protected from a stormy sea.

Once outside, Bone locked the cell door and said, 'That's how I find him every time I go in there. Don't worry, he won't hear. Oblivious to everything once he gets his nose stuck into that thing.'

They started walking to the prison entrance.

'So there's nothing whatsoever left?' Bone said. 'Not that it would be even the slightest use to him now.'

'No, nothing,' Pye said.

'But you thought this Holywell Street thing might be something?'

'Not really,' Pye said. 'It's just another dirty little line running back to Fowler, that's all.'

'Perhaps it's just as well,' Bone said.

'Of course.'

Bone let them out of the building and into one of the exercise yards.

'This witness business,' Bone said as they walked outside. 'It means a lot to him.'

Pye nodded.

'And all this meeting-his-mother-in-Heaven nonsense – I honestly think he believes it, I really do.'

Just as you or I might believe it if we were convinced our own lost wives were waiting there for us? 'I can see that,' Pye said. It was raining lightly, but the sky above them was cloudless and blue.

'One of the newspaper reports said the Russians were sending back trainloads of watches, candlesticks, cutlery, glassware, you name it – back to Russia,' Bone said. 'Said they were going to strip Germany to the bones before they were through with it. You can't blame them. It said somewhere else that they'd be scrapping with *us* next. Us and the Yanks. Even Churchill sounded worried on that score.' He paused and turned up his face to the falling rain. 'You'd think everyone would be exhausted by now, that they'd just want to sit down and forget about it all, or lie down and fall asleep until everything was completely over and done with.'

'I know,' Pye said. He felt the same sparse rain on his own forehead and cheeks. 'I know.'

31

FRANKIE DOLL STOOD IN THE DEPTHS OF THE SHADOW IN the space beneath the staircase at the end of the hallway of the house on Warwick Street. He had been there for an hour. It felt like longer to Frankie Doll. Much longer. It was two in the morning, and he was waiting for Laura to come home, hopefully alone. It had been nearly a week since he'd last seen her, sitting by the window and hiding her bruised face from him.

And twenty-four hours since Tommy Fowler had burned Julian Beazley to death in his Holywell Street studio. And that, too, seemed like much, much longer ago to Frankie Doll.

Ever since his visit to Billy Leach and the discovery of Tommy Fowler's secret, Frankie Doll had stayed away from Laura, and he had stayed away from the Regency and every other one of Fowler's bars and clubs and knocking shops and gambling dens. He had even fooled himself into believing that he had stayed away from Tommy Fowler himself.

It was why he had come to Warwick Street at this time of the night – the middle of Tommy Fowler's working day. It was why he had walked past the door half a dozen times and then waited in another deep shadow opposite it, watching to see if Laura arrived; watching, too, for anyone he recognized from the Regency who might have followed her there on Tommy Fowler's orders in the hope of being led to Frankie Doll.

Frankie Doll's best guess was that Fowler would send the Sweeney boy. Because he was teaching Frankie Doll a lesson, and because Frankie Doll needed to understand that. But what Frankie Doll didn't know – and why he was waiting for Laura now – was whether or not Fowler had learned from Beazley what the pair of them were intending. The problem now for Frankie Doll was that with every one of those passing minutes, and following his days of absence from the Regency, Tommy Fowler's suspicions would be multiplying and per-haps growing ever more vengeance-worthy. It was a lot for Frankie Doll to have to take in and consider. Everywhere he looked, it seemed to him, these opposing forces were gathering in ever-tightening circles around him.

And still those minutes ticked slowly by. The building was cold. He could feel the coldness of the tiled floor through the thin soles of his shoes. He could feel the damp coolness of the wall through the palms of his hands. His breath clouded slightly in the night air. He wondered how much longer he would have to wait before either Laura appeared and he revealed himself to her, or he found the courage to climb up to her room and knock on her door.

If Tommy Fowler *was* looking for him, then the room upstairs might be a baited trap. He might have panicked when he was approached by the detective on Holywell Street, but, he reassured himself, he had surely regained *some* measure of composure and reason since then. Surely. At least *now* he was thinking straight.

He was distracted from all these cold and circling thoughts

by the sudden opening of a door further along the hallway. A man appeared, followed by one of the girls. The man was slipping on his coat and talking over his shoulder to her. The girl was half his age and half his size and she stood beyond the threshold of her room wearing only a dressing gown. She was smoking, helping the man with his coat, and the man talked non-stop to her, making arrangements for the next time. Eventually, she kissed him and pushed him further out into the hallway, quickly shutting the door on him.

The man stood for a moment and then walked to the front door, passing only a few feet from where Frankie Doll stood and held his breath.

As the man finally left, the inner door opened again and the girl came back out into the hallway. She had fastened her hair back and looked even younger than before.

'You waiting for somebody?' she said to Frankie Doll.

'I'm not hiding,' Frankie Doll said, feeling ridiculous.

'I never said you were. What is it, then – shyness?' She laughed at this.

Frankie Doll left his hiding place. 'It's me,' he said. 'Frankie Doll.' He stepped into the dim yellow light coming from her room and saw the sudden look of alarm on her face.

'What you doing here?' she said. 'Of all places.'

And Frankie Doll knew immediately that most of his desperate and frantic guessing over the past twenty-four hours had been correct.

'I came to see Laura,' he said. Why else would he be there?

'She thought – forget it.'

'Thought what? That I'd gone, that something had happened to me?' He wanted to sound bold and dismissive.

'Something like that,' the girl said.

'Is she back from the Regency yet?'

'The Regency? She hasn't been in that place for a good few days now.'

'Oh?' Her bruising must surely have gone down by now.

'Ever since . . .'

Frankie Doll waited, but whatever it was, she didn't want to say it.

'Ever since I went away for a few days?'

'That's it – ever since you went away for a few days. She's up there now, all by herself.'

'I was on my way up to her,' Frankie Doll said. Not hiding, not weighing up his chances, not holding his breath in the dark and trying to make out all those circling, forming outlines getting ever closer to him. On his way up to see Laura.

He moved to the bottom of the stairs and looked into the space above him.

'You ought to keep an eye out,' the girl said, almost involuntarily.

'Oh?' For Tommy Fowler? 'Why?' He waited for her to explain.

'I'm just saying, that's all.' She went back into her room, once again casting Frankie Doll into darkness.

Frankie Doll went quickly and silently up the three flights of stairs. He arrived at Laura's door, saw that no light showed beneath it, and knocked quietly.

He pressed his ear to the door and heard something inside.

'It's me,' he said, his voice barely a whisper. More noise.

A moment later, the latch was drawn and a key turned. The door opened a few inches and Laura looked out at him.

Frankie Doll went quickly in to her and locked the door behind him.

Laura, too, was in her dressing gown. She looked as though she'd been sleeping, her hair hanging over her face.

'I meant to come sooner,' Frankie Doll said to her.

'No, you didn't,' she said. 'You were looking after number one. As per. That's all you ever do these days.' Her voice sounded strange, and she finally brushed back her hair to reveal to him all her new bruises, along with the line of stitches which ran across her bottom lip and into the loose flesh between her mouth and chin.

'Who—?' Frankie Doll began to say.

'Don't,' she told him.

Frankie Doll's first, uncontainable thought was that the boy from Billericay had got wind of his visit to Billy Leach and had returned to look for him, finding Laura instead.

Laura told him to turn off the overhead bulb, and then switched on the lamp by her bed. She pulled the thin eiderdown over her legs. Frankie Doll sat in the chair opposite her.

'And just in case you were wondering . . .' she said, and pulled up both her sleeves to reveal the bruises on her arms.

'Laura, I—'

'Don't,' she said again, more forcibly this time.

They sat and looked at each other in silence for another of those long, cold minutes.

Frankie Doll wondered if she wanted him to go and sit beside her on the bed, to put his arm around her, to hold and try to comfort her and reassure her. But supposing her bruises were still painful – they *looked* painful – and supposing she hurt elsewhere.

Laura touched a finger to her stitched lip and then examined it.

'It looks . . .' Frankie Doll began to say.

'I think that's the point, don't you?' she said. 'A working girl with a bleeding mouth and a body covered in bruises who can hardly sit down or stand up, let alone lie down.'

'I didn't mean to—'

'You never do,' she said.

'Who was it?' he finally asked her.

She looked at him with an expression of surprise and disgust on her face. 'You're pathetic,' she said. And for the first time ever, Frankie Doll saw that he had absolutely no power whatsoever over her.

'The boy from Essex?' he said.

'You've got no idea, have you? No idea whatsoever. *You* did this, Frankie Doll. You.'

Meaning Tommy Fowler.

'Fowler,' Frankie Doll said.

She applauded him, three slow claps.

'Fowler himself?' he said.

She stopped clapping. 'What do you think? Fowler did what he always does – he watched, and, occasionally, he smiled.'

'Who did the stitches?'

'Meaning did I go to the hospital or the police?'

Frankie Doll could only nod.

'One of the new girls used to be a nurse. Handy, that. As you can imagine.'

Frankie Doll looked around him for something to drink.

'The last drink I had, I almost passed out with the pain,' Laura said.

'Your lip.'

'The nurse gave me some painkillers. Military stuff. American. They're good tablets. Costly, but they work. If I want, I can dissolve them and use a syringe. Fowler even left me the money for them on the way out. That, and the usual advice about hospitals and the law.'

'Was he here looking for me?' Frankie Doll said. He wondered if she would applaud him again. 'Did he say anything?'

'What do you mean, did he say anything? He said a lot, and most of it while all this was happening.'

'But you had no idea where I was,' Frankie Doll said.

'And it took him an hour to be convinced of that.' She took a packet of pills from the table and put one in her mouth, tipping back her head to swallow it dry.

'Beazley's dead,' Frankie Doll said.

'Give the man a coconut. And according to Fowler, you and him were like that' – she attempted to cross her forefinger and index-finger, wincing at the pain this caused her.

So Tommy Fowler knew everything.

'The police were at Holywell Street,' Frankie Doll said.

'And that means what, exactly?'

Perhaps Billy Leach had called Fowler a minute after Frankie Doll had left Paddington and told him about all the unnecessary questions his employee had been asking.

'There's a bottle under the sink,' Laura said.

Frankie Doll found this and poured himself a drink.

'You should have stayed well away,' she said. 'Steered well clear.'

Was that a note of sympathy in her voice?

'It would have meant leaving London,' Frankie Doll said. He had only ever left London three times in his entire life.

'You should still have gone.'

Gone where? 'And never come back – is that what you're saying?'

'It's what Fowler said you'd do.'

Frankie Doll shook his head. 'The thing with Fowler—'

But before he could finish the sentence, the door was kicked open, shattering its frame, and before either of them could respond to this, Tommy Fowler came into the room, followed by two other men.

'Surprise,' Fowler said. He wore his hat and a camel-coloured coat which hung unbuttoned over his shoulders, his arms loose inside it. He went first to Laura, where she sat on the bed, and stood with his leg touching her arm. He nudged her and she winced again at the pain this caused her.

'You look as though you've been in the wars,' he said. He turned to the two men. 'She's been in the wars. Criminal, the things that are happening these days.' He motioned for one of the men to shut the damaged door and then to stand against it. The second man went to stand by the window.

Tommy Fowler then looked slowly around the room, and finally at Frankie Doll, who still sat with the glass in his hand. 'Hope we're not interrupting anything here,' he said. 'Remind me – you are?'

'Listen, Mister—' Frankie Doll said.

'Ah, now I remember. Didn't you use to work for me? Weren't you once a grateful employee who was well paid and well treated and with everything he ever wanted at his fingertips?'

Frankie Doll nodded.

'"Yes, Mister Fowler, I was" would be nicer.'

The man at the door laughed.

'Yes, Mister Fowler, I was. I mean I—'

'You here visiting Laura?' Tommy Fowler said. 'You concerned about her having been in the wars as well, are you?'

Frankie Doll nodded again.

'What is it they say – that time heals everything?' He turned to Laura. 'You still taking the tablets I gave you?'

Laura nodded.

'They're good stuff, the best. Make sure you hang on to some for when the pain gets really bad. There isn't a pain in the world those particular pills won't cure. Worth remembering, that. For the future. A world filled with pain, and people crying out for a cure. *Well* worth remembering.'

Frankie Doll looked up at the remark, and the man at the door laughed again.

Tommy Fowler pulled up a chair to sit close to Frankie Doll.

'I was beginning to think you'd gone for good, Frankie boy. Disappeared. Whoosh.' He threw up his hands. 'That what you were planning? Especially after all the trouble your little photographer friend's had recently.'

'I never said anything,' Frankie Doll said.

'Never said anything about what? To who?'

'The detective at Holywell Street.'

'What detective? What's at Holywell Street? Never heard of the place. What are you talking about?' He looked to the two others. 'Either of you two ever heard of – where did you say again?'

'Holywell Street,' Frankie Doll said.

'Holywell Street?'

One man shrugged; the other said, 'Where's that, then?'

'See?' Fowler said to Frankie Doll. 'We're all in the dark on this one. Though I have to say, *you* seem to know a great deal about it. What is it they say – a little knowledge and all that? Still, we're a long way from – where was it again?'

'Holywell Street,' Frankie Doll said.

'A long way from Holywell Street here.' Fowler took the glass from Frankie Doll's hand, sniffed at it, pulled a face and then put it back between Frankie Doll's rigid fingers. 'Although perhaps it does explain one thing – ask me what it explains – I've forgotten your name again. What am I like? Memory like a sieve. It's almost as though you've disappeared already, as though you never even existed in the first place. I'm waiting.'

'Frankie Doll,' Frankie Doll said. He wondered why saying his own name made him feel so humiliated.

'That's the one – Frankie Doll. Go on.'

Frankie Doll didn't understand him.

'Ask me what all this Holywell Street business might help to explain.'

'What?' Frankie Doll said.

'It might help to explain why a particularly annoying and persistent little detective has been to the Regency three times in the past twenty-four hours. In fact, now that I come to think of it, I do believe he even mentioned you by name. You, personally. Small world, eh? Coming to the Regency and leaving his squad of size tens plodding up and down in front of the entrance all day and all night long. You can see how that might not be good for business. All sorts of questions, he was asking. Questions about this, that and the other. He was making me feel quite uncomfortable by the time he'd finished. And all of this in the Regency, the one place I've always called "home". Well?'

'Right,' Frankie Doll said.

'He says, "Right",' Tommy Fowler said to the two men.

'I mean yes, I can see,' Frankie Doll said.

'He says, "Yes, he can see",' Tommy Fowler said to the men. He turned back to Laura. 'And how about you? Can you see how that might not be the best thing all round as far as business is concerned? *My* business, that is.'

'I suppose so,' Laura said.

And without the slightest warning or indication, Tommy Fowler swung his hand at her and caught her squarely across her face, causing her to fall sideways on to the bed. When she pushed herself up there was fresh blood on her lip and chin along the line of stitches.

Frankie Doll half rose from his chair and Fowler turned back to him and pointed at him. 'You either finish what you've started or you sit back down,' he said.

Neither of the other men moved during any of this.

Frankie Doll sat back down.

'Finish your drink,' Fowler said to him.

Frankie Doll emptied the glass.

'Tell me – what was it you didn't understand?' Fowler said to him.

'Understand?'

'About me. What did you think you and that ungrateful little ponce and his camera were ever going to do without my say-so?'

'It wasn't like—'

Tommy Fowler swung his arm again, this time stopping an inch short of Laura's face.

'Don't tell me what it *wasn't* like,' he said. 'Tell me it was all his idea, if you like. I can certainly see that he was the one with all the expertise.'

But it was beyond Frankie Doll to say anything.

'It's like I was saying to Billy Leach only a few hours ago,'

Fowler said. 'The world's changing, Billy, and you and me, we've got to change with it. Does that make sense to you, Frankie – a changing world, survival of the fittest, to the victor the spoils, and all that?'

Frankie Doll could only nod. Short of saying outright that Billy Leach had told him everything, Fowler couldn't have made himself any clearer.

'Good,' Fowler said. 'So we're all up to scratch on that particular score.'

'What do you want me to do?' Frankie Doll said.

'Do? You? I wouldn't trust you to wipe the dog shit off my shoes. And believe me, Frankie, there's a lot of it around these days.'

'To put things right,' Frankie Doll said. Was this him being brave again? Bold? He nodded at Laura. 'She doesn't deserve any of this.' He tried to catch Laura's eye, but she resisted looking at him.

'To wipe the slate clean, you mean?' Tommy Fowler said. 'Something like that? Is that what you're saying? Is that what you're asking me? I won't say "begging".'

Frankie Doll nodded. Now he didn't even have to speak to feel the depth and heat of his humiliation.

'Let me think,' Tommy Fowler said, and he took a piece of paper from his breast pocket and gave it to Frankie Doll.

It was an address.

'The boy with the lip lives there. He's got something of mine.' He made his hand into a gun and pointed it at Frankie Doll. 'Something you might need in helping me sort out the problem of that persistent little policeman you pointed in my direction. I'd ask *him* to do it for me – the boy with the lip, that is, and, believe me, he'd jump at the opportunity – but all of a sudden I see that it might be a job for somebody more experienced. Somebody, shall we say, with more to repay, and certainly with more to lose.'

Somebody disposable, Frankie Doll thought. But killing a policeman? Even threatening a policeman? It wasn't Tommy Fowler's style. And it was only happening now because Tommy Fowler had the man to do it and because there was no other way out of any of this for either Frankie Doll or Laura.

'Me?' Frankie Doll said.

'You,' Tommy Fowler said. 'Now eat it.'

'Eat it?'

'The piece of paper.'

Frankie Doll looked at the address again and started to tear the paper into small pieces.

'Eating it would make me happier,' Tommy Fowler said. 'Or perhaps Laura here is feeling peckish.'

Frankie Doll ate the pieces of paper.

'Open wide,' Tommy Fowler said when he'd finished. He pushed a finger into Frankie Doll's mouth and slid out a final tiny piece of wet paper, putting this on his own tongue and then chewing it as though it were something rare and delicious.

'If I do this for you, then—'

'Not *if*,' Tommy Fowler said. 'When.'

'About Laura.'

'About Laura what? She's a good-looking girl. Or she was. And she will be again, I'm sure of it. Let's look on the bright side, shall we? Go on – what about her? I'll doubt she'll want to come with you, if that's what you were going to suggest. In fact, I think it's best all round if she stays exactly where she is until all of this is sorted out, don't you? Besides, she's still in pain; she's not going anywhere. And speaking of pain.' Tommy Fowler motioned to the man at the window, who came to him and laid a packet of powder and a syringe on the table. 'Same stuff you had earlier,' he said to Laura. 'A little bit stronger, perhaps.' Turning back to Frankie Doll, he said, 'So – are we all clear on that?'

Frankie Doll nodded again.

'Don't blame yourself,' Tommy Fowler said to him, patting his shoulder. 'You forgot, that's all. You forgot who I am. And you forgot that I see everything, hear everything, know about everything that's going on. Even all those things going on behind my back. I'm like a dog, I am, Frankie, a dog, forever sniffing the air for a smell of something. I get a particular scent and I just can't let go of it.' He raised his face and sniffed the air. 'See?' he said. 'See?'

32

'CAN YOU IMAGINE?' CROWLEY SAID TO RUBY NOLAN. 'I honestly hoped Rose might give birth to a monster. My first-born child. I believed I might possess some influence over the unborn foetus. Lilith would have been forty-one in two months' time. Nuit Ma Ahathoor Hecate Sappho Jezebel Lilith. She was two years old. Typhus. Rangoon. I didn't learn about it until weeks afterwards.' He clasped a hand to his brow.

'A monster?' Ruby said. 'What kind of monster?'

'Any kind, I suppose. I was flexing muscles I had never before used. Muscles I have flexed ever since, though I often wonder to what true end.' He could see that this constant reminiscing was once again boring the girl.

It was almost midnight. And in two days and seven hours, Peter Tait would be hanged and the ceremonies would be over. And only then would Crowley know if he had been successful or not. The penultimate incantation would take place in seven hours' time, forty-eight hours before the death, followed by the final rite as the lever was thrown on the trapdoor and the condemned man simultaneously let out his dying breath.

'How will you know?' Ruby asked him.

'How will I know what?'

'The exact time.'

'Pentonville has a clock that chimes. It governs everything in the place. The authorities are assiduous in these things. A few minutes here and there are not important until that final invocation, when seconds will count. Silver will come from the prison an hour beforehand with his watch accurately set to their clock.'

'And then what?'

'Who can say? No one before me has attempted what I am attempting. And if anyone *has* been successful, then they have certainly kept their mouth shut.' Besides, who else *deserved* to succeed more than he did?

'So you think there are others attempting to do the same thing?' she said. 'Others like you?'

'There may be others,' Crowley said. 'Others engaged on the same quest and in their own ways. But none are like me. No one possesses the knowledge I possess, the potency, the desire.'

Across the room, Silver, who had appeared to be sleeping on the bed, tutted loudly and opened his eyes.

'He's awake,' Ruby said.

It was clear to Crowley that the girl resented Silver's presence, that she had become accustomed to being alone with him, beyond Silver's critical gaze.

'He'll know the precise time because he knows that I, at least, am dependable,' Silver said pointedly. He settled his hands across his stomach and closed his eyes again.

Ruby Nolan had arrived unannounced an hour earlier, disappointed to find Silver already there. In truth, Silver had been on the point of leaving, having spent several hours with

383

Crowley helping him to prepare himself for this penultimate effort. But upon the girl's arrival, he had decided to stay longer, both to her annoyance and to Crowley's equally apparent amusement. He had heard everything the girl had said to Crowley as he had lain on the bed with his eyes closed.

As he listened to Crowley and the girl now, Joshua Silver knew that he would be much happier when this was all over and done with, when Crowley had made and then failed at this one last, deluded attempt at immortality, and when the girl, upon finally seeing Crowley for what he truly was and realizing that there was nothing to be gained for herself, cut her losses and detached herself from this man old enough and decrepit enough to be her grandfather.

The thought made Silver smile. He felt the pocket watch beneath his hands. He would not stay the whole night, only long enough to determine more of the girl's scheming ways and to add his own tempering presence to Crowley's excesses.

Silver understood only too well what a final opportunity this was for the pair of them – himself and Crowley – and his first impulse upon the girl's arrival had been to turn her away, to save his friend from the inevitable humiliation and embarrassment. But – and Joshua Silver had given this even greater thought over the past few days – supposing the girl stayed and ensured that that humiliation and embarrassment – Crowley's *disgrace* almost – was even *more* painful, even *more* complete? What then? Perhaps *then* Crowley might accept his failure and abandon his so-called quest for good. Perhaps then, if he fell a long way and landed hard, he would finally abandon this life of endless striving, and the pair of them might at last move out of the city – back to Bournemouth or Torquay or Hastings, say – and live out their lives there, creating and sharing new interests, unnoticed, unhounded, forgotten. Two old men growing even older. Two old men supporting and encouraging each other as they wandered together towards that cloudy horizon of ordinary death.

But if all of this passed through Joshua Silver's mind as he rested on the bed and listened to Crowley and the girl, then he was careful not to whisper a breath of it. He himself, he had decided, would say a prayer for Tait – a man put to death after months of judicial process, when all over the world there were now smouldering pits of the slaughtered, innocent dead – and then afterwards try to convince himself that the man had indeed been guilty of the crime for which he had been condemned.

He was distracted from these thoughts by the girl, who had come closer to the bed, and who was now standing looking down at him.

'Catch all that, did you?' she said in a low voice.

'Perfectly,' Silver told her, even though he hadn't heard much beyond Crowley's ridiculous opening remarks. 'He was telling you about his first, lost daughter. Name any one of his other children for me.' He kept his eyes carefully closed.

'What?'

'Aleister's other children. Name any one of them. Or his wives, official and otherwise. Or perhaps I should say "women".' All his other little whores, gold-diggers and attention-seekers.'

'I don't get you,' she said, taking a step away from him.

Silver opened his eyes and looked up at her. 'Oh, I think you "get" me perfectly,' he said. 'In fact, I doubt if there's anything of all this – of everything you've pushed your way into – that you don't *get* in one way or another, or which you haven't already started scheming to turn to your own advantage.'

'"Scheming"?' Ruby Nolan said, and then laughed. She had already made a list of the addresses of the newspapers and magazines she had read, made notes of the names of the journalists and editors who had shown an interest in Crowley. 'You're just jealous,' she said. She knew this was unlikely, too.

'Because you pay attention to him and not to me? I was married for—'

'So? What does that have to do with anything? Anybody can be married. It doesn't mean to say that they're happy, or that they've *achieved* anything. You could have been married for fifty years and still not have had what me and him might have had.'

And again, Silver wanted to laugh at her, at her self-delusion, at her gross overestimation of her true value and significance to Crowley.

Crowley himself, he saw, was watching this exchange closely and grinning at everything he saw and heard.

'"What me and him might have had",' Silver mimicked. 'It's a small word – "might".'

'Ask him,' she said. 'Last time I was here he called me his scarlet woman. Ask him.'

'It's true,' Crowley called to Silver. 'And she does possess some remarkable attributes and qualities.'

Silver shook his head at this. 'You're starting to sound like a washed-up music-hall turn,' he said to Crowley, at which Crowley nodded his agreement. Turning back to the girl, Silver said, 'Sex, you mean. Another small word.' And one that Silver would never have uttered in the girl's presence if he had given it even a second's thought.

Crowley laughed at hearing this, seeing what an obvious trap Silver had wandered into. 'A certain sinuous compliance and grace, shall we say? A willingness to be . . . employed. I shan't yet call it "devotion", but surely *you* get my meaning.'

'Of course,' Silver said. And he knew, too, why Crowley was saying all this to him now within the girl's hearing.

'Then my envy knows no bounds,' he said to Crowley, and Crowley spun his hand like a gracious victor.

'In fact,' Crowley said. 'My dear . . .'

Ruby Nolan turned to look at him. 'What?' she said, suspicious of what she had just missed between the two of them.

'No,' Crowley said, as though deciding against what he had been about to suggest to her. 'It would be too presumptuous of me. I must not presume on your sense of duty or obligation.'

Only Silver heard the faltering note of mock uncertainty in Crowley's voice, and he quickly guessed what Crowley would suggest next. 'No,' he said firmly.

'But my dear friend.'

'*Absolument pas. Ne le suggère pas à la petite salope.*'

'What?' Ruby Nolan said.

'Aleister, no,' Silver said again. 'Please.'

The city was full of French soldiers, or at least it had been up until the Invasion, and so the girl probably knew the lingo when she heard it; not the meaning, just the lingo.

'*Mais pourquoi pas?*' Crowley said to Silver. '*Tu ne l'aurais pas refusé tout de même, si on te l'avait proposé.*'

This time, Silver knew from Crowley's tone that he was not being serious, that his friend was teasing him.

'What?' Ruby Nolan said again. 'What?' Like a fading echo.

'My apologies,' Crowley said to Silver. 'My sincere apologies. I go too far. I never learn.'

'Go too far in what?' Ruby said. 'Besides, what was all that mumbo-jumbo about? *Parlez-vous français?* I'm not *entirely* stupid, you know?'

'No,' Silver said, his eyes still on Crowley.

'And besides,' Ruby went on, turning back to Silver, 'if it's *real* mumbo-jumbo you want, you should be here when he starts up with all his spook talk. I bet there's not a man alive can make head or tail of that gobbledygook.'

That's the whole point, Silver thought. 'No, I suppose not,' he said. 'And, believe me, you're honoured to be allowed to be present when it happens.' It was something he himself had always avoided, but he could easily imagine the appeal of it to her.

'Right,' Ruby said. 'Well,' and, 'Then.'

'Please, accept my apology,' Silver said. It was an apology more to Crowley than to her, and he knew Crowley would understand this.

'See,' Crowley called to her. 'He apologizes.'

'What for?' And again, she had no real idea of what had just happened, of the offer made and refused. 'All that French stuff,' she said. 'I never knew you could speak it.'

'I speak three languages apart from this one,' Silver said.

But the girl hadn't been speaking to him.

'Then, perhaps,' Crowley suggested, 'I should engage the tongue more fully when we are alone. You might learn something.'

Silver finally pushed himself upright and swung his legs to the floor, waiting for the blood to flow and to feel his toes when he moved them. He rubbed a hand over his thighs to help the process.

Ruby returned to sit beside Crowley.

'I wouldn't mind,' she said. 'Learning a bit.'

'We'll see,' Crowley said.

'Who knows?' she said. 'Two of us talking it – it might even help with everything.' She put her hand on his arm.

'Of course it might,' Crowley said.

Silver finally rose to his feet.

'Are you leaving?' Crowley asked him.

And despite everything that had just happened, Silver heard the genuine note of regret in his friend's voice.

'*Tout cela sera bientôt terminé,*' Crowley said. '*Tu le comprendes bien, j'espère.*'

'*Bien sûr que oui,*' Silver said. All over and done with and the girl gone the way of all the others. *But then what?*

'There you both go again,' Ruby said. 'A regular double act. Perhaps I should invite a few of the other girls round. They'd love this. Some of them have a real thing for the Frogs.'

'We're hardly young, handsome French soldiers,' Silver said to her.

'I suppose not. But with a bit of' – she rubbed her fingers and thumb together – 'the proper encouragement . . .'

Crowley laughed at the suggestion. 'How about it, Joshua? Do you think you and I might come up with the proper *encouragement*?'

'What *I* think,' Silver said firmly to Crowley, 'is that there are plenty of other things you might like – need – to consider first. The world is full of men making promises they have neither the intention nor the ability to keep.' He smiled as he said all this, his meaning clear.

'And I've met most of them,' Ruby Nolan said, causing all three of them to laugh at this sudden release of tension.

Silver picked up his jacket and coat and scarf. It may have

been early May but he still felt the cold in his bones. And it was already well past midnight.

Crowley, too, began to push himself up from where he sat.

'Stay where you are,' Silver told him. 'You'll no doubt need all your energy for later.'

'Here, what's he suggesting?' Ruby said, feigning anger and expecting another laugh, which this time was slow in coming.

'Precisely,' Silver said to Crowley, ensuring he, at least, understood him.

'I hear you,' Crowley said. 'Energy. Reserves. Harnessing.'

'One more heart attack and you'll wish you'd listened a little more closely.' Like all of Silver's rebuttals, it was a gentle and reasonable one, and one born of genuine concern.

Crowley held out his hand and Silver took it, removing his glove first.

'Afterwards,' Crowley said. 'And assuming success . . .' And then he faltered, suddenly unable to continue.

'Afterwards, what?' Silver said. He saw the uncertainty – the anguish almost – that creased his friend's already creased brow.

'Nothing,' Crowley said. 'I merely . . . it's just that . . .'

'That you believe – what? – that things will change irrevocably between us? That you will succeed and I, perforce, will be left behind, forgotten?'

'What's he talking about?' Ruby asked Crowley, but neither man could answer her.

'I don't know,' Crowley said eventually, speaking directly to Silver, and emerging only slowly from his own tangle of uncertain, unhappy thoughts. 'But just then, taking and holding your hand – I don't know . . .'

Silver could only guess at what Crowley was trying to say to him. 'I suppose we'll all just have to wait and see,' he said. Their two hands separated. *You'll fail. You'll fail like you have always failed. And this time when you fail I will be the only one still here and waiting for you and ready and able to comfort you in that failure. You'll fail and* nothing whatsoever *will change between us. Nothing whatsoever.*

'I suppose so,' Crowley said.

Silver opened the door and felt the cold air of the landing on his face.

'The eighth,' Crowley said.

'On the stroke of six at the latest,' Silver said. 'I'll be here with my watch perfectly synchronized. You have my word.'

A moment later he was at the flimsy bannister, looking down into the lower reaches of the house. The door was closed behind him, and he heard Crowley's mumbled voice and the forced laughter of the girl. He thought of his own lost wife. Forty-three years. The pair of them had spoken French to each other. Everyone called it 'the language of love', but it was really just a flimsy gown to be occasionally thrown over the mechanics of love. A scent to mask all those other odours. There was more laughter, followed by an exclamation of surprise from the girl.

Silver walked along the landing and down the first flight of stairs. The night's constellations were framed briefly above him in a small skylight, but quickly lost as he continued walking. By then, all he could hear was the girl's distant voice and laughter, distorted and muted by the walls and floors through which it came to him, and wreathed now in the noise of his own laboured breathing.

33

FRANKIE DOLL STOOD IN THE STREET AND LOOKED UP AT the house in front of him. It was almost midnight, and with the exception of a solitary high window, the whole place was in darkness.

A day had passed since Tommy Fowler had told him what to do, how to redeem himself, and Frankie Doll had spent most of that time with Laura. Her bruises were already changing colour, her wounds slowly healing; and the stitches in her lip and chin would be removed in a fortnight's time by the girl downstairs who had been a nurse, and who, in all likelihood, had been the girl in the hallway – the one who had let Tommy Fowler know that Frankie Doll had finally turned up.

A fortnight. Fourteen days. It seemed like the far distant future to Frankie Doll.

But every single part of Frankie Doll's future had already disappeared ahead of him. He knew that. Of course he knew that. All his prospects and preparations – as scant and as vague and as buoyed by false hope as they had always been – had now unravelled and drifted and faded all around him. And all his plans had been torn into pieces as small as those tiny scraps of paper that Tommy Fowler had forced him to swallow. He had sacrificed Beazley, he had sacrificed Laura, and now – unless there *was* a God, and that God was on Frankie Doll's side and was watching over him and ready to intervene on his behalf – he was about to sacrifice himself. It had been a simple enough bargain – do what Tommy Fowler told him to do, then leave Laura behind, and she would be safe. Do what Tommy Fowler told him to do and then live with the consequences. Or, in Frankie Doll's case . . .

He looked up at the solitary window and knew without checking the bells and labels in the porch that this was where Sweeney lived. First Tait had pulled an imaginary trigger for Tommy Fowler, and now here *he* was, Frankie Doll, about to do the same again, only this time for real. A lost beginning, a confused middle and an unpredictable ending, and all part of the same convoluted tale. And even though he knew that he still wasn't thinking straight, the irony of all this was not entirely lost on Frankie Doll.

Or perhaps it was time for Frankie Doll to start considering his other options, whatever they might be. Looking on the bright side, he certainly had more room for manoeuvre than poor old Tait had ever had. And he was still alive, still of *some* use to Tommy Fowler. And he still knew what he knew. And Laura was alive and recovering; there was always that to add to the equation. So, surely, if he had survived for this long, and after everything that had happened during the past few weeks, then there must be *some* hope for him. The chances were that Tommy Fowler would never have caught up with him in the first place if he'd followed his instinct and stayed as far away from Laura as possible. After all, what kind of sacrifice would *that* have been?

And soon he would have Tommy Fowler's gun in his hand.

It must be worth *something* to Frankie Doll, must count for *something* on that increasingly promising-looking side of the equation.

So, all that was required of Frankie Doll now was to retrieve the gun from Sweeney, keep his own prints off it, and then take charge again of his own destiny. Perhaps he could still disappear for a few months, let everything and everyone calm down, let the war end and everything change in that particular direction, and then perhaps even go to see the detective he'd met at Holywell Street, the one Tommy Fowler intended him meeting anyway.

Deciding the time had finally come, Frankie Doll went to the doorway of the house, found the bell marked 'Sweeney', pressed it and held it for thirty seconds.

After which, he stepped back into the street and looked up. The window of the illuminated room was raised and a woman looked down at him.

'Sweeney,' Frankie Doll shouted up to her. 'Tell him Fowler sent me.'

A figure then appeared beside her and looked down at Frankie Doll. Sweeney.

'Sweeney?' Frankie Doll called up to him. 'Mister Fowler sent me.'

Sweeney gave no answer.

'Something he wanted me to pick up from you,' Frankie Doll shouted, looking back and forth along the dark, empty street.

'At this time of night?' Sweeney eventually called down to him.

'You know Tommy,' Frankie Doll said, but quietly this time. From 'Mister Fowler' to 'Tommy'. Clever, that. Spoke volumes. And Frankie Doll had hardly had to give it a second thought.

Sweeney withdrew and pulled down the window.

A minute later, a dim light showed through the taped-up glass of the door, followed by an approaching outline.

Frankie Doll spent that minute wondering how to do this, how to approach this little upstart, what to say to him. He was uncertain how much Sweeney knew – about either the chain of events that had brought Frankie Doll here, or what a juncture in the lives of the two men this meeting and exchange represented.

The first thing Frankie Doll saw when Sweeney opened the door and looked out at him was the boy's crooked lip, and all he could think about was Laura's own stitched-up mouth.

'You're Frankie Doll,' Sweeney said to him.

'And you're something Sweeney,' Frankie Doll said. 'So? Tommy sent me for the you-know-what. Let me in.' Sweeney might be good enough to take the thing home and hide it somewhere, but when it needed to be used – *used* – then Frankie Doll was the man Tommy Fowler had turned to.

'It's gone midnight,' Sweeney said. He had not climbed into his own cold bed until four in the morning for the past fortnight.

'Oh, right,' Frankie Doll said. 'I'll make an appointment, shall I? Come back later when it's more fucking convenient for you?' He pushed past the boy and into the hallway. 'Up here, is it?' He started climbing the stairs and Sweeney ran to catch up with him.

'You weren't asleep, were you?' Frankie Doll said, looking up and down at Sweeney's shabby suit and his soiled collar and loose tie.

'Just in,' Sweeney said. He knew full well how many of Frankie Doll's former responsibilities Tommy Fowler had transferred to him during that fortnight. 'Besides, I thought—'

'Thought what – thought me and Tommy had come to blows? Perhaps that's what he *wanted* you to think. And believe me, that's never going to happen. We're still big friends, me and Tommy. So don't you go worrying yourself on that particular score.'

And the vicious little bastard was still hiding out in Billericay, and Frankie Doll knew who he was and what he'd done, and the boy Tait wasn't hanged yet. And besides, even when he was, didn't that just make things worse for Tommy do-this-for-me-Frankie-and-we'll-wipe-the-slate-clean Fowler? Frankie Doll smiled at the thought of all the unplayed cards he still held. In fact, it was beginning to look to him like his return to see Laura had been the only true mistake he'd ever made, and not much of a mistake at that when you thought about it. He'd been concerned for the girl; it's the kind of man he was.

'What's so funny?' Sweeney asked him.

'What's so funny? I'll tell you what's so funny,' Frankie Doll said, without any real idea of what to add, but then said, 'What's so funny is you thinking you're turning into Tommy Fowler's right-hand man. What's so funny is you thinking you can just step in and pick up the scraps he used to throw to me.'

'I don't,' Sweeney said.

It had seemed a good come-back to Frankie Doll and he was reluctant to let the point go now just because Sweeney had *sounded* so honest. He stopped on the first landing and waited for the boy to catch up with him.

'Two more flights,' Sweeney told him.

Frankie Doll looked along the landings they passed, each one of them receding quickly into darkness. The air was as stale as the air on the landings and the stairways of the Warwick Street house, and he again thought briefly about Laura.

'There,' Sweeney told him, pointing to an open doorway which cast both a dim yellow light and the shadow of the woman who stood in it and watched the two men approach.

Frankie Doll's first thought was that this was Sweeney's mother.

'This is Veronica,' Sweeney said.

'And she is?' Frankie Doll looked at the woman.

Sweeney hesitated before answering. 'A friend,' he said.

'*His* friend,' Veronica said, as though making a considerably greater point, as though she hadn't been disappointed by Sweeney's hesitation in answering this stranger. Her first thought when the bell had sounded was that it was the little Irish tart come back to cause more trouble. And now here was this man who looked as though he could be just as much trouble if he put his mind to it. She knew from long experience that you could take against some people within seconds of meeting them.

'Pleased to meet you, *Veronica*,' Frankie Doll said to her. 'Hope I haven't interrupted anything – you know – by turning up unannounced like this.' He smiled at her and then at Sweeney. He went past her into the attic room and both Sweeney and the woman came in after him.

Frankie Doll sat in the room's only comfortable chair and looked around him. He watched as Sweeney and Veronica sat together on the small settee.

'You can go now,' Frankie Doll said to the woman.

'This is my room,' she told him.

This surprised Frankie Doll and he looked again at everything it contained. 'I can see that now,' he said. He wondered how old she was. She wore a lot of make-up, thickly applied. The bulb was dim. He wondered what Sweeney had meant by 'friend'. There was something of the gypsy about her. He wondered what *she* had meant by telling him that she was Sweeney's friend. His first guess was mid-forties, his second mid-fifties.

'I live next door,' Sweeney said, as though this explained everything, which, of course, it did.

'We've got some business,' Frankie Doll said to the woman. 'Me and him. I'm here on behalf of a mutual friend.'

'Mister high-and-mighty Tommy Fowler sent you, you mean?' Veronica said. 'I wouldn't trust that little crook as far as I could spit. Bent as a three-quid note, that one. He'll get what's coming to him, you mark my words.'

Frankie Doll saw the crystal ball on its stand on the sideboard; he saw the room and the three of them turned into a globe, bulb-lit from within. He moved his arm to see the figure inside the glass ball do the same. That was him – a tiny Frankie Doll inside the glass, moving his arm. He had hardly been listening to the woman. Something about Tommy Fowler getting what was coming to him. Well, she'd got that much right, at least.

'Button it,' he said to her, and then to Sweeney, 'You going to let her get away with flapping her big mouth off like that? I doubt if Tommy – sorry, Mister Fowler to you – would be happy to know she was whispering this poison into your ear every time you came in here to have your tea leaves read.' It was a funny crack and so Frankie Doll laughed.

The remark had the desired effect on Sweeney, and he looked at Veronica, uncertain what to say to her.

After a few seconds of this awkward silence, Frankie Doll said. 'That's more like it – peace and quiet.'

'She doesn't mean anything by it,' Sweeney said.

'*She* might not, but what it *does* mean, is that *you*'ve been blabbing your twisted little mouth off to her about business which is none of her concern. I'm sure Tommy would also be unhappy to hear that.'

'You leave his mouth out of it,' Veronica said sharply.

'What?' She had undermined Frankie Doll's threat completely.

'His mouth. That's not his fault. There's plenty of people a lot worse off than him. How come you're so bloody perfect all of a sudden?'

What? Frankie Doll wondered how they had come so swiftly on to this other path. He wondered if he'd even been referring to Sweeney's split lip in the first place. A further vision of Laura and her stitched-up mouth crossed his mind.

'He didn't mean anything by it,' Sweeney said to the woman.

In response, she stroked his shoulder and smiled at him. She *behaved* like his mother. And he behaved like her young and vulnerable son. She protected him, that was it. Or perhaps there *was* more going on between them, something Frankie Doll could easily guess at. *Sick*, he thought to himself. *Sick*. And perhaps she only mothered him and protected him because she felt sorry for him on account of his mouth. He had always known there was something *off* about the boy, and perhaps this was it. Whatever it was, it was something else to add to that positive side of the equation that would finally prise him free of Tommy Fowler.

'You should listen to her,' he said to Sweeney. 'There's a lot of bad people out there, sick people.'

'The whole world's sick,' Veronica said, bowing her head as she spoke.

'What?'

'The world. I said the whole world's sick.'

As sick as you and him? Frankie Doll thought. *As sick as you two?* 'What's with the crystal ball?' he asked her.

'She tells fortunes,' Sweeney said. Turning to Veronica, he said, 'Tell him.'

'I have a gift,' she said. 'That's all.'

'She inherited it from her mother.'

'A gift?' Frankie Doll said.

'The crystal ball, palms, the tarot,' she said.

She *was* a gypsy. He looked at her earrings and at the tangle of cheap and gaudy necklaces she wore.

'She could look into *your* future,' Sweeney said, with something now approaching enthusiasm in his voice.

'*Him?*' Veronica said.

Frankie Doll felt the word like a slap across his face. 'Business first,' he said. 'I'm here for that thing Tommy Fowler gave to you.'

'What's he talking about?' Veronica asked Sweeney. 'What thing?'

'It's nothing,' Sweeney told her. 'Just something I'm looking after, keeping safe.'

'Is it here?' Frankie Doll looked around again.

'Next door,' Sweeney said.

'Then be a good little boy and go and fetch it. You know Mister Fowler – not a man who likes to be kept waiting.'

'No, and not a man who—' Veronica began to say.

'Don't,' Frankie Doll shouted at her, pointing directly at her mouth.

'It's all right,' Sweeney told her. 'I'll go and get it. You two wait here.'

'Why would *I* be going anywhere?' Veronica said.

'Don't make it sound as though you're doing anybody any favours,' Frankie Doll told her.

'Right,' Sweeney said, and he left the room, leaving Frankie Doll and this gypsy fortune-teller sitting in another awkward silence until he returned a minute later with the gun wrapped in a cloth in his hand.

Frankie Doll took it from him, squeezed the cloth to determine its contents and then put it on the floor beside his chair.

'What is it?' Veronica asked Sweeney.

'None of your business, that's what it is,' Frankie Doll told her.

'A gun,' Sweeney said at the same time.

'A what?' Veronica said. 'A gun?' She looked disbelievingly at Sweeney.

As did Frankie Doll, who said, 'I think Mister Fowler is going to want more than a few words when all of this is over and done with, don't you?'

'All of *what*'s over and done with?' Veronica asked him.

'*This.* All of this. Everything. Go and give your crystal ball a rub if you want the details.'

'How long have you had that thing in there?' Veronica asked Sweeney.

'A few days,' Sweeney told her. 'That's all.'

'Is it loaded?'

Sweeney nodded.

'Not much good without the bullets, is it?' Frankie Doll said.

Veronica cast him another scornful look. 'Oh, so you're a killer now, are you? Killer for hire. A hired gun. You're not just an errand boy, then; you're a real live killer. Next you'll be telling me you've got a tommy-gun at home. Where is it, under the bed next to your piss-pot?' She laughed at this.

'Mister Fowler—' Sweeney began to say.

'I'm sick and tired of hearing about *Mister* Fowler,' Veronica said.

'Don't you two love birds fall out on my account,' Frankie Doll said, smiling. 'I'm just the errand boy, remember?'

'We're not—' Sweeney said.

'Not what?' Frankie Doll said. He looked at the woman and saw the flash of longing in her dark-ringed eyes. *Thought so.*

'Me and him,' she said.

'You and him what?'

'We're not . . .' She looked fondly at Sweeney, who was by then sitting back beside her.

'I'll believe you,' Frankie Doll said. 'Thousands wouldn't.'

None of them spoke for a moment.

Then Sweeney said, 'She was thinking of going to live in Brighton.'

'It'd suit her, that would, Brighton,' Frankie Doll said. 'Full of charlatans and shysters, that place.'

'To open a bed and breakfast,' Sweeney said.

'Then why doesn't she just go? Oh, I forgot – because it would mean leaving her dream-boat lover-boy behind. Then perhaps you should go with her. I bet they see a lot of that sort of thing down in *Brighton*. In fact, I bet they see a lot of *all* sorts of things in that place. The pair of you should get the next train down there, take your crystal balls, buckets and spades with you. Because, let's face it, Sweeney boy, there isn't going to be much left over for you here once Mister Fowler gets wind of everything you've been shooting your mouth off about.'

Veronica's face was now twisted with anger at hearing Frankie Doll say all this. And everything he'd said had found its mark.

Sweeney put his hand across her back. 'He doesn't mean any of it,' he said to her. Turning to Frankie Doll, he said, 'Tell her you don't mean it, that you were only joking.'

'He's right,' Frankie Doll said to her. 'Everything's just one big joke to me. In fact, that's what everything is to everybody these days – one big joke.'

He stopped talking after that, and gradually the woman's anger subsided, helped by the cupping motions of Sweeney's hand on her shoulder. Frankie Doll watched this, seeing how close she was to reaching up and holding Sweeney's fingers.

To reassert his control, Frankie Doll picked up the cloth-bound gun, spinning the material until the revolver was revealed and in his hand and pointing at the pair of them.

Veronica screamed involuntarily, and Sweeney pulled her closer to him and held up his hand in front of her face.

'Now, that's *proper* magic,' Frankie Doll said, waving the gun from side to side.

'Put it down,' Sweeney said to him.

Frankie Doll watched Veronica. 'That what you want too, is it?'

Veronica said nothing, allowing Sweeney to hold her and to hide her face from the pointing gun.

'It's a' – Frankie Doll realized he didn't know what make of gun it was – 'gun. I'm sitting three feet away from you. You think you're going to catch the bullet in your hand? You think it isn't going to go straight through your sweaty little palm and then smash into her gyppo face? Fortune-teller? I bet she won't see *that* one coming.' He laughed again and then laid the gun in his lap. Damn – first his prints all over the handle and now gun oil on his trousers. Or perhaps the oil was all in the cloth, which he'd also handled. Or perhaps the oil wouldn't be there in any real quantity.

Sweeney slowly lowered his hand and moved apart from Veronica. 'You want to be more careful,' he said to Frankie Doll.

'You sound very brave all of a sudden,' Frankie Doll said. He had never fired a live bullet before, any bullet.

'Anyway,' Veronica said, 'what do you want it for?'

And for an instant, Frankie Doll actually considered telling her, telling them both – no names or details, of course – but telling them all the same. 'That's for me to know and you to find out,' he said.

'Big man,' Veronica said under her breath.

Frankie Doll pointed the gun again. 'What?'

'You heard me,' she said, this time looking directly at him. 'I said you're a big man. But only when you're pointing that thing. Go on, then, shoot it.' She held out her arms to him. 'Go on. Even *you* couldn't miss at three feet.' She laughed at him.

'Don't,' Sweeney said, though whether to Frankie Doll or Veronica, Frankie Doll was uncertain.

'Then tell her to shut up,' Frankie Doll told him.

'No – *you* tell me to shut up,' Veronica said. 'You're the one with the gun. *You* tell me.'

'Just put it down,' Sweeney said.

Frankie Doll knew he wasn't going to shoot. 'Fair enough,' he said. 'Fair enough, you win.' And he put the gun down again. 'Let's all just calm down, shall we?'

Veronica shook her head. 'You should tell Tommy Fowler what happened here,' she said to Sweeney. 'I doubt if he'd be too happy to hear all about this little carry-on.'

She was right: it was true. Or perhaps Frankie Doll's threat to tell Tommy Fowler about Sweeney's loose tongue was simply cancelled out by this counter-threat. He could see that Sweeney was giving the matter some thought, too.

'Will you bring it back here?' Sweeney asked him. 'Afterwards?'

'After what?' Frankie Doll said.

'After whatever it is you want it for.'

'Perhaps he's going to stick up the Bank of England,' Veronica said. 'According to the papers, they're printing money like there's no tomorrow. Something to do with the peacetime economy.'

'Right on the nose,' Frankie Doll said. 'That's exactly what I want it for.' Veronica leaned closer to him, and then, just as Frankie Doll expected her to say something else clever, she reached out and grabbed his hand.

Frankie Doll's first thought was that she was trying to get to the gun, but instead she grabbed his hand in both of her own and held it tightly, pulling him off balance and making it impossible for him to escape from her grasp.

'Stop struggling,' she told him. 'Give me your hand.'

'What for?'

'What do you think, what for?'

She wanted to read his palm. All this *gift* claptrap. And so Frankie Doll relaxed and stopped trying to pull himself free of her. 'Fair enough,' he told her. 'Let's see just how wrong you can be.'

He turned his hand palm upwards and supported it in her own. She looked more closely at it, angling it towards the dim light and stroking her thumb over the smooth, shallow bowl of Frankie Doll's palm.

'Go on, then,' Frankie Doll told her. 'Tell me what you see. Health, wealth and happiness, I imagine. As much of the second as you like. A big house in the country, is it? Kids? Christ, how many?' He looked over Veronica's head at Sweeney as he said all this. How many times had she done the same for *him*? How many times had he *let* her do it? Did he actually *believe* in all this hocus pocus? Was it even—

Veronica suddenly let go of him, drawing back and putting the hand which a second ago had been searching the creases of Frankie Doll's palm over her mouth.

'What?' Frankie Doll said. 'What? You want me to cross your palm with silver?'

But Veronica didn't answer him.

'What?' Frankie Doll said again.

'You should just go,' Veronica said, the words dry in her mouth. 'Now. Just leave. Just go and never come back here.'

Her voice, its sudden dryness and the note of alarm, caught Frankie Doll short, and he pulled his hand back and looked at it. It looked exactly as it had always looked. What was she telling him? What had she seen there? Something big? Something serious? What? There wasn't anything *to* see.

Everything was exactly the same as it had always been.

'Tell me,' he said to her.

'I can't,' Veronica said. 'I can't. You should just go.'

Can't? Go? Were the two things connected? Frankie Doll was confused.

'Tell me,' he said to her again.

With her free hand, Veronica now covered her eyes. She started murmuring to herself, her voice lost behind the fingers still over her mouth. She began rocking slightly, back and forth, her eyes still shut and firmly covered.

'Tell her,' Frankie Doll shouted at Sweeney, who himself hardly knew how to respond to what he had just seen.

Sweeney put his hand back on Veronica's shoulder and she shouted out and pulled away from him, too.

Frankie Doll picked up the gun and again pointed it at the pair of them, his finger along the trigger guard, swinging it from one to the other.

'Put it down,' Sweeney shouted at him. 'Can't you see – she's *seen* something. In your palm. She's seen something and it's upset her.'

'I know she's *seen* something,' Frankie Doll shouted back at him. 'What I'm telling you to do now is to tell her to tell me *what* she's seen. *Tell her.*' He leaned closer to Veronica and jabbed her forearm and the back of her hand with the gun. 'Tell her. Tell her to tell me.'

And seeing this – Frankie Doll prodding Veronica with the gun – Sweeney screamed at him to get away from her, from the pair of them. He lunged at Frankie Doll and grabbed the gun by its barrel, twisting it painfully from Frankie Doll's grip.

Veronica, meanwhile, her eyes and mouth still covered,

started crying, wailing almost, and her rocking became more agitated. She was near-hysterical now, and Frankie Doll didn't know what to do. And so he grabbed her arms and pulled her hands away from her face and shouted even louder at her to tell him what she'd seen. And still struggling, Veronica screamed at him, pulled her hands free and then clamped them back to her face. There were already red marks on her cheeks and around her eyes. And as she did all this, Sweeney started clubbing at Frankie Doll's hands with the gun, not even holding it by its handle, holding it by its barrel as though it were just a piece of metal, anything to inflict hurt on Frankie Doll and to force him away from Veronica.

And then, amid this confused tangle of struggling bodies, of flailing arms and grabbing hands, and as all three of them shouted and screamed at each other, the gun suddenly fired, and there was a scattered flash, a burst of acrid smoke and a sharp and reverberating explosion which deafened and then silenced and then froze them all.

And after the sparks and the smoke and the noise there was a sudden spray of wetness, and a warm, vaporous splatter of blood which covered all their faces.

It was a second, less, and then Frankie Doll was the first to fall out of this tangle of arms and bodies and faces and back into the chair in which he sat. He rubbed a hand across his eyes and then his mouth and forehead. His palm turned red with the blood there, but he felt no pain and he knew that it wasn't his blood.

And after he had fallen back into his chair, so the knot of the three of them quickly unravelled and he saw Sweeney and Veronica fall back on to the settee. Sweeney still held the gun. There was blood across his chin and lips – a clean line across his mouth and cheeks which gave him the appearance of a carefully painted savage.

And from Sweeney, Frankie Doll looked to the fortune-teller, to Veronica. She sat slumped with her head back, her long black hair over her face. She looked as though her whole chest had been painted red. She made a single, sudden gasping sound and then fell silent. Blood ran briefly from her open mouth down on to her red chest, into the elaborate lace collar of her blouse and the necklaces still rattling and settling there.

Sweeney started calling her name and shaking her. He wanted to know what had happened, what had happened, what had happened, over and over, shouting at her and shaking her and pushing at her with the hand which still held the gun.

Frankie Doll watched all this for a few seconds, and then he got up and ran to the door, pulling it open and looking out. The house remained dark and silent.

'What are you doing?' Sweeney shouted at him. 'Where are you going? She needs help. Send for help. She needs help. An ambulance. Go and find an ambulance. She's been shot.'

And this desperate, pointless pleading was all that Frankie Doll heard as he ran down the endless flights of stairs and along the endless narrow landings to the front door of the house and then out beneath the porch and down the steps and along the pitch-black street. And then as he ran along another pitch-black street just like it, and another after that, and another after that. Street after street after street, with the darkness ahead of him always visible, forever beckoning, forever drawing him on and on and on into its own cold and empty heart.

And Frankie Doll ran like this – for minutes, for hours –
until he was finally exhausted, barely conscious of where he
was, knowing only that his lungs were burning and that his
heart was beating fit to burst, and that every limb and muscle
and sinew and fibre of his entire being was trembling with
the exertion of his escape, and that his blood was coursing
through his every artery and vein like the fire it had become,
and raging like a furnace against the walls of his own sorry,
saved and precious skin.

34

'Is that it, then?' Ruby Nolan said to Crowley. 'Is it finished?'

'Not quite,' Crowley said. He looked beyond her to the rising light at the window.

'The hanging, you mean?'

Crowley looked at the watch he wore. It was almost five in the morning. Silver would be back in an hour with his own perfectly synchronized watch, and an hour after that the boy would be hanged.

And after that . . .

The girl was clearly undecided about whether to stay or not.

'I feel a certain . . .' Crowley trailed off.

'A certain what?' She rubbed at a mark he'd made on her calf.

'Satisfaction,' Crowley said, but absently, as though uncertain of what he meant by the word.

The girl pulled up one of her stockings. She saw where this had snagged, and she swore.

'What?' Crowley said.

She showed him the ladder in the nylon.

'It's a small price to pay,' he told her. 'Are you complaining?'

411

He looked directly at her. What did she have to complain about? She had just been afforded the privilege of participating in the event of a lifetime. The rite was almost completed – a further single mouthed sentence as the clock struck seven – and there she was, rubbing at her small bruises and complaining about a tear in her cheap stockings.

'Your nails are too long,' she said to him.

He curled his fingers into his palm and looked down at them. His nails were always long, and of late they had grown even thicker and more discoloured. The nails of the fingers where he held his cigarettes were brown, the others on the same hand a darkening yellow.

'I used to sharpen them,' he said, again absently, his confused thoughts still elsewhere.

'You did what?'

'To inflict pain. Necessary pain. During the rituals. And you'd be surprised how many of my partners derived no small satisfaction from that pain.'

'If you say so,' she said, still concentrating on her stocking.

'Another, shall we say, heightening of the senses, a focusing of the process.' He looked at her. He could see she had little idea of what he was telling her. Her bare leg was white, the same tone from her crotch to her toes. And shapeless, or so it suddenly seemed to him. 'Two hours,' he said. 'Less.'

He wanted to tell her to leave, that she had played her own small and worthless part in everything, and that now she was useless to him. Her role was over. Perhaps he might desire her in the future, but who could say what that future held for any of them? Who could say – those two short hours ahead – what transformation was about to take place, what reawakening, what resurgence of power and will? Perhaps it *would* be akin to a great fountain of life and vigour and energy rising within him, and perhaps he would want her again immediately afterwards as a test of that new-found energy and vigour and desire. Perhaps her being there, and his performance with her so soon after the last, would be all the proof he needed to convince himself that he had finally succeeded.

'You were still too rough,' she said, distracting him from these thoughts.

He would stop thinking of her by her name, he decided. It would help to separate them, and then for him to detach himself completely from her when the time came. Few believed him when he insisted that the memory of some of the women he had known fifty years earlier was a hundred times more potent than the actual presence of the woman who was with him there and then, even a woman like Ruby Nolan now.

You're a whore, he thought, but said nothing. *Rough?* He was seventy years old. She didn't know the meaning of the word. He had lived the lives of a dozen men in reaching that age. She should have seen him when all those other women were queuing up to feed off him and absorb even the smallest part of the power he once possessed. Opportunists and true believers alike, they had always been there, always been obedient to him, always come back for more of whatever he was offering to them.

Perhaps his fortunes had once counted for something, but many of them had possessed fortunes of their own, and so for those at least, money could not have played the smallest part in their attachment to him. And some of them had had nothing – literally nothing except the clothes they stood up in – and they too had played their part. He had not believed how compliant and debased some of them would allow themselves to become in his presence as his various rituals began. He had not believed what they would submit themselves to, and then endure, how they would so easily and willingly bend to his every cruelty and whim.

The girl was talking again. Something about the radiogram, an announcement. But that was all there ever were these days – announcements. Everybody needed to be kept in touch, kept in line. Announcements of victories. Victory after victory, success after success. A never-ending parade of the things. Announcements of preparations. Preparations for celebrations, for everything that was to come.

He looked down at his feet. His trousers were still unbelted and loose around his knees. His shrunken, flaccid organ was lost between his thighs and the overhang of his stomach where he sat in the soft chair. He pulled his trousers up, fastening his fly buttons and tucking his shirt into his lost waist.

She was watching him closely, working out, perhaps, how the balance had tipped for or against her now that she no longer had a part to play. She watched him and then she smiled, and in that fleeting, calculating gesture, he suddenly saw much more. He didn't know *what* he had seen, exactly, just that there was something – something she alone understood and took pleasure in.

Whatever it was, it was beyond Crowley to ask her directly, especially now. And besides, in a little under two hours none of this would be of the slightest consequence to him. He would achieve everything he had ever hoped and striven to achieve, and every favour and reward in the world would be his to dispense and bestow. Another two hours, and *then* let them all see with perfect clarity where they stood. Because *then*, wherever they believed *they* stood, he, Aleister Edward Crowley – Perdurabo – He Who Shall Endure – He Who *Had* Endured – would be standing firmly and immovably at their centre.

She was still talking. The darkness in the window beyond her was failing. It was true what they said about the hours immediately before the dawn, before that first glimmer of the rising light of a new day. It was true, too, what they said about hope and despair and the scarcely discernible line which divided them. He wondered briefly why men were hanged and shot at dawn, why men who saw that day coming waited for it. Why were hope and expectation so endlessly reborn? Why was the brightening sky filled with so much hope and expectation which was all so seldom realized? The morning star – the star of fallen angels.

'What language was it?'

This time the girl's voice surprised him. She was beside him where he sat. She smoothed down the front of his shirt, pulled his jacket shut and fastened the buttons, and he acceded to all this without pushing her away. It was a small act of kindness, he supposed, a consideration, a final intimacy between them.

'Pardon?' he said.

'You were in a world of your own,' she said. 'I asked you what language you were talking – shouting – while we were – you know . . .'

'A mixture of tongues,' he said. Whatever he told her would be far beyond her comprehension, neither a lie nor a truth, and something which would always better serve his own purpose when these people without the faintest idea asked their pointless, stupid questions.

'Tongues?' she said.

Whore.

'You sounded . . .'

He waited for her to finish. Everything was a clue.

'You sounded different,' she said. 'Like someone else completely.' She finished fastening his buttons, and then tugged at the material at each of his shoulders. He had owned the jacket for thirty years, and for twenty-nine of those it had been too tight for him.

'In what way?' he asked her. 'In what way different?'

'You sounded – younger – more forceful – I don't know.'

He wondered if she was lying to him, telling him only what she imagined he wanted to hear. She still wanted to be part of everything. And the last thing she would want was for him to believe that she was part of his failure. Was *that* why she was saying it? Was that why she had earlier smiled and then wiped that same smile from her lips an instant later?

'Perhaps the very act . . .' Crowley suggested.

'Act? I wasn't acting. I—'

'I know what you were doing,' Crowley said. In the past he would have relished this kind of talk, but not now. The room – according to the rite he had all but just completed in it – had become a shrine, a sacred place, and the ceremony he had commenced there three weeks earlier could do nothing now except move unstoppably to its climax. All those small, scattered pieces becoming whole again.

'You know what I mean,' he said to her.

He wondered how many others had heard her say exactly the same words. Perhaps she usually waited until they were about to leave her, their wallets in their hands, all passion spent. It was a phrase he had always appreciated. Because that's what passion was – a thing to be released, something to be offered up as forcibly and as completely as possible. And how many millions of men didn't possess even the faintest notion of that in their lives? And life, too, Aleister Edward Crowley also knew better than most, was itself a storm, something to be confronted and challenged, something to be fought and conquered; never something to be merely endured or, worse, avoided or regretted.

He felt a sudden heat in his hands and chest and he held up his hands to look at them.

'What is it?' she asked him. She looked at him as though he were about to grab hold of her.

'I felt something,' he said. Something coursing through him.

'What? Is it working? Already?'

But even as he considered this, the heat subsided and he lowered his hands back into his lap.

'What?' she said again. 'Something connected to our – to the ceremony?'

'Possibly,' he said. And then an instant later he felt a sudden pain in his chest. And this, too, came and went as quickly and as unexpectedly as the heat had come and gone.

This time, the girl said nothing; instead she continued watching him closely.

'Perhaps you've done too much,' she suggested, smiling at all this implied.

Crowley resisted the urge to slap her across her face. 'Perhaps,' he said.

On the mantel above the empty fireplace the heavy clock struck six, and neither of them spoke as the evenly spaced notes were sounded, their duration doubled by their dying hum in the quiet of the room.

Six. An hour had passed so swiftly. And soon Silver would be there with his synchronized watch.

'It's getting light,' the girl said.

Outside, the early May sky was already filled with the rising sunlight.

Crowley nodded. It was the longest she had stayed with him. Silver had a key for both the front door and the door of Crowley's room; there would be no bell. The first they would know of his arrival would be the man himself letting himself in and holding out his precious watch to them.

Silence returned to the room.

Once, Crowley had believed that there was no end to the darkness in the world – the darkness of night and the darkness of shadow and those secretive and destructive darknesses that all men carried inside themselves – but now, unexpectedly, he found himself more inclined to favour these coming dawns, these coming days of hope and expectation and brightening light.

The war would soon be over, even in the Far East, and perhaps that would be the brightest light of all. At least until the next time. And afterwards, the world would seek to banish all those lesser, converging darknesses, and the brilliant and inescapable sun of the New Age would shine endlessly down upon them all.

'What are you thinking about?' the girl asked him. She too was looking at the window and at the light rising in the east as it finally gave some true form and outline to the buildings and trees outside.

35

ARTHUR BONE LOOKED UP FROM WHERE HE SAT WITH Peter Tait. A distant door had just been opened and then closed. A door beyond a door beyond a door. He glanced at Tait, who appeared to have heard nothing, and who sat, as usual, hunched over the table and his Bible.

Bone pushed back his chair. A second door, and now he could hear distant footsteps. Faint, but discernible, and moving in a single direction. The Governor and Simpson the chaplain.

'I think you ought to . . .' he said to Tait. He rose to his feet and gestured to the boy.

The pair of them had been sitting like that for the past three hours, since before four, when Bone had arrived early and taken over from Lynch.

He hadn't slept all night, walking from his home to the prison through the dim light of that final morning. A few men, strangers to him, had acknowledged him as he'd walked, and he'd returned their anonymous greetings. And just as there was a new day in the mild spring air, so there was also something else – something he heard in the voices of those few others, something he could see and smell and feel in the near-empty streets through which he passed on his journey to the prison.

He saw what a matter of luck and chance the war had been for most people – those noisy rockets and falling bombs – and how some streets remained completely untouched while others had been reduced to mounds of rubble, piles of scorched timber and new paths through the ruins. Half a street gone completely, half a street as perfect as it had been at the start of it all; lives lost, lives diverted, and lives put on hold; and lives which had continued as though the whole dirty, bloody business had never happened. He heard birdsong and the night cries of cats in the darkness.

At the table, Peter Tait finally looked up at him.

Bone beckoned again and Tait stood up and presented himself for Bone's inspection. He pushed his chair beneath the table, positioning its wooden back in line with the table's edge. The same as Bone's. He waited for Bone to say something, for his approval.

'At last,' Bone said. 'You're learning.'

And Tait smiled at the words.

Then he picked up the Bible and put it in his pocket.

Two days earlier he had asked Bone to ask the Governor if he'd be allowed to take the book to the gallows with him. At first the request had been refused. Regulations. And then, after a brief discussion with Simpson, permission was granted. Tait would be allowed to walk to the gallows with the Bible in his pocket, and this would afterwards be taken from him and held by the chaplain until it was claimed.

Part of Bone's argument to the Governor was that there would be no one coming to claim anything of Tait's, and that ever since hearing of his failed appeal, the book had calmed and steadied him while he'd waited. Apart from his clothes, shoes and an empty wallet, Tait had no other possessions.

Upon his arrival at the prison entrance, Bone had passed through the crowd already gathered there in the darkness – the usual word-spreaders, do-gooders and assorted campaigners – holding vigil for the condemned man. Some had tried to detain him and ask him questions, but Bone had held up his arms and passed through them like a man wading through water up to his chest.

A man standing on a crate had shouted down at him, asking him what the past six years had all been about if *this* was being allowed to happen. A woman young enough to be Bone's granddaughter had waved a placard in his face and then spat at his feet. Bone had said nothing to either of them.

A group of women at the prison wall held up a banner announcing that they were the mothers of lost sons – sons killed in the war, Bone assumed – and that they wanted no more mothers – they meant Tait's mother – to have to suffer and endure what they had suffered and endured. Bone neither diverted from his course nor put them right on that particular score. Or perhaps – and the thought only then occurred to Bone and caused him to falter on his course through the women – or perhaps Tait's mother *did* know what was happening to her abandoned son. Perhaps she had known all along and had been watching and waiting with all those others who were finally showing an interest in the boy's case. Perhaps – *perhaps* – she was even in the crowd now, as close to her son – her baby, her boy – as she had ever been. Bone regained his step and resisted the urge to look around him. The women by the wall began chanting as he continued through them.

A man beside him asked him if he was the hangman, and this too Bone ignored. 'I bet you are,' the man hissed in his ear. 'You look the sort.' He shouted to those around him that Bone was the hangman and there was a moment of silence. Concerned that others might believe the man, Bone unfastened the top few buttons of his coat to reveal the uniform beneath. 'Oh,' the man said, disappointed. 'You *look* like a hangman.' He turned away and pushed back into the restless crowd.

By the wall, the grieving mothers fell silent as Bone finally arrived at the prison entrance and pressed the bell. 'Shame on you,' a woman called to him. She held a candle in a jar and had a photograph of her own lost son in uniform pinned to her coat.

Bone was relieved to hear the bolts being drawn, and then to finally step into the peace and calm of the prison.

The man who opened the door grabbed Bone's arm and pulled him inside. 'You all right?' he said.

'Nothing we haven't all seen before,' Bone told him.

'Not me,' the man said. 'This is my first.'

Bone heard the note of barely suppressed excitement in the man's voice.

The man held out his hand to Bone and Bone reciprocated before realizing that this was not what the man had intended. He was missing three fingers on the hand.

'Italy,' the man said. 'Anzio.'

'Right,' Bone said and nodded at him. Everybody had their trophies. The world was soon going to be full of these men and their stories and their foreign places and the weight of loss and remembering they would never afterwards be able to either properly bear or fully shed.

Bone left him and went into the guard wing, hung up his coat and hat, clocked on, and then went straight to Tait.

Lynch was asleep in the chair in the corridor beside Tait's door. At Bone's approach, the man rubbed his face and looked at his watch. 'You're keen,' he said through a yawn.

Bone looked into the cell and saw Tait sitting hunched at the table. There was nothing Bone could say to Lynch that the boy wouldn't hear. Big day. Lots to do. Best be ready. Better early than late. Unexpected eventualities. Although, in all likelihood, the boy would hear nothing of any of this as he continued to scrutinize the tiny print of the book inches from his face.

Only after Bone had gone into the cell, and after Lynch had closed the door behind him, did Tait finally look up at him.

'Here I am,' Bone said, and was then caught off-guard by the look of both relief and gratitude on Tait's face.

'I knew you'd get here early,' Tait said, rising and holding out his hand to Bone.

'Yes, well,' Bone said. 'Things to sort. You need someone who knows what they're doing. You don't want things going arse over – well, you know – not on a day like this.'

Tait smiled at the phrase.

'I'd catch a rocket even for breathing the word,' Bone said. He motioned for Tait to sit back down.

And they had been sitting together and waiting like this until the first of those distant doors had sounded, and those footsteps had started towards them along all those corridors.

'I think you ought to . . .' Bone said.

Tait rose and pulled his jacket straight. 'How do I look?' he said.

'You look just fine, son,' Bone told him.

Then Tait, too, heard the approaching footsteps and a flicker of uncertainty crossed his face. 'What will . . . ?' he began to say.

'You just follow my lead,' Bone said quickly and firmly. 'That's why I'm here. You just watch me. *Me*, Bone. Watch and follow, and nothing will go wrong. I'll keep you on the straight and narrow for this one.' He motioned to the Bible on the table. 'You going to pick that up and put it in your pocket, then? Be a shame to forget it after all this time.'

He knew that once the Governor and the chaplain entered the cell there would be no time for all these little incidentals, no time for questions beyond the Governor's solitary 'Ready?' to Bone, and certainly no time for even the slightest hesitation or delay. Like clockwork – that was how things would move from then onwards. Like clockwork. They would be like marching soldiers, no diversion, no moving out of line or step, no room whatsoever for wavering or indecision.

Another door was opened and closed, and Bone knew exactly how far away the approaching men now were.

Tait picked up the Bible and pulled out its slender scarlet ribbon. He drew this flat between his thumb and forefinger and then slid it back into the book at a particular place. At the place where the girl – whoever she might have been – had once pencilled in and then lost her name, but of which a faint and discernible imprint still remained to Tait's discerning eye. Then he put the book in his pocket and patted it where it lay.

Bone ran his hands down the boy's lapels, tugging at his cuffs and then brushing imaginary dust from his shoulders.

'Dust,' he said. 'Can't have you looking all . . .' He brushed again, the lightest touch of his fingers. He felt the boy straighten himself, press his arms to his sides and raise his chin slightly. 'Good lad,' Bone told him. 'You'll do.'

Another smile.

He could save this boy, look after him. He could save this boy and the world would be a better place for it. He could save this boy and he could save himself at the same time.

The thought rushed through him like a bomb blast and left him feeling dizzy. He closed his eyes for a second and pulled his hands away from Tait.

'You all right, Mister Bone?' Tait asked him.

Bone opened his eyes. 'Me?' he said. 'Never better. Don't you worry about me.' He took a step back from the empty table.

The footsteps were now in the corridor outside.

Tait looked over Bone's shoulder at the door.

'You ready?' Bone asked him, and Tait smiled again, closed his eyes briefly, and then nodded.

'Officer Bone.' It was the Governor. 'Are we—?'

'All present and correct, sir,' Bone said, oblivious to the face the Governor pulled at hearing the words.

Beside the Governor stood Simpson, his own much larger Bible held open between his hands. He was caressing the book and reading from it, his eyes closed, the murmured words flowing in a stream as though passing up from his hands and through his arms and chest to his mouth and then out into the room, where they drifted like motes of warm, holy dust around the four of them.

The Governor took a folded sheet of paper from his inside pocket, put on his glasses, which he carried around his neck on a slender black cord, carefully unfolded the sheet of paper and read from it.

Tait again looked suddenly anxious at this, but Bone caught his eye and silently shushed him.

The Governor finished reading. He refolded the paper and pushed it just as carefully back into his pocket. He then took out a leather strap and handed this quickly to Bone.

Bone took it and went to Tait, deftly drawing the boy's hands behind his back.

'Remember what we talked about,' he whispered in Tait's ear, and Tait nodded once. 'Good boy, good lad.' Bone finished tying the strap. Another would be fastened around Tait's waist at the gallows, and his bound hands would be secured to this.

'All ready,' Bone said to the Governor, and the Governor immediately turned and walked out of the cell, followed by Simpson, who had not for a second faltered in his practised murmuring.

'We need to get going,' Bone whispered to Tait, holding the palm of his hand to the boy's back, relieved when Tait started walking in the wake of the two men.

The four of them walked along the corridor, and Tait looked briefly over his shoulder at the room he was leaving behind him.

'I'm still here, lad,' Bone said to him. 'You just keep walking.'

The pace of the four men never slowed. Doors were opened ahead of them and then locked behind them. It was three minutes to seven, give or take a few seconds. The route of this walk, the shortness of the journey, had long since been calculated. No other occupied cells to pass. Not even a word from the doorkeepers, these silent witnesses to Tait's last journey on God's Earth.

A final door, opened, passed through, closed behind.

And there was the gallows, as simple and as stark and as efficient-looking as it always was. A wooden platform, a metal beam, supports, and a coiled noose held in a collar of leather.

And standing a short distance beyond it were several other men – six in all – including Detective Inspector Ernest Pye.

The man caught Bone's eye as he entered the room immediately behind Tait, and the two of them acknowledged each other.

Tait, too, saw Pye and smiled at him. He turned to Bone and said, 'He came, see?'

'I see,' Bone said.

There was no talking in the room, only the endless murmuring of Simpson, until that too finally stopped, and the man took his place amid the other officiating witnesses and waited in silence with his head bowed and his eyes closed. It had long since occurred to Bone that the man never once looked in the eye the men he was leading to their deaths. *All right for some*, he thought. *Pity it wasn't an option for them all*. He came to a halt in his own preordained position, a final gentle stamp of his foot like another of those soldiers on parade.

Tait continued a step further, and Bone grabbed his arm and held him in place.

Another guard came to them, fastened a broad leather belt around Tait's waist and secured his bound hands to this. A further restraint was equally swiftly fastened around the boy's ankles, almost flicked into place and then pulled tight, causing Tait to lose his balance and stumble for a moment. But Bone held him steady by his arms.

'Careful,' Bone said, but more to the man at Tait's feet than to the boy himself.

Then Simpson came forward and made a cross in front of Tait's face.

Bone looked again to Ernest Pye, who was watching everything closely and without blinking.

That's right, you keep looking, Bone thought. *You keep looking. You could have prevented this. You could have done your job properly in the first place and none of this would ever have happened. So you keep watching.*

He knew the moment the thought occurred to him that it was an unjust one, and that perhaps he and Ernest Pye alone in a nation of millions knew that the boy was innocent. Well, Pye, himself and those few others who had used the boy for their own ends and who had then happily let him come to the gallows. He wondered if Pye was thinking the same thing. It was possible, likely even.

He signalled his apology to the man, and something in Pye's eyes, something in the way the detective briefly bowed and then raised his head, told Bone that Pye understood him perfectly.

Simpson finally raised his head, nodded at the men around him and then returned the two paces back to the edge of the gallows platform.

Now the Governor was speaking again.

The warder who had put on the belt came forward with a folded cloth bag, which he opened and quickly slid over Tait's head, pulling its edges down to his collar. This was when other men might panic or shout out in surprise.

But not Tait.

'Good lad,' Bone said again, the words now less than a whisper between them.

'My Bible, Mister Bone,' Tait whispered back to him.

'Still safe in your pocket,' Bone said. 'It's still there.' After-wards, he had decided, he would ask Simpson for the book and then keep it in remembrance of the boy.

Then he and the other warder moved Tait forward on to the trap-door.

The coiled noose in its loose leather ring was put over the boy's head by the other man, and then Bone pulled it tighter to his neck.

'You take care, now,' he mouthed through the material of the bag into the boy's ear, and he heard Tait say, 'Thank you,' to him the instant before he stepped back.

The boy stood perfectly upright and rigid on the platform.

A third man came to the nearby lever, took hold of it in both his hands and turned to the Governor.

The Governor held up his arm in front of his face and looked at his watch, holding back his jacket sleeve and the cuff of his shirt to keep it in clear view.

The room was almost silent again – the breathing of men, the creak of leather shoes, shuffling feet, the noise of the boards upon which they all stood and waited.

Bone glanced again at Pye and then both men turned to look at the boy.

A moment later, the silence was broken by the first distant note of the prison clock striking seven.

And scarcely had this first chime sounded before the Governor pulled down his cuff and then his jacket sleeve and then lowered his arm to his side and turned to the man at the lever and closed his eyes and inclined his head an inch.

And hardly had the second chime begun to sound than all of this was done and the man at the lever clasped tight its handle and pulled the steel arm of the lever towards him until it struck the rim of its socket and the two hinged, oiled halves of the trap-door swung open beneath Tait's feet and he dropped without a sound between them, falling into that second chime, and with the rope uncoiling to its full released length and stiffening and juddering and then swinging slightly with its settling weight below. The sound of Peter Tait's breaking neck was lost to the scrape of the metal bolt, the crack of the lever hitting its waiting slot, the clatter of the two swinging halves of the trap-door, and the suddenly released breath of all the surrounding, watching men.

Ernest Pye, Arthur Bone noticed, raised a hand to his forehead and swiftly crossed himself.

36

THE CLOCK ON THE MANTEL FINISHED CHIMING AND THE two old men and the girl sitting beneath it looked hard at it and then silently counted the seconds into the reverberating silence which followed.

Ruby Nolan was the first to speak. 'What happens now?' she said.

Joshua Silver turned away from the clock and looked at Crowley, who remained slumped in his chair with his eyes tightly closed – either because he had now abandoned himself to some genuine and all-consuming process of transformation, or – as Silver already knew was considerably more likely – because he simply could not bear to open them and to look out at the same unaltered world which still lay all around him, and within which he too remained undeniably unchanged.

He waited, his hand hovering over Crowley's, ready to lower it and hold his friend at the first indication of Crowley's terrible realization of this final failure and defeat.

'Aleister?' he said after a minute, his voice hoarse.

He had been back there since soon after six, waiting with Crowley and the girl, having walked all the way from Pentonville. He had hoped to sleep for a few hours before

431

visiting the prison to listen for its clock, but this had proved impossible.

The first thing he had done upon arriving at Coleherne Road was to transfer the exact time of his pocket watch to the clock on the mantel. And so they were all now connected – even the girl in her own small way – all now connected and waiting.

'Aleister?'

Crowley slowly opened his eyes and looked up at him. 'My dear friend,' he said. He raised his hand a few inches and then laid it back down.

Close to them both, the girl said, 'I'm still here. Invisible, am I?'

She seemed agitated to Silver, nervous. Drugs, perhaps. Perhaps something she'd shared with Crowley during his absence. Perhaps something she'd taken to keep herself awake and alert through that long night. Perhaps it was why Crowley himself seemed so lethargic now.

Crowley looked at the room around them. 'I've failed,' he said, but instead of the despair and anguish Silver had expected, Crowley seemed strangely resigned to this.

'It may be too early to tell,' Silver said, but with little true conviction. The boy would still be on the end of his rope, perhaps still swinging or twisting from side to side, perhaps not even dead yet, perhaps still alive. Perhaps *that* was why Crowley had not yet felt anything. Perhaps there had been some delay, and perhaps the boy was still alive, and so perhaps whatever Crowley had expected to happen had yet to take place; perhaps it was still imminent; perhaps it was even happening now. Or perhaps the watch and then the clock had gained a few seconds. How long had passed? Could he still not hear the lost echo of the final chime in the small room? Could he still not feel its smallest vibrations in the calm air? Besides, how long did a man take to die on the end of a rope? Presumably the authorities decided that a certain amount of time had to pass, and perhaps this official interval had not yet elapsed. Perhaps they were all now stuck in a kind of limbo until that officially designated time was counted out.

Silver might have put all these racing thoughts into words and then suggested everything to Crowley, but he didn't; instead, he stayed silent and kept everything to himself, waiting and watching, his hand now firmly clasped to the back of Crowley's own.

'I've failed,' Crowley repeated, this time the two words more mouthed than spoken.

'What's he saying?' Ruby Nolan asked Silver. She was pacing back and forth in front of the cold fireplace, barely pausing in her restless motion to look at the two men or to listen any more closely to what they were saying.

'You tried,' Silver tried to reassure Crowley, but knew this was no consolation.

'All my long life . . .' Crowley said.

'What's he saying?' Ruby Nolan said again, but again she made no effort to either come any closer to them or to stop her agitated pacing and listen.

'Rest,' Silver told Crowley, and he let go of his hand. He rose from beside his friend and went to the girl. He grabbed her arm and told her to keep still.

At first, the gesture angered Ruby Nolan, but then she stopped trying to pull herself free of Silver and simply smiled at him.

'Or what?' she said. 'What are *you* going to do?' She

motioned to Crowley. 'Do you think you're going to do what *he* imagined he was actually up to doing with me? It's pathetic. *He's* pathetic. He wasn't capable of *anything*. Stories, that's all. Big man. Him and all his women, all his so-called slaves and followers – stories, that's all they ever were, stories.'

'You're wrong,' Silver said to her, but again without conviction.

She finally pulled herself free of him, and then she pushed him hard in his chest, causing him to stagger back a few paces.

'The pair of you. You're as pathetic as he is. Look at you. Oh, and don't worry – I know all there is to know about *you*. And I certainly know as much as I need to know about *him* to make it worth my while where the newspapers are concerned. Wait until *they* get an earful of everything that's been happening here.'

Silver heard the venom in her voice and remained silent, unwilling to provoke her further.

Behind him, alerted by the girl's raised voice and what she was threatening, Crowley was now watching the pair of them.

'Why don't you go back to him?' Ruby Nolan said to Silver. 'You and him, you deserve each other. Who else have you got? Nobody, that's who. Nobody and nothing.'

'He honestly thought you—' Silver began to say.

'He thought I what? That I believed all this clap-trap, all this mumbo-jumbo, all this devil-worshipping rubbish, that I wanted any part whatsoever in it all? What? What did he believe?'

She must have believed some of it, Silver thought to himself. *Or why else would she have stayed? Why else would she have allowed Crowley to involve her as he had done? Why else would she have done those things Crowley said she'd done? It surely can't all have been born of uncertain need and desperate compliance. Or was it all just that – all just more of Crowley's exaggerated and self-serving boasting? Were the habits and practices of a lifetime so impossible to shed?*

The girl came back to Silver and held her face close to him, another cold smile fixed on her lips. 'Besides,' she said, pausing, her eyes flicking from side to side. 'There's that poor boy to consider now. It looks like *he* died for nothing. I bet the newspapers *and* the authorities would like to hear about that little set-up, don't you?' She paused again. 'What, you thought I didn't know about any of that?' She glanced at Crowley. 'Surprising what comes out when – you know.'

Silver didn't know how to respond to this. Perhaps Crowley *had* told her all about the condemned boy's part in everything. Or perhaps he'd said just enough for her to ask the right questions elsewhere – back in Soho, for instance, back in the world she inhabited, back in *her* world. But however she had come by the information, he knew that it was now the biggest threat to the pair of them.

'See?' she said to Silver. 'See? It's not as though the authorities and the newspapers *wouldn't* be interested in the part played by that' – she motioned to Crowley – 'poor old exhausted – what was it? – oh, that's right, that poor old exhausted "Beast" over there, is it? I imagine they'll be fighting to get to me to hear what I've got to tell them. "Monster"? Don't make me laugh. Look at him, sitting there with all his grubby little plans in shreds and tatters all around him, and with his flies undone and his trousers covered in stains.'

Silver knew that there was a great deal of truth in what she was saying, even if much of what she was threatening

435

was only then occurring to her. Or perhaps this had been her plan all along – to wait and see what Crowley might achieve and then to run to the newspapers with everything she knew, everything she had seen, and, presumably, everything she had been forced against her will to participate in. Either way – success or failure – her own reward would be great.

'"Demon"?' she said, and laughed. 'They should see him now.' She went to Crowley and put her face close to his. 'I was just telling the struck-off little quack here: they should see you now, see what a pathetic old windbag you've become. Wait until they hear what I've got to tell them. That poor, innocent boy, hanged for no good reason, and all because *you* wanted to pretend you could do something you've already spent fifty years failing to come even close to achieving. Nobody's going to look very kindly on you after they hear about all that, are they?' She pretended to think. 'Still, I suppose they'll have an empty cell up at Pentonville they can put you in for the rest of your days. Not that there's going to be many of them left, by the look of things. Shut the door and throw away the key – that would be my guess. Unless they decide to leave the gallows where it is and get some more use out of it, that is. Always an option, I suppose, especially in these unsettled times.'

In his chair, Crowley tried to respond to this. He raised his arm and pointed at her. He started to speak, but his words were unintelligible and weighted with exhaustion.

'What?' she said, leaning closer to him so that her breasts were again revealed. 'Giving you ideas, am I? Remembering the last time you had these in your hands, are you?' She cupped her breasts and held them even closer to Crowley's face, almost touching him.

'Stop it,' Silver shouted at her. 'Leave him alone. He's exhausted. This thing has taken everything out of him. You have no idea.'

The final invocation had lasted only seconds – a single mouthed sentence as the clock on the mantel had started to strike.

'No – *you* shut up, quack,' Ruby Nolan shouted back at Silver. '*I'm* the one who's wasted everything. The things I've done, the things I've let *him* do, the things he *forced* me to do. I'm entitled, I'm owed, he owes me. And one way or another, I'm going to get what I deserve. I'll get it from him, or I'll get it from the papers, but however I get it, and whatever it amounts to, I'm going to make sure I get everything that's coming to me.'

'Don't,' Silver said to her. 'Otherwise—'

'Otherwise what? He'll put one of his curses on me? One of his spells? Like the spell he put on me to make me do the things I did? Look at him – he can't even sit up straight or wipe the dribble from his own chin. Otherwise what? Otherwise he'll curse me and I'll go to Hell? I had enough of all that back at home. Why do you think I came here in the first place? Besides, if anyone deserves a few words with the Devil, I'd be the first in line.'

'Don't,' Silver said again.

Why didn't she just go and leave the two of them alone? Leave them alone to recover, to rest, to wait for everything to pass and for the world to stop shaking and to right itself again? Why didn't she just go back to where she belonged and let him take care of his friend like he had always done? Take care of him, help him to recover his strength and his health, and perhaps even something of his lost conviction, and then for the two of them to continue together along the same badly marked and poorly lit path which forever stretched ahead of them these days. Why didn't she just go and let all of this happen?

Silver guessed then that it had also been her intention to benefit in other ways from Crowley's hoped-for success, and that her anger was further fuelled by her disappointment at all she believed she had lost as a result of his failure. All she needed now were the eager ears of all those waiting editors – and Horatio Bottomley would surely outbid them all for this final opportunity to nail Crowley to the cross he had spent his whole life erecting.

She would tell the papers everything, and afterwards Crowley would spend his final few years – perhaps not even that – hounded and ridiculed and persecuted again. War or no war, the world would always choose its easy targets and its ready victims.

Even if she went and left the two of them alone for only a few days – even if she gave them that much grace – then perhaps Silver could get Crowley out of the flat and then empty it so that no one would know they had ever been there, let alone know where they had gone.

But even as he considered this, Silver knew that he wasn't thinking straight. Those editors already knew where Crowley lived; it was what had led the girl to him in the first place, and not a single one of them would pass up this opportunity to do to him what they had always done to him.

She finally left him and went back to the mantel, putting her hand on the clock still sitting there.

'Ten past,' she said. 'He'll have stopped swinging by now. Perhaps they've already cut the poor little sod down. Perhaps he's been cut down and carted away to wherever it is they're going to bury him and forget all about him.'

It was still the thought of the hanged boy that concerned Silver the most, and he tried to work out how much she could actually prove of what she was suggesting. But nothing came to him – his head was still full of all these other considerations – and so he decided to be bold. He went back to Crowley and crouched beside him.

Turning to look at the girl, he said, 'You can't prove a thing. Not where the boy's concerned. He was going to hang anyway. Everybody in London knows that. Perhaps Aleister just convinced – deluded – himself that he could somehow use the hanging to his own advantage.' He felt sure that he was finally stopping her where she stood.

But again Ruby Nolan simply smiled at all he said. And when he'd finished, she put a finger to her lips and waited. 'Finished?' she said to him.

Silver nodded, surprised and disappointed by his sudden acquiescence after everything he'd just attempted.

Beside him, Crowley mumbled again.

'You're forgetting Tommy Fowler,' she said. 'The first thing *he*'ll have done is cover his own back.'

'He won't be able to deny that—'

'That you and the "Antichrist" here visited him?'

'Exactly,' Silver said.

She shook her head. 'You're not listening to what I'm saying,' she said. 'Perhaps he won't be able to deny that, but what he *will* say, if pushed, is that he thought he was doing both Crowley and poor old Tait a favour in getting the Bible to him.'

She knew about the Bible.

She saw the look on his face and her smile broadened. 'That's right,' she said. 'The Bible. And I don't imagine it will take too much effort to find it and then for the law to go through it with one of those fine-tooth combs they're always going on about.'

'There's nothing in it,' Silver said, but too quickly.

'And besides,' Ruby Nolan went on, 'you don't imagine that Tommy Fowler *didn't* want the poor sod to hang, do you? Ask me, he was depending on Crowley telling him the truth for once when he said that by using the boy to his own ends, his appeal would fail and he would definitely be strung up.' She held up her palms to Silver. 'I can see you haven't really given any of this much thought. At least not like me, you haven't. And then, of course, there's Sweeney to consider.'

'Who's Sweeney?' Silver said, alarmed by the speed with which she was now moving ahead of him.

'Who's Sweeney? He's the boy with the split lip.' She pulled a face to suggest this. 'Very suggestible. Happy to tell a girl anything if she showed him the slightest bit of attention. And what he didn't tell me – a bit slow, in his own way, if you ask me; just the way Tommy Fowler likes them – then all those newspaper and magazine articles filled in the blanks.'

'He knew you'd come to him deliberately,' Silver said, indicating Crowley.

'Of course he did. He knew it, and I *knew* he knew it. It was as much of a game to me as it was to him. Not that I'll tell the papers any of that, of course. As far as they're concerned, I found myself irresistibly lured to this place, as though I was being drawn here against my will. I can see it now. They'll probably even want a decent photograph of me to go with all the lurid details.'

'The Bible wouldn't prove anything conclusively,' Silver said, still struggling to maintain some small measure of defiance in the face of all these revelations.

She put a hand on her exposed breasts. 'Oh dear, did I forget to say?' she said. 'Suppose there *was* a name in that little book. And suppose all this drum-beating and bell-ringing hocus pocus has been taking place while that name was sitting there all this time.'

'What?' Silver said, struggling now to grasp what she was telling him, how far ahead of him she had suddenly just moved. 'Yours?' The word dried in his mouth.

She put her finger back to her lip. 'Now let me think,' she said slowly.

Beside Silver, Crowley said, 'Her name? Where?'

'In the Bible,' Silver said. It was the last thing he wanted to say.

Crowley opened his eyes wide and looked at the girl standing at the hearth. He attempted to frame his response, but failed, and then sagged where he sat, struggling for breath.

Silver pulled the collar from Crowley's neck, feeling it tear in his hand. He pressed his ear to Crowley's chest and heard the rapid and erratic beating of his heart.

Eventually, Crowley grew calm and his breathing became more regular.

Silver left him and went back to the girl. 'You don't have the first idea what you've done,' he said to her.

'And you do?' she said. 'Are you telling me now that you had every faith in what he was doing, that you knew he'd succeed?'

'Perhaps not,' he said. 'But that was his last opportunity.'

'His last opportunity to do what, exactly? To make a

bigger and even more pathetic fool of himself? Of you both? What in God's name did he think was going to happen? What's *ever* happened, what has he *ever* achieved? I'll tell you what – a lot of nothing, that's what. It's all up here' – she tapped her temple – 'as far as he's concerned. I meet his sort every single day of the week. All that money, all those women, all that other stuff – all he ever achieved with *any* of it was to please himself, make himself feel good, make out he was something he never was. Read the papers; it's all there in black and white. All he ever needed around him were weak people desperate to believe in something their own sorry little lives didn't give them. People like you, in fact. And don't deny it – I can see by your face that I'm right. All he ever needed were people telling him how wonderful he was.' She made her hand into a clacking mouth and held it to Silver's face. 'And he conned *you* as much as he conned the rest of them; more, probably. *They* were all in it for some sort of rubbed-off glory or power. What did *you* ever get out of it? Nothing – that's what. You call yourself his friend? Don't make me laugh. He used you, that's all. Just like he used everybody else. All those weak, desperate people, and all *he* has to do is click his fingers and they all come running. *You* could have stopped all this before it was ever started, but what did you do? Nothing, that's what, absolutely nothing. You let him talk you into it, and then afterwards all you ever did was hold his hand and nod your head and do everything he told you to do, like the obedient little dog you are.' She was shouting now, her own breathing loud and erratic. 'So you can see just how many precious stories I'll have to tell to the papers, what evidence I'll have to show them. Perhaps I might even go back round to Sweeney's and tell him how much I've missed him, what a fool I was not to have been with *him* all this time, and find out how much more *he* knows about all of this. Let's face it, he's probably the only visitor poor little Tait had while he was waiting for the rope. Perhaps Sweeney might even want to come straight round here and sort the pair of you out for everything Crowley forced me to do while I was under his evil spell.' She pushed a finger hard into Silver's chest. 'So, like I said, old man, you haven't really got the first idea about any of this, not the first idea.'

She started to laugh at him and Silver felt the spray of her saliva on his face.

And before he knew what he was doing, what was happening, Joshua Silver felt his hand close around the heavy clock on the mantel alongside her laughing head, and he felt his grip tighten, felt the solid weight of the clock in his palm and beneath his fingers. And still without thinking or truly understanding what he was doing, he swung the clock with every ounce of angry strength he possessed into the side of her laughing head, and he felt the released energy of that short, sudden blow, and then the impact of metal, glass and malachite on bone and flesh, and the jarring pain which ran back through his fingers and wrist to his shoulder.

And the girl stopped laughing then, and her eyes widened briefly and she gave a solitary dry 'Oh' of painless surprise and fell instantly silent.

The only thought now in Joshua Silver's head was that he had finally stopped her talking, finally stopped her mockery and her laughter and all her threat-making, that he had silenced her, and that there was now the opportunity of a new beginning, a chance to stand briefly upright in that silence and stillness and for them all to catch their breath, for them all to begin again.

He felt the clock fall from his grasp and then shatter in the ash-strewn hearth, its glass breaking, its shining innards scattering noisily across the floor.

The girl remained standing where he had struck her, looking hard into his eyes, her lips forming the same simple word over and over but nothing coming out. She looked surprised, anxious, suddenly undecided about something she had been about to say or do.

And then she seemed to simply disappear from Silver's view, falling at his feet into the hearth. And though she was only inches from him, she fell without touching him, without any more of her hot, wet breath on his face, and without grabbing hold of him and either trying to keep herself upright or dragging him down with her as she fell.

And as he stood like that, looking down at the fallen girl and hearing only the painful rasp of Crowley's tortured breathing, Joshua Silver began to discern another sound – a sound coming into the room from outside. And though at first he was unable to make out this distant noise, it continued and grew louder until eventually he realized that what he was hearing was the sound of countless church bells all being separately and simultaneously rung, countless peals, near and distant, gathering and then merging to a single underlying rhythm, and growing ever louder and more insistent as the seconds and then the minutes passed, and seeming to Joshua Silver like nothing less than the powerful wind of an approaching storm rising effortlessly to its destructive crescendo.

And finally realizing what this sound signified, what it

heralded and what it brought rushing unstoppably towards him, Joshua Silver turned from Crowley and the girl to the window and the world outside, closed his eyes and then slowly raised and held out his arms to embrace that approaching storm of Peace in all its long-awaited and ferocious beauty.

Robert Edric was born in 1956. His novels include *Winter Garden* (1986 James Tait Black Prize winner), *A New Ice Age* (runner-up for the 1986 *Guardian* Fiction Prize), *The Book of the Heathen* (shortlisted for the 2001 WHSmith Literary Award), *Peacetime* (longlisted for the Booker Prize 2002), *Gathering the Water* (longlisted for the Booker Prize 2006) and *In Zodiac Light*, which was shortlisted for the Dublin Impac Prize 2010. His most recent novel is *The Devil's Beat*. He lives in Yorkshire.